Ancient Magic— ~~Book Evil~~ *. . .*

Francesca gasped and looked up, startled and frightened, at the intruder who filled the mouth of the tomb. She scrambled up frantically, trying to cover her nakedness. "What are you doing here, Murad?" she cried, her voice quivering, her eyes huge with fear. "What do you want?"

"Nothing, dear English teacher, except what you gave to the French doctor." His voice was as slimy as a serpent as he started toward her. "My father will be most interested to know what his beloved English lady does behind his back. She turns up her nose at Elfi Bey in disdain and then defiles the pharaohs' tombs with a worthless foreigner." He laughed vilely and ripped the clothing from her hands. "Why are you trying to hide from your pupil?" he sneered. "Surely you would not deny Elfi Bey's son a lesson in your English ways? That is why you are my father's servant—to teach his only son."

Screaming wildly, Francesca fought to escape from his loathsome touch. But he grabbed her arm and twisted it brutally behind her back.

"Scream! Scream if you like, English lady, for there is no one to heed you but the ancient ghosts. Your Frenchman is on his way to Thebes by now, and that ox Osari cannot hear you. Not today, you foreign whore!"

"What do you mean, Murad? Tell me what you have done with Osari," Francesca pleaded.

But the boy just flung his head back and laughed, a drunken, triumphant, crazed peal of victory—and revenge. . . .

Also by Angelica Aimes from Pinnacle Books:

Samantha

FRANCESCA

Angelica Aimes

PINNACLE BOOKS • **LOS ANGELES**

This is a work of fiction. All the characters and events portrayed in this book are fictional, and any resemblance to real people or incidents is purely coincidental.

FRANCESCA

An original Pinnacle Books edition, published for the first time anywhere.

First printing, December 1978

ISBN: 0-523-40387-9

Cover illustration by Bill Maughan

Printed in the United States of America

PINNACLE BOOKS, INC.
2029 Century Park East
Los Angeles, California 90067

BOOK I— *The Cousins*

Chapter One

Clarissa Dorset stole a sidelong glance at the tall, fair young man who stood at her side straight as a ramrod and strong as the empire, and her heart leaped happily. Malcolm Lord Harrod was everything she had ever wanted and in a few brief moments he would be hers, for better for worse, for richer for poorer, in sickness and in health, to love, honor, cherish and obey until death do them part.

Clarissa spoke the words clearly and crisply as the Archbishop of Canterbury smiled benevolently down on the handsome young couple. Her sweet, high voice rang like a crystal bell in the great nave of Westminster Abbey and her eyes shimmered like the candles on the high altar.

Clarissa was so tiny and delicate that she seemed scarcely old enough for marriage. Golden ringlets framed her heart-shaped face like a halo and set off her violet eyes and rosebud mouth. Only her strong, pert chin hinted that behind the angelic face was a girl well used to having her own way. Its determined tilt said: *I know what I want and I shall get it by hook or by crook*. And she most certainly had. She had wanted Malcolm and she had allowed nothing—and no one—to stand in her way of marrying him.

But Malcolm never suspected any of this. A man not blinded by love might have recognized the firm chin as a sign of willfulness, but to Malcolm it was simply adorable. To him Clarissa was unlike any of the other girls in London. She was madcap, unpredictable and incorrigible, and it was just these qualities that he found so irresistible. He knew she was capricious, headstrong and spoiled, and he was looking forward to spoiling her more. She was made to be pampered and doted on, and he was already planning the extravagant gifts he would lavish upon her.

As he gazed down at the radiant slip of a girl he was about to take as his wife, Malcolm's laughing blue eyes filled with admiration. Clarissa looked like a china doll in her satin wedding gown. The fitted bodice hugged her full, round breasts enticingly. Clusters of pearl roses were appliquéd on the full skirt and spilled down on the tiered train, which fanned out behind her, filling the wide cathedral aisle.

The train must be three times as long as she is, Malcolm thought fondly. Although a lace mantilla hid all but the tip of her upturned nose and the point of her pert chin, he could not take his eyes off his beautiful bride.

Malcolm had known Clarissa and her cousin Francesca forever. As children, the three had been inseparable. They had played together and learned to ride together. They had exchanged innocent confidences, teased and tiffed. But it was only this past year, when Clarissa had returned from school on the continent, that he realized for the first time how truly enchanting she was. He felt like a man who had been standing on a hill of gold and had never looked down.

How blind I was, Malcolm thought as he took Clarissa's hand in his and promised to love, cherish and support her from this day forward.

He spoke firmly, his big, strong hand clasping her petite one, his adoring eyes lost in her violet pools. "I,

4

Malcolm Lord Harrod, take this woman to be my lawful, wedded wife." And as he spoke he slipped a wide gold wedding band on her finger.

Clarissa gave his hand a loving squeeze and bowed her head. The Archbishop pronounced the benediction. The organ music welled. At last they were man and wife.

Jeremy Dorset cleared his throat self-consciously as Malcolm and Clarissa turned to begin the long recessional march. For all her faults, and no one knew them better, Clarissa was his daughter. Even though she had always been her mother's favorite and even though he knew all too well that young Malcolm would have his hands full, still Jeremy Dorset could not deny the rush of paternal pride that filled his heart as Clarissa started down the aisle of Westminster Abbey on the arm of her handsome new husband.

She is the most beautiful, most radiant bride I have ever seen, he thought, and for the moment he forgot his worries about his spoiled, headstrong daughter and the guilt he felt for leaving her upbringing in the hands of his over-indulgent wife.

Beside Jeremy, Genevieve Dorset wiped the tears of happiness and pride from her eyes. She had always harbored the highest hopes for her only daughter and today she was seeing them fulfilled. *They make a picture-book couple in a fairytale wedding,* she thought to herself, and, could they have read Genevieve's mind, all of the friends and relatives who had gathered to witness the blessed union would have agreed with her. All save one.

One guest was not seeing the bride and bridegroom as Genevieve did—Clarissa enchanting in her long, white wedding gown; Malcolm handsome in his midnight-blue waistcoat and white silk cravat. In the pew behind the Dorsets, the lovely, still alluring Lady Andrea Marlowe was stripping the bridegroom naked in her mind. She was seeing every sinew of his young, bare body.

Lady Marlowe was imagining the easy, convincing words he had used to turn the girl's head, the professions of undying love he'd sworn to make her surrender. She pictured Malcolm undressing the girl, his skilled fingers fondling her long, lissome body. She visualized his bold stare as he gazed hungrily on the flesh that no man had ever seen before, and the girl's shyness as she gave herself trustingly to him, pledging all her love with the gift of her flesh.

As he passed her pew with his new bride at his side, Lady Marlowe imagined Malcolm, his body naked and demanding, mounting the innocent girl and drawing forth the bloody token of her purity.

But Lady Marlowe's handsome face never once betrayed her bitter thoughts. From the moment she entered Westminster Cathedral, a smile that seemed chiseled in marble had adorned her lovely mouth, and she remained as cool and composed as a Greek statue as she watched her niece float down the aisle on the arm of the man who had violated her own daughter—Clarissa's cousin, Francesca.

Chapter Two

"Aunt Andrea," Clarissa gushed, kissing Lady Marlowe on the cheek, "I am so glad you came. I think if only dear Francesca could be with us as well, this would be the very happiest day of my life."

Lady Marlowe looked at her niece sharply, astounded by the girl's audacity. When she finally spoke, her voice was as dry and icy as the champagne she sipped. "As you well know, Clarissa, Francesca is even now on her way to Egypt for an indefinite stay."

"Yes, of course, Mother told me," Clarissa went on undaunted. Her eyes, wide and innocent, looked directly into Lady Marlowe's own. "Still, Aunt Andrea, it was my fondest wish that Francesca would be here, sharing this wonderful moment with me. We spent so many of our childhood hours together imagining our weddings . . ."

Lady Marlowe cut off her niece brusquely. "Yes, my dear, I am sure you did. Francesca planning, and you plotting." She brushed by Clarissa and reached her hand to Malcolm. "A lovely wedding, Lord Harrod, my congratulations," she said smoothly.

Malcolm took her outstretched hand in both of his. "Lady Marlowe, I hope you will try to understand . . ." he began. But something indefinable in her demeanor stopped him from saying more, and he simply bowed low and murmured, "Thank you."

Lady Marlowe glided away from Clarissa and Malcolm, weaving gracefully between groups of friends and well-wishers, pausing to nod to one and exchange a word of greeting with another. But her mind was occupied—miles and miles away with Francesca, who might have been the bride today, but instead was somewhere on the open sea, fleeing to a strange and distant land to escape her broken heart.

Did Clarissa know that her cousin had given more than her consent to Malcolm, Lady Marlowe wondered. Did she know that the man she just married had extracted tangible, physical proof of Francesca's love? He had possessed her. He had used her. He had taken her body as well as her heart and then cast her aside, breaking his pledge of marriage to be free for this very day. Could Clarissa know this and still marry the wretch?

Lady Marlowe had never been close to her niece. She really only knew Clarissa through her daughter's eyes, and Francesca would forgive Clarissa anything and make a million excuses for her if she had to. But Lady Marlowe was a shrewder judge than her naïve daughter. An angelic countenance and a wide-eyed gaze were not enough to convince her of her niece's innocence. Yet could Clarissa know the truth and still dare to speak so brazenly to her aunt?

Lady Marlowe was not sure. She needed to collect her thoughts calmly. The wedding had been an ordeal, but she felt that she had comported herself decently for the sake of the family and now she wanted only to get away from the gushing wedding guests.

"Beautiful bride, lovely wedding," she murmured abstractly, as she threaded her way among them, edging slowly towards the sanctuary of the library. She knew that the dark panelled room would afford her a few moments of solitude. But, before she could reach it, she was intercepted by her sister, Genevieve Dorset.

"At last, Andrea, even you must be convinced that Clarissa and Lord Harrod were made for each other. Please, dear, let's let bygones be bygones and be grateful that it was never more than a harmless flirtation between Francesca and the young man."

Genevieve looked up at her sister hopefully. Her ample form was wedged into yards of purple taffeta. Her face was florid from the excitement of the day and her eyes, as round and violet as Clarissa's, were glazed.

"You know, Andrea, as well as I," she went on, barely pausing to catch her breath, "that one day Francesca will find true love, as Clarissa has this day. I only wish she had not run off to Egypt, of all places, in that dramatic fashion. Clarissa did so want her to be her maid of honor. You know it still saddens me to remember that you would not come back from Paris for my wedding to Jeremy."

Genevieve sighed deeply, her big bosom rising and falling like the Roman Empire. "They really are made for each other, Andrea," she said, beaming lovingly across the room at the handsome couple. "Remember how they played together as children. It was always Malcolm and Clarissa, with Francesca tagging along."

"You mean, I suppose, that Francesca was always the odd one out, the third, the extra," Lady Marlowe paused, "as I have been all these years with you and Jeremy."

"Why, Andrea, what an extraordinary thing to say. What ever do you mean?" Genevieve asked.

"Nothing, Genevieve, nothing," Lady Marlowe answered quickly, "except that history does have a strange way of repeating itself, don't you think? Now, if you will excuse me, I think I will slip into the library. The reception has, of course, been delightful, but I would like a few tranquil moments to compose myself."

Genevieve Dorset shook her head in bewilderment. Even as children she and her sister had never been close, and the years only served to widen the gap. Andrea was three years her senior, but to Genevieve it seemed more like a generation.

Andrea had always been the beautiful sister—cool, aloof, and stunning. Genevieve, plainer and plumper, had hovered in her shadow, always hoping some day that she would be transformed into a swan, as lovely as Andrea had been on her wedding day.

Andrea had been only eighteen, Genevieve an awkward fifteen, but the memory was etched forever in her mind. She was a beautiful bride—yes, Genevieve admitted to herself reluctantly, more beautiful even than Clarissa today. But, except for their titles, the bridegroom was no Malcolm.

Lord Marlowe was rich and powerful—quite a catch, their mother thought. But he was also fifty years older than Andrea. Genevieve remembered the tearful scenes vividly. Andrea begged and pleaded with her mother not to make her marry the ugly, old lord. But her mother was determined and so, like a lamb to the slaughter, Andrea went to her wedding, showing a brave, lovely face to the world. Her full, young figure and flashing green eyes seemed somehow unconstrained by either the virginal white wedding gown or the wizened old man who waited at the altar to claim her.

The young Lady Marlowe was a widow within the year. Although Genevieve never dared to question her sister about the unfortunate marriage, talk was that the enchanting bride would allow her old husband a glimpse of her beauty but would never enter his bed. So taken was he with the promise she proferred that he could not contain himself. He chased her from castle room to castle room until the strain of the chase and the anticipation proved too much for his ancient heart.

Genevieve Dorset watched her still arresting sister until the library door closed behind her. She had always admired and envied Andrea; but now, she thought, the irony was that her daughter was by far the prettier. Although she was truly fond of Francesca and wished her nothing but happiness and good health, Genevieve could not help but gloat a little. The two cousins had grown up like sisters and her daughter had won the handsome young man.

Lady Marlowe sighed deeply as she closed the library door behind her. She blamed herself for what had happened to Francesca. Her generous, loving daughter was destined to make the same tragic mistake she had made—a mistake that broke her heart twenty years before. Now, she thought disconsolately, Francesca had become a wanderer as I have been for these past twenty years, a wanderer always trying to escape her own heart.

Lady Marlowe's mind was so far away that she did not notice her brother-in-law sitting in the shadows. But Jeremy Dorset read the anguish that was printed so clearly on his sister-in-law's bewitching face and he was filled with remorse.

"Dear Andrea," he said comfortingly as he rose to greet her, "it is not as terrible as you are imagining, believe me. This time, at least, I agree with Genevieve. Clarissa and Malcolm make a grand couple."

He took her hand and, kissing her cheek tenderly, led her to one of the deep leather chairs by the fire-

11

place. "Believe me, Andrea, the boy is a good lad, in spite of what he may have done. But he is not a match for Francesca. They could never have been happy together."

"I should never have brought Francesca into this world, Jeremy," Lady Marlowe answered gloomily. "She is doomed like her mother—foredoomed at birth to make the same tragic mistake I made, to break her own heart and live with the shattered shards forever." Lady Marlowe paused for a moment. "At least there is no issue from her heartbreak," she added softly, "for that I am thankful."

"My dear," Jeremy said, soothingly, "you mustn't talk like this, or even think this way."

"I mustn't, Jeremy?" Lady Marlowe's voice was suddenly cold and angry. "Do you realize how many years I have been listening to 'Andrea, you mustn't, we mustn't'? I often wonder what ever became of the impetuous young man who once said to me, 'My darling, we must, we must, no matter what happens to us tomorrow.'"

Jeremy Dorset looked at her sadly. She was even more beautiful now, he thought, than she had been in her youth.

"I will tell you what happened to him, Jeremy," she went on bitterly. "Living with the wrong woman killed him, and living with your dear Clarissa will do the same to Malcolm—not that I care what happens to the rotter."

"I am surprised at you, Andrea," Jeremy chided her gently. "A woman with your experience of the world, your charm and allure, cannot be so naive. Surely, you of all people know that it is not whom one lives *with* that destroys a man, it is whom one lives—must live—*without*."

Jeremy stood in front of his sister-in-law, studying

12

her beautiful face for some hint of what was in her heart. He was a tall, slender man with soft brown eyes and a shock of gray hair, the kind of man more often described as distinguished than handsome. Somewhere along the way he had lost the irrepressible enthusiasm of his youth and had grown withdrawn and introspective. He had not aged as well as his sister-in-law and now as he studied her loveliness, he felt much more than his forty-five years.

Jeremy wished with all his heart that Andrea was wrong about Clarissa and Malcolm. Too many members of his family had been cheated out of their happiness. He did not want the same thing to happen to either Clarissa or Francesca.

Even today at his daughter's wedding, the thought of her loving, tomboyish cousin made him glow with warmth. Genevieve had often accused him of favoring Francesca over their own daughter and, although he always denied it stoutly, he knew she was right.

He loved Francesca in a way he could never love Clarissa. Francesca was a companion for him. In the evenings she would sit for hours reading in this very library with him, and when they were in the country she would go on long walks with him through the woodlands. She always seemed to know when to be quiet with him and when to give vent to her own mischievous spirit.

Clarissa, on the other hand, was a pretty toy who would preen and pose for him when there was something she wanted. But she had always been her mama's girl. She was a willful and petulant child and she had grown into a willful, petulant young lady. Jeremy knew it was his own fault. He had never made any attempt to discipline the girl or to curb her mother's pampering. Then, too, when Clarissa wanted something, she was very hard to resist.

13

Young Malcolm will have his hands full, Jeremy thought darkly, *but he seems to be an amiable, easygoing chap. I hope Clarissa does not break his spirit before he has learned how to handle her.*

Jeremy began to pace the length of the library distractedly. "You are right, Andrea, we have not lived our lives well. We have made too many mistakes—too many mistakes to undo now. But the worst of it is we continue in our erring ways. Why didn't I talk with my daughter before this day of all days? Why didn't I warn young Malcolm to be firm with Clarissa, firm yet patient with my girl? It is the very least a father could do. Dear God," he prayed, "I hope Genevieve has prepared her for this night. For all her madcap ways, Clarissa is, underneath, a very proper, very conventional girl."

But Jeremy Dorset's remorse had come too late to save Malcolm and Clarissa, for the barouche that would take them to their honeymoon castle was even then waiting in front of Dorset House.

Chapter Three

Malcolm Lord Harrod was easy prey for a designing woman. Tall, blond and slimly built, he was handsome in an indolent, sleepy-eyed way. His blue eyes glimmered mischievously through half-closed lids and his casual, carefree manner made him popular with everyone.

As the second son of the wealthy Lord Harrod, Malcolm was not expected to be as serious and highminded as his elder brother. But when his father and brother both died suddenly within weeks of each other, Malcolm found himself heir to the title. He was taken up by the Prince of Wales and soon became a regular in Prinnie's wild, fun-loving circle. For, as Francesca Fairchild had discovered much to her heartache, Malcolm was very much a man of the world with all the tastes and appetites of a twenty-seven-year-old dandy.

Francesca had fallen in love with Malcolm when he was just a second son. Clarissa set her sights on him when he became Lord Harrod.

Although the cousins had grown up like sisters, they had little in common except the lustrous golden color of their hair. Francesca was lithe and lean, with a slender, boyish figure, long straight hair and deep brown eyes set behind wide cheekbones. Clarissa was a delicate porcelain doll, with a small yet voluptuous

15

body, an enchanting elfin face and translucent ivory skin marred only by the tiny row of freckles that ran across the bridge of her nose.

Francesca was generous and passionate, shy yet playful. Clarissa was a golden girl with a heart of ice. Spoiled by her mother, allowed to run wild by her father, she had grown up to be a wily young woman with looks, brains and authority. But she managed to conceal this well beneath a pixie charm, which could melt the most austere heart. She could be captivating when she wanted to be and a thorough bitch when she chose.

Even though she was younger by several months, Francesca always stood up for her cousin and made excuses for her nasty habits. But Clarissa resented Francesca's defense. She was self-confident to the point of arrogance, and, when she returned from school on the continent and became aware of the power she could wield over men, she was more than ready to use it against her cousin.

With her beauty and impish charm, Clarissa became the toast of London. A dozen eligible young men vied for her attention and affections. But she would give her hand and her heart to only one, and it only steeled her resolve that Malcolm Lord Harrod was Francesca's fiancé.

Today was Clarissa's crowning moment. But now that she had won her prize, she was unwilling to pay the price of victory.

As the new Lord and Lady Harrod rode in their elegant barouche to their country estate in Hertford, Malcolm's mind filled with pictures of the bliss he would soon know. He was totally mesmerized by Clarissa. She fascinated him. She tormented him. He was in her thrall, completely seduced by her fragile beauty and her mercurial nature.

At one moment, snuggling up to him in the carriage, she was a playful, delightful little girl, tickling his nose with her ermine muff. At the next, she was a daring woman of the world, driving him wild with desire for the charms she flaunted so freely. With her merciless teasing and risqué manner, Clarissa had deceived Malcolm into believing that she was as eager for this wedding night as he.

Malcolm was so avid for the long-anticipated moment that, when they reached Hertford Manor, he scooped up his tiny bride in his arms and carried her into the castle, up the wide oaken stairway to the master suite. As he deposited her on the big fourposter, he murmured warmly, "Later we will have a lovely supper, just we two, and I will give you a tour of your new castle; but first, my darling, we will become one. Nothing can keep me from you now."

Clarissa was uncertain and afraid of what Malcolm had in mind. Her eyes were as wide as tea saucers as she gazed up at him and he lost himself in their violet depths. Dropping to his knee, he bent over her delicate Valentine face and covered her sweet bow mouth with his own. Gone were the chaste kisses of their courtship as he gave vent to the steamy passion that he had contained within himself for this very moment.

Malcolm was a healthy, arduous young man, wellknown in the best brothels of London, and he thought, from Clarissa's wild ways, plunging decolletage and daring talk, that she had tasted some of the joys of the flesh herself. When she tried demurely to avoid his embrace, he thought she was teasing him, toying with his emotions as she had done so often in their whirlwind courtship, and her vixen charm drove him wilder with desire.

His mouth enveloped hers with a deep, passionate

17

kiss. His hands groped feverishly with her handsome peach traveling dress, trying to reach beneath its folds to the flesh she had always denied him. All his long-suppressed desire welled up inside him as he fought her camisoles and corsets for a touch of the round, rosy breasts they protected.

But Clarissa was not teasing this time. She was thoroughly unprepared for Malcolm's sudden onslaught and equally ignorant of her duty now that she was his wife. She had pictured herself as the glamorous, young Lady Harrod taking a promenade on the arm of her handsome husband, riding beside him in their carriage, entertaining at the head of his table or dancing at the royal balls. But this other side of marriage was unknown to her.

Her mother had not told her what to expect in her marriage bed and she was frightened of the impassioned young man, now frantically tearing at her clothing. Where, she wondered fearfully, was the cool, casual dandy she had wed just hours before? What terrible schemes did he have planned for her? What foul carnal desires burned in his heart?

Scared and uncertain and wishing her mother had joined them for this honeymoon, Clarissa screamed in terror and wriggled her way out of her husband's loving grasp. Rolling over to the far side of the bed out of his reach, she began to sob uncontrollably.

Poor Malcolm, distraught at the sight of Clarissa's tears, was disconsolate. "Clarissa, my dearest girl, what have I done wrong? Please do not cry. I will do anything to make those tears dry up and your violet eyes smile at me again. Was I too impetuous, darling? If I was, it is only because I love you so very much I cannot wait to make you my lady."

He reached across the bed and drew her to him. Cradling her in his arms like a child, he continued to

18

whisper gently in her ear. "Was I clumsy? If I was rough, if I bruised your beautiful lips with mine, it was only to show you the strength of my love for you. Did I act too hastily? If I did, it was only because every moment waking and sleeping I have thought of nothing else, nothing except making you my own, nothing except this moment when you would become my wife, truly and totally, and I would give my body and soul for your love."

Stifling a sob, Clarissa looked up lovingly into Malcolm's contrite eyes. She felt safe and secure in his arms, with his gentle voice droning comfortingly in her ear. Maybe he will be as content to remain just this way as I am, she thought hopefully, and, like the canny woman she was, she nestled more snugly into the crook of his arm and smiled angelically up at him. "I think the excitement of our wedding has made me tired," she whispered. "Can you forgive me, Malcolm?"

Malcolm kissed the tears on her delicate cheeks gently and brushed a wisp of curls off of her forehead. "Of course, my darling. It is I who should be begging forgiveness from you. I will send old Margaret up to help you into a hot tub. The bath will refresh and relax you. Later, when you are comfortably in bed, I will come back. That is a promise," he murmured softly and, laying her down gently on the bed, he kissed the top of her head and went off to fetch his faithful nanny.

Malcolm's parting words rang in Clarissa's head as old Margaret, clutching and clacking all the while, helped her out of her traveling dress and into a steaming bath. Clarissa dallied in the hot tub as long as she could and then dallied even longer over her toilet.

"Now, don't you be afraid, my pretty young lady,"

19

old Margaret soothed. She was too wise not to notice what Clarissa was up to. "Master Malcolm is a gentleman, you can rest assured of that. All he wants from you is what men and women are doing all over the world every night of the year, and sometimes in the afternoons as well, I suspect."

But Clarissa was too impudent to heed the words of a servant. She dismissed Margaret perfunctorily. "That will be all, thank you. If I want anything else, I will ring."

"Yes, madam," old Margaret said anxiously. "I hope I have not spoken out of turn. I did not mean to offend you." She backed toward the door, closing it softly behind her and bumped right into Master Malcolm who was pacing anxiously in front of his wife's room.

"Ah, Margaret, how is my beautiful bride feeling now?"

"She is as pretty as a picture, Master Malcolm," Margaret answered evasively.

"That she is. But, Margaret, is she rested? Is she," Malcolm stammered, "is she ready for me now do you think?"

Margaret looked at the young lord sympathetically. "Ah, Master Malcolm, she said, patting him on the arm, "give her a little while longer. A lot of young brides are frightened on their wedding night. It is not you, child. It is the facts of life. They don't know what to expect and they have probably heard some terrible old wives' tales that have given them an awful scare. It is a hard lot being a woman. Be patient with the girl. She has everything to learn yet, and you are her only teacher."

Malcolm was grateful for the old woman's kind words. He tried to heed her advice, but each minute seemed to pass like an hour. He bathed, groomed

20

himself carefully, and changed into a silk dressing gown. Finally, he could not wait a second longer.

Knocking lightly on the door, he entered Clarissa's chamber. Malcolm caught his breath at the apparition before him. The room was in darkness except for a single candle, which cast an ethereal light across the bed where Clarissa lay in a mass of downy pillows. Her blonde ringlets, still damp from the bath, clung to her forehead. Her fair porcelain skin still glowed from the warm water. One full, round breast had escaped from the confines of her white batiste nightdress.

The round, perfect globe seemed to beckon to Malcolm, as it rose and fell with the even breath of Orpheus. The gentle rising and falling motion hypnotized him and drew him irresistibly to her side. He bent over his sleeping bride, his fingers poised to touch the heaving flesh he had pictured so many times in his mind, when Clarissa opened her eyes.

Gasping with embarrassment, she pulled the coverlets up tightly around her neck. "Malcolm," she cried in horror, "what *do* you think you are doing?"

"Nothing to hurt you, my darling. I was only admiring your perfect breast, as I admire your perfect face or your perfect hands," he said softly, slipping into bed beside her. He kissed her eyes tenderly. "There is nothing to be afraid of, Clarissa. Men and women have been mating since the beginning of time. Surely you know that."

Clarissa looked at him apprehensively. "What do you want me to do, Malcolm? What do you want to do to me?" she asked fearfully.

"Nothing that you won't like, darling," he said putting an arm around her and drawing her to him reassuringly. He could feel every curve of her full, round body through the sheer nightdress. He wanted to

21

throw off the covers, strip off her nightdress, and taste his fair love at last. But he tried to control his hunger.

Malcolm was unprepared for Clarissa's coldness and uncertain of how to handle her obvious ignorance. But remembering old Margaret's wise words, he tried to behave like a tender teacher.

"Perhaps, darling," he began slowly, "if I tell you what a man and woman do together, you will not be so frightened. I always suspected that you knew, because you were always so daring and flirtatious, always surrounded by a bevy of young men, but I am glad you don't. I am glad I am the only one who will ever teach you the joys of love. We will discover them together," he whispered.

He tried to loosen the sheets from around her neck as he spoke, but Clarissa clung to them desperately and so he groped beneath them, his strong hands running the length of her small form. He could feel her body stiffen beneath his touch, but still he perservered gently, patiently.

"Inside here," Malcolm murmured as he brushed his hand lightly across her mound of Venus, "you have a wonderful secret garden which no one has ever visited and I, I have a seed, many seeds, to plant in that garden. Look at me, Clarissa," he whispered, letting go of her and drawing the linen sheets away from his body. He lay on his back and opened his dressing gown. "Look at me," he whispered again with all the confidence and pride of a young man. He cupped his genitals in the palm of his hand as if to display himself better for his bride. "The seed I have for you is in here," he whispered.

Much to Malcolm's consternation, Clarissa gasped in horror when her eyes fell on his looming manhood, now swollen to immense proportions and throbbing uncontrollably with his long-suppressed desire.

"Oh, my darling," he begged, his voice hoarse with passion, "don't make me wait another moment to possess you."

But the more enthusiastic Malcolm became, the more frightened and distraught Clarissa grew. The foul deed her husband proposed shocked her. She imagined Malcolm's strong body crushing her own fragile one, driving straight through her delicate frame and she grew pale and weak at the very thought, until she was on the verge of swooning.

Seeing that, rather than quieting Clarissa's fears, he had served only to aggravate them, Malcolm drew away from her. He was afraid now to even lay a finger on her for fear that his touch would disgust her. Discouraged and aching with his unanswered love, he lay back and withdrew into his own thoughts.

Clarissa's horror at the idea of consummating their marriage, her unresponsiveness to his every caress were so great that as he lay beside his bride on his wedding night, Malcolm could not help but remember Francesca.

She was never as beautiful as Clarissa, but when she told him she loved him, she told him with more than words. She told him with her entire being, with her heart, her breasts, her loins, her purity. Nothing mattered to her—not the conventions of the day, her reputation or her future—because she believed that nothing could stop their love. For a moment Malcolm felt dejected as he remembered how he had used and abused the girl. But then Clarissa, seeing how far her husband had drifted from her, quickly nuzzled towards him. Curling up in his warm arms, she turned on her honey charm again.

Clarissa was confident that she could stay coyly wrapped in his warm embrace. But Malcolm could withstand just so much of Clarissa's flirtatiousness, especially on his wedding night. When she reached up her cherry mouth to kiss him, he answered with a mighty hunger. His tongue parted her lips and when her pearly teeth closed down on it drawing forth his warm, thick blood, he threw back the covers. Rolling over on his delicate bride, his hungry mouth sucked on the bud of her perfect rosebud breast.

"Don't be afraid, darling, you will like it, I promise. I promise. I can't wait any longer to make you mine," he murmured, trying to raise her nightdress.

Malcolm was quaking with desire for Clarissa's beautiful flesh. Her skin was petal-soft and fair. Her full ripe body held the answers to a man's sweetest dreams, and it was about to be his. He yearned to hold her lush nakedness, to caress every inch of her virgin territory. But she would have none of his advances.

Clarissa never did what she didn't want to do—and she most definitely did not want any part of the obscene things that her new husband seemed bent on.

She was tiny. But what she lacked in brawn, she made up for in willfulness. Her angelic bride's face contorted in a spiteful grimace, she fought like an alley cat—hissing, spitting, clawing, biting—to keep Malcolm from accomplishing his foul intent. She would not have his ugly, horrid rod touching her. But the harder she fought the bigger and more furious it grew.

By nature, the young Lord Harrod was the gentlest, most easygoing of men, but he was driven to a violent, brutal passion by his bride's rejection. Crazed with desire to have her at long last, he forced himself on her. Clarissa raked her long, sharp nails across her husband's face as he mounted her but he would not be stopped. His steaming rod broke through her clenched thighs. She screamed wildly as he tore

24

through the veil of virginity that had guarded her chastity and, scratched and bloodied, consummated their union.

And so, against her will, Clarissa Dorset became Lady Harrod in a brutal wedding night that she would never forget—or forgive.

Chapter Four

Francesca Fairchild stood on the topdeck of the S.S. *Georgiana* as it sailed toward the ancient, unknown world that she hoped would open up a new life for her. There in Egypt, amid the monuments to the durability and awesome egoism of mankind, she hoped to regain some of her own lost pride and confidence.

A wide-brimmed, sea-green bonnet covered her long golden hair and shadowed her strange, haunted face. There was an unusual, compelling quality about Francesca, which, once discovered, was rarely forgotten. Hers was not a face to turn a man's head, but one that would haunt his dreams long after other prettier girls had been kissed and forgotten.

Her deep-set, velvet-brown eyes gazed out at the world from behind cheekbones as high and wide as a mountain range. Her forehead was high and broad as well, and she wore her long, straight, sun-kissed hair pulled back off her face in a knot, highlighting the strength of her fine, dramatic features. Her nose was thin and straight and a trifle too long; her mouth wide and a trifle too full. Her long, lissome body was as straight as a boy's and just as lean, yet she moved with her mother's willowy, fluid grace as if she were floating rather than walking, and she had the quickness and shyness of a deer. In repose she seemed serious, but when she smiled, her face lit up as brightly as the sun suddenly emerging through a blanket of clouds.

She would never be as pretty as her cousin Clarissa or as tantalizingly beautiful as her mother Andrea, yet there was a deep, penetrating look in her eyes that could sear a man's heart and puncture his posturings. Francesca was not a girl to be taken lightly or forgotten easily. But Malcolm Lord Harrod had not yet learned the full dimension of her power.

The S.S. *Georgiana* sailed toward the island of Pharus, where the great pharaoh Ptolemy II had constructed the lighthouse that was one of the seven wonders of the ancient world, bringing Francesca ever closer to her strange, new life. It was an exciting, risky adventure for a young Englishwoman to dare, yet Francesca's thoughts were far from her new life. They were back in London where, she knew, at that very moment, the man she had given her heart to was sealing his troth to her dearly loved cousin, Clarissa.

The day was overcast to match Francesca's mood, gray and heavy with clouds. The choppy sea was like an irritable old man banging at the boat in distemper. But the wedding rose as clearly in her mind as a summer day in Brighton.

In her mind's eye it was as perfect as a fairytale. She imagined that the sun had broken through the incessant London gloom and burned off the fog to bring Clarissa and Malcolm a balmy, sky-blue day. The bride was a vision of loveliness in yards and yards of snow-white satin. Her eyes shone with rapture as she beamed on her bridegroom. Her flaxen curls were lightly covered with a lace mantilla twice as long as she was. And at her side was the tall, laughing, carefree man to whom she herself had given her heart.

27

Francesca sighed deeply. She knew she was farther from Malcolm's thoughts than any ship could take her. Her small bosom was heavy with the weight of her suppressed emotion and tears welled up in her dark eyes. But she refused to give into her heartache.

Francesca did not begrudge Clarissa and Malcolm their happiness. Quite the contrary. But the pain of first love was too fresh to be forgotten and every memory, every picture, made the wound ache anew. Malcolm was her first love—and, like everyone who is in love for the first time, she had believed it was forever and was now convinced she would never love again.

Although she tried to distract herself with thoughts of the new world that was opening before her, Francesca's mind kept returning to Malcolm and Clarissa. Try as she might to banish the thought from her mind, she kept picturing Malcolm coming to Clarissa with the first glow of evening. Had Clarissa given herself to him before this night, she wondered? And immediately she answered her own question. No, Clarissa was too clever by far to make the same foolish mistake she had made. Francesca knew her cousin too well to have any doubts on that score. Had he pleaded with Clarissa as he had pleaded with her? How did she resist his earnest entreaties, Francesca marveled? Would he touch Clarissa as he had touched her?

For a terrible, desperate moment, Francesca could again feel Malcolm's hands on her body and see his warm, sky-blue eyes, so sincere and guileless as they looked into hers that unforgettable evening, when he had taken her for his own in the very house where, this day, he and Clarissa had greeted their wedding guests.

Every detail of that fateful night was etched in

28

Francesca's memory. Malcolm had gone to Heretsford Manor for a fortnight. Although he had left just three days before, each hour had stretched out interminably as if weeks had already separated them. Aunt Genevieve was in France visiting Clarissa. Uncle Jeremy and Francesca were alone in the big house. They had finished a quiet dinner and were sitting in the library reading. The house was silent except for the occasional crackling of a log in the fire. Francesca was making a valiant effort to concentrate on her reading, but try as she might she could not keep her mind on the page before her. Uncle Jeremy had noticed her nervousness but wisely made no mention of it, when suddenly, unexpectedly, Malcolm was being announced.

Francesca had blushed to the roots of her golden hair with excitement and her heart leaped joyfully when he rushed in, glowing with the chill evening air and his desire to see her again. Striving mightily to contain their happiness, they greeted each other correctly. Malcolm settled down in a broad wing chair to exchange pleasantries with Uncle Jeremy.

But after a few moments Jeremy smiled indulgently. "Malcolm, my boy," he laughed, "I know you did not rush all the way back to London to discuss the health of your father's Herefords with me this evening."

"But sir," Malcolm began to protest politely.

"You need not apologize, my boy. I am old, but not so old that I cannot still remember what it was like to be twenty-six years of age and wear my heart on my sleeve."

Francesca had blushed again at her uncle's uncharacteristically outspoken words, but this only made him chuckle more. "The evening is still young," he said, "but I have a long day ahead of me tomorrow.

So if you will excuse me Malcolm, I think I will retire early. I trust you will forgive me if I leave Francesca to see you out. Of course if my wife, Genevieve, were home she would think such conduct shocking." He looked from one to the other and smiled again. "Which is all the more reason to take advantage of this opportunity for a few moments alone together with no curious chaperon eavesdropping on your every word."

As the door closed behind Uncle Jeremy, Francesca felt suddenly very shy and awkward. The big house was too quiet. The silence settled around them, insulating them. A shiver of delicious yet frightening apprehension swept through her body and she lowered her eyes bashfully to avoid looking at Malcolm. She had not said more than a dozen words since he had arrived and he'd mistaken her quietness for disinterest.

"Francesca, aren't you glad to see me?" he asked. He stood in front of the fire, facing her but still she avoided meeting his eyes. "I thought you would be surprised and happy to see me," he said. "But I see from the coolness of your reception that I was wrong. I hope my eagerness has not offended you." A cold, correct note had crept into his voice and the hurt was clear in his eyes.

The torrent of emotions that had been swirling in Francesca's heart was loosed when she saw how wounded he was, mistaking her shy silence for aloofness. "Oh, no, no, Malcolm," she cried. "I don't think I could have stood two full weeks without so much as a glimpse of you. These three days have been so long, so utterly empty without you. Even the sun has not come out since you left. I could not concentrate on anything. Poor Uncle Jeremy has been quite beside himself, I fear, although he has been kind enough not

30

to draw attention to my obvious state of melancholy."

"Francesca, if you only knew how my heart soars to hear those words," Malcolm grinned. "I made some feeble excuse to mother this morning and rushed back to town. I fear I was frightfully rude, but I could not help myself. I could not stay away from you another second. I have not even been home to freshen up so anxious was I to see you smile again."

He stood in front of her beaming broadly and held out both his hands to her. "Please, Francesca, let me embrace you," he whispered ardently. "I have waited so long for a moment when we could be alone together and I could take you in my arms and feel the warmth of your body light up my own." As he spoke, he drew her to him, clasping her firmly against his strong, lean body. "I want to hold you forever, Francesca, and never let you go. I never want a day to pass without you in my arms."

Francesca knew that Malcolm was a familiar figure in the fashionable clubs of London where certain women dispensed their favors freely. But at that moment she did not remember anything that might give her pause or make her act with caution.

She had never been in a man's arms before. She had never felt a man's embrace, and now, after the lonely days without him, any natural caution (of which she never had a great abundance) was lost. Malcolm's warm breath in her ear sent shivers of excitement coursing through her. His lean body pressed tightly against her own banished every thought from her head. Before she knew what was happening, his eager lips were encircling her own and she was answering him with all the abandon of a first love that one always thinks will endure forever.

Ever since Francesca could remember, she had been certain that she would marry Malcolm one day.

They had carved their initials on the elm in the garden when she was eight, and Francesca had never even thought of another boy since then. During the last two years with Clarissa away at school on the continent, Malcolm and she had grown even closer. Yet an element of shyness had grown up between them that had never existed before, as Francesca became more and more aware of the unfamiliar stirrings within her body when they were together.

Tentatively at first, Malcolm's lips met hers and, then, emboldened by the passion of her response, he pressed her closer to him until their bodies were as one and their lips were joined in a long, lingering embrace. For the first time, Francesca tasted a man's special flavor and with her own generous, unrestrained kiss she gave Malcolm her heart, her soul, and every fiber of her innocent, trusting nature.

Overwhelmed by the unexpected gift of love Francesca was giving him, Malcolm hesitated. Her unsuspecting lips were arousing his ardor to a pitch that no kisses alone, however passionate, could satisfy. Moved as much by the deep emotion he had awakened in her as by his own desire, he drew away from her. "Francesca," he asked earnestly, "am I the first man you have ever kissed?"

She nodded her head, suddenly embarrassed and afraid that her kiss had disappointed him.

"The first man, the only man?" he asked wondrously.

Again she nodded shyly.

"Oh, Francesca, Francesca," he cried, overcome by the passion of the innocent girl, "then you burn for me as I do for you! You love me! Your lips have yearned to reach out for mine!"

"Yes, Malcolm, yes," she whispered, but her words

were lost in the torrent of kisses he showered on her mouth and eyes and neck.

"I knew you cared for me, but I thought it was as an old friend," he marveled. "I never dared hoped that I could be anything else to you."

Francesca smiled at him. Love lit her face and glowed from her eyes. "I love you, Malcolm," she said simply. "I think I have always loved you, ever since I was five and you were nine. You helped me up when I fell off Duchess and kissed my forehead where I had banged it." She stroked his cheek tenderly. "Kiss me again, my love," she whispered.

"I never want to stop kissing you," he answered. "I never want to let you out of my arms." And again his lips enveloped hers and his tongue delved deeply into the coolness of her mouth. She accepted it eagerly and answered it with her own in a kiss that seemed to repeat every word they had spoken.

Malcolm had gone much further than he had intended to when he called on Francesca that evening, much further than he had ever dreamed possible. Now, almost before he knew what he was saying, the words were pouring out of his mouth as rapidly as his kisses.

"Francesca," he heard himself ask as if in a dream, "will you marry me? Please say you will be my wife. I love you as I have never loved another woman. Tell me you love me, Francesca. Tell me you will be mine." He had gone too far to turn back now, even if he had wanted to. He had to possess her. His body was bursting with desire.

"I do with my whole heart and I will forever and ever," she answered and, as if to seal her promise, she surrendered herself to his lips and he consumed her with a kiss that in its intensity and abandon he believed gave him claim to even more.

33

He drew away from her and taking her face in his hands, he gazed intently into her dark, velvet eyes. "Francesca, how can I be sure you love me?" he asked her. "What will you do to show me that you love me truly and totally, me and no other?"

"I will do anything, Malcolm," she replied, "anything you want to prove my love, anything you ask." His questioning voice had surprised and upset her. "Do you want me to wake up Uncle Jeremy and tell him? Or rush out into the street and shout my love so that all of London will know it? Or wear a veil over my eyes so that I will not look, even in passing, at any man but you?"

Malcolm smiled at Francesca tenderly. "All of these things," he said, "and none of them. It is something less dramatic, but much more important to me. Something you can do now, just for me, that will remain forever between us. It will be ours alone."

"What is it, Malcolm?" she asked, still uncertain of what was in his mind.

He whispered his desire in her ear and his words sent shivers up her spine. "Let me look on your beauty, just for a moment."

Francesca blushed scarlet and hid her face in Malcolm's chest. "Here, tonight?" she whispered shyly.

"Here, now, my darling. Here, before the fire so that its glow will keep you warm. I will not touch you," he swore. "That is my solemn oath. I want you to give your beauty to me, to pledge it to me with this act, as proof of your love. Only this and nothing more."

"But Malcolm, I have never . . ."

He interrupted her almost angrily. "A moment ago you pledged your love to me. Now you will deny me the one small thing that I ask you to do to prove the truth of your words. How can I believe in such a

34

love? There is nothing I would not do for you. Nothing I would not sacrifice. If you asked me to fight a war for you, to conquer a nation, to give my life, I would. But you will not even allow me a glimpse of your beauty."

"No, no, Malcolm," Francesca protested. "I would do anything you asked, anything to prove that I love you. It is just . . . I have never . . ."

"I know, I know, darling," Malcolm spoke more gently now. "You are shy. No man has ever gazed on your loveliness before—and no man but I ever shall again." He stroked her golden hair. "Don't be afraid. You are so beautiful, you should be proud to show me your beauty."

"What . . ." Francesca hesitated, "how much do you want to see?" she whispered bashfully and Malcolm knew he had won.

He kissed her lightly, lingeringly, on the lips. "I want to see all of you," he murmured. "Please my love, just this one thing and I will not ask anything more. I will snuff out the candles and turn away and not look until you call me."

Francesca hesitated for a moment and then, turning away from him, she began to undress with shaking fingers. While she was disrobing, Malcolm turned the key in the library door and snuffed out the candles. Quickly, quietly, he stripped off his own clothes. Not daring to move for fear she would change her mind, he stood naked in the shadows by the door until he heard her call him softly. Then he stepped forward.

Thinking that she had probably stripped down to her chemise and petticoats, he was unprepared for what he saw. For Francesca was as good as her word. She stood bashfully, her head bowed, while the glow of the fire bathed her long, slender body in its reddish light.

Her skin was as smooth and creamy as a calla lily. Her breasts were small but firm and perfectly shaped. Prominent hip bones angled out from her tall, slim body as if standing guard on each side of her smooth belly.

His eyes lingered longingly on her nakedness, moving down from her breasts to her small waist, following her flat belly to the dark triangle that crowned her long, shapely legs. As his eyes inched lower and lower, he rose, until, when he finally stepped from the shadows, he was as large as he had ever been in any raucous night of carousing.

"I would not ask you to do anything that I would not do myself," he whispered, his voice hoarse with desire. "Please, I beg you, release me from my promise. Let me hold you. Just for a moment, let me feel your flesh pressed against mine."

He came slowly toward her until he stood only inches away. Then he took her hands and slowly, almost imperceptibly, he drew her to him until her nipples were brushing his chest and his manhood was caressing her thighs. His eager fingers stroked her back seductively and his yearning body undulated erotically against hers.

Francesca's cool face flushed and her body clung lovingly to his. *This must be heaven,* she thought enraptured, as his strong arms entwined her and his lean, muscular body met hers. Soon his lips, his mouth, his tongue were again searching hers and his immense member was insinuating itself between her innocent thighs.

Slowly, sensually, he rotated his body against hers, rubbing against her other lips and sending such strange and wonderful feelings surging through her limbs that her thighs began to quake and she felt a thick, warm moisture between her legs.

"Oh, Francesca, my love, my life," Malcolm murmured, "don't make me wait another second. Be my wife, my happiness, now, forever, this very night unto eternity. Let me take you, let me make you mine."

"But, Malcolm," Francesca whispered, "shouldn't we wait until our wedding night? How can we do this before we are married?"

Even as she spoke, Francesca could feel Malcolm's hot breath on her neck and his lips burning a path to her ear. It was difficult for her to concentrate on anything or to remember what was right and what was wrong.

"You are right, my darling, you are right, and sweet and pure. We will be married first," Malcolm said. He knelt down in front of her and, pressing his cheek against her downy crown, he said, "I do solemnly swear to make Francesca Fairchild my wife in a holy act of matrimony, right here, right now."

He drew Francesca down until she was kneeling in front of him and kissed her lips softly. "If we become man and wife now, then after tonight, no matter what may happen, nothing and no one can keep us apart."

"Do you love me, Malcolm?" Francesca asked, all her hopes and fears and dreams posed in those four simple words.

"I do," he answered, pressing Francesca back until she was lying outstretched and there, on Jeremy Dorset's best Oriental carpet, as the fire flickered and danced in the grate, Malcolm had his way.

He mounted Francesca eagerly and with anxious hands reached down and spread her tremulous thighs. He penetrated her slowly until he could feel the unmistakable curtain of her innocence before him, then

37

gently he pushed himself through it and entered the virgin world that no man had ever known before.

What Francesca lacked in skill and experience, she made up for in the complete trust of her lovemaking. Every movement of her body proclaimed her love and her willingness to give whatever would please Malcolm.

In her innocent, guileless way, she believed they were now man and wife. Nothing could keep them apart, Malcolm said, but her happiness was short-lived. For the very next day, Malcolm received word that his brother had been killed in a tragic riding accident. He rushed to the side of his ailing father, who unable to withstand the terrible shock of his eldest son's death, followed just two weeks later.

When, after a proper period of mourning, Malcolm returned to London, he was the handsome young Lord Harrod, lionized by every ambitious beauty in town, and none more so than Clarissa Dorset who had herself just recently returned home. Her two years on the continent had given Clarissa an exciting, daring, demeanor that entranced Malcolm. He was so dazzled by the petite beauty with the charm of a fairy queen, the delicacy of a porcelain figurine and the promise of a nymphet that he never looked back. His promises were forgotten; his vows sheepishly renounced.

Wiping away the tears that filled her eyes and spilled down her cheeks, Francesca stared out to sea, looking for the first trace of the new land toward which she was sailing. In her mind's eye she saw instead the circle of blood that stained her Uncle Jeremy's Oriental carpet. She remembered her terrible fear when she discovered it that fateful night, the indelible sign of her union with Malcolm—all that was left of her virginity—and she remembered how Malcolm had laughed at her fear.

"Don't worry, darling, no one will ever notice it," he had said reassuringly. "By morning it will have dried and merged with the patterns and colors of the carpet. No one will ever know it is there except the two of us. It will always remain as a sign and a proof of our love, and one day our children and grandchildren will play right here, where they all began."

As the S.S. *Georgiana* sailed eastward through the Mediterranean Sea, Francesca thought of Malcolm's light words and joyous laughter, and she hoped that there was something special—something locked away in a dusty far corner of his heart—that would remain forever theirs.

Chapter Five

Francesca Fairchild was a dishonored woman. Yet
she bore no grudge. Her wounded heart bled for the
man she had given herself to, but she felt oddly
thankful that she had discovered, before the bonds of
marriage inextricably bound them, that Malcolm had
never truly plighted his love to her.

Although it was her deepest wish that Clarissa
would find with him the joy and happiness she had
always hoped would be hers, Francesca would not
soon again give herself so trustingly to another man.

Malcolm and Uncle Jeremy were the only men
Francesca had ever been close to. She had never seen
her father. She did not even know who he was. As a
child, whenever she asked about her papa, her Aunt
Genevieve Dorset would try to distract her attention
with the promise of a new doll or a special treat at
tea.

The little girl's pathetic questions tore at Genevieve's soft heart, but she knew little more about the
man than Francesca herself. Andrea simply refused to
discuss the matter with her sister.

All Genevieve knew was that immediately after the
funeral of the ugly old Lord Marlowe, Andrea moved
to the continent. Although Genevieve wrote to her sister, begging her to return the following year for her
own wedding to the young barrister she was be-

trothed to, Andrea did not return to England for the event. In fact it was not until six years later that Andrea came home again, bringing with her a four-year-old daughter, Francesca, fathered, she claimed, by a French nobleman, a rake whose name she anglicized to Fairchild.

Lady Marlowe was more alluring than ever, but she had grown into a restless, hungry spirit. She was not content to remain in England long and, during her frequent trips back to the continent, little Francesca Fairchild lived with her Uncle and Aunt Dorset.

Francesca had always been fatherless. Now she was homeless as well. In a desperate effort to overcome her broken heart and to prove to herself that she could stand alone, she was traveling to Egypt to live in the palace of the governor of Cairo and serve as governess and English tutor for his children.

The opportunity had come quite by chance and Francesca had seized it. It was the hand of fortune, she thought. But to her Aunt Genevieve, it was shocking that a young woman of her station and means would even consider accepting such a position, or even setting foot in a heathen land where the men had many wives in harems, and everyone prayed to Allah.

Even Francesca's unusually liberal and broadminded mother opposed the trip. Lady Marlowe urged her daughter to travel with her to France, to visit Paris where the charismatic young General Napoleon Bonaparte had just routed the revolutionary Directors and proclaimed himself First Consul.

Only Jeremy Dorset condoned Francesca's proposed adventure, and, in the end, his cool judgment won out.

Jeremy had sparked Francesca's interest in the

home of the ancient pharaohs. His old friend, Sir John Stuart had been serving as the British commander-in-chief in Egypt. He was sent to the Middle East after Bonaparte's conquest of Cairo to oversee the orderly evacuation of the British forces. When Sir John returned to London following the Peace of Amiens, he brought Elfi Bey, the Mameluke chieftain and governor of Cairo, back with him. Elfi Bey was anxious to plead his case directly to King George III. He hoped to convince the British monarch and the Parliament that it was in their best interests to support the Mamelukes against both the Ottoman invaders from Turkey and the French forces of General Bonaparte.

It was Sir John who had mentioned the Mameluke leader's desire to secure a British governess for his children. He had hoped that Jeremy would be able to suggest an eligible woman, but he never suspected for a moment that the young woman would be Dorset's own niece, Francesca.

Initially, Sir John was as shocked by the prospect as Genevieve. But, when he became convinced of Francesca's determination and of his old friend's unwavering support for the idea, he tried to assure the girl's mother and aunt she would be in safe hands. To ease his own conscience, he sent advance word to Major Misset, the consular representative he had left behind in Cairo, to make absolutely certain that no harm or misfortune would come to the young English girl who was arriving on the S.S. *Georgiana*.

As the steamer carried her closer and closer to her new life in Egypt, Francesca went over again what Sir John had told her about her prospective employer—Elfi Bey.

Elfi Bey was a prince—or bey—of the Mameluke tribe, an elite corps of powerful warriors who had controlled Egypt for almost six centuries. Their courage was legendary. Their wealth immeasurable. They dressed in brilliant colors and lived in sumptuous palaces. They rode the fleetest Arabian stallions, claimed the most beautiful women for their harems, and brandished glittering arms encrusted with precious gems.

The Mamelukes were not native Egyptians. Sometime in the early thirteenth century, the Egyptian sultan had imported some twelve thousand of the sturdiest young men he could find from the Caucasus Mountain region of Eastern Europe to be the heart of his army. Most of the young men were Georgian or Circassian. With their fair skin and massive size, they stood out in sharp contrast to the small, dark natives, and soon they became known as the Mamelukes. Although Mameluke is an Arabic word meaning "bought man," they were not slaves in any commonly understood sense of the word. For the Mamelukes were never content to serve any master but themselves.

They murdered the sultan and established their own despotic dynasty. For three hundred years, until the Turkish invasion of Egypt in 1516, the native Egyptians remained under their iron fist and, even then, although the Ottoman Empire claimed Egypt as its own, the Mamelukes remained the only true masters of the country.

A Turkish pasha, or governor, was appointed to rule Egypt and the country was divided into twenty-four provinces, but each was under the control of a bey elected by an assembly of Mamelukes called the Grand Divan. Although the beys were notorious for fighting and intriguing against each other, still they gradually consolidated their power until they possessed absolute control over the Turkish pasha himself.

The arrival at the Ottoman Citadel of a herald

clothed in black and riding a donkey, with the command, "Inzil ya Pasha"—"Descend, oh Pasha"—was enough to unseat the Turkish governor. And even Bonaparte's conquest of Cairo had not succeeded in destroying the awesome power of the Mameluke beys.

Sir John did not trust the Mamelukes—particularly Elfi Bey—for a moment. But he hoped to restore Britain's power in the Middle East by supporting them and he was imperious enough to believe that the barbarian prince would not dare mistreat an English woman who was under the direct protection of the British crown. And so Sir John did not impart his deepest fears to either Jeremy Dorset or his niece.

Chapter Six

The sturdy *Georgiana* carried Francesca down the coast of France and Portugal, through the narrow Strait of Gibraltar, into the Mediterranean Sea. *It is the clearest, greenest water I have ever seen,* Francesca thought as the ship moved in a south-easterly direction towards Alexandria.

From her reading Francesca knew that the ancient Egyptian port had been a magnificent city, named for its founder, Alexander the Great. In ancient times it was the largest city in the West, larger even than Carthage. It was the capital of the Ptolemies, the center of much of the Mediterranean trade, and an important seat of Hellenistic culture. For centuries Alexandria had been a fabled cosmopolitan metropolis. Its elaborate pleasure resorts were as famous throughout the ancient world as its royal libraries, which housed a vast collection of seven hundred thousand rolls. The famous Greek mathematician, Euclid, came to its great university. The distinguished anatomist, Herophilus, founded a medical school there. Under the Roman Empire it became the biggest provincial capital, and it was there, in Alexandria, where the famous lovers, Antony and Cleopatra, died.

Francesca's first glimpse of Alexandria from the topdeck of the *Georgiana* was of Pompey's Pillar, a tall, granite shaft silhouetted against a cloudless blue sky. This only heightened her romantic picture of the city, for she had no way of knowing that the pillar was one of the few remnants that remained of the ancient community. But once she disembarked from the *Georgiana*, her dreams faded quickly.

The fascinating metropolis she'd read about had declined until it was now small and seedy—a treeless city of dirty, unpaved streets and unbearable heat. The air was so dry that she developed an unquenchable thirst. The oppressive heat made her feel tired and sluggish all the time.

Alexandria was nothing like Francesca had imagined and she could not leave it soon enough. She stayed just two days to rest from her long sea voyage before beginning the second leg of her journey.

Francesca was to travel overland from Alexandria to Rosetta at the mouth of the delta and then proceed by boat up the Nile, accompanied all the way by Sergeant Crawford, the British maritime representative in Alexandria whom Major Misset had ordered to provide her with safe escort. But when they met at the gate of the city to start their journey, Francesca was surprised to find that the officer had only requisitioned a pair of dromedaries and a contingent of native servants.

"Well, Sergeant, how do we proceed from here?" she asked quizzically as she looked around her for some sign of a horse or carriage. "Do we walk?"

"Heavens, no, Miss Fairchild," the young officer replied seriously. He was a most solicitous but pompous young man. "We proceed from here to Rosetta by dromedary."

"Do you ride, ma'am?" he asked hastily, noting Francesca's apprehensive face.

"Only horses, I am afraid to say. I have not had

much exposure to camels in Hyde Park," she added ruefully.

But if there was one thing Sergeant Crawford lacked it was a sense of humor and he took every word of Francesca's literally. "It was horses I was referring to, Miss Fairchild. If you are a skilled equestrian, you will find riding a dromedary is as easy as sitting in a rocking chair." After so long in this isolated post, he was both uncomfortable and excited to be in the company of an English girl again and he tried to sound very worldly and mature.

Francesca looked uncertainly at the spindly-legged, hump-backed creatures, wondering how she would ever be able to mount such a tall beast. But the native boy who was holding the reins grinned at her and tapped the camels across their front legs with his stick. The beasts squatted down obediently, their long legs tucked neatly under their bodies.

Sergeant Crawford helped Francesca onto the back of one and mounted the other himself. The native boy jerked the beasts' heads up slightly and with great dignity the camels rose and soon Alexandria was far behind them.

On the first day they rode through desert that seemed to stretch on forever. The sun was merciless. The dry, scorching heat burned their eyelids and parched their throats. But at last they came to the sea and the road turned into a glorious, crescent-shaped beach, broken only by a narrow channel of water, which connected the pure Mediterranean and the brackish water of Lake Idku. A small ferry carried them across the channel.

The last few miles brought them once again into the desert, but this only served to heighten Francesca's pleasure when at last they reached Rosetta. It was a striking contrast to Alexandria. The

47

city bloomed with gardens, orchards and fertile fields. The streets were paved and the comfortable homes of the European merchants looked out on the waterfront.

Rosetta sat at the mouth of the Nile River where the delta soil was rich and dark and a profusion of variegated flowers flourished. But to one observer who watched her arrival under the escort of Sergeant Crawford, Francesca stood out in the city like a sunflower in the desert.

Pierre du Bellenfant recognized Sergeant Crawford immediately and he knew without a doubt that the Englishman would never introduce him to his charge. Just the month before, when he arrived in Alexandria, Bellenfant had relieved the sergeant of a fortnight's pay in a friendly game of cards. Although it was won fairly and squarely, he suspected that the officer was not a man to forget or forgive a sound drubbing. But he did not need Crawford's help.

Moments after he watched Francesca ride into town, the handsome Frenchman made it his business to find out who she was and he laughed silently to himself at what he discovered about her.

Pierre du Bellenfant had been planning to leave for Cairo in the morning but when the sergeant and his fair prize arrived, he decided to postpone his departure. Francesca's presence intrigued him. What kind of woman, he wondered, would travel alone to Egypt, without husband, father, or relative of any kind, to become the governess for Elfi Bey? Either she was exceptionally daring or exceptionally foolish. But either way she could be very useful to him in the matter which had brought him to Egypt.

For Pierre du Bellenfant needed an unsuspecting ally in the palace of Elfi Bey.

Chapter Seven

After the heat and dust of Alexandria, Rosetta seemed like a lush oasis to Francesca and, for the first time since leaving England, she began to relax from the traumatic emotional events that had precipitated her journey, and from the long sea voyage that had brought her so many miles from home.

With his characteristic thoroughnesss, Sergeant Crawford had arranged for them to rest for five days in the home of a prosperous British merchant in Rosetta, and the cozy though modest cottage was like a tonic for Francesca.

Although she had enjoyed viewing the strange new world from her high seat on the dromedary's back, she was never able to adjust to the sudden, frightening, lurching motion one experiences when the camel stops and buckles his front legs beneath him to allow his passenger to dismount. She was happy to trust her own legs again and to fall asleep once more in a soft feather bed.

Francesca slept more soundly than she had in months. She woke up refreshed and invigorated, and filled with enthusiasm to begin her new life. After a hearty breakfast, she ran up to her hostess's sitting room to pay her respects and inquire after her health. But to her consternation, she found that Lady Chumley was not alone. A tall, dark man was bending over her chaise longe. Her dressing gown was open and the man's hand was on her bare chest.

Surprised and embarrassed, Francesca turned hastily to leave, hoping that her entrance had gone unnoticed, when Mrs. Chumley's bright voice stopped her.

"Don't run off, my dear," she called cheerfully as if there was nothing untoward or awkward in the scene Francesca had unwittingly interrupted. "We are just about finished and you must make the acquaintance of the most handsome man in Rosetta before he dashes off to Cairo and loses himself in some ancient temple or other."

"The temple I am most interested in, Madame, is the one more beautiful, more perfectly constructed, more intricate than any made by man. It is the temple of a beautiful woman's body."

His voice was soft and low, yet each word reached across the room to Francesca like a musical note. His English was perfect, but he spoke more like an American than a Britisher, with just an intriguing trace of an accent. As he spoke, he turned toward Francesca and, though her eyes were riveted on the floor to avoid looking again at the scene she had interrupted, she could feel his eyes on her body and she knew that his words, so carefully chosen and clearly enunciated, were meant for her, and her cheeks flushed at his boldness.

Mrs. Chumley saw her guest's acute embarrassment, but she was in no hurry to alleviate it. In fact, she was secretly pleased and flattered as she imagined what was going through Francesca's mind. She'd had the same thoughts herself on more than one occasion and, after all, she told herself, thoughts never hurt anyone so why not enjoy them.

Mrs. Chumley laughed coquettishly. She was a

large woman, fleshy and florid, and her girlish titter increased Francesca's uneasiness. Unable to retreat yet unwilling to advance, Francesca still stood hesitantly at the door.

"Pierre, you really are an incorrigible rascal," Mrs. Chumley cooed, "and you are making me forget my manners. What ever will Miss Fairchild think seeing your hand on my bosom, and then hearing your naughty talk. Why, I haven't even introduced you two yet, have I?"

The dark visitor interrupted smoothly with a slight bow toward Francesca. "Miss Fairchild, allow me to introduce myself. I am Pierre du Bellenfant."

Francesca raised her eyes and found herself looking into a pair of frank, and frankly amused, gray eyes. *He is laughing at me for being so hopelessly unsophisticated,* she thought. *Clarissa would not be standing here like a tree that has suddenly taken root in her hostess's boudoir.*

"I am pleased to make your acquaintance," Francesca replied stiffly, but the words echoed leadenly in her ears.

Monsieur du Bellenfant's amusement spread from his eyes and he flashed a wide, dazzling smile at her. "The pleasure, I assure you, Mademoiselle, is entirely my own," he said. "Now if you will be kind enough to permit me one moment longer with Mrs. Chumley, then I will leave you to enjoy her gracious company."

The Frenchman turned back to the chaise lounge and pressed Mrs. Chumley's hand in his. He held it silently in his own, completely absorbed, as if he had forgotten Francesca's presence. But Mrs. Chumley, seemingly unmoved by his intimate behavior, began to chirp again.

"Come, Miss Fairchild," she said warmly, "you need not stand at the door all morning. Do sit on the sofa

51

there," she gestured with her free hand, "and make yourself comfortable. I want to tell you all about the dinner party that Mr. Chumley and I have planned in your honor this evening. Of course, it will be nothing as grand as the dinners you are accustomed to attending in London, but for a tiny outpost like Rosetta . . . well, my dear, I am afraid it is the best we can do."

"I am sure it will be as delightful as any dinner I have ever attended, Mrs. Chumley," Francesca replied gracefully.

At Francesca's encouraging words, Mrs. Chumley abandoned any pretense of humility. "Well," she admitted, "I can tell you it will be an occasion that will not soon be forgotten around here. It is not every week we have an honored guest like yourself visiting—and your mother a titled lady, I am told."

"Nor a visitor as lovely to look at," the Frenchman added. He relinquished Mrs. Chumley's hand and turned to Francesca, the same bemused expression on his face.

Francesca lowered her eyes again to avoid his cool gaze. He sighed dramatically. "Ah, ladies, I am afraid I have stayed far too long. Mrs. Chumley, I will look in on you again tomorrow if you like, although I find nothing that should cause you alarm. Mademoiselle Fairchild, I hope we will meet again while you are in Egypt."

"But surely, Pierre," Mrs. Chumley interrupted, "we will see you before tomorrow. You cannot have forgotten the dinner for Miss Fairchild this evening?"

"I do not believe I have received an invitation to your party, Madame," he answered smoothly, "but if I may take your kind words as a request for my presence, then I would be enchanted to attend."

"Of course you received an invitation, Pierre. I

wrote it myself. You are always so absent-minded about these things," Mrs. Chumley scolded.

"You are undoubtedly correct, Madame. My faults are legion," he said, bending over her outstretched hand and kissing it lightly. Then turning to Francesca, he bowed. "Until this evening, Mademoiselle."

Francesca met his devilish gray eyes for an instant, then she turned away. She had never met a man with so disconcertingly frank a gaze. He had not for a moment appeared embarrassed. He had not tried to disguise his business with Mrs. Chumley or offered any excuse for his presence in her boudoir. He had not even seemed concerned in the slightest when Francesca discovered them together in such a compromising position.

Mrs. Chumley was one thing. Francesca could tell at a glance that she was a weak, frivolous woman who might even be proud to be caught with an undeniably handsome man much younger than she. But the Frenchman was quite clearly a gentleman, albeit certainly unlike any English gentleman Francesca had ever known.

Her heart was too filled with memories of Malcolm to be moved by any other. But no man or woman could see Pierre du Bellenfant and fail to note his splendid appearance. He was the only man Francesca had ever seen whom she would have to call beautiful—truly beautiful in the fullest sense of the word.

There was no hint of softness or femininity in his face, yet the words that are usually reserved to describe a startling woman seemed to fit him as no others could. He was much more than handsome. His body was as supremely proportioned as the finest sculpture. His noble head was a perfect globe and his features looked as if they had been carved by a master artisan. He was like a priceless statue of a god—

Apollo perhaps, or Icarus—who had suddenly come to life.

But Francesca remembered his devilish gray eyes and thought to herself warily, *Pierre du Bellenfant might look like a god, but he is every inch a man.*

Chapter Eight

Francesca decided that it was not her place to interfere in the domestic relations of her host and hostess and so she tried to dismiss the disturbing episode of the morning from her mind. In fact, she did not think about Pierre du Bellenfant again until that evening at the dinner party which the Chumleys gave in her honor.

Francesca was discussing her forthcoming trip up the Nile with her host when the Frenchman appeared suddenly at her side and greeted Mr. Chumley with a great show of warmth. The boldness with which the scoundrel confronted the husband he had just cuckolded astounded Francesca. She did not want to be a party to his impudence, but Mr. Chumley did not allow her an opportunity to escape.

"My wife tells me, Miss Fairchild," he said, "that you made the acquaintance of our distinguished French guest this morning, so you will forgive me if I do not repeat the introductions."

"We have met," Francesca replied icily.

Pierre du Bellenfant took note of her frosty tone. *"Enchanté, toujours,"* he replied coolly and with a slight bow he moved on, mingling easily with the other guests. His frank, demanding eyes were masked behind a suave, mannered air which he wore like a veneer. Francesca found it distinctly annoying. In fact everything about the rogue infuriated her at this brief second meeting. She felt like denouncing the audacious scoundrel to poor Mr. Chumley who was rambling on, never suspecting the Frenchman's dark deeds.

"My wife is a very sickly woman," Mr. Chumley was saying. "She has been ever since we married thirty-five years ago. She must have seen one hundred doctors over the years—and not only physicians, but faith healers, holy men who prayed for cures, scientists with chemical potions. It would not surprise me if some of them were witch doctors," he confided. "Now Dr. Bellenfant is her latest and she has never been better. No quackery about him."

"Pierre du Bellenfant is your wife's personal physician?" Francesca asked incredulously, as the true meaning of the morning's scene slowly dawned on her. She blushed at her own foolishness, but Mr. Chumley did not notice her embarrassment.

"He is not only her physician," he answered, "but Mrs. Chumley swears he is the best she has ever had. Although he is a Frenchman, I understand he learned his doctoring in America. It is our bad luck that he will be leaving Rosetta within the week—around the same time you are, now that I think of it, Miss Fairchild—and destined for Cairo, as are you."

"Perhaps we will come across each other again in Cairo," Francesca said, only by way of conversation for she had no interest in furthering her acquaintance with the doctor. But her words gave Mr. Chumley an idea.

"By Jove," he exclaimed, "I never thought of it until this moment. Dr. Bellenfant could escort you to Cairo and deliver you to Major Misset himself. The doctor knows the area well—was here with Bonaparte, they

56

tell me. Quite a hero he was in the Battle of the Pyramids."

Mr. Chumley saw the apprehensive look on Francesca's face and patted her arm reassuringly. "Granted, Miss Fairchild, the doctor is a bit of a looker—a lady's man I guess you would call him—but you would be in safe hands. He is the son of a duke, you know, an educated man and a gentleman. He would never take advantage of a lady like yourself."

Mr. Chumley was the kind of man who was content with the smallest accomplishments and he was very pleased with himself for thinking of this new plan for Francesca.

"It would save Sergeant Crawford a long trip up and back," he went on encouragingly. "Why just this afternoon the sergeant was saying that he could ill afford the time. He is very concerned about being away from his post for more than a day or two at a stretch, and this long absence worries him, especially in these precarious times. Why, the country has never truly settled down since Bonaparte's landing in '78. It's been one side winning and then another—more than a man can keep straight. We had the French Revolutionary Army bivouacked right here in this town. Then Lord Nelson and our own royal navy, God bless King George, routing the upstarts from Alexandria, and the Mameluke beys skirmishing and plotting all the while—and all that in five short years. We are longing for a return to tranquil times.

"Mind you, Miss Fairchild, I have no desire to put the fear of the Lord in you, but it is no bed of roses you have come to," he warned ominously.

"You believe, then, Mr. Chumley, that Cairo is too dangerous a city for a young woman like myself?" Francesca asked sharply.

Chumley had heard terrible tales about the Mame-

57

luke beys. Their cruelty was as legendary as their courage. But it was not his business to tell the girl this. Her trip had Major Misset's blessing, and who was he to question the consul?

"Don't you be getting frightened by anything I say, now. It is just an old man's tongue wagging," he said, trying unconvincingly to gloss over his dark words. "Rest assured that the consul would not allow you to go to Cairo if he were not one humdred percent sure that you would be in the best of hands.

"Come now, Miss Fairchild," he exclaimed, obviously relieved to find a way to end their unfortunate conversation, "there are Sergeant Crawford and the doctor. We must tell them about my plan for you."

"Perhaps," Francesca began diplomatically, "since all the arrangements have already been made, it would be wiser if I continued with my original itinerary."

"Nonsense, my girl. Just you leave the talking to me and you won't have a worry in the world," he said heartily, as he steered Francesca across the room toward the two men.

"I hope there are no ill feelings between us from our meeting in Alexandria," Bellenfant was saying as they approached.

"Certainly not," Crawford answered gruffly.

The resentment he denied showed clearly in his voice and the Frenchman replied with a mock seriousness that was lost on the officer. "If there are, I would be less than a gentleman if I did not give you an opportunity to satisfy yourself now that we meet again."

"What are you proposing, sir?"

"Why another game of chance; what else?" the doctor responded lightly.

Sergeant Crawford reddened with anger as he realized that he had fallen into the Frenchman's suave trap. His purse could not afford another loss and his pride could bear the damage even less.

"I have no time for that," he bristled; then added pompously, "the safety of a young woman is in my hands."

"By any chance, would this be the fortunate lady?" Bellenfant asked sarcastically as he turned to greet Francesca and her host.

Sergeant Crawford's hackles rose but he held his tongue now that a lady was present. Unlike Pierre du Bellenfant, Sergeant Crawford was always shy with women he had not paid for. He envied the Frenchman's ease. More than anything else, he wanted women to think he was charming and polished, but they always seemed to be laughing at him. Francesca was different. She was gentle and did not make him feel awkward. He thought it was probably because she was not a pretty girl. The prettier they were, the more foolish they made him feel.

"Well, Crawford," Mr. Chumley began, "has the doctor here been telling you that he is leaving for Cairo this week? Quite a coincidence, isn't it? When I saw the two of you together, I remembered our little conversation this afternoon. Perfect timing, I call it, and it will save you from the long trip to Cairo, after all."

Sergeant Crawford looked blank. "I'm not sure I understand your meaning, Chumley," he said.

"I believe, Sergeant," the doctor interjected, "that our host is proposing that I relieve you of your duty of escorting Miss Fairchild to Cairo and shoulder the happy burden in your place, an exchange from which, I have no doubt, I emerge once again the luckier man. What do you say? Shall I accompany Miss Fairchild to Cairo while you return post haste to Alexandria to answer the call of duty and country?"

"Oh, I don't think that I could agree to any such arrangement," Sergeant Crawford blustered. "I have my orders you know, direct from Major Misset. I am responsible for this young lady's safe conduct."

The doctor feigned shock. "Are you suggesting, Sergeant, that Miss Fairchild's conduct is something less than it should be?"

"How dare you, sir!" Crawford replied furiously.

Francesca did not like to see the poor, well-meaning sergeant made mock of, yet she smiled in spite of herself. He was like a great moose at the mercy of a sleek panther. "I think, Dr. Bellenfant, that it may be your conduct that gives Sergeant Crawford pause," she said gently.

"You mean to say that Sergeant Crawford is impugning my honor?" he said, pretending to be shocked. "Why, Crawford, I give you my word as a Frenchman and a gentleman that I will not seduce Miss Fairchild into a game of chance."

"But Major Misset . . ." Sergeant Crawford began to protest.

"And," the doctor interrupted, "I further swear that I will deliver her myself into the arms of the distinguished major. I will go even beyond that. If the good major is discomposed because you are not at Miss Fairchild's side, I will further swear that, as your personal physician, I ordered you for reasons of health to return to your command and insisted on taking your place as Miss Fairchild's personal escort."

Sergeant Crawford looked at the doctor in bewilderment. Then, as if he had suddenly seen a vision, he burst out triumphantly, "Aha! That is just what worries me, Bellenfant. If you would swear a falsehood to

Major Misset, how can I trust your word as a gentleman that Miss Fairchild will be safe in your hands?"

"Ah, Crawford, that is a dilemma, isn't it? But it is one which I must leave you and your countrymen here to solve. If you will excuse me . . ." Pierre du Bellenfant bowed deeply to Francesca and left the three Britishers staring after him.

Francesca did not see the doctor again to speak to until he was taking his leave.

"I hope, Miss Fairchild," he said, "that you will help Sergeant Crawford resolve his dilemma in a way that will not condemn me to a solitary river voyage."

Francesca was not sure whether his words were sincerely felt or were mere gallantry, but she was touched by their graciousness and by the grave way in which he spoke them.

Chapter Nine

Pierre du Bellenfant smiled to himself, pleased with his unexpected success. He delighted in each subtle nuance and small victory that brought him slowly but surely closer to the successful completion of his mission. But the young doctor would have ample time to savor his triumphs later. Now he had to concentrate his full attention on the problem at hand—namely how best to gain the confidence and, if need be, the affection of Miss Francesca Fairchild during the voyage to Cairo.

He had observed her closely but discreetly at the Chumleys' dinner party and had detected a strain of sadness in her that not even her most gracious efforts at cordiality could mask completely from his penetrating eyes.

Pierre du Bellenfant not only knew each curve and intimate crevice of a woman's body, as a physician he was privy to women's most closely guarded secrets. He had learned to distinguish the pain in their hearts from the imaginary ills they complained of and used as excuses to pull the curtains around their beds and hide their anguish from the world.

Beneath Francesca's innate shyness and reserve, he sensed the heartbreak that she was fleeing. Whatever else there was to discover about her—whether she was a courageous woman or a fool to undertake the position she had—he was sure he would find out soon enough.

The Chumleys' dinner had worked out far better than Pierre ever dared hope. He had virtually been offered the girl on a silver platter. *If Sergeant Crawford ever realizes what a plum he has handed me,* Pierre thought, not without a tinge of humor, *he will come galloping from Alexandria to try to reclaim his charge. And if Major Misset ever discovers the depth of his sergeant's stupidity, someone's hide will receive a tanning that will smart for a lifetime.*

But it was too late to stop him now, for a graceful white-sailed chebek was carrying Pierre and Francesca up the slow-moving Nile through the verdant delta land.

In the week she spent aboard the small barque, Francesca came to be grateful that Pierre du Bellenfant was at her side, and not the well-intentioned but eminently dull Sergeant Crawford. She could not imagine a better companion. The reservations with which she'd begun the Nile journey were soon forgotten. If the handsome doctor was a rogue and a rascal, he showed no sign of it in his behavior to her.

She found him to be gay but never raucous, considerate but never fawning, appreciative of her as a woman yet never suggestive. Best of all, he seemed to know the country and its people as well as the most expert guide, and when he looked out at the forty centuries of history that stretched before them, he looked with the eyes of a true romantic.

At last Francesca was entering the legendary world that she and her Uncle Jeremy had read so much about. She could see women washing clothes in the river and water buffalo ploughing the fields along its banks, and she thought that life in the primitive villages they were passing could not have changed at all in centuries. Sailing up the Nile of the pharaohs, of Antony and Cleopatra, following the same route that the Greek Herodotus had taken to write his great history of Egypt, she felt like a part of history herself. She was awed by the experience and eager to drink in every detail; yet, at the same time, she could hardly believe it was really happening to her.

Seeing how quick Francesca's mind was and how her eyes grew wide with wonder when he talked about the country and its history, Pierre filled her with stories. He told her about his first trip to Egypt five years before when he was a major in the conquering army of General Bonaparte and faced the Mameluke beys at the Battle of the Pyramids, the site of which they would pass on the last day of their river journey.

"The Mamelukes were lined up against the Nile, resplendently costumed in vivid silk gowns of every color in the rainbow," he said, his gray eyes flashing at the memory. "The brilliant morning sun glinted off their helmets, off the swords and scimitars they waved, and off the crescents and globes atop the sumptuous tents they'd pitched behind them. Their Arabian steeds pawed the desert sand and reared their sleek heads as if they were impatient for battle. The Mamelukes made a brilliant spectacle, but as a foe they were easily vanquished. In twenty-four hours the battle was over and we marched into Cairo and claimed it for the new Republic of France."

Pierre spoke proudly of their conquest and of the work of the scientists and scholars General Bonaparte had brought to Egypt along with his troops. He told Francesca about a fine-grained basalt tablet they had found near Rosetta. "It was inscribed two hundred years before the birth of Christ," he said excitedly, "and may very possibly be the key that will finally unlock the secret picture writing that the ancient Egyptians carved on every statue and monument."

When Pierre described Egypt's treasures and hidden possibilities, his bon vivant image seemed to drop away and Francesca glimpsed a different man—a man of strength and action and deep passions. During their voyage together she observed him in every mood—playful, brooding, intense, exhilarated, solitary—and she realized that her first impression had been correct. He was truly beautiful.

His every movement, even his hands, revealed a grace that any woman would envy, yet he was intensely virile, broad-shouldered and darkly handsome. His hair was blacker than midnight and thick with curls. His features were patrician. He had none of Malcolm's languid ease. His body exuded strength and energy, yet, Francesca thought, there was something obscurely alarming in its coiled, controlled power, and something disturbing in his compelling gray eyes. Some dark passion seemed buried within him and when he remembered it, his eyes turned smoky. He was frightening then but strangely exciting, and a tingle of delicious fear ran down her spine as she imagined what an angry Pierre du Bellenfant would be like.

It was the evening of the third night. Francesca sat in the prow of the chebek lost in her thoughts of Pierre. Why had he come back to Egypt? she wondered. How, if his father was truly a nobleman, had he escaped the wrath of Robespierre and his furious rebels? She shuddered at the thought of Pierre's noble head bowed beneath the democratic blade of the guillotine.

The air was cool, the water dark below. The moon, full and white above, slipped in and out of the cloud-strewn sky, casting Francesca in darkness one moment and then, in the next instant, bathing her in its eerie light. At first, protected by the deep shadows, she thought she was alone, but gradually, as the moon illuminated the deck, she became aware of another presence.

Pierre was lying on his back, his arms linked behind his head. His grave face was fixed on hers with an expression she had never seen before and did not understand. But she had the eerie feeling that he had been reading her mind, and she flushed both at her thoughts and at the knowledge that he knew them.

Her cheeks turned pink and he smiled at her. "What are you thinking that makes you blush, Miss Fairchild?" he asked gently.

And she, thinking that he was teasing her, blushed even deeper and bowed her head. Pierre marveled at her wonderful contradictions—so strong and courageous to dare this dangerous adventure, yet so shy and guileless that her cheeks would redden at the slightest provocation.

"You are never more lovely to me than when your cheeks turn pink," he said. "I remember at our first meeting you were blushing."

Francesca laughed and the happy notes rippled across the Nile. "I was so foolish."

"Why do you say that?"

"I thought that I had burst in on you and Mrs. Chumley . . ."

"But you did."

"Well, I did, of course, although I was sure that I knocked. But I thought that you and Mrs. Chumley were . . . were . . ." she hesitated, unsure of what word to use. She had never talked about such an intimate thing with any man, even Malcolm.

"Were making love, Miss Fairchild?"

"Yes," she added.

66

"Why are those words so difficult for you to say?" he asked softly. "They are simple words which describe what is indescribable." His gray eyes were fixed on hers and they were so frank, so unflinching, that they seemed to penetrate her heart and see her deepest secret. Tears of shame and longing welled in her eyes and Pierre, seeing her sudden, terrible sadness, was deeply moved and saddened himself.

"Francesca, Francesca," he whispered, his voice deep and vibrant. "I shall never call you Miss Fairchild again. Once when I was six or seven, my father told me that somewhere, he knew not where, I had a sister—or was it a cousin?—whose name was Francesca. Did he tell me or did I dream it? I have never been certain. But I always imagined her. In my dreams she had long golden hair like yours, and eyes as soft as velvet like yours. She was slim and laughing and she loved me."

The shadows had fallen over Pierre again. Francesca could only distinguish his form vaguely in the darkness, but she felt as if she were seeing him more clearly than she ever had—than he had ever allowed her to—before. At that moment he seemed vulnerable and unprotected. He had dropped his mask of the gay lady's man, and lay beside her more naked than Malcolm had ever been. "Let me be your sister," she urged him tenderly.

Although he smiled at her, his eyes were cloudy and sad. "Have you ever been in love, Francesca?" he asked. "Have you ever made love in the moonlight?" His words drifted over the river to her.

Protected by the darkness and by the almost mystical aura of closeness he had woven around them, she said, "Yes, Pierre, once I loved and I made love." She paused, holding her breath, listening for some response from him, but the only reply was an ibis calling to her mate across the dark desert sky. "It was not in the moonlight but in the light of the fire," she whispered, half to herself, half to the forgiving night, as the memory of Malcolm once again flooded over her.

The silent night closed in around them and they drifted wordlessly on the black river.

"Do you love him, Francesca?" Pierre asked finally.

She breathed deeply, as if to either summon her strength or hold back her emotions. "Yes, I do." The evening breeze carried her whispered answer to him. "He was, he is . . ."

"Does it matter who he was or is?" Pierre interrupted sharply. His words sounded cruel to her and made her regret her confession. But then he spoke again, so tenderly that Francesca's eyes filled with tears.

"If it matters, Francesca, then don't tell me who he is," he said. "Keep your love inviolate, untarnished by anyone but him. It is yours and his—a private thing, a treasure to cherish together in your hearts."

Francesca yearned to unburden her heartache to him. *This beautiful, mysterious, god-like man will understand my sorrow and my loss,* she thought, but he had made further confession impossible.

In the darkness Pierre could not see Francesca clearly, but every instinct in his body told him that she was crying. Still he made no move to comfort her. He lay on his back staring up into the starless sky, so silent, so motionless, that she thought he had fallen asleep.

When at last he spoke, he seemed to be talking to himself or addressing the ancient dieties that had guarded the river for centuries. Francesca strained to hear his words. She felt like an intruder, eavesdropping on a very private confession.

"I have never made love," he said. "Ah, yes, I have known women, too many to count or even to remember, and they have been good. I discovered their mysterious powers from a Yankee barmaid. Kate her name was—old Kate. She had breasts so large she could smother a man and limbs so strong she could imprison him for life if she wanted. But she was a wise woman and a good teacher, and I—I was a good pupil. When she taught me everything she knew, she turned me out of her bed. She would have been proud of me, Kate would." He paused wearily. "For I have lusted and I have sated myself, quenching my thirst at women's eternal fountain. But I have never made *love*. I have never *known* love."

The river lapped at the side of the boat, otherwise the night was silent. *How sorely I have misjudged him*, Francesca thought. His words had moved her deeply. They seemed to her as frank as his eyes had been when they first looked into hers and she felt that for a precious moment she had glimpsed another person's soul.

If Francesca had been more sophisticated, she might have suspected that the doctor's touching confession was nothing more than a skillful performance enacted to weaken her defenses—an unprincipled rogue's shrewd ploy to win her for a night. But cynicism and suspicion were alien to Francesca's trusting nature. She accepted Pierre at his word and was deeply moved by his confidences. She wished that she could find the right words to comfort him, the right way to banish the sadness that she had seen in his eyes.

But as she wondered what she could say or do to soothe him, Pierre spoke again and this time his words shocked her as profoundly as his earlier ones had moved her.

"Will you lie with me tonight, Francesca?" he asked turning to her. The moonlight played on her face and he saw the surprise and consternation written clearly on it.

"No, no, Francesca, not as you think. Lie with me here, just as we are. Alone yet together, apart yet so close. Give me only your hand," he whispered, reaching out for hers, "and we will be bound by the tenuous thread of our fingertips, and by history which we can never escape—the history of this country that presses around us, insulating us in its ancient cocoon, and our own histories that we carry inexorably in our hearts."

Francesca's fingers reached out and touched his and the soft music of his words lulled her into a sweet, dream-filled sleep.

Pierre kissed the hand he held and smiled at the sleeping girl. *She is lovely,* he thought, *in her own special way, and deeply sensual for all her innocence.* She was not foolish as he had first imagined. She was valiant and wounded and, he suspected, she must be impetuous to have given her love and generous not to have extorted the payment of marriage from her lover. She would make a strong ally for him.

But Pierre was not thinking of that now. He was wondering if she had lusted for the man she loved—if she still lusted for him. He wondered if she dreamed of her lover and woke in the night hungry with desire. And he wished that she had never known a man's love.

70

Chapter Ten

When Francesca woke up, she found herself tucked snugly into her own berth.

"You fell sound asleep," Pierre said later that morning by way of explanation. "I think my conversation worked better than any sleeping powder could. Perhaps I should try to find a way to bottle my words and peddle them as Dr. Bellenfant's Magic Slumber Dust," he joked.

"Don't be silly, Pierre," Francesca said laughingly, "I heard every word you said. But I guess," she added ruefully, "I would make a terrible companion for a night watch. There I was seeing the sun rise over the desert with you—but only in my dreams."

"I watched you, that was companionship enough," he said gallantly.

Pierre was once again the gay, charming rogue. Now that she had seen his other side, it seemed to Francesca that he deliberately assumed this pose because it was an easy, convenient disguise to hide behind. *Yet why is he hiding from me?* she wondered. *Why is he disappearing again just when he had showed me his true self?*

Francesca could never go back. In their shadowed evening talk, Pierre had pierced her natural reserve. He had penetrated the shy demeanor with which she faced the world and she could never again be anything but her natural self with him. He was delighted by the change in her. It was as if he had opened a pigeon's cage and out flew a brilliant minah bird.

In the remaining days of their river journey, Pierre always played the roué—bold, irrepressible, fun-loving. But Francesca was simply Francesca and he discovered how lovely and sensitive she was, impulsive and generous, quick to laugh or cry, quick to give her heart, he suspected. She put no price, no demands on the affection she gave.

She was not as serious as he had thought, nor he as superficial as she had assumed. Francesca knew she would miss his gaiety and companionship when they parted, and, as each moment brought them closer to their destination, Pierre grew increasingly concerned for the safety of this very special girl he had discovered. Finally, on the last day of their journey, he warned Francesca about the Mameluke beys, and about Elfi Bey in particular.

"I cannot deflect you from the course you have chosen, Francesca, but at least I can prevent you from going like a lamb into a wolf's den," he said. "The Mamelukes are as fierce as they are fearless. They boast that they can sever a head with a single blow, and they have neither friendships nor family bonds to stay their hand. For the most promising young Mamelukes are not the natural sons of the chieftains. Like the reigning beys and the beys for generations before them, these youths were taken from their homes in the Caucasus when they were eight or nine and trained to be warriors. Destruction and domination are all that they know."

Pierre was more serious than Francesca had ever seen him and his ominous words chilled her to the bone. Nothing Sir John had told her had prepared her for this, yet she knew that Pierre understood this exotic country and its customs far better than most Europeans.

"Why do not the natural sons of the beys succeed their fathers?" she questioned him.

Pierre studied her gravely. "The ways of the Mamelukes are very different from the ways of the English. They have many concubines of every race and color who bear them numerous children. But they marry only their own kind and almost never father a legitimate son. You see, Francesca, the Mameluke wives are as ambitious and cunning as their husbands. They understand that a woman's beauty is her keenest weapon and they will do anything to preserve it for as long as they can—even abort their children. The few Mamelukes who are privileged because of their birth are held in contempt by the many who earn their position by their courage and connivance."

He paused for a moment, uncertain of how much more to tell Francesca. For his own selfish reasons he did not want to frighten her so much that she would abandon her position and turn back. But she waited for him to continue with such brave, resolute eyes and such a trusting expression that he was forced to plunge on.

"Elfi Bey is one of the many. He is reputed to be the most powerful and most fearsome of all the beys—and he earned that reputation by his deeds. To him every man exists to be bested, every woman to be possessed. He is arrogant and proud, obstinate and bold. Yet he has a taste for fine music, plays chess like a master, and welcomes the most distinguished and cultivated visitors to his splendid palaces in Cairo and Thebes.

"I am telling you all this, not to frighten you, Francesca, but to warn you to be on your guard. Elfi Bey is a shrewd and clever man. He knows that if he

73

treats you poorly, he will endanger his position with the British. But he is also primitive and cold-blooded. I cannot be at your side every moment, nor can Major Misset—although you will see more of me than you imagine," he added cryptically, "You must be alert and careful, for a bey's palace is a hotbed of envy and intrigue."

Pierre's dire warning cast a pall over the final hours of their Nile journey. Although the evening was cool and inviting, Francesca slept fitfully. Her mind was churning with his alarming words and the unanswered question they raised: If the Mameluke beys fathered no children, why then had she been employed as a governess and English teacher?

Chapter Eleven

Pierre roused Francesca at dawn. The night haze was beginning to lift, releasing the stately palms that lined the shore from its dark embrace. A lone ibis waded in the shallow water where the Nile lapped at the fertile bank. And the fiery disk of the sun slipped over the horizon, coloring the distant, gray dunes of the Sahara a rosy hue.

Francesca gazed in wonder at forty centuries of recorded history. To her right rose the Great Pyramids of the Pharaoh, massive triangles of mystery and majesty looming out of the barren desert sands. To her left glittered the one thousand minarets of Cairo, the fabled city that would be her new home now.

Within its thick, protective walls, Cairo was already beginning to awaken. The great gates that locked the city in at night were open. Peddlers and street vendors jostled each other for the best spots in the crowded bazaar. Caravans carrying ivory and gold from Africa, china and ostrich shells from Asia, streamed into the city to barter their exotic wares for cotton and grain. They came from as far away as India and Timbuktu to trade in the city's teeming bazaar and haggle in the shops of its skilled silversmiths, potters and leatherworkers whose workmanship was famed far and wide.

Cairo was a labyrinth of narrow, unpaved streets, which in a few hours would be a solid mass of flesh—shrewd shysters hawking their wares; merchants hunting for the most favorable exchange; women of the street, their faces veiled, their salable goods exposed; bands of hungry, naked children begging for coins, and packs of scavaging dogs attacking the garbage that was strewn everywhere.

But Cairo was also one of the holy centers of Islam. Huge granite mosques, built with the stones of ancient Egyptian monuments to the honor of the Moslem god Allah, were everywhere, their gilt domes shimmering under the relentless sun, their graceful minarets soaring into the heavens.

Francesca was overwhelmed by the strangeness of the place and by the noise and bustle of its narrow streets, as Pierre guided her through the thronged city to the imposing, white stucco residence of the British consul. He refused to let her out of his sight until he had delivered her personally into the hands of Major Misset.

The major, a short, sallow-faced man with a bald pate and a thickening waistline, greeted Francesca correctly but cautiously and listened attentively as she explained why a dashing Frenchman was at her side instead of Sergeant Crawford.

Major Misset did not attempt to disguise his displeasure at this unexpected turn of events. He made it clear to Pierre that no Frenchman was welcome in his consulate.

For an instant Pierre's gray eyes flashed angrily, but he refused to take umbrage. The last thing he wanted in his delicate position was to provoke the British consul on his first day in Cairo. He had won over Francesca and gained entry to Elfi Bey's court. That was victory enough for now.

"I understand your position, Major Misset, and I take no offense," he said coolly. "Miss Fairchild," he bowed formally. "It has been an honor and a great pleasure to escort you."

But Francesca, angered and embarrassed by the major's rudeness, said pointedly, "I shall not say good-bye to you, Pierre, because I hope that I shall see you again—and often. After all, you are the only friend I have in Cairo."

Pierre took her hand and brought it to his lips. Then, speaking very softly for her ears alone, he answered, "Friend or foe, you could not keep me away."

She could not read the expression in his eyes and his cryptic words disturbed her. But with the major's baleful glance fixed upon them, she decided to remain silent.

Francesca was glad she'd held her tongue, because, once Pierre had taken his leave, Major Misset began to question her closely about him. If he had not been so insolent to Pierre or so arrogant in his cross-examination, she would have willingly told him anything he wanted to know. But now she deflected his inquiries frostily. Yet, even as she did, Francesca realized for the first time that—other than his name, his profession and his intimate midnight confession—she actually knew very little about Dr. Pierre du Bellenfant.

He had a reputation on three continents as an adventurer, gambler and rogue. It was said that his medical specialty was beautiful women who repaid him for his excellent care a hundred times over, or until he tired of them. But if the true story of Dr. Pierre du Bellenfant were known, it would come as a surprise to those who dismissed him so lightly.

He was the only son of Georges Duc du Bellenfant, the last of a noble family that traced its ancestry directly back to Charlemagne, and of a gay, light-hearted American girl named Lucy Barnes, who fell utterly in love with the dashing young French officer the first time she saw him. To her stern Yankee father the Duc was an enemy who had come to the colonies to fight with the savage redskins against his British brothers in the French and Indian War, and he forbade the marriage. But Lucy was as stubborn as her father and very much in love. She eloped with the handsome officer.

From that day forth old Lucius Barnes decreed that her name would never be spoken in his house again. Although she was his favorite daughter, the only one of his children he truly cared for, he never relented and the old manse never again rang with the laughter that was like music to his ears, and the smile that to him was brighter than the sun never shone in his hallways again.

When Pierre was born, Lucy wrote to her father, telling him she had given birth to a son and was living in Paris with her husband, and begging his forgiveness. Lucius Barnes steamed the letter open over the tea kettle, read it, resealed it, and sent it back. Lucy thought he had refused to open it and she never wrote again.

Over the years, the frequent indiscretions of Georges Duc du Bellenfant became common gossip in the salons and cafes of Paris. But if Lucy ever regretted her hasty elopement or rued her marriage, few ever knew it. Outwardly she appeared radiantly happy, glowing with life and with love for her husband. Yet each new liaison that reached her ears was like a knife in her heart.

Lucy was too proud to plead for her husband's love or to chastise him for his amours. If her love was not enough to bind Georges to her, then she felt the fault must lie with her. But no matter how hard she tried to please him or how satisfied he seemed, she would always hear again—if not that week then the next or the next—of another dalliance, another affair, another mistress whom the Duc had presented with an expensive bibelot, another lady he had courted at Versailles.

In her sadness Lucy turned to Pierre, pouring out all her love on her small son who, even at a very early age, sensed in her violent outpouring of affection a terrible sorrow. Usually though, she was filled with laughter and gaiety and he loved her completely. She taught him to speak English and filled him with exciting stories of the land where she was born. She told him about the enormous animals that roamed there called buffalo, and the red-skinned people who lived in tents in the woodlands and killed the buffalo with their bows and arrows, and she always promised Pierre that some day she would take him home with her.

On his sixteenth birthday, Pierre discovered, suddenly and brutally, the reason for his mother's sadness. Deciding that he was old enough to prove himself a man, he paid his first visit to a Parisian salon. He tried to appear nonchalant and sophisticated, but he was awkward and shy as he entered the long-imagined sanctum of the notorious Madame Surret. The salon was more decadent than anything he had pictured. In a softly lit, mirrored room draped in red damask, perhaps a dozen or more women, their faces painted, their bodies free of any artificial constraints, lounged on sumptuous brocade pillows. Some lay with men, others alone in positions that revealed them to their greatest advantage, and displayed the wares they were selling.

A large redhead called to Pierre. Cupping a bare

79

breast in her hand and pointing it at him, she teased, "Is this what you are looking for, son?"

Pierre had never seen a woman's flesh before, not even his mother's, and his excitement mounted along with his embarrassment. The redhead got up, laughing, and moved toward the stairs. "Come on," she called over her shoulder, "and I will give you all the milk you can drink."

All Pierre had to do was follow the girl up the stairs and he would finally discover the forbidden secrets a woman possessed. As he started after her, he saw on the landing above him, impudently squeezing the fleshy, bare breasts of a raven-haired whore, his own father.

Pierre fled, shocked and angry, and from that day he turned irrevocably against his father. When the revolution broke out, he joined the side of the rebels and called himself Citizen Enfant in defiance of his father and the noble lineage of which he was so proud.

Not even his mother's tears or remonstrances could bring him to make peace with his father. "I am a democrat like you, Mother," he told her. "I renounce the aristocrats—each and all of them without distinction or exception."

After King Louis was executed and the guillotine's blade dripped with the blood of noble men and women, the Duc decided to flee to the safety of England. He pleaded with his son to help them escape, if only for his mother's sake. But even then Pierre refused to give his assistance.

"Each aristocrat," he spat out the word contemptuously as if it was dirt, "will be judged by what he has done for the Republic—and for its children. As for Mother, she will be safe among the citizens for she is one of us." Pierre suffered from the arrogance and blind confidence of youth.

Georges Duc du Bellenfant was as passionate and volatile as his son. He slapped Pierre sharply for his insolent words and his dark eyes glowered. "Citizen Enfant," he said coldly, "you are no longer welcome in this nobleman's home."

Pierre did not see his parents again until one night several weeks later in the midst of the Reign of Terror. He was caught up in the hysterical force of a mob that was raping and burning indiscriminately in the name of *liberté, equalité, fraternité.* Revolted by what he was witnessing, Pierre tried to separate himself from the unruly throng. As he did he caught a glimpse of the new focus of the mob's anger. The leaders had intercepted a couple trying to flee with their servants and were bent on a bloody revenge.

Stupid aristocrats, he thought. *They can never escape the glorious revolution.* Then suddenly, he recognized the woman's rich auburn hair. Pierre screamed wildly and tried to fight his way through the crazed citizens, but their bodies formed a solid block of flesh. He might as well have been trying to push through a granite wall and still he fought savagely to reach his mother.

He heard his father lash out furiously, condemning all citizens as craven cowards and bullies. But his voice was abruptly silenced. Burly, red-faced men grabbed Lucy Barnes roughly. Shouting gross obscenities, they ripped off her gown and exposed her still fair flesh. Her desperate screams mingled with Pierre's, but he was helpless to protect her or to save her. Silver blades glinted in the moonlight and slashed off the nipples which had nursed him. Maddened by the sight of her blood, the angry mob surged forward. Lucy Barnes's limp body was knocked to the cobblestones and fell beneath the feet of the stampeding crowd.

Pierre struggled to free himself from the crazed mob but he was caught in the vortex and carried forward, over his mother's crushed body. Finally he was able to flatten himself against a wall until the last of the throng had rushed by him. Then, sick with revulsion at himself and his fellow citizens, he turned back to look for his mother.

He found her, just steps from her own home. She was trampled beyond recognition. Little was left except her auburn hair. Tears streaming down his face, he gathered up in his arms what remained of his beautiful mother. He carried her home and wrapped her mangled corpse in a linen sheet. Under the cover of darkness, he dug a grave with his bare hands and laid Lucy Barnes to rest.

The next day Pierre du Bellenfant fled to America. He never saw his father again or discovered what fate befell him. But wherever he went, however far he roamed, he could still feel his mother's crushed body in his arms. Disgusted and desolate, he blamed himself for her terrible death.

Pierre made his way from the port of Boston across the northeast to the Mississippi and down the great river to New Orleans. In the rough-and-ready new world where every boy was a man and no questions were asked about who you were or where you were going, Pierre became a man.

He learned about women in a one-room shack behind the Golden Spur Saloon from a barmaid named Kate. He was an explorer in the new world and her generously endowed body was like a topographical map. She had breasts as high as the Smokies, a stomach as vast as the Great Plains, hair as red as a forest of maples in autumn, and a great canyon—a well at which many men had wished.

Around the Golden Spur she was known as "Kiss 'em Again" and "One of a Kind" Kate. There wasn't a gambler in New Orleans who could whip her at poker and, if she wasn't teaching Pierre the one thing, she was teaching him the other. When he got so good he could beat her at the gaming table and surprise her in bed, she christened him "Lucky Pierre" and told him it was time to move on.

Kate's lessons served him well. In the lusty frontier towns and on the river boats, there was no slicker gambler than Lucky Pierre. His flashing gray eyes and handsome face brought him any woman he wanted. His skill at cards brought him silver dollars and silk shirts. But nothing he did, nowhere he traveled, eradicated the terrible memory of his mother's death. One day he decided to find her home.

He gambled his way across the south to Kentucky and near the town of Lexington he located the old Lucius Barnes estate. It was a handsome, white-pillared mansion, which stood at the end of a long drive of locust trees. In the front pasture a pair of matching chestnut fillies grazed on the bluegrass; otherwise the place looked deserted.

Pierre leaned against the fence, trying to picture his mother running through the field, her lustrous auburn hair blowing freely in the wind. He was so deeply lost in his thoughts that he did not hear the carriage coming up the road behind him until it turned into the drive. A white-haired old man leaned out and waved his hand as if to shoo him away.

This must be my grandfather, Lucius Barnes, the man who banished my mother from his home, Pierre thought. He stared at the old man, looking for some glimmer of recognition, some trace of Lucy Barnes in the weathered face. Memories of his mother flooded Pierre's mind and he did not even hear the old man order his black driver to crack the whip at the arrogant youth.

Pierre felt the sting of cold leather bite his cheek. A sudden stab of pain shot through his head.

"That is to teach you not to come nosing around where you don't belong," Lucius Barnes warned.

Pierre touched his face and felt the warm, sticky blood on his fingers. He looked at the bitter, dried-up old man in the carriage and he knew his grandfather had spoken the truth. He did not belong here. He was too much his father's son.

Pierre went north from Kentucky. He had grown weary of the vagabond life and impatient with himself. He had to accept the bitter truth at last. There was no way he could ever avenge his mother's death. But if he had failed to save her, at least he could try to save others.

Pierre du Bellenfant enrolled in the school of medicine at Harvard College and in the evenings, as Lucky Pierre the Mississippi Riverboat Gambler, he earned the money to pay the tuition.

When the revolutionists were replaced and the young Corsican general, Napoleon Bonaparte, began his rise to power, Pierre returned to Paris, arriving just in time to join the forces that were preparing for the Egyptian Campaign.

At the Battle of the Pyramids he distinguished himself by his valor and daring. He was named Bonaparte's aide-de-camp and promoted to major. The general quickly realized that Major du Bellenfant was more than a fearless soldier. He exhibited a keen intelligence that cut to the heart of an issue and the courage to carry out the most difficult assignment and he soon became a valued adviser.

84

Now that General Bonaparte had seized the reins of power in France, his trusted aide had suddenly come back to Egypt. He was traveling unofficially, as a private tourist not as a representative of Napoleon, he said. His stated reasons for the journey were to see more of the land he had come to love; and to study the treasures of its antiquity for which he had developed a deep interest on his first visit.

But Napoleon dreamed of creating a vast French empire, greater than any England had ever controlled, and it seemed unlikely to Major Misset that General Bonaparte's visions of empire and Dr. du Bellenfant's arrival in Egypt were unrelated.

Chapter Twelve

The morning after her arrival Francesca dressed in her finest day dress and bonnet to meet Elfi Bey. Although she appeared calm and composed, she was more nervous than she ever had been before. Pierre's alarming warning rang ominously in her mind, but she was determined not to be defeated even before she had begun her new life.

Only Francesca's extreme pallor revealed her apprehension. But even if he had been concerned about the state of her emotions, Major Misset was not the man to detect such a subtle sign of her fear. As they rode in his elegant carriage through the swarming streets of Cairo with runners bearing heavy sticks proceeding them to beat a path through the crowds, he broached the delicate subject that he had been reserving until this last moment alone with the girl.

"You are in a unique position to render a great service to your country, Miss Fairchild," he began diplomatically. He hoped through subtle flattery to appeal to her feminine vanity. "The Mamelukes are a strong ally of the British in Egypt, and an important one in thwarting the little French general's grandiose ambitions in this part of the world."

"I am not sure I understand your meaning, Major," Francesca said.

"Surely, Miss Fairchild, I do not have to spell out

each detail to a young lady as bright and clever as yourself. Suffice to say that our continued—and, I might add, improved—friendship with the Mamelukes is very much in the interests of England. I am sure King George would be most appreciative of any service you perform for Elfi Bey to cement that friendship. Though I hesitate to speak critically of our friends, these Mamelukes do not share an Englishman's sense of honor. They turn from one ally to another as easily as the wind changes. If your position with Elfi Bey is an intimate one, it could give us a clear advantage."

Francesca looked at the little major with a mixture of incredulity and disgust. *To have my safety resting in his conniving hands will not make me sleep easy,* she thought, but she would not be intimidated or compromised by this Machiavellian man. She glared at him icily. "I think I understand your message, Major Misset. But I wonder if Sir John will. We shall see when I write to him this evening."

Major Misset glared back at her. "Very well, Miss Fairchild. At least we both now understand each other."

Francesca had no time to consider the major's words or reply to them, because the carriage had already entered the lush palace grounds. The contrast between the paradise that stretched before them and what she had seen of Cairo was astounding. Terraced gardens studded with fruit and palm trees extended on all sides as far as the eye could see. Ornate fountains spewed their crystal water in front of a graceful open-air colonnade.

The palace itself was designed like a sumptuous Moorish castle. Cool white stucco walls rose in high-ceilinged rooms. The doorways were arched. The floors were inlaid with colorful mosaics in intricate patterns. A sweeping staircase of polished granite from Aswan, along with alabaster and marble, rose in the broad foyer through which Francesca and Major Misset passed. Thick, gilded doors opened slowly before them and two gigantic Nubian slaves motioned to them to enter. Each was about seven feet tall and was clad only in velvet knickers. Their shiny black torsos were bare, their heads were shaved, and they wore no stockings or shoes.

Major Misset knew the protocol of Elfi Bey's court well. "Just do what I do," he whispered, taking Francesca's arm, and together they entered a huge reception room. It must have been one hundred feet wide and twice that long. In the center an immense fountain bubbled. At the far end on a raised dais lay Elfi Bey.

He was lounging on a silk divan. A score of slaves and concubines surrounded him, feeding him fruit and fanning him with long ostrich plumes while the tarabookah wailed the monotonous Arab music. The male slaves were dressed like the Nubians; the women as scantily clad. Layers of veils concealed their faces, but the diaphanous fabrics that draped the rest of their bodies revealed more than they covered. Jeweled bracelets encrusted their arms and their ankles gleamed with golden bangles.

Elfi Bey clapped his hands twice. The music stopped. The slaves and concubines retreated to the rear of the dais. He rose from the divan and stretched his arms out toward them in an expansive gesture of greeting. His deep voice boomed through the enormous room.

"Dear Major Misset, at last you have brought me my English teacher."

Lying on the divan, Elfi Bey seemed like an average size man, but when he rose Francesca was astonished. He was a colossus, as tall as his Nubian slaves and just as powerfully built, splendidly costumed in a fine muslin shirt and brilliant vest. His feet were bare beneath his billowing silk trousers. An emerald turban was wrapped around his head and buckled at his waist in a golden sheath was a magnificent saber with a handle made of rhinoceros horn.

"Miss Fairchild," he said with a deep, flourishing bow, "I hope you have had an easy journey and will find my home comfortable, my character agreeable, my children well-disciplined and my country engaging."

Francesca smiled at his little speech, so obviously rehearsed and yet appealing in its simplicity.

"Good," he said, seeing her smile. "You like it here. You will stay. No more need for Major Misset," he announced as if the Englishman had already gone.

"As you wish, Elfi Bey," Major Misset said. "But I shall be at Miss Fairchild's call for however long she remains in Egypt."

"Thank you, Major," Francesca said coolly, "for everything."

Their eyes locked for a moment, then Major Misset bowed low and backed slowly out of the great hall. Francesca waited, not daring to move a muscle, as Elfi Bey's pale, fierce eyes appraised her boldly, almost challenging any person to question his right. A long scar in the curved shape of a scimitar cut across one cheekbone and a full, blond beard covered the lower half of his face.

Alone with this wild, uncivilized chieftain, Francesca realized at last how very far she had gone to escape from Malcolm and the heartache he had caused her. For a moment, standing by herself in the midst of the great reception room under the awesome scrutiny of a man whose face told her clearly that he would not stand being disobeyed or defied, she wished with all her heart that that one fateful evening had never happened. But Francesca had little time for regrets.

Once again Elfi Bey clapped his great hands twice. The gilded doors opened wide and a troop of a dozen little children filed in, followed by a thin, sallow-skinned young man whom Francesca judged to be about her own age. The children lined up in front of the dais where the proud bey stood with his arms folded and prostrated themselves at his feet. The young man was as fair as Francesca herself. The other children were every color and hue—deep chocolate, shiny ebony, and the brown-skinned olive shade of the Mediterraneans.

Elfi Bey clapped a third time and they scrambled up, smiling and giggling, except for the young man whose sulky, sour expression never changed. "These are your pupils, English teacher. My many children," the bey said waving at the little boys and girls, "that I make with my concubines. I no longer remember what little one comes out of what woman. But it is no matter, because this is my one son." He indicated the sulky young man. "I am like your English gentlemen—one wife and one heir to everything I have." The bey threw out his arms as if to embrace the universe and claim it for his son. "You will teach my son well," he commanded. "My children, as you like. I have prepared a schoolroom for you with English pens and notebooks, which I brought myself from London."

"It pleases me very much to know that, Your Highness," Francesca replied, "and since I brought some of my own books, we should be well-supplied."

"Good. Then you begin at once," he ordered.

"This very moment?"

"Yes. Now."

"But surely, Elfi Bey, you will allow me a few hours to settle myself in the apartment that you have chosen to provide for me and to accustom myself to my new surroundings."

He waved away her objections with a sweep of his hand. "Later, later. First the class. Is very important, speaking English. You must teach my son to speak like one of your English lords."

Francesca smiled. This was why he had brought her all the way from London. "I will do my very best."

"Good." He beamed with evident satisfaction. "I may even let you teach me more English words."

"You speak very well already," Francesca said.

"I do. It is right. You are very smart to see that. Now you are dismissed. Go to the classroom, teacher."

"Very well," Francesca laughed and beckoned to her new pupils. "Come along, children; we may as well not lose another precious moment."

"Wait, teacher!" Elfi Bey's command resounded in every corner of the room.

Francesca turned back. He clapped his hands again and all the children scrambled to their knees, bowing low before their father until their foreheads touched the floor. He motioned Francesca to do the same, but she looked at him in astonishment.

"Why do you remain standing?" he questioned sharply. "Now you are in my house. I am your master."

Elfi Bey's fierce eyes flashed angrily but Francesca was certainly not going to prostrate herself before any man, let alone this savage chieftain. *Better to stand up to him from the very start,* she thought, *no matter what the consequences are.*

"Elfi Bey," she said, her voice clear and firm, "your

91

English is very good, but there are many shades of meaning in my language which one only learns after much study." She hesitated a moment, then, summoning all her courage, she continued. "For instance, there is a considerable difference between the words employer and master. You are my employer and in any matters which concern the education of your children, I will defer to you. But no man is my master."

Francesca curtsied deeply. She had made her stand and now she was anxious to escape before he had time to vent the full measure of his wrath. "Come children," she called and beckoning them to follow, she turned and led her charges out of the reception room, leaving Elfi Bey, his arms still folded across his chest, staring after her in amazement.

Her impudence angered him and, at the same time, amused him. He liked the English woman's spirit, he decided. But even more, he looked forward to breaking it.

Chapter Thirteen

In the weeks and months that passed, Francesca grew to love the little children, and to love teaching them. She was given a lavish apartment in a separate wing of the palace, which afforded her the utmost privacy, and servants to dress and undress her, bathe her, wait on her, bring her meals, and attend to her every need or desire. Osari, a huge Nubian slave, was assigned to be her personal bodyguard. He stood watch at her apartment door and whenever she ventured from it, he was at her side.

Francesca even came to like and respect Elfi Bey. At first he would devise cunning ways to try to force her to become like the other women in his household with whom he did whatever he wished. But Francesca somehow always managed to elude his grasp. She had not the slightest intention of joining Elfi Bey's harem.

Francesca was determined to maintain her independence even in that distinctly tyrannical employ and she realized that the bey was shrewd enough not to push her too far for fear of jeopardizing his favored political position with the British.

Once they had tested each other and the point beyond which neither one would go had been firmly established, Elfi Bey and his English schoolmarm settled into a pleasantly antagonistic relationship. They were often at swords' point, but each knew their swords would never cross. Francesca was grateful for his restraint and Elfi Bey grew to look forward to his daily parry and thrust with the cool, young English woman. He wanted to conquer her.

Elfi Bey was a man in his late fifties, but the years had not diminished his appetites. He could not force Francesca. No woman was worth endangering his power and wealth. So he tried in his own way to win her. Since she was the only woman he had not taken at will, courting proved a great challenge to him. His unique method of wooing consisted primarily in pointing out to Francesca how inferior women were to men and, by implication suggesting that they should all be happy to submit to a strong master.

In the English lessons he now insisted on taking each day, Elfi Bey would usually brush aside the exercises Francesca had planned for him, and regale her instead with stories about the great Mamelukes of the past. One of his favorite allegories was the grisly tale of Shajaret-ed-Durr, the only woman who ever sat on a Moslem throne.

"Many hundreds of years ago," Elfii Bey would invariably begin, "there lived a slave woman named Shajaret-ed-Durr, who came to the bed of the great Sultan of Egypt, Salah-ed-Din al Ayyubi. Her sole ambition was to possess the power and the strength of a man; but she was so beautiful, so inventive, that the Sultan was blind to her designs. He freed her and made her his wife, and in due course she presented him with a son.

"While the boy was still at his nurse's breast, the great Sultan died and Shajaret-ed-Durr sat on his throne and proclaimed herself Sultana. She ruled

Egypt for eighty days before my ancestors, the Mameluke warriors, exercised their supreme authority and overthrew her. They named one of their own, Izzedin Aybak, Sultan. But the woman was not easily destroyed.

"Abandoning her infant son, she married the new Sultan and, while he was leading his troops in war, she once again ruled this land. Yet for all her ambition, Shajaret was still only a woman and, one day, overwhelmed by feminine jealousy, she had her Mameluke husband slain.

"The murder of a Mameluke husband will never go long unavenged and one day the slave woman of Izzedin Aybak's first wife seized the murderess and beat her to death with her own wooden shoes. From that day to this, Egypt has been ruled by the Mamelukes—without the help of any woman.

"I tell you this story, Miss Fairchild," Elfi Bey would always conclude, "so that you will remember what happens when a woman is not broken early, when she begins to think she is as powerful and able as a man and her head grows so big that she believes it is not her business to serve."

Francesca only smiled at the bey. She knew better than to let his tales enrage her. On the trip from Rosetta to Cairo, Pierre had laughed off his promise to Sergeant Crawford and taught her the rudiments of poker as it was played on the Mississippi riverboats. Now she applied the rules he taught her in her dealings with Elfi Bey. She never tried to beat him at his own game because she knew he had stacked the cards. Instead she tried to finesse him. But the more successful she was, the more jealous she made Elfi Bey's first wife.

Iasman watched with mounting envy as her husband lavished more and more of his attention on the English teacher. Local custom excluded her from much of her husband's life, but the bold foreign woman knew no such restraints. Nothing seemed forbidden to her. Riding, feasting, entertaining—she was conspicuous at the bey's side.

Iasman was ignored while the English woman was indulged. She was shunted aside and the other was given the place of honor at the bey's right hand. Ever since the Feast of the Prophet, whenever she entered the seraglio, she thought she could hear the muffled titters of the concubines.

The celebration of Mohammed's birthday had lasted for three days and three nights. The city became an immense carnival. Every square and corner held some entertainment—snake jugglers, singers, trained bears and monkeys, poets reciting their verse. At night torches and huge candelabra illuminated the festivities; revelers danced in the streets; and through the swarm of celebrators the Moslem holy men wound their weird procession. Fakirs and dervishes, their long hair streaming, their scrawny bodies nearly naked, seized women at random from the crowds to make their chosen vessels, and the women were honored to be taken.

On the third night Elfi Bey gave an elaborate feast with snake charmers and belly dancers to entertain his guests and gigantic round copper trays of rice, meats and delicacies of every sort in which all could plunge their hands freely. It was the most lavish spectacle the palace had ever known and it was given to praise Mohammed, and to welcome and honor the English teacher.

Nothing had ever aroused Iasman's anger more than this lavish display for another woman. To her it was a public affront. If she had been jealous before, now she was consumed by a deadly hatred for Francesca. And Iasman's emnity was as dangerous as her husband's.

Chapter Fourteen

"Miss English Teacher, I have come to rescue you from pens and primers and carry you off to the land of the pharaohs."

Francesca smiled happily. Pierre du Bellenfant's parting words had not been spoken idly. He had become so much a part of her life that she could not imagine a week without him anymore than she could imagine a week without daylight.

"Although I am sorely tempted to escape with you, I should not desert my classroom again today, Pierre."

Pierre looked at her with an expression of exaggerated grief, which made Francesca laugh merrily.

"I have been waiting for this terrible day when you tired of my company."

"And I have been waiting for the terrible day when you tired of mine."

"It is impossible to even imagine such a time, Francesca."

"Then your imagination must be far weaker than mine, for I think of it often. In fact, I sometimes think that you tired of me long ago and your continued visits are just a pretext to call on Elfi Bey."

Although they were spoken lightly, Francesca's words had the bite of truth. For it had not escaped her attention that whenever Pierre called on her he always contrived to see Elfi Bey as well.

Pierre looked at her gravely. "So, you know after all. I hoped you would never discover my secret."

"What secret?" Francesca asked anxiously.

He took her hand and patted it gently. "Francesca, you are a wonderful companion. But Elfi Bey . . ." He raised his eyebrows and smiled broadly. "Ah, Elfi Bey, the beard, the great wide shoulders . . . irresistible!"

Francesca smiled in spite of herself. Pierre was utterly shameless and irrepressible, and she was never quite sure when he was serious and when he was joking. But there was no one she would rather be with.

He had taken her to the site of the ancient Heliopolis, where a great temple of the sun once stood, and to the Island of Roda, where the pharoah's daughter discovered the infant Moses hidden in the reeds. He opened her eyes to the wonders of Egypt and helped close the wound that Malcolm had left in her heart. No doctor could have prescribed a better salve for her heartache than Pierre's delightful but undemanding company.

Francesca had matured in her new life. Thrust into an alien world with no family or friends to turn to for support, she had learned how to live with people whom hitherto she thought only existed in storybooks. The experience gave her confidence in her own strength and independence, and gradually she began to realize that perhaps in fleeing from Malcolm, she had gained more than she had lost. It was a slow, often painful, process of realization, and far from complete. First love—or the dream of it—is not an easy one to let go, and Francesca still could not admit that Malcolm answered the child's fancy in her and not the woman's need. In the meantime, Pierre du Bellenfant was willing to be whatever she wanted him to be.

He took her hand and laughed easily. "Today, Francesca, I am prepared to sacrifice myself on the altar of friendship. We will go to Giza and climb to the very peak of the Great Pyramid. There, on top of the ancient world, you cannot be jealous of the attention I lavish on the beautiful bey."

Francesca's face glowed with excitement at the prospect.

"There is one condition, though," Pierre said. "You must leave Osari here. He looms like a great black shadow over every moment I spend with you and today I am determined to see you alone. You will have the shadow of the pyramids to protect you from my evil designs."

"Nothing will keep Osari from my side, and least of all you." Francesca's face colored lightly. "Elfi Bey is jealous of the time I spend with you. It is he who doubts your intentions, not I. I would trust you, Pierre, if we were on a boat on the Nile, condemned to sail alone, up and down the river forever."

"Would that be such a harsh sentence for you, Francesca?"

The color in her face deepened and her cheeks burned under his frank, questioning gaze. Francesca was certain that his gray eyes could read the answer clearly. She would trust Pierre but she was not sure she would trust herself.

Each day Francesca looked forward more eagerly to the time they would spend together. She felt her pulse quicken whenever he entered the room and a glance of his frank eyes could make her blush. But she clung to the memory of Malcolm and turned a deaf ear on the language of her heart.

Instinctively, Francesca was protecting herself from being hurt again. She saw plainly that Pierre cared for her as a friend, or, at most, as the sister he had

100

never known, and sometimes she truly did wonder if his only interest in her was Elfi Bey.

That unspoken answer, which she had never even admitted to herself before, seemed to lie between them as they rode toward Giza. Once outside the gates of Cairo, the desert stretched like an infinite ocean of sand as far as the eye could see. The sudden change from the teeming city streets to the vast silent space was startling. Nothing moved; no trace of life except the two of them riding silently across the dunes, the shadow of Osari always behind them, and ahead the pyramids, eternal shelter of the ancient kings, beckoning the curious visitors.

The closer they rode, the more gigantic the pyramids grew. The Great Pyramid of Cheops alone covered eleven acres and towered three times as high as a church steeple. Beside the awesome monument petty fears and confusions were lost.

It took Pierre and Francesca almost half an hour to climb the tiered stones. Some of the steps were as much as four feet high, but Pierre climbed ahead and lifted Francesca easily up the steepest tiers. The giant Osari grew smaller and smaller with each step, until he was no bigger than a fly waiting at the base below for them, and then they were at the summit.

At the last step, Pierre did not relinquish Francesca, but held her for an extra moment. His hands were sure and firm at her waist and she felt his dry, cool breath on her face. It was a glorious, cloudless blue day and they were truly on the top of the world.

They looked out on the domes and minarets of Cairo; on the long ribbon of the Nile and its rich valley; on the boundless sands imprinted with each wind, each tempest and gentle breeze that blows; and on the range of pyramids and tombs extending along its edge to the ruined city of Memphis. And they were bound once more by history—the history of the land they surveyed, and the history of their hearts.

Francesca looked up at Pierre. Her lips were only inches from his. They were soft and willing and held the promise of a kiss. She felt his hands tighten at her waist and he bent to take her kiss. Then he hesitated. His eyes grew cloudy and he released her. But in that instant Francesca knew that her first love was still to be discovered.

Chapter Fifteen

Like a clock, every Tuesday at 4:00 P.M. Major Misset called on Francesca. They sipped syrupy Turkish coffee from small white cups and discussed the news they had received from England. At the end of the hour Major Misset always said, "I trust you are cooperating in every way with the bey, Miss Fairchild." To which Francesca always replied, "His English is improving each week."

"And what do you hear from the French doctor?" the major would ask next. "He is always a welcome friend," Francesca would answer. Then, as punctually as he arrived, Major Misset departed.

Francesca wished the mail from home was as dependable as the major. Each week she hoped that he would have a letter for her and, when he did, she would read it again and again. Aunt Genevieve, though flighty and foolish, had a heart as big as the Atlantic and she corresponded faithfully with her niece. Her large cursive script filled pages of onion skin with the newest gossip. The latest teas, dinners and draperies were all reported in the minutest detail. But, other than to say in one letter that she was well and was expecting a child, Aunt Genevieve made only the most fleeting mention of Clarissa. Uncle Jeremy's letters were less frequent but just as discreet, and Clarissa herself never wrote.

Only her mother's letters brought news of Clarissa and Malcolm, and Francesca read the latest missive with a sinking heart.

"Although Clarissa is expecting in the winter," Lady Marlowe wrote, "from your Aunt Genevieve's ceaseless hand-wringing and river of tears, I surmise the storybook couple are drifting perilously close to a rocky shore. Malcolm is only now beginning to discover what a little vixen he took for his bride. She seems quite determined to make a fool of herself and of him throughout the city. Even in her very private condition, she engages in public displays of emotion that bring chagrin and embarrassment on the entire family. Perhaps motherhood will effect a salutory change in your dear cousin."

Even allowing for her mother's powerful prejudice against Clarissa, her letter worried Francesca. She wanted to send some word of encouragement and comfort. But under the circumstances she dared not write directly to Clarissa and Malcolm for fear her intentions might be misunderstood. She had to content herself with appending a few short paragraphs for Clarissa to her letters to her Aunt Genevieve.

Just months before it had seemed as if Clarissa had everything to live for, and she herself had nothing. Now Francesca saw how foolish and immature she had been. As the only Western woman in Elfi Bey's palace, she held a unique position and enjoyed a special privilege. Since the women of Egypt were secluded from the world and kept in their husbands' seraglios with faces veiled, Francesca was forced to measure herself against men each day. Her mettle was tested and tempered.

Only two things clouded her new life: the restrictiveness of her life in Cairo and the relentless hostility of Elfi Bey's son. Murad was a pitiful shadow of his father. His face was as weak as his father's was strong. His body as limpid as his father's was virile. He had the beak of a hawk for a nose, small, watery blue eyes and little or nothing for a chin.

Looking at him sometimes, Elfi Bey wondered how Murad could have come from his own loins. He scorned his son and taunted him for his weakness. But he was his son nonetheless—his only son—and one day he would be even greater than his father. It was not enough for Murad to become a powerful bey, he must be an educated gentleman as well. That was why Elfi Bey had brought the English teacher from London.

Murad was terrified of his father. He hated Elfi Bey and resented him, but in one respect he was clearly his father's son. Murad was intrigued by Francesca. He had never been drawn to a woman before. But her cool British manner and long, slim figure attracted him as much as the boys he usually favored. He mocked her and goaded her in the classroom to hide his secret desire and he stalked her in the palace halls. He followed her like a snake, slithering along the walls and hiding in the gardens coiled to spring when she passed, always slyly eluding Osari's watchful eye. None was aware of his evil desire except his mother, Iasman.

At first, when she discovered her son's secret, she was furious. Then her scheming mind began to spin. Iasman had aborted all of the children she conceived except this one, knowing that a son would bind Elfi Bey to her even after he had tired of her youthful body. She had prayed to Allah that the child she carried would be a male and when her prayers were answered, she used her son like a sword to strike at his father whenever she felt slighted.

Nothing had ever humiliated her more than the attention Elfi Bey paid to the English teacher. He neglected his wives, acted the old fool over the young stranger, and got nothing in return. Angry and jealous, Iasman contrived a fiendish plot to teach her husband a lesson. With a single blow it would drive the teacher from the palace and turn her son into a man at last.

Iasman summoned the boy to her chamber. "Murad, my son," she said, "it is time that you prove to your father that you are a man—not just any man, Murad, but one who is his equal and worthy heir."

"Do not talk to me about impossible things, Mother. No matter what valiant deeds I performed my father would only laugh at me more. He is so blind, Mother, why does he never see me for what I am?"

"And what are you, my son?"

"I am, as you have always told me, superior to every man and demanding obedience of all."

Iasman watched her son's face closely. He was an arrogant, proud prince for all his weakness. "Listen to your mother, Murad," she promised, "and you will not hear your father's voice raised in scorn or anger against you again, and it will be you and not the English teacher who will sit at his right hand on the next Feast of the Prophet Mohammed.

"You must give up the slave boys you love. They are the pleasure of a youth, Murad. If you want Elfi Bey to look on you as a man, then you must act like a man. You like the fair English woman."

"No, Mother . . ." Murad began to protest his indifference, but Iasman stopped him.

"You cannot hide the secrets of your heart from your mother, my son. I read them in your eyes. You want the foreign woman, Murad. Take her. Be the son of your father. How proud Elfi Bey will be when he discovers that his son has tamed the bold English

106

teacher. He cannot laugh again at a man who does what he has failed to do."

Murad's pale little eyes leered hungrily but he hesitated. He was weak and scared. "I can never do what you ask, Mother. The brute Osari is always at her side."

Inwardly the queen cursed her son's cowardice, but her words were honeyed poison. "Do not think of Osari, Murad. When the time comes, I will take care of the slave. Think of the English teacher's white body, as slender as lean as a boy's. Whatever you do to your slaves, you can do to her as well. It will not be so different, you will see."

Murad did not have the courage to do his mother's bidding, but her words burned like embers inside him and a night came when her promise was remembered.

On that fateful evening he was passing through the gardens when he heard the English teacher's sweet voice and the answering laughter of Elfi Bey and the French doctor. He was jealous of the doctor. He wanted Elfi Bey to laugh easily with him and the girl to flush when he smiled at her. Above all, he wanted his father to treat him like a man just this once.

Trying to appear casual and indifferent, Murad strode across the terrace toward them. But when Elfi Bey saw his son approaching like a preening peacock, he drained his tumbler of liquor in disgust.

"Doctor, teacher, see the simpering sissy there," he bellowed drunkenly. "He calls himself my son. Look at him. He belongs in my harem, not at my table. Dance, Murad," he jibed cruelly, "show us your fine belly and hips."

Humiliated and enraged, Murad turned and flew into the palace, deaf to Francesca's urgent cries to stop him.

"Wait, Murad, wait," she called after him, disgusted by Elfi Bey's brutal taunting.

But it was too late. Murad had made his decision.

Still shaking with rage and shame, he knelt before his mother and buried his face in her lap. "If you can occupy Osari for a day, I swear by Allah I will do as you ask," he vowed.

Chapter Sixteen

.

Francesca yearned for the freedom she had known in England. The fabled city of Cairo lay all around her but she was not allowed to browse through its shops and bazaars without a great entourage to protect her. Both Pierre and Elfi Bey warned her repeatedly of the dangers a woman faced alone in Cairo, but after the disgusting scene with Murad, Francesca had to escape the oppressive palace. Disguising herself in the long, formless dress and heavy veils of an Arab woman, she slipped past Osari. Once outside the serene palace grounds, she followed the milling crowds through the great wooden gate of the city.

Caravans of camels and heavily laden donkeys carried their merchandise to the bazaar. Barefoot men in long caftans, their skin swarthy, their features bold, bore huge clay urns on their turbaned heads. Bearded old men squatted in doorways smoking water pipes. Others idled in the open cafes drinking the powerful, sweet Turkish coffee.

The only women Francesca saw were dirty and scantily clad. Their eyes were smeared with kohl. Their fingernails were painted a gaudy red, and their calves were bare. Except for the veils that covered their faces, their only garment was a loose, soiled shirt, which they opened to display themselves shamelessly to any promising customer. Hundreds of naked children, their bellies distended horribly with hunger, slipped in and out among the crowd. One little waif with enormous, sad eyes begged Francesca for a coin. When she produced the coveted piece of silver, she was instantly surrounded by dirty, brown bodies, their scrawny, skeletal arms outstretched, whining and pleading for more. It was all Francesca could do to free herself from their hungry grasp, and, even then, a dozen or more pursued her, clutching at her skirts and entreating her pathetically.

The jostling crowds carried her deeper into the bazaar. The aromas were tantalizing. Sweet spices mingled in the close hot air with the odor of burning oil from the vendors' carts. The monotonous, mournful music of the tarabookah wailed through the cries of hawking peddlers and haggling customers.

Francesca wandered aimlessly through the labyrinth of narrow streets and crowded stalls. There were bolts of colorful cotton for sale; exquisite rugs hanging in doorways and piled high in the squares; elaborate funerary urns, tiny carved amulets and precious scarabs, all plundered from the ancient tombs. Even mummies had a price in the bazaars of Cairo.

As Francesca browsed through the antiquities, the distinctive, singsong call of the muzzerin rang across the city. The Moslem Egyptians' daily ritual of worship always moved her. Three times each day, from the top of the minarets the muzzerin called the faithful to prayer. No matter where they were or what they were doing, the Arabs answered the sacred call. Even in the crowded bazaar they lay down their prayer mats and facing Mecca, the holy birthplace of the Prophet Mohammed, they prostrated themselves on the ground.

All work and commerce stop and a nation bows to its God, Francesca thought with awe. *Can there be a*

110

more stirring sight anywhere in the world than this public display of faith?

As she looked at the crouched figures, marveling at the power of their belief, she suddenly became aware of dark, shocked eyes, peering up at her from every side. With her heavily veiled face and long black dress, the Moslems assumed she was one of them.

Francesca glanced around nervously, unsure of what to do or where to turn. But there, in the middle of the bazaar, surrounded by the accusing eyes of the faithful, she had little choice. She had to kneel to Allah. The street was filthy and unpaved and the stench of the garbage and of the animal and human dung was overwhelming. Fighting back a wave of nausea, she crouched in the dirt and prayed to whatever God would hear her to make the dreadful moment pass swiftly.

Her prayer answered, Francesca lingered in the bazaar, choosing a striking black scarab ring for her mother, a length of fine cloth for her Aunt Genevieve and a precious gold charm for Clarissa. She was exhilarated by her daring adventure and resolved not to let the dire warnings of Pierre and Elfi Bey dissuade her again from exploring the intriguing city. While she was completing her purchases and thinking how groundless their fears were, a strange procession was coming toward her from the great Mosque of Al Azhar. A line of weird men was wending its way through the narrow streets, prancing crazily, their long hair streaming behind them, their filthy bodies half-naked.

Francesca stared at the bizarre sight in astonishment. She had never before encountered the Moslem fakirs and dervishes who were so holy that they were believed to be in a state of permanent ecstasy and were allowed to behave however they chose to. Nothing was forbidden them, even in the public streets.

As the strange procession passed, a scrawny old fakir leaped out of the holy ranks and began to whirl around Francesca, chanting and dancing wildly. A few scraps of clothing clung to his bony shoulders, but his vital parts were totally bare.

Francesca stood stock still, too shocked to move, as the holy man circled crazily, grasping and manipulating himself lewdly until his old, shriveled member was the thickest part of his body. Prancing closer, he lunged for her, clawing at her heavy dress. She screamed in horror and tried to run, but there was no avenue of escape. Instead of moving to save her from the crazed holy man, the devout Moslem onlookers formed a tight circle around her, hemming her in completely.

In spite of his age, the fakir was spry and wiry and much stronger than he appeared. He grabbed Francesca around the waist with one arm and with the other he tore at her clothing. His stench was foul and his fingers with their long yellow nails were like the talons of a vulture. She struggled fiercely against the disgusting old man but her heel caught in her voluminous skirts and she fell backwards into the dung-strewn street. With an obscene cry of delight, the fakir pounced on his helpless victim and ripped open her dress, exposing the precious object of his desire.

Overcome by fear and by the fetid odor of his filthy body, Francesca began to grow faint. She was too weak to save herself and she despaired of being rescued by any of the swarthy, turbaned men who encircled her. She felt the threat of the fakir's lust against her thigh and struggled to regain her ebbing strength. But she could not resist his defilement.

Francesca swooned, shutting out her unbearable fate in the only way she could, and as she did, a great black arm reached through the circle of impassive onlookers and seized the holy man by his long, matted hair.

Osari flung the fakir aside, brushing him away as if he were one of the millions of flies that festered in the bazaar, and scooped Francesca up in his powerful arms. Although he had committed an unpardonable sacrilege, the Nubian slave was so huge no one dared to stop him. Moving swiftly through the crowd, he carried the unconscious girl to the bey's waiting carriage. The stunned throng scattered, screaming and scrambling to avoid the mighty hoofs as he whipped the horses and galloped away, bringing Francesca home to the safety of the palace.

Osari carried her to her apartment, where all her servants gathered to attend her. Her body seemed to be burning up, and they bathed her with cool, scented oils. But, despite their best ministrations, she never awoke. She lay like a corpse, her body drenched in sweat, her fever so high she raged deliriously. Elfi Bey visited her bed hourly, only to retreat each time, shaking his head in dismay. His doctors applied every poultice and remedy they knew, but nothing roused the girl from her deathly slumber or lowered her raging fever.

"She suffers from the plague," they warned Elfi Bey ominously. "The whole household will be contaminated."

The shameful incident with the fakir had already cost Elfi Bey many bags of gold. It was scandalous for a woman to refuse a holy man who had chosen to make her his sacred vessel, and even more unforgivable for a slave to strike him. Powerful though he was, such a public display of irreverence could weaken his position dangerously unless injured feelings were assuaged with the soothing glitter of coins.

Now the terrible bubonic plague was threatening his household. Wandering through the bazaar, the doctors said, the girl had contracted this deadliest of ills that was making its annual devastating journey across the country, claiming the lives of thousands as it went. The bey always escaped the worst of the plague by moving his entourage up the Nile to his palace in Thebes. But Francesca's illness was delaying his departure.

Finally, after three days and three nights, Elfi Bey called in Dr. Pierre du Bellenfant.

Chapter Seventeen

Dr. du Bellenfant stood at her bedside and looked down at his new patient. Her cheeks were flushed, as they were when he first saw her. Her long, golden hair was undone and lay in a tousled mass on her pillow, framing her face. He bent over the bed and with the back of his hand he felt Francesca's fevered brow. Then he raised each eyelid gently and looked into their unseeing brown depths. With tender fingers he examined her throat and neck. He called her name, repeating it again and again, willing her to hear him, willing her eyes to open. But she remained unconscious.

Slowly, almost reluctantly, as if he was about to uncover a mystery he had long cherished, as if he was afraid the reality would be less wondrous than the dream. Pierre turned down the coverlets. Again he hesitated, unwilling to violate her privacy. He tried to retain the cool, clinical, professional manner he had been forced to learn, as every physician did, in order to survive the terrible agony of body and soul he was called upon to witness. But his hands trembled as he raised Francesca's cherry-blossom pink nightdress, until her long, slim body lay exposed and vulnerable before him.

There was no sound in the room except for her labored breathing. Pierre stood for a moment that seemed to linger suspended in time and space, gazing at her nakedness. It might have been a second or an hour. Time had stopped. The world stood still on its axis and was scorched by the sun. His heart stopped. His soul was seared eternally by her smooth, spare beauty.

He had seen hundreds of women before. He had known them as a doctor and a lover—half-clothed and naked; young girls and old; dark and fair; bold, voluptuous women who were eager to receive him; women with breasts that could suckle the nation and rumps as broad as the delta. But none stirred him like Francesca's slender form.

He sat down on the side of her bed and pressed his ear against her chest to catch the beating of her heart and felt the velvety curve of her shy nipple against the rim of his ear. Her small breasts were like the buds of a delicate flower, pink and promising. His fingers pressed firmly into her smooth flesh, probing for some clue to her illness. Her belly was supple and flat. Her skin was as soft as a baby's and as golden as honey. His hands moved on, examining the hard triangle that jutted up to protect her cavern of love. As his fingers tangled in the fine chestnut hair that crowned it, torrential desire stormed in his loins, driving everything else out of his mind.

For the first time, Pierre wished he had not taken the Hippocratic Oath of the physician. Francesca was his patient and he was her doctor. He could not defile his sacred trust. But neither could he ignore the passions that her body aroused within him. He was a doctor, but first he was a man and he was in love.

Did it happen on the boat to Cairo? Or the first day he saw her ride into Rosetta, cool and straight beside the blustering sergeant? Was it the next morning when she burst into Mrs. Chumley's chamber, blushing and modest? He didn't know when it was. He knew only that he had never loved anyone or desired anyone as he loved and desired Francesca.

In the beginning he had intended to use her and, if in the bargain he had the opportunity to sample her charms, well, he was never the man to refuse a woman anything. But her strange haunting beauty and loving nature had taken possession of him and with each day she consumed him more.

He wanted all of her, body and soul, heart and mind, flesh and spirit. Nothing less could satisfy him. Yet he could not declare his love anymore than he could deny it. As long as he remained in Egypt, there was nothing he could offer her and no promises he could make. But something else held Pierre back as well. Even at the top of the pyramid with the promise of a kiss on her lips, he could not forget the secret she had confided as the dark Nile waters lapped around them.

For months he had held himself back and released his desire after he left her. He bestowed his mark on every belly dancer in Cairo and on the wives of half the European merchants. Once they had succumbed to his seductive charms and experienced the ardor and skill of his lovemaking, they looked forward to another housecall from the handsome young doctor. For each time he imagined it was Francesca and his passion knew no bounds.

Now, as his hungry eyes swept over her naked body, Pierre thought he could possess her as he had so long wanted to and she would never know. With trembling hands and a terrible lust mounting in his loins, he parted her long, silky thighs and continued his examination. He felt each side of her hidden mouth; then, opening her lips, he explored her secret sanctuary. Only the depth of his love kept him from releasing the torrent of passion inside him, as he completed his careful probe.

When he was finished, he sat for a moment drinking in her loveliness. Her scent was on his fingers, more fragrant than a lily but not as pure or undefiled. His gray eyes smoked and, if his hand trembled now, it was with fury as he thought of the man who had known her, the man she loved.

Fiercely, possessively, Pierre cradled her in his arms, crushing her against him as if the tighter he held her the more he could make her his own, and in his jealousy he pictured Francesca's lovemaking. If she loved, it would be with abandon. No inhibitions or restraints would stop her from giving herself to her love.

There is nothing left to give me that she has not already bestowed on another, he thought bitterly. Laying her down on the bed again, he turned her over on her stomach and completed his examination. Her narrow back tapered into a slim waist then blossomed into round, shapely globes. The left one shone like satin in the morning light but the right one glared raw and ugly. Cursing the sacred fakir for his lechery, Pierre examined the painful abrasion. It had been thoroughly cleaned and dressed and was healing well. There was nothing more he could do for Francesca. Plunged in grief, he covered her helpless body. Then, unable to hold himself back any longer, he clung to her, kissing her and burying his face in her golden hair.

When Pierre rose to leave Francesca his gray eyes were cloudy and his cheeks were stained with tears. He had wept, as he had not wept since his mother's death, for the treasure that he had explored but would never possess. For that morning he received a message from General Bonaparte to return immediately to Paris.

Chapter Eighteen

Francesca lay in her lavish apartment so far from
home and family, from everything and everyone she
held dear. Locked in a silent world, not knowing
where she was or who she was, unable to speak or
hear or even wake up, she dreamed that the ancient
Egyptian sun god, Ra, reached down from the sky
and caressed her naked breasts, her belly and thighs.
Wherever he touched, the sun rays seeped into her
body and warmed her, and she basked in their
healing power. When her flesh tingled and glowed,
she turned on her stomach and allowed the rays to
caress her back and her bare buttocks and she luxuriated in its warmth.

Then Francesca dreamed that the great sun god
leaned down from the sky. He kissed her hair and
warm drops rained on it like a summer shower
through the woods. At the end of the rain was a vivid
rainbow. Blinking her eyes from its brilliant light, she
turned. The rainbow faded and she saw Pierre standing over her. His gray eyes were soft and he was crying. She thought he whispered, *"Adieu, adieu, mon
amour."*

When Francesca awoke the next morning, it was
not Pierre who was standing over her but Elfi Bey.

"At last, Miss Fairchild," he boomed, "you have decided to come back to us. We welcome you."

"Where have I been? What have I done?" Francesca's voice was so weak and soft that Elfi Bey had to strain to hear her words.

He was relieved to see that she had returned at last to the land of the living. But, after the terrible fright she had given him and the near scandal she had caused, he had no intention of letting his relief show.

"What have you done?" he repeated sharply. "You have defied me. You disobeyed my orders and ran through the city bringing shame on my house. Where have you been?" He shrugged. "Dreaming of golden rivers and silver skies; who can say? Osari rescued you from the bazaar and carried you back in his arms. For four days and four nights you have lain silent as death. I feared it was the plague. But your French doctor friend thought not."

"He was here?" she whispered weakly.

"Yes, yes. Yesterday. He said I should take you away from Cairo before it is too late. The plague is everywhere. Thousands lie dead. We leave for my palace in Thebes in the morning."

Elfi Bey spoke gruffly to hide his concern, but Francesca did not hear him. She had drifted off again, dreams of Pierre twisting and tumbling through her troubled sleep. Each time she woke, she looked for him hopefully, but only Osari kept watch at her bedside.

At dawn Francesca was bundled in blankets and lifted to a satin bed slung between bamboo poles. Four slaves raised the poles to their shoulders. With Osari at their head, they carried her to the river where Elfi Bey waited to receive her. He had sent his wives, concubines and children ahead to Thebes two days before to escape the plague, but he had lingered behind anxiously, afraid to take Francesca on the two hundred mile river voyage and reluctant to leave her in Cairo. Only Dr. du Bellenfant's reassuring words had convinced him that she could bear the strain of the trip.

When the sun was a pale orb, peeking up from behind the pyramids of Giza, Elfi Bey's opulent barge began its majestic way up the Nile, signal flags flying stern and aft. Propped up on a mound of pillows, Francesca watched the ancient triangles grow slowly smaller and her eyes filled with tears.

"When will we return, Elfi Bey?" she asked. A great sob choked her frail voice.

"The river must rise and flood the land. After, when it has returned quietly to its bed, we come back. Then you will be strong again and filled with smiles."

Elfi Bey spoke hopefully but he did not believe his own words. Francesca was practically lost in the bundle of blankets. Only her face was visible and it was as thin as a papyrus reed and as white as the moon. He looked down at her, anxiety etched on his strong features, and remembered Major Misset's warning: "No harm must come to this girl, Elfi Bey. Remember, she is the special ward of Sir John Stuart himself." But a resonant, confident voice cut through his dire thoughts.

"Don't worry, Your Highness, the voyage will be good for the patient's health. She will be feeling well enough to give you an English lesson before we reach Asyut."

Francesca could never mistake the deep, vibrant voice that she had feared she would not hear again for weeks or even months.

"Pierre," she called happily, but her voice was so feeble only the river could hear her cry of delight.

He was standing beside them, handsome and cool, as if he did not have a concern in the world, a dazzling smile lighting his noble face and devilish eyes.

"No terrible plague will descend on your house, Elfi Bey. As I told you yesterday, Miss Fairchild is suffering from nothing more severe than shock."

Elfi Bey turned to the Frenchman menacingly. He had insisted Pierre accompany them to Thebes to insure that Francesca received the best care he could provide for her.

"I hope you are right, Dr. du Bellenfant, because I am making you responsible for Miss Fairchild's wellbeing," he snarled. "Whatever happens to her on this voyage, you must answer to me for. I commend her into your hands."

His eyes flashed menacingly. The veneer of charm he always wore for his European friends was forgotten and he was the primitive, ruthless desert fox who looked on all men as threats to be defied and all women as desires to be satisfied at will.

Though a gentleman and an aristocrat, Pierre du Bellenfant was no less dangerous than the desert chief. He allowed no man to cow him and no woman to trifle with him. But he had no interest in warring with the bey and everything to gain by deflecting his anger.

"If that is a challenge, Your Highness," he said with an impudent grin, "then I accept it with delight. If it is a command, then I will brook no man's interference in obeying it, no matter how exalted his station," he quipped mockingly.

Elfi Bey glared at him. There on his barge, surrounded by his slaves, nothing prevented him from cutting the bold, young doctor down with one stroke. But he admired his flair and audacity and he needed him to take care of the girl.

"It is your physician's duty, Doctor du Bellenfant to restore Miss Fairchild to health," he cautioned sternly.

"A duty much too agreeable to ever shirk, I assure you, Elfi Bey."

Pierre had agreed to make the trip with the utmost reluctance. It would be a fortnight before arrangements for his return to France were complete, yet he knew each moment he spent with Francesca would only prolong the agony of departure. Although he cherished each instant he shared with her, Pierre knew that it would make the eternity he was doomed to live without her even more unbearable.

Chapter Nineteen

Elfi Bey's dahabeah was as luxuriously appointed as his palace and Francesca and Pierre traveled up the Nile in opulent style. About fifty miles beyond Cairo the scenery began to change. The rich delta valley gave way on the one side to the mountains of Moqattam and on the other to the desert, which encroached almost to the very banks of the river.

As they advanced into Upper Egypt they observed a way of life along the banks that had not changed for centuries. Arab men, wearing only a wreath of grass to cover their loins, drew water to irrigate their fields in round baskets that were attached to the end of a long pole. Huge crocodiles, as long as twenty feet, which were once worshipped by the ancient Egyptians as sacred creatures, dozed lazily on sand bars, basking in the sun. Hundreds of pigeons, wild geese and ducks flew overhead and pelicans pecked at the shore, filling their large bills greedily.

Pierre's prediction proved accurate and by the time they reached Asyut, which lay midway between Cairo and Thebes in the heart of one of the lushest Nile valleys, Francesca's strength was returning rapidly. Seeing her steady improvement put Elfi Bey in such a warm, expansive humor that he even joked openly about her escapade.

"Miss Fairchild, if you plan to continue to live

among us, you must learn to accept our ways. When I was in your country, out of courtesy to my hosts, I drank tea as cold as an English night and served with milk—a barbaric custom, in my opinion. But I did as the Englishman does while accepting the hospitality of his country. You must learn to do likewise," he teased. "In my country a woman who comes under the lecherous eye of a holy man is blessed. She believes that to be—how do you say it? To be entered? Do I make myself clear?"

"Quite clear, Your Highness," Francesca replied, blushing at his directness.

"Ah, then, to be entered and plundered by such a sacred man is an honor and brings her closer to Allah."

Francesca's dark eyes burned hotly. Although his outspoken words embarrassed her, she was not easily subdued when it came to a matter of honor or principle, and she retorted vehemently. "I certainly do not mean to question or criticize your Moslem faith, Elfi Bey, but I would rather go directly to my eternal rest with Allah than bear the advances of your unholy fakirs."

Elfi Bey laughed heartily. "Then, you have only one thing to do. You must obey my command. When I say you can not leave the palace alone, my word is the law."

Francesca bristled at the challenge of this man who still wanted to be her lord and master.

"But that is in Cairo," he hastened to assure her. "In Thebes it is much different, very safe, and so I have decided to give you a gift. It will make you free like the wind and fly like the birds."

"Oh no, Your Highness, I could not accept a gift . . ." Francesca began to protest.

Elfi Bey raised his hand. "Stop. It is decided. I

126

make a gift to you of a stallion of pure Arab blood, as fleet as the current and as black as the night."

"My own Arabian stallion?" Francesca gasped in surprise and her eyes sparkled brightly.

Pleased with himself for making her so happy, he declared grandly, "He is yours, Miss Fairchild—if you swear one promise. Whenever you ride him, Osari will be at your side."

"But Elfi Bey . . ."

"No more words," he commanded. "It is finished."

Francesca could barely contain her excitement. A pure Arabian stallion, black as night and her very own! She and Clarissa had learned to ride as soon as they could walk. Sometimes they thought they had been born on horses. For as long as she could remember, they had galloped together, racing through the pastures of Marlowe Castle, leaping fences, each trying to outdare the other.

"My own Arabian," she whispered to herself. "Oh Clarissa, I do wish you were here."

Chapter Twenty

The trip up the Nile was tranquil in spite of the volatile tempers of Elfi Bey and Pierre du Bellenfant. Francesca gained in strength each day and she bubbled with excitement over the promised Arabian. Basking in her delight, Elfi Bey was at his most expansive and charming. But Pierre was uncharacteristically quiet and withdrawn. He was solicitous and always courteous, but distant, as if he had drawn a shade over their good humor.

Pierre sat on deck for hours staring out at the passing world. Beyond Asyut, the river widened and the valley narrowed. The fertile strip of palm groves and orchards wedged between water and mountains, the little feluccas with their huge latteen sails that crowded the river, and the simple papyrus reed canoes that served the villager's needs seemed to interest him more than his companions.

Sometimes Francesca found him studying her, his gray eyes dark and shadowed with sadness. But he always turned away silently and resumed his solitary contemplation. Which was the real Pierre, she wondered, this brooding god she could not reach? The rakish doctor she knew in Cairo? The deep, passionate man she had glimpsed on the trip from Rosetta?

Each one moved her in a different way, gently awakening her heart from the long, melancholy sleep in which Malcolm had plunged it, touching deeper chords than any man had ever reached.

Francesca worried that she had inherited her mother's fickle heart. Although she loved Lady Marlowe as one would adore a distant goddess and envied her charm and beauty, she did not want to be like her, gliding from one lover to another like a bee in search of nectar. She did not want a host of passing lovers; she wanted to give her heart to one perfect man.

Once she had believed that man was Malcolm, but since her trip to Giza with Pierre, Francesca could not force herself to believe that any longer. Her emotions were too clear to deny. She had wanted Pierre's kiss and she was hurt by his refusal. Was she so unattractive? In her dreams he treated her like the woman he desired above all others, kissing her and stroking her hair. But when he was with her, he never even seemed to notice that she was a woman.

On the trip to Thebes his aloofness swept like a cold draft across her excitement. But he seemed to become easier as they drew nearer to the ancient city, and, by the time they rounded the last bend in the Nile and Luxor and Karnak suddenly stretched out before them, his dark mood had lifted.

The fertile fields spread green and lush on both sides and overlooking them towered the ruined cities of antiquity, each constructed on a colossal scale. To the east stood the temple of Luxor, built on the river bank to the great god Amun, the Hidden One. A pair of granite obelisks more than eighty feet tall soared above its gateway. The slim, pointed pillars were covered with pictures and hieroglyphics and the mighty temple facade was entirely sculpted with the battle scenes of an ancient Egyptian warrior.

As magnificent as it was, Luxor was just a prelude to the earth-brick city of Karnak, a world of temples that stretched three miles beyond at the end of a long avenue of sphinxes, some broken and partially covered by the encroaching desert sands, but all still holding tightly to their eternal secrets.

No one could look at Karnak's maze of sanctuaries, pylons and walls embellished with figures of kings and dieties without feeling humble. Francesca thought they had entered an astonishing world of giants. She marveled at the greatness of the people who had constructed these mighty cities fourteen hundred years before the birth of Christ and at the power of the ancient gods who had inspired the majestic monuments.

But Luxor and Karnak were only half the ruins of Thebes. On the west bank of the Nile in the midst of the broad floodplain sat two colossal statues of Amenhotep III, the imperial visages chipped and scarred by the ravages of time, and beyond them stretched the desolate Valley of the Kings, the burial place of the ancient pharaohs.

"I remember the first time I saw these marvels," Pierre said quietly. "I was leading a corps of General Bonaparte's troops from Cairo to Aswan. We were dusty and tired when we rounded this bend in the river. The march had been long and difficult and tempers were short. But to a man we stopped dead in amazement. Nothing had prepared us for the wondrous sight we beheld. Spontaneous applause burst out through the ranks and, without an order being given, the drums rolled and the men presented arms."

Elfi Bey beamed proudly, pleased that the treasures of his land had so impressed the foreign conquerors.

"It is well that you only looked with admiration, Dr. du Bellenfant," he said. "Many men are not content to admire with their eyes alone. They take what pleases them from the royal tombs that lie to the west, in the great Valley of the Kings. But their greed does not go unpunished. These bold thieves are examined with a stick on the soles of their feet. If they do not admit their crime, they are examined again with the birch and the screw and then with the stick again."

"You have nothing to fear from us Frenchmen, Your Highness," Pierre replied. "Although your antiquities are awesome, we are more interested in stealing from your living treasures. A Frenchman would rather claim a jewel from the navel of one of your tantalizing belly dancers than a lifeless mummy of the noblest ancestry."

Pierre's eyes glinted devilishly. His melancholy mood had lifted and he seemed again the dazzling rogue.

Elfi Bey's great laugh boomed across the river. "And you, Doctor, confess! How many of our living treasures have you looted? I am told you have not left very many for your compatriots."

"Perhaps you should apply the birch treatment to exact his confession, Elfi Bey," Francesca cut in sharply. She spoke lightly but the thoughts of what he had been doing all those months while she had been falling in love with him made her heart sink. No wonder Pierre had no interest in her when he had a city of exotic, exciting women to choose from.

Pierre smiled ruefully. "Torture will not be necessary. I confess freely. One plunders these beautiful treasures like a beggar snatching at coins, greedily, indiscriminately, rubies, sapphires, onyx, garnets, scarabs, until one day one finds a perfect jewel. Then all the others you have stolen seem no more precious than the sands of the desert."

"Ah, Dr. du Bellenfant, you must tell us the name of the jewel you have discovered," Elfi Bey urged.

"To make me confess that you would have to follow Miss Fairchild's urging and even then, birches and screws together could not force me to give up that secret."

"She is so precious you would guard her identity with your life?" Elfi Bey challenged.

"With due respect, Your Highness," Pierre replied smoothly, "when two men share such a secret, one must end up the loser. Would you lead me to your treasure and trust that I would not plunder it as well?"

Elfi Bey laughed heartily. "One way or another I will discover your secret, Dr. du Bellenfant," he warned. "But I have time for that, and eyes all over Cairo."

"Your eyes would better serve you, Elfi Bey, if they uncovered the secret power of Mehamet Ali," Pierre rejoined cunningly.

His audacious words angered the bey, whose good humor suddenly turned sour. "That traitor Mehamet," he growled, "with his false heart and butcher's hands. He has turned against us Mamelukes and gone to the side of the Turks again."

"What is the cause of his treachery, Your Highness?" Pierre asked innocently.

"Mehamet Ali wants only one thing: To be governor in my place." Elfi Bey's mood turned as murderous as a desert storm. "Only on the river do I have peace," he stormed angrily. "Behind me in Cairo the treacherous Mehamet plots to take my command.

132

Ahead in Thebes my wife and concubines scheme to be first in my bed and my son, Murad, flesh of my loins, simpering like a girl and dreaming of how to avenge me, sticks like a dagger in my heart."

Chapter Twenty-One

Francesca named him Nightsong and the stallion was all that Elfi Bey had promised—pitch black, sleek as satin, and so swift that Pierre could barely keep pace with her as they rode out to survey the ruins of ancient Thebes.

Cantering away from the river and the mud-brick villages that clustered on its bank, through fields of cotton and clover where aged buffalo worked the water wheels, they came to what was once the most magnificent city in the world, long before Athens was civilized or Rome was built.

They rode slowly, inspecting the gigantic pillars and statues that lay fallen and half-buried in the sand, and the remains of the columned temples with their elaborate wall sculptures, all once connected by an avenue of sphinxes similar to the one across the river at Karnak.

The colossal seated figures of Amenhotep—damaged but still awesome, the granite whitened like skeletal bones under the scorching African sun—dwarfed them as they stopped beneath them, gazing in wonder at the overpowering colossus and the vast desert that stretched behind it.

Spurring their horses again, Pierre and Francesca rode on, leaving the ancient land of the living behind them, entering the vast city of the dead. The desert sands flew and the dry wind whipped their hair as they galloped together, yet separate, each locked in his own thoughts, into the Valley of the Kings.

Few words had passed between them, since they arrived at Thebes. Pierre had grown remote again and Francesca hesitated to intrude upon him. But even in the face of his aloofness, she could not contain the exuberance that filled her, just being with him in this giant, ruined world of legend.

In the Valley of the Kings they reined their horses to explore the royal burial chambers, which Elfi Bey assured them were hidden in the sides of the Theban mountain.

"We seem to have lost Osari," Pierre said casually as he dismounted.

Francesca laughed. "I hope you are more observant when tending to your patients, Doctor," she joked. "Osari never started out with us. For the first time I can remember he was not at his post by my door this morning. I looked for him everywhere because I promised Elfi Bey I would not ride without him, but I could not find him."

Francesca smiled at Pierre, her eyes shining as brilliantly as the sun, and jumped lightly off Nightsong like a boy. "Anyway, I didn't think I would need Osari's protection today since I have you to guard me," she added.

To gallop in the desert, she had abandoned her full riding skirts and jacket in favor of trim tan trousers and a tunic that freed her body and revealed its subtle curves. Her hair was long and free and glinted in the sun. She was so radiant and full of life that Pierre felt a terrible sense of desolation sweep over him. He longed to take her in his arms and never let her go but he only allowed himself to take her hand.

"You should not trust me to guard you, Francesca,"

135

he said softly. His voice was grave and he squeezed her hand tightly as if he was afraid that he would lose her forever if he let go.

"Tell me what is troubling you, Pierre," Francesca urged gently as they walked down the burial valley. "You have been so quiet and distant since we left Cairo."

"It is nothing, really. These majestic ruins reduce our worst worries to petty cares and our deepest emotions to selfish whims."

She studied his perfect profile, as beautifully chiseled as the colossus they had passed. "There is one emotion, at least, that not even the most awesome temple can diminish."

"You would know more about that than I," he interrupted coldly. He let go of her hand and concentrated his attention on the landscape, looking for some break in the vista that would indicate a hidden tomb.

"Perhaps, Pierre," Francesca said hesitantly, "your expectations are more than any woman can fill." She tried to ignore his cruel jibe and lighten the cloud of depression that had enveloped him for most of the journey.

"No, Francesca," his deep voice was rich with emotion. "I have found a girl who fulfills my wildest dreams, but I have never known her love and never will. That is for another time, perhaps, another life," he said cryptically. "For now, there is only this."

Pierre reached into his pocket and took out a gold chain with a black scarab on it. Carved on the stone in perfect replica was the face of the sphinx—cool, wise and secretive. It must have been made by a royal artisan centuries and centuries before.

"It is exquisite, Pierre," Francesca whispered, hushed with admiration for its ancient perfection,

"Put it on, Francesca, if you like it. It is for you. I

could not give you anything as grand as an Arabian stallion," he said with a tinge of jealousy, "but I wanted you to have some small remembrance of the time we've spent together."

"I am thrilled with it, Pierre," she smiled brilliantly as she clasped the scarab around her neck. "But must it be a remembrance?"

He held her with his eyes. "I leave for Cairo tonight, Francesca, and from there I go immediately to Paris."

His eyes were naked, holding nothing back from her and, as she looked into their gray depths, she realized she had not been dreaming. "Au revoir, mon amour," he'd said.

Impulsively, she threw her arms around his neck, confused and excited by the unexpected emotion he was revealing. "I won't let you go, Pierre," she cried.

He hugged her to him, holding her tightly, and looked lovingly into her strangely beautiful face.

"What is there about you, Francesca, that haunts me waking and sleeping, whose smile fills me with joy, whose aloof gaze is like a knife in my heart," he asked wondrously.

Francesca clung to him, knowing in Pierre's embrace, she was where she had always belonged, where she would always belong. She had traveled so far and discovered so much. But it seemed that everything in her life, even Malcolm, had been contrived to bring her into his arms at last.

Tears of joy and relief filled her eyes. All the heartache and shame, all the uncertainty that she had stored in her heart, washed away with her tears.

"Pierre," she whispered, looking up at him lovingly through the fine mist of tears, "his name was Malcolm. But it doesn't matter anymore. It hasn't mattered for a long time now."

Pierre pressed her closer. "I have waited so long, hoping to hear those words," he murmured gruffly, barely able to trust his voice.

His lips reached down for hers and he kissed her tenderly, fighting to hold back the tempest of desire that her words unloosed. But when he felt the ardor of her response, he could not restrain himself any longer. He plunged his tongue between her full, yielding lips, driving it deeper and deeper. The intensity of his love was so great, nothing could stop him from consummating it now. She felt his immense desire surge hard and hungrily against her and she longed to know the depth of his love and to receive its fullness.

"My love girl," Pierre murmured. His voice was low and warm with the anticipation of untasted pleasures. "I have searched for you so long and so far, and now that I have found you at last, I must leave you. I cannot promise you anything, Francesca. I cannot ask you to be my wife and I have no right to ask you to wait for me. I can only beg you to love me and hope and dream, and one day I will come back to you."

"No, Pierre, I don't want you to go," she cried again and again.

"I don't want to go, but I must," he murmured, stroking her silky hair and held her quietly. "If you want me, I will come back, Francesca, no matter how long it takes."

They kissed again, and there in the desolate Valley of the Kings, there was no tomorrow. There was only then and now and forever, and a love that could not be denied.

He smiled at her. "Do you love me enough to risk the curse of the pharaohs?"

"We will rescue them from their eternal slumber with our love and give them a brief reprieve," she smiled back at him and her eyes held the promise of all he desired.

He took her hand and led her back to a low, narrow entrance in the side of the hill that he had noticed as they passed. Lighting a torch, he led the way into the royal tomb. The contrast was startling. They stepped from the barren desert into the most exquisite room Francesca had ever seen. It was twenty feet square. Every wall was painted with detailed scenes describing the life of the honored dead, and the colors were so sharp, it looked as if it had just been completed that morning. A broken sarcophagus lay in the corner, evidence that tomb robbers had been there before them. They had stepped back into history.

"It is so eerily beautiful," Francesca whispered in amazement.

"Just as you are," Pierre replied, and there, surrounded by ancient secrets, they explored the oldest mystery of all—the mystery of love.

Pierre took Francesca's face in his hands and, raising it towards him, he kissed her deep, velvet eyes and her eyelids and her hair. He ran his thumb along the curve of her lips, tracing their outline gently, and following it with a kiss.

Slowly, as if in a dream, his passions and desire suspended tantalizingly, he lifted her tunic over her head and let it drop to the floor. He unlaced her bodice with the same unhurried motion and slipped it off her shoulders. Her small, round breasts thrust towards him as if they were reaching for his touch, and he caressed them longingly.

This is all a woman needs to be beautiful; no more, he thought as he stroked their perfect circumference. Then he reached down and took one in his mouth. His tongue circled lightly before his mouth closed over her pink bud. He sucked it gently, then more

139

hungrily until he felt the soft nipple contract and harden between his lips. His teeth sank slowly into her tender petals and she groaned with pleasure. Her fingers entwined in his dark curly hair, urging him for more.

Although Pierre had waited so long for Francesca, he did not hurry. He savored each moment, each touch of her flesh, not knowing how long he would have to hold to this single memory. He released her breast and she leaned on his back as he bent down and pulled off her riding boots and stockings. Francesca felt an exquisite tremor of excitement when he began to unbutton her trousers. He opened them slowly and drew them down until only her silk bloomers covered her nakedness. She felt his strong hands stroking the inside of her thighs, higher, ever higher, until he reached the prize he sought. Then his fingers were between her legs and through the silk she felt his sweet caresses. A strange, wonderful sensation, like nothing she had ever known before, swept through her and she shivered uncontrollably.

Suddenly they were kissing fiercely, passionately and his hands were possessing her, caressing her bare belly and buttocks, squeezing them lovingly. She pressed against his body, every inch of her flesh straining for his. His silk shirt was soft and sensual against her bare breasts, his trousers rough against her legs. But she didn't care how they felt, she wanted only the feel of his flesh against hers. She wanted to merge with him completely.

With unsure fingers, Francesca opened Pierre's shirt and, stripping it off, she ran her hands lovingly down his broad bare chest. Her fingers tingled at the touch of his naked flesh.

"Go on, Francesca," he urged when she reached the rim of his belt. "Claim your love."

140

His voice was deep with passion and she did as he asked. Trembling with desire, she unbuttoned his trousers and he helped her undress him until finally they faced each other naked and unashamed, each drinking in the other's coveted flesh.

"You are beautiful, Francesca," he said.

"No, you are," she answered and she reached out and caressed him, touching his broad, strong shoulders, running her fingers through the fine black curls that spread across his muscular chest. His buttocks were round and firm, his thighs thick and powerful, and rising between them was the full measure of his love.

"Touch me, Francesca," he whispered hoarsely, and her fingers strayed down his belly and stroked him shyly, surprised by his smoothness and thickness. She thought he was so enormous, he would fit the colossus of Amenhotep. But when Pierre spread his cloak for her to lie on, she was not afraid, because she knew that he had been saving all his love for her.

For an instant he loomed over her, huge and hungry with desire, and then she drew him into her arms. He lay on top of her, caressing her body with his own, until she tingled with a delicious anticipation.

He smiled at her with his wondrous gray eyes. "I love you, Francesca," he murmured, "now and forever."

She answered with a kiss that held much more than a promise and he took her then, entering her with a thrust of passion so powerful that she cried out. Then he began to move slowly, plumbing the depths of her love, awakening passions in her that she had never even suspected.

When he felt her begin to respond fully, he thrust faster, driving her on, firing her with his seething desire. Oblivious to everything except the terrible, magical feeling that was overwhelming her, Francesca clutched frantically at his back and buttocks. Her nails sank into his flesh in her hunger to possess him and be possessed, and she arched her back to meet his demanding love.

Their bodies one, their passions indivisible, they exploded together, proclaiming their love at last in a wild burst of bliss, and they clung together, laughing and weeping with joy, long after it was over. In the deep afterglow of love, Francesca covered his face with happy kisses, unable to stop touching and caressing him. She had never imagined anything could be like this.

"If this is the pharaohs' curse, I don't think I could bear their blessing," she said.

Pierre laughed lovingly. "Don't you know it is bad luck to blaspheme?" He held her closer, marveling at the passion he had discovered in her spare, cool body, and she felt his desire begin to rise again.

"Woe to the living who disturb the kingdom of the dead." She intoned the ancient curse impishly, teasing him for his Latin superstitiousness.

He gazed into her shining eyes, "Were you like this before, Francesca?" he asked.

She didn't hesitate or turn away from his penetrating eyes. "Never!" she answered easily. Whatever she had done with Malcolm, it was nothing like this. Then, the emotion of being alone with a man for the first time and of the marriage vows they exchanged had excited her more than the act itself.

"Tell me truthfully, have you ever behaved this way with any man?" Pierre demanded again. He wanted to believe her but he couldn't. She was so generous with her love that he could not imagine her holding anything back. His eyes darkened with anger and he held her possessively.

The veiled strain of violence she sensed in his hands and in his accusing eyes was thrilling yet oddly dangerous and Francesca hesitated, uncertain of how to explain what Malcolm had been to her, yet anxious for him to understand that it was nothing like this. "We grew up together," she said slowly. "I always dreamed we would marry. He was a part of my life for so long, I never thought of any other man, until I met you." She looked up at him, her eyes filled with love. "Can you forgive me, Pierre, for not waiting for you?"

He saw then that it was true. Her love was a precious gift given to him alone, of all men. "If you *will* wait for me," he answered, his voice choked with emotion,

Francesca fought to hold back her tears. "Wait for you?" she cried in anguish. "How can you go now, Pierre, after . . . after this?"

"I must go, my love. I cannot tell you why, but I have a duty to my country which I must obey. Believe me, Francesca, if there were any way I could stay, I would seize it."

They lay silent together, clasped in each other's arms.

"If you must go," Francesca said softly, "then leave now—quickly, before we have time to think about it anymore or else I do not think I could bear to let you go."

"I can't leave you here alone, Francesca, and slink away like a thief. How will I know if you are safe? What if something happened to you, how could I live?"

"Please, Pierre," she pleaded, "grant me this one request. I cannot bear a prolonged leavetaking. Go quickly and I will follow soon after you. Nightsong will carry me back to the palace swiftly and safely."

143

"If this is truly what you want, then I must leave now, while there is still daylight to guide you back. But I wish you would not ask me to do this, Francesca."

"It is the only way."

Pierre smiled into her dark, sad eyes and caressed her cheek lightly. "Very well, my heart, until I return then," he murmured.

He kissed her tenderly for the last time but she clung to his lips, pouring out all the deep love and unsuspected passion that had lain buried inside her.

"*Mon Dieu*, Francesca," he groaned as he felt the fire raging between his legs again, "how can I ever leave you—even for a moment?"

"Don't," she whispered huskily. Her innocent flesh burned with desire. "Come to me again, just once more," she begged. "I want you so much, I can't let you go, not yet, not now."

She opened her legs to receive his love, raising them high around his back as he thrust into her fully, wildly—driven beyond thought, beyond control, beyond any lust he had ever known by the passions he had awakened in her.

Abandoning herself to their love and her lust, Francesca met his most powerful thrusts with her own. They drove together, one flesh, one raging fire, consumed with a tempestuous passion, until their searing desires burst forth together and with a glorious cry they lay back, exhausted, ecstatic, wet with their love.

"Is this how you plundered all those living treasures?" Francesca smiled.

"No, this is how I claim only the most perfect jewel of all," Pierre replied. He pressed her close, listening to her heart beat fast against his own.

Her new love made her radiant and he was moved

144

by her innocence, by the sense of discovery with which she caressed him and responded to his touch. Suddenly he thought, "This girl will probably hurt me." But the flicker of fear that he had never felt with any other woman, no matter how devious or demanding, was forgotten in the fullness of her embrace.

"Can you wait for me, Francesca?" he asked.

"No, I can't wait a second for you."

"Nor I," he laughed deeply.

"*Can* you wait for me, my love girl?" he asked again.

"No, but I will—forever."

He kissed her fiercely and got up, quickly pulling on his clothes. Francesca did not watch. She could not.

"*Adieu, mon amour,*" Pierre whispered, a note of wild, uncontrollable passion in his voice, and then he was gone.

Pierre never looked back, knowing that if he did he would be lost. But if he had turned just once, he would have seen a shadow fall across the entrance of the tomb and known that they had not escaped the curse of the pharaohs.

Chapter Twenty-Two

"Come back to me, my love. Come back to me soon," Francesca said. She spoke aloud, still lying as Pierre had left her, believing that she was alone with the kings and noblemen who had lain buried for century after century in the Valley of the Kings, the ancient city of the dead that, for a moment suspended in history, she and Pierre had transformed into a city of life, a temple of love.

But there was one other who heard her words.

"Were you calling me, my English teacher?" he mocked. His tone was lewd and insinuating. His glazed eyes were riveted on her thighs, a leering grin smeared across his pasty face.

Francesca gasped and looked up, startled and frightened, at the intruder who filled the mouth of the tomb. Murad's trousers were open and he was holding himself.

Francesca scrambled up frantically, trying to cover her nakedness. "What are you doing here, Murad?" she cried, her voice quivering, her eyes huge with fear. "What do you want?"

"Nothing, dear English teacher, except what you gave to the French doctor." His voice was as slimy as a serpent as he started toward Francesca.

"No, Murad, don't!" she pleaded.

"Why? Is a son of a Mameluke bey less worthy

than a French lecher? Is he not good enough for his teacher, for his father's servant?" he spat viciously. "My father will be most interested to know what his beloved English lady does behind his back. She turns up her nose at Elfi Bey in disdain and then defiles the pharoahs' tombs with a worthless foreigner."

"Murad, you do not understand. It is not as it seems." Francesca tried to speak calmly, hoping to quiet the aroused, embittered young man.

"No, you can deny nothing. For months I have waited for this moment. You never knew it—you and your Frenchman—because I am so clever, but I followed you all the way from the palace. I waited and I watched you. I saw the Frenchman mount you. I crept closer until I could see the fine hair on his strong buttocks . . ."

Murad had abstained too long from his slave boys and the sight of Pierre's athletic body, each muscle perfectly toned, poised and supple, tense and powerfully coiled astride Francesca, had fired his lust. As Pierre's passion rose and he thrust faster and harder into Francesca, Murad had whipped his member into a frenzy of excitement until he spilled over violently. The thought of Pierre's body aroused him again and he lunged for Francesca.

He laughed vilely and ripped the clothing from her hands. "Why are you trying to hide from your pupil?" he sneered.

Francesca felt the rough wool of his cloak scratch her bare flesh as he grabbed her breasts savagely.

"Surely you would not deny Elfi Bey's son a lesson in your English ways? That is why you are my father's servant—to teach his only son," Murad snarled.

Screaming wildly, Francesca fought to escape from his loathsome touch. But he grabbed her arm and twisted it brutally behind her back,

"Scream! Scream if you like, English lady, for there is no one to heed you but the ancient ghosts. Your Frenchman is on his way to Thebes by now and that ox Osari can not hear you. Not today, you foreign whore," he gloated. "My mother has seen to that."

"What do you mean, Murad? Tell me what you have done with Osari," Francesca pleaded.

But the boy just flung his head back and laughed, a drunken, triumphant, crazed peal of victory and revenge.

Suddenly, seeing a chance to escape, Francesca twisted free of his grip and ran out of the temple. Blindly, naked as the day she was born, she fled through the city of the dead, desperate to reach Nightsong before Murad could catch her. But in her terror, all sense of direction gone, she did not run towards the stallion, and the fertile valley land. She fled in the opposite direction, into the vast and barren desert wasteland.

Murad's crazy laugh faded in the distance, and still Francesca ran. The desert stretched around her, on all sides an infinite emptiness. The sun was a furious ball, falling in the west, turning the gray sands blood red. Panting and breathless, she strained to catch some sound of his footsteps behind her, but there was none. A deathlike silence enveloped her and at last she dared to stop. She was terrified, lost and exhausted, but she had escaped. He had not followed her into the desert.

Tears of relief welled in Francesca's eyes and her heart filled with thanksgiving for her deliverance. But even as it did, she suddenly heard the steady, rhythmic pounding of a horse's hooves, galloping towards her. She began to run again, forcing herself on, consumed by a single desire—to escape Murad. Her throat parched, her naked body drenched in sweat,

Francesca stumbled ahead. But the horse gained ground easily, rapidly closing the distance between them, and she heard the dreaded laughter again.

"Did you think I would let you escape so easily, my English teacher?" Murad's cunning voice cut through her desperate hopes like a sword in her bosom and his cold leather whip cracked across her naked back. The force of the blow thrust her forward, but still she staggered on. Again and again, his cruel whip tore open her bare tender flesh. Blood spurted from her back and buttocks She tried to scream, but no sound would come from her dry throat. She tried to run faster, but her exhausted legs could carry her no farther.

Murad leaped off his horse and overtook her in a stride. Grabbing her long golden hair, now wet and dark with sweat, he spun her around and spat in her face like an angry cat. Francesca fought back viciously. Summoning some mysterious reserve of strength she never knew she possessed, she bit and clawed savagely. But tooth and nail were her only weapons and they were no match for Murad's vengeance.

All the shame, the insults and humiliations he had suffered from his father, all the years of stored fury, were released on the helpless girl who had taken the place of honor at Elfi Bey's right hand—the place that belonged by right of position and birth to his mother and himself. He beat her face and breasts, pounding her again and again with clenched fists, until, bruised and bloody, she fell face down in the sand. When she tried to rise again, he unsheathed his saber and, with the full force of his fury, he brought its heavy hilt down across the back of her head.

Francesca fell forward in the sand. She felt herself spinning faster and faster and faster, spiraling help-

149

lessly down into a bottomless black abyss. But Murad's sadistic pleasure was not satisfied.

"When I have finished with you, English teacher, you will not be fit for my father's stable, let alone his table," he cried triumphantly and, opening his trousers, he mounted Francesca's helpless body.

For a moment he swung over her, gloating obscenely. *Mother was right,* he thought, *she is as lean and firm as a boy.* Then seizing her buttocks brutally, he drove his angry purple member between them, lashing Francesca over and over until she was torn and bloodied and his fury exploded inside her.

His revenge against his father complete, Murad got up and flipped Francesca's limp body over with the toe of his boot. Her eyes and mouth were filled with sand and grains stuck to her cold, clammy body. She had not known the full measure of his cruelty, and no more pain, no humiliation could reach her now.

He kicked her bruised ribs to awaken her, but noting no sign of life he bent over her motionless body and yanked the scarab sphinx from around her neck.

"A memento for the bey," he shouted into the Valley of the Kings, "and an offering to this necropolis of our royal ancestors." He kicked Francesca's limp body again. Then he mounted his horse and, waving the scarab aloft like a knight's pennant, Murad rode triumphantly back toward Thebes.

Chapter Twenty-Three

There was nothing as far as the eye could see in any direction. The sky was a glaring bright blue, unbroken by even a wisp of cumulous. The sun was a white shimmering disk, brilliant and merciless. The sand burned, barren and infinite and lifeless. Not a shrub, not a leaf, no trace of animal or man moved on its vast horizon.

Francesca stirred slightly. Her head throbbed painfully, her bruised body ached. Sand ground painfully in the open wounds on her back and buttocks and stuck in the blood that caked them. Her parched lips moved in an uncontrollable sucking motion of which she was not even aware. She was too weak to wonder where she was or what had happened to her. Still only barely conscious yet urged by some primitive instinct for survival, she struggled to her knees and began to crawl through the endless desert, inch by painful inch.

"Water, water!" She kept forming the word over and over again on her dry lips as she crawled forward on her hands and knees, too weak to walk or even stand. But with each agonizing foot she moved away from the river, away from the Valley of the Kings, deeper and deeper into the relentless heart of the desert, into the path of an onrushing khasmin.

Francesca had lain unconscious through the night

and in the cool cover of darkness she had been safe. But now the sun was high, firing the desert like an oven. As she crawled, the burning sand torturing her palms and knees, a hot, dry sandstorm rose suddenly on the horizon, a solid mass ten thousand feet high sweeping toward her like a great brown wall of dust. If the khasmin did not crush her with its driving force, she would surely suffocate in its thick sands.

Francesca lay flat on her stomach and buried her face in the desert, trying to protect herself from the enveloping storm. The khasmin was so thick that even the sun could not penetrate it and it rolled over her, plunging her into total blackness. The hot, dry dust filled her nostrils. It parched her throat and scorched her swollen tongue, and ground like emery against the bare skin of her back and legs.

The khasmin passed as swiftly as it had appeared. The sun broke through the dust and Francesca turned and saw the sand wall behind her, moving relentlessly forward, enveloping everything in its sweep, leaving nothing behind but a fine film of dust that clung in the air.

The sun glared again, blistering her fair skin. But there was no way to escape its white heat. The torturous thirst crazed her mind. She couldn't speak, she couldn't weep, she couldn't remember, and when she couldn't crawl on her hands and knees any longer, she crawled on her stomach. But the sand scorched her tender belly and breasts and the grains cut into her nipples until they were raw and bleeding.

Francesca craved desperately for water—even a single drop to wet her scorched tongue. But she could not struggle another inch. Her eyes burned yet she strained for some sign of life that would indicate an oasis, and in the distance through a blue haze, she saw him riding toward her, strong and beautiful as a god. She did not have to fight anymore. He had come back to her. He would take her in his arms and shelter her from the heartless desert and the brutal sun.

Francesca's parched, cracked lips smiled, forming a single word, "Pierre," and she surrendered herself to the merciless desert, deceived by the cruel mirage of her love.

Chapter Twenty-Four

The curse of the pharaohs haunted Pierre as he rode north toward Cairo. He could not refuse the one thing it was in his power to grant Francesca, and so he had left her as she wished, alone and defenseless, without a backwards glance. But neither could he clear his mind of the ancient threat. Finally, unable to quell the premonition of danger than rankled in his heart, he wheeled his horse around and galloped back toward the Valley of the Kings.

As he passed the line where the fertile river valley met the encroaching desert, he saw a rider coming toward him. In the fading evening light he could not distinguish the figure clearly but he was sure it must be Francesca. With a thrill of joy, he spurred his mount onward. But, as the distance between them closed, he saw that there were two horses, both saddled and bridled, and a lone rider.

The empty horse was a black beauty, high-spirited and nervous, straining at the lead. The rider whipped the wild stallion cruelly and he reared up, whinnying angrily.

"Nightsong!" Pierre cried.

He galloped faster and reined sharply in front of the startled son of Elfi Bey.

"Murad," he demanded tautly, "what are you doing with this horse?"

154

"I am bringing it back to my father's palace. I found the beast straying in the valley to the west," Murad answered. His lying voice was slow and whining.

"Didn't you see Miss Fairchild in the valley, Murad?" Pierre questioned, unconvinced by the boy's story.

A nasty smile played at the corners of Murad's mouth. "I saw no one but the ghosts of the dead."

He spurred his horse and tried to ride on but Pierre blocked the path.

"Where is Miss Fairchild, Murad?" he shouted angrily. "What are you doing with her horse?"

The young Mameluke blanched and his hands began to shake. The brave, brutal bully was suddenly a craven quiver of fear.

"I am the son of Elfi Bey," he shrieked, "let me pass."

"Not until you tell me what you are doing with Nightsong." Pierre seized the bridle of Murad's horse and, as he did, his hand closed around the scarab sphinx he had given to Francesca. He had returned in time to revenge her, but not to save her.

"I have told you," Murad whined fearfully, "now let me pass."

Pierre's eyes were smoldering infernos. "Liar!" he cried. He swung savagely and with a single, powerful blow, he knocked Murad off his horse. Then he leaped out of his saddle and towered over Murad, who lay terrified in the dusty road.

"Where is Miss Fairchild, Murad?" he shouted anher?" he demanded furiously.

"Nothing! I have not seen the English teacher." Murad cringed in the dust.

"Then how did you get this?" Pierre opened his hand and dangled the scarab in front of Murad. "If

155

anything has happened to that girl, you shall pay with your life," he threatened.

The wily Mameluke leered gleefully, for he saw that Pierre was unarmed. "We will see soon enough who shall exact payment," he said, and, rolling away suddenly, he unsheathed his saber and scrambled to his feet.

"Now I am ready to listen to your brave words and threats." He laughed arrogantly and came toward Pierre with his sword drawn. "On your knees, Doctor," he commanded. "I am going to make you grovel in the dust as you have made me."

Pierre never flinched. Carefully, coolly, he measured the distance between himself and Murad and began circling slowly, never allowing him to draw closer.

"Where is Francesca?" he asked again. His voice was low and insistent. His fury was contained now, cold and lethal. As he circled his prey, he kept repeating the question, slowly, persistently, waiting for Murad to make the first move.

Suddenly Nightsong whinnied sharply in warning. Pierre crouched low just as Murad lunged for him. The boy sailed over his coiled body and fell head over heels in the sand. Pierre was on him in an instant, wrestling him fiercely for the sword. Sweating and groaning, they rolled together, locked in a deadly embrace. But even in his desperation, Murad was no match for the Frenchman.

Pierre seized the saber and sprang to his feet. Pulling Murad to his knees by his hair, he held the blade against his throat. "Where is she? What have you done to her?" he demanded again.

Murad stammered. Pierre pressed the blade closer against his neck. Murad felt the cold, sharp metal on his skin. "She's dead," he blurted.

"Liar!" Pierre shouted furiously. "I will kill you for less than that." He pulled Murad's hair harder and nicked his neck with the saber.

Blood spurted out on the blade and Murad screamed, "She is dead. I killed her. I swear it on my mother's grave, I killed the English teacher." He began to weep pitifully. "I did not want to. I meant no harm. Please, please, grant me mercy." He clasped Pierre's knees, trembling with terror. "I will do anything, anything you ask, only spare my life," he begged.

Pierre looked down at the craven man. His handsome face was contorted with violent rage. Francesca dead. He would not believe it.

"No, no!" he cried, shaking Murad viciously by the hair. His strong, muscular body seethed with anger. "I will slit your throat for your lies."

"I swear it is the truth. May Allah turn my mother to stone if I lie. I followed you from the palace," Murad confessed in terror. "I watched you in the tomb and, when you left, I tried to take her. But she would not have me. She fought me like a wild beast, all claws, but I had her anyway. I had what my father could never get." He was hysterical, gloating and uncontrolled, crazed with fear.

Pierre stared incredulously at the boy, shocked and repulsed by his confession. He spoke softly at first, his voice, low and deep, rising louder and louder like gathering thunder, until he was raining abuse on Murad. "Scum, swine, vermin, bully, coward, weasel, worm. I should beat you. I should torture you. I should cut off your genitals and choke your lies with them. I should slit your throat and watch you bleed slowly until every drop of life is drained from your body."

157

Pierre's cold, white fury was even more terrifying than his angry rage.

"I will do anything," the weeping boy pleaded. "I will be your slave, only have mercy. I beg you, have mercy."

Pierre heard the sound of horsemen galloping toward them, but he did not turn or waiver. "What mercy did you have, Murad?" he asked coldly.

His fierce gray eyes glinted like steel and he drove the saber through the Mameluke's heart with a thrust so brutal the sword's point came through the other side. Cursing himself for leaving Francesca, he drew the sword from Murad's heart and leaped on the back of Nightsong. With the bloody saber waving, Pierre faced the oncoming horsemen.

Elfi Bey, with Osari at his side and a dozen fierce Mameluke warriors behind him, reined in his horse roughly when he saw the sword the Frenchman brandished. The black Damascus steel of the blade and the curved solid gold filigreed handle were unmistakable. It was the saber he had given to his son the first and only time he had tried to lead the boy into battle.

Elfi Bey looked at the sword still dripping with freshly spilled blood and at the furious foreigner who waved it like a victory banner. Then behind the Frenchman, lying face down in the dust, Elfi Bey saw the lifeless body of his only son.

"Murad, my son!" the old bey cried. His anguished words caught and strangled in his throat as he charged Pierre.

They faced each other astride their Arabian mounts. Elfi Bey, resplendent in a brilliant turban and flowing silk gown, was old but he was still fierce enough to sever a head with a single reverse blow. He was a man of enormous courage and daring and he was fighting for his honor—to avenge his son, killed ignobly with his own sword. The Mameluke prince was heroic and determined and, if he won, he would be merciless.

Pierre du Bellenfant, dusty and bloodstained, was young and courageous and daring. He fought with the furious abandon of a man who does not know fear. There was no risk too great to dare because he had nothing to lose, nothing to gain. He didn't care if he lived or died.

They fought fiercely, charging and wheeling, attacking and retreating. Elfi bey was like a mounted armory, a djerid in hand, a battle axe and a pair of scimitars in his belt. But he could not contend with the Frenchman who had no arms except the bloody saber and nothing left to live for, nothing to protect.

First the long, sharpened palm branch fell, then the battle axe. But the old chief would not concede defeat. Grasping the reins between his teeth, he unsheathed both scimitars and charged again, but one by one, he lost both weapons.

Pierre was a healer not a killer. Enough had been lost in this day, more than any man could measure. He blamed himself for Francesca's death. Her blood was on his hands as surely as Murad's. He wanted no more murder.

When he had stripped Elfi Bey of even his dagger, Pierre cried to the old man, "Enough! I have no quarrel with you, Elfi Bey."

He threw Murad's saber into the sand and, wheeling Nightsong around he galloped away.

But Elfi Bey was still armed with his honor—his strongest weapon of all. He could not allow his son's death to go unavenged.

"After him," he shouted to his horsemen, "and don't dare to turn back unless the Frenchman's head is on your spear."

He watched alertly until the last rider was lost in the distance, then the powerful chieftain slumped in his saddle, a tired, defeated old man. He didn't look at the faithful Nubian who remained at his side. He just waved him away sadly.

"Go, Osari, if you must," he said, his voice flat and dry. "But if you find the girl, do not bring her back to my palace—and do not return yourself. This day you are a free man."

Osari's loyalty was not divided. Without a word or so much as a blink of his eyes, he rode into the Valley of the Kings.

Alone with his son at last, Elfi Bey knelt in the desert sand. He held Murad in his arms, pressing the boy against his bosom, and for the first time in his sixty-three years, the proud Mameluke prince wept.

Chapter Twenty-Five

"But of course you knew the Frenchman was a spy for Bonaparte. We uncovered his dangerous little game about a month ago. We thought we had him firmly in our trap but he somehow managed to slip through our web and escape from Egypt with his life. A pity, in my opinion."

Major Misset pressed his fingertips together and propped them under his chin. "It seems," he went on, "that General Bonaparte remains unconvinced by his first defeat in Egypt. He is anxious to try again. The little Napoleon fancies himself another Alexander who is destined to conquer the world. Dr. du Bellenfant's mission was to turn the Mamelukes against us through bribery, false promises, or . . ." He cleared his throat theatrically. "Or any other means he could. He was most successful with Elfi Bey—at least until the last days.

"It is my hope that, in view of your, er, your intimate position in the bey's palace, you will be able to furnish us with additional information on the activities of Dr. du Bellenfant."

Major Misset paused and regarded the girl sharply. His eyes were as cold as dead fish. "It is clear, Miss Fairchild," he said, "that Pierre du Bellenfant used you to gain entry to Elfi Bey. You should not feel

161

bound by any ties of friendship to protect the scoundrel."

Francesca had not liked the major at their first meeting and nothing he had ever said or done had changed that initial impression.

"What exactly would you like to know, Major Misset?" she asked.

Although her voice was cool, behind the poised and haughty surface Francesca was numb. The major's revelations startled and shocked her. Perhaps Pierre *was* a spy. That at least would explain his precipitous departure. But she refused to even think that he had used her or that his lovemaking was nothing more than a duty performed for his country and for his consul, General Bonaparte. Only Pierre himself could ever make her believe that.

Major Misset calculated her response shrewdly. He did not think he would elicit any information from the girl. He certainly never had before. Yet he suspected that she was at the heart of the discord that had shattered Elfi Bey's power.

"It is my considered opinion, Miss Fairchild," he said, "that the sudden departure of Pierre du Bellenfant and the abrupt collapse of Elfi Bey's power are not unconnected. I hoped that perhaps you would confirm my suspicion or," he paused reflectively, "at the very least cast some light on the issue."

Francesca chose each word carefully, determined not to allow a trace of the emotion that was in her heart to sound in her voice.

"I can only say, Major Misset, that the last time I saw Elfi Bey he was as strong and imposing as ever. The same—and more—is true of Dr. du Bellenfant. Now, if that is all, Major, I hope you will excuse me. I have not yet regained my strength completely, and I tire very easily."

162

"Ah, of course. I am sorry that I detained you so long on matters that are of such little interest or concern to you," he said sarcastically. "But there is just one more thing, Miss Fairchild, if you would permit me?"

"What is it, Major?" Francesca asked coldly.

"May I ask why you left the employ of Elfi Bey so hastily?"

Francesca fixed Major Misset with a frosty smile. "Certainly, Major, although you will be sorely disappointed by my answer for it contains no mystery or intrigue at all. I simply tired of life in Thebes and yearned for the excitement of Cairo. On the return voyage, I carelessly took too much sun. My long convalescence delayed the trip for some weeks, but now I am pleased to report that I am enjoying my sojourn with Mehamet Ali who was kind enough to offer me his hospitality when I arrived back in Cairo."

"Yes, very kind, very kind indeed," the major answered drily. "Let me compliment you, Miss Fairchild, on the enviable talent you possess for earning the protection of the most powerful men in Egypt."

Francesca rose and faced the consul defiantly. Her dark eyes flashed angrily at the insinuation in his words. "Good friends are a rare and valuable possession in his city, Major Misset," she replied pointedly and, picking up the packet of letters he had held for her, she swept out of his office without so much as a "good afternoon."

The faithful Osari waited for her at the consul's door. He never allowed her out of his sight now, and Francesca never complained about his attentiveness. She owed him her life.

For two days and two nights Osari had ridden across the desert, searching for Francesca, but he found no

163

trace of her, no track in the vast, sandy wasteland. On the third night, despairing of ever finding her dead or alive, he camped at the Great Oasis. There, in the tent of a Bedouin chief, he found her. She lay naked and nearly dead on the bare ground, her blistered, scorched flesh raw and uncovered, her heart beating so faintly that he was not sure she was alive.

The Bedouin had scooped her up in the desert to sell in the white slave trade. If she recovered, her long, golden hair alone would bring him a handsome profit. But it did not seem as if Francesca would ever wake up. In another day, another hour, the chief feared, she would be dead, and so he willingly traded her to the Nubian in exchange for a spear. He even threw in a shawl to cover her with, and was sure he had gotten the better of the bargain.

Osari wrapped Francesca in the shawl and carried her in front of him as he rode east to Dendera. In the shadow of the ancient temple, shaded by the Nile, he raised a tent. He cleaned her burnt and lacerated body, annointed it with oils and bandaged her until she looked like an ancient mummy. Then he wove a mat of palm leaves and placed her gently on it. He forced cool water through her parched lips and each day he rubbed fresh linament on her wounds and bandaged her carefully again.

For many days Francesca was unaware of Osari's care. She thought she was back in England, swimming in a cool, blue lake with Clarissa and Malcolm and their baby boy. Her recovery was slow and painful, but Osari nursed her patiently and, when she was finally able to travel, they returned to Cairo.

Osari had his own strong, though primitive, sense of honor. He would not reveal to anyone, even Francesca, how he had become a free man. The

164

secret of Murad's ignoble death and Elfi Bey's heart-break was not his to tell.

Believing Murad still alive, Francesca lived each day in fear that he would find her again. There was only one place in Egypt where she would be safe— one place where the son of Elfi Bey would not dare to trespass—the palace of the hated Mehamet Ali.

Chapter Twenty-Six

The marks on Francesca's flesh were beginning to fade but the internal scars would never dissolve. She dreaded the day when Elfi Bey's entourage returned to Cairo and rarely ventured out of Mehamet Ali's palace, even with Osari at her side, for fear of Murad.

During her long, slow recovery, Francesca lived like a mole. Her only companions were Osari and the letters from home that Major Misset had delivered to her. She read them over and over until the sheets were dog-eared and thin, savoring each word. But as always, the only news of Clarissa and Malcolm came from Lady Marlowe and saddened Francesca's heart.

"My darling daughter," she began, "I am writing to you from Paris where the bold little general has routed the revolutionaries and installed himself as high commander or some such title. Each day he seems to grow bolder and it would not even surprise me if he dared to proclaim himself king or even emperor of France, if only to make his fair, faithless Josephine a royal empress. Ah, such is the weakness of men that no amount of greatness can protect them from the power of an enterprising woman!

"I left London a fortnight ago with that thought fresh in my mind after a painful visit with Lord and Lady Harrod. Not even your Aunt Genevieve's most ardent pleas prevented Clarissa from making a public display of herself on every possible occasion. Malcolm seems to have aged a decade or more since their marriage. He puts up a brave front for the sake of the family—and particularly of his little son, who is quite the picture of his mother with large violet eyes and golden curls. But he seems to have accepted the fact that Clarissa cannot be controlled and spends as much time as possible now attending to his seat in the House of Lords.

"If your cousin's impossible behavior were confined to her chambers, I would not go on so. But her public displays are not only humiliating to Malcolm, they have taken their toll on your aunt and uncle as well. Genevieve of course is still making excuses for the girl or closing her mind entirely to her outrageous behavior, but poor Jeremy suffers grievously. Clarissa's antics are a terrible strain on his health.

"It would tear at your heartstrings, Francesca, if you saw your uncle now. He has grown quite feeble in your absence and often does not leave his chambers for days at a time. The doctors can do little for him. They say he has lost his will to fight. Clarissa is such a disappointment to him, and you so far away, and everything else he sacrificed so many, many years ago.

"But enough, dear daughter, of my morose family notes. One day you will know the full details, but, there is plenty of time for that. Paris is gray today and that always sends me into a dark mood. Humor me once more. You are always in my thoughts and in my heart, usually perched gracefully on the back of one of those extraordinary dromedaries. I think of visiting you in your new palace home, although I cannot understand why you left the employ of the bey when every letter sounded so happy and filled with enthusiasm. But it is just a frivolous dream. I know I shall never make the voyage."

Francesca folded the letter and sat staring out the window into the palace gardens. The palm trees were waving in the gentle breeze. She thought of the first time she saw one. The tall, bare trunk with the stiff formal growth at the top, the wide green leaves bowing oddly, looked so novel to her foreign eyes and she marveled at the Arab boys as they shinnied up and slid down seconds later bearing the round, brown-haired fruit they called coconuts. Now she could scarcely picture the elms and woodlands of England. That other world and everyone in it, their lives, their troubles, their joys, their disappointments, seemed distant and foreign now, yet still so dear to her heart.

She was living in a limbo between waking and sleeping. She felt sometimes as if she was holding her breath, not daring to release it until Pierre came back to her. He was always in her mind, his name on her lips, his smile in her heart, his touch on her skin.

Paris is gray today; as gray as his eyes? Francesca wondered. What would he do when he heard about Murad? Would he still want her when he knew that other hands had touched her and abused her when his seed was still fresh in her loins?

Francesca tortured herself with these questions. But she had no reason to, for Pierre du Bellenfant had no intention of ever returning to Egypt.

Chapter Twenty-Seven

Mehamet Ali was more than willing to grant Francesca sanctuary, when she returned to Cairo. While she had been hovering between life and death, he had done what nations had failed to do for centuries. He had cracked the power of the Mameluke beys and was conspiring how best to finish the job he had begun.

Elfi Bey, until then the most fearsome power in Egypt, was a broken man, humiliated by the success of his enemy and by his failure to avenge the death of his son. Although the Mameluke chief dared not show his face in Cairo, Mehamet Ali was still wary of the desert fox, skulking in Upper Egypt waiting for his chance to strike. As long as Elfi Bey lived he was a threat to the new pasha.

Anxious to learn every detail of his old foe's swift collapse and to uncover any sly schemes he was devising in revenge, Mehamet Ali welcomed Francesca into his palace. He was wiser than Major Misset and did not press her for information at first, but bided his time patiently. When she was settled comfortably in his palace and her strength had begun to return, he confronted her at last.

"Miss Fairchild, I trust you are enjoying your visit with me," Mehamet Ali began smoothly.

"Very much, Your Excellency," she replied, "you are most kind to grant me your hospitality."

"Ah," he said with a crafty smile, "I would like to show you as much hospitality as Elfi Bey did, if you would permit me."

Mehamet Ali did not want to provoke the ire of the British by forcing himself on this cool, long-limbed woman, but he was eager for the intimacy he was sure the Mameluke had enjoyed.

"I assure you, Mehamet Ali, you are no less gracious than my former employer," she replied diplomatically.

"We shall see about that, Miss Fairchild," he promised, "but first you must tell me what you know about the violent death of the bey's only son, Murad."

Francesca blanched, unable to disguise her shock. "Murad is dead?" she whispered.

"You did not know?"

"No, Your Excellency," she stammered. "I . . . I had no idea."

Mehamet Ali eyed her shrewdly. "How extraordinary," he replied. "One would think that a person who held such a position of privilege in Elfi Bey's household would know of such a . . . a family tragedy. The boy was killed with his own sword and his death goes unavenged. Although a dozen of the bey's fiercest and swiftest guards were sent to catch the murderer and bring his head back to Thebes on a pole, he escaped without a trace."

Francesca shuddered involuntarily. "Is the identity of the murderer known?"

"That is all I know of the story." Mehamet Ali paused, then said, "I am told the boy was weak and cruel."

"Yes, he was both." Francesca's voice was flat and hard.

The pasha scrutinized her closely, watching the changing emotions in her face. "Enough of these dark stories," he said finally. "In London, Miss Fairchild, I am sure you do not have to listen to such bloody tales of intrigue. Tell me about your great country and why you came to Egypt. I am very interested to know more of the West."

Francesca smiled wanly. In spite of his smooth words, Mehmamet Ali was a brilliant barbarian, shrewder and even more ruthless than Elfi Bey. *I have gone from the skillet to the fire*, she thought fleetingly, but she could not concentrate on her dangerous host now. Her mind was fixed on Murad.

The picture of him standing in the entrance of the tomb, lewd and exposed, mocking her love for Pierre, was etched forever in her memory. The knowledge that he had watched them had soiled their lovemaking, and she could not think of it now without seeing his leering, pasty face.

Francesca remembered each second that he stalked her in the tomb as if it were hours. She could still feel his hands on her breasts, tearing away her clothing, and she shuddered with revulsion as she recalled it. She felt herself running again, running desperately through the desert. At night she would wake up from a nightmare of that flight, trembling with fear, her body cold with sweat, and she would hear the sound of hoof beats coming closer and his wild laughter screaming in her brain.

Now it was over. She had nothing to fear from Murad again. But she felt no gladness at the news of his death—only an unutterable sense of relief and a strange twinge of loss. Did he ravish her or did he just beat her and leave her to die?

Now Francesca would never know.

Chapter Twenty-Eight

Mehamet Ali had not spoken idly. His interest in the West was genuine and he was eager to introduce its advanced techniques to his primitive country. The new pasha brought European doctors to Cairo to cure the ill, engineers to harness the impetuous Nile, and agriculturists to help cultivate the fields. Encouraged by his advances and intrigued by what they had read of ancient Egypt, more and more Europeans dared the voyage. But Pierre du Bellenfant was not among them and Mehamet Ali's demands on Francesca, though always subtly couched, became more insistent each day.

To escape from the palace and to wile away the long, lonely days until Pierre's return, Francesca began to join the excursions of curious travelers that were becoming a frequent event along the Nile. At first she used the trips to the ancient cities as an excuse to avoid the pasha's intimacies. But as the weeks grew to months, she became absorbed in the expeditions and, with Osari at her side, she began to devote all her time and energy to exploring the lost world of the pharaohs.

Keeping meticulous notes of every artifact and relic she found, Francesca dug through what was once the mighty city of Memphis. Although almost nothing remained of its temples and palaces, the ruins offered far more than any single explorer could fathom. Before Alexandria was built, Memphis had been the foremost city in Egypt. Now palm trees grew where the ancient city once flourished. But in the groves Francesca found mounds of ruins to study. In the encroaching desert sands she unearthed fragments of statues that had once towered as impressively as any in Thebes, and behind the site of the city she explored the pyramids and royal tombs. She even stumbled on a catacombs of birds where the sacred ibis, worshiped as a god by the ancient Egyptians, lay as perfectly mummified as any great pharaoh.

But Francesca never ventured farther south than Memphis. In spite of the glorious ruined cities of Luxor and Karnak, which she had glimpsed from Elfi Bey's barge, she could not bring herself to return to the scene of her love and her defilement. The frightening memories that were her legacy from Murad still haunted her dreams. Yet Francesca knew that, unless she returned one day to Thebes, the terror of his brutal attack would dog her life forever. There was no other way to rid herself of his ghost.

Finally, in spite of Osari's direst warnings, Francesca forced herself to go back. She made her singular pilgrimage in a chebek, very much like the one she had taken with Pierre from Rosetta to Cairo. Her fear hung like a caul over the voyage all the way from Memphis, mounting steadily the farther south they sailed.

At the last bend in the Nile before Thebes, she stood at the prow, trembling with apprehension, yet anxious to savor again the sudden splendor of Luxor and Karnak. The river was empty except for a richly appointed barge that was sailing down the Nile toward her. Francesca did not recognize the ship until it was nearly alongside her much smaller one. Then she saw at the helm the once mighty Mameluke prince.

Elfi Bey's fair beard was now pure white. His flashing eyes were vacant and dull. The only remnant of his splendor was the brilliant orange turban that swathed his great head. Little remained of his power and even less of his command. A skirmish with another old bey in the distant desert, where it made no difference who was victor or who was vanquished, was all that was left to him.

As their ships passed on the river, their eyes met briefly and held each other. Where was the arrogant, handsome chieftain who had ordered her to bow before him? Where was the quick, demanding English pupil who had wanted his son to speak like a British lord?

A rush of memories and of sadness flooded over Francesca and, in that instant when her eyes met Elfi Bey's, she realized how much more had died than a weak, cruel boy. The old Mameluke turned away and Francesca knew nothing remained for her to fear.

Although she and Osari returned to Upper Egypt many times, she never saw Elfi Bey again. The months turned into a year and the cycle of seasons began anew. Francesca continued to live in the pasha's palace, maintaining her precarious position as a guest. She studied and dug in the ancient ruined cities and she waited for Pierre.

His words were carved in her heart: "I promise I will come back to you, no matter how long it takes." And so she waited. She received regular letters from England, but not a word or a message from Pierre.

More and more Europeans journeyed to Egypt but he was never one of the visitors to the pasha's palace. Finally, one spring, before the Nile had begun to rise and threaten the valley again with its annual flooding, Francesca received a letter from her Aunt Genevieve.

"My dear niece," she wrote. "It breaks my heart to send you this sad news. Your Uncle Jeremy has taken a turn for the worse. His doctors offer little hope that he will last through the fall, and he, of course, knows very well that his time is short. He never was an easy man to deceive, not that I ever wanted to hide more from him than the purchase of an extravagant new bonnet. Francesca dear, your uncle has but one wish—to see you before he dies."

Francesca read her aunt's letter and she was filled with a devastating sense of loss. She had waited almost two years for Pierre without a word or message of any kind. Major Misset's sly words had begun to gnaw at her heart. *Could he have been using me—nothing more?* she wondered. *Could I mean nothing to him? Could he be that way with every woman?*

Francesca could not believe it, nor could she erase the nagging doubt from her mind. But neither mattered now. Duty called her as it had called him and she must answer.

BOOK II—*The Homecoming*

Chapter Twenty-Nine

Lady Clarissa Harrod looked forward with loathing to the return of her cousin Francesca. When they were growing up together, she always thought of Francesca as a planet oribiting her sun—not too clever, but absolutely loyal. In a world where schemers and conspirers throve, her fidelity was a constant. Later, when they were both old enough to turn a young man's head, it still never occurred to her that Francesca could be a threat. She stole Malcolm easily, and never gave it a second thought, until one day to her profound shock, she discovered Francesca's treachery.

From the first Clarissa's marriage was little more than a charade. She never forgave Malcolm for the cruelty of their wedding night and every day, in every way possible, she tried to punish him for it.

Malcolm never understood what terrible crime he had committed against his wife. At first he teased her for her prudishness and tried to coax her with his tender caresses. Finally he began to insist on his rights as a husband. He would sit in the library long into the night, a bottle of port at his side for company, and drink until he had emptied it. Then, drunk and aroused and uncontrollable, Lord Harrod would stumble into his wife's bed and storm her closely guarded fortress. Overriding her objections, he would take what pleasure he wished.

In the mornings he would repent and plead for forgiveness, promising Clarissa that if she allowed him an occasional night in her bed, it would never happen again. But each incident just drove her further from him.

Clarissa tried to torment her husband by exhibiting her voluptuous body before any man who caught her eye. She chose diaphanous gowns of the palest chiffons that revealed more of her creamy flesh and full breasts than they covered, and stayed at balls dancing until dawn.

Clarissa's outrageous behavior and public displays embarrassed Malcolm, but he laughed them off as harmless flirtations because he knew her secret. She was a romantic only as far as the bedroom door and then she had no further interest or desire. She was cold and sexless, and, one night after he had finished a bottle of port and was well into a second, he told her so.

Drunk and raging when Clarissa refused him yet again, Malcolm lashed out at her with furious words.

"I should never have married you," he shouted, "you are no more a woman than that doll." He seized the porcelain figure she always kept on her bed and hurled it across the room at her. "I should have married your cousin. Francesca was a real woman. She knew how to love. You . . . you are nothing but a toy, a plaything."

"For one so enamored, your engagement was certainly short-lived," Clarissa retorted coldly. She hated Malcolm when he was in a drunken rage and struck back at him any way she could.

"You saw to that."

"Yes, I did—unfortunately," she mocked, "so how

would you know how womanly my cousin is, Lord Harrod?"

"How do you think I know, Clarissa?" Malcolm rejoined bitterly. "The only way a man ever finds out what a woman truly is—by lying with her."

Clarissa's face turned ashen. Her big violet eyes stared unbelievingly at her husband.

"Does that shock you, Clarissa? Does it offend your delicate, dainty little soul? If it does, then why did you marry me? Surely, you don't expect me to believe that you did not know we were lovers. Yes, Clarissa, lovers!" he raged furiously. "You will never be anyone's lover. You are incapable of caring for anyone except yourself. I am through with your pretending. I am finished with your little girl games. You knew, Clarissa, but it did not stop you from having your way. Nothing ever stops you."

Clarissa glared at Malcolm, still speechless. His brutal, arrogant admission was worse than a blow, worse even than what he had done to her on their wedding night. She never considered what had goaded her genial, easy-going husband to such a cruel tirade.

Blind with fury, Clarissa could think only of the lovers. Although the engagement had never been formally announced, she knew Malcolm and Francesca were planning to marry but she never suspected that her cousin . . . It was too disgusting to even think of.

Malcolm's harsh words festered in her heart, turning her fury to scorn and then to hate. From that day on Clarissa did everything she could to hurt her husband as deeply as he had hurt her, yet Malcolm would not rise to her bait. Only the ultimate step, the one he believed she would never take, would pay him back in full measure.

Chapter Thirty

Genevieve Dorset's plump, pretty face was haggard and her full, matronly figure sagged with exhaustion.

"Please, you must get some rest, Genevieve," her sister urged. "Jeremy is sleeping now. Let me sit with him. If there is any change, I will send for you immediately. You know the doctor said he can linger like this for several weeks."

Genevieve looked up at her sister wearily. "Very well, but just for an hour, Andrea. I must be at his side when he wakes again."

"Don't worry, dear. I promise I will call you."

Lady Marlowe squeezed her tired sister's hand reassuringly as she took her place at Jeremy Dorset's bedside. She stared dry-eyed at the frail, ashen man who lay propped on the pillows. He had once been so supple and strong, she thought. Though Jeremy had never been a handsome man, he had possessed more charm than dozens of men twice as good-looking whom she had known through the years.

Where were they now? Where had all those long, lonely years gone? Was this all that was left to them—a painful, prolonged slipping away of life until only one feeble thread remained, tying an old man to all who loved him and all that he held dear?

Lady Marlowe shuddered in the face of their fragile mortality. *There was a time when we never would have believed that we could come to this,* she thought, *Genevieve, Jeremy, Clarissa, Francesca and I bound by complex ties known only to us two.* She took the dying man's hand, so thin and delicate now it looked almost transparent. The afternoon sun angled in thin shafts through the partially drawn curtains.

"Jeremy," she called in her warm, low voice. She held his hand in both of hers and leaned close to him.

"Jeremy," she called again. "It is Andrea. Can you hear me? I have come to stay with you."

Lady Marlowe paused, her eyes never stirring for a moment from her brother-in-law's face. The nurse and doctor had warned that he should not be disturbed but she called to him again, pressing his hand lightly in hers, willing him to wake up, to go back with her again to Paris if only for a last fleeting moment.

"Jeremy," she called again. His eyelids fluttered lightly and then opened slowly. But he seemed not to see her.

"Jeremy, it is Andrea," she said again.

The dying man looked at the beautiful face bent over him and smiled. "Andrea! Andrea! Are you sure you are not an angel sent to guide me home?" he asked. "You always looked like an angel, but . . ." His voice trailed off.

"I remember, Jeremy. But looks are happily deceiving, you always used to say."

She felt his thin hand squeeze hers weakly and he smiled at her again.

"I want to talk, Andrea, now while I still have a little time left," he said.

"Are you strong enough?"

"I must be." His voice was surprisingly firm. "I will

183

not ask you to forgive me, Andrea. You never have in all these years and I know, that no matter what you say now, in your heart you never will. But there is one thing you must promise me. When Francesca comes home, you must tell her everything. She has a right to know the truth about us—about all of us. I would like to tell her myself but I am afraid I will not last that long. Andrea, this is what I would tell her, if I could," he said.

Jeremy Dorset breathed heavily in short, quick gasps as if he was struggling for air, then he began to speak again, slowly but intently. Lady Marlowe stroked his hand as he talked. The light in the room grew dim and the murmur of his voice grew fainter. Still Jeremy went on. When he was finished speaking, he sank back in the pillows and looked at Andrea Marlowe. Her green eyes that had tempted so many men were filled with tears.

"I will tell Francesca, Jeremy, I swear to you I will," she vowed.

Jeremy smiled at her weakly. "Where is she now?" he asked.

"Somewhere in the Mediterranean. She should arrive home within the week," Lady Marlowe answered and the unspoken words hung in the air between them, *if you can last that long.*

"And Clarissa? Where is my Clarissa?" he asked.

"I am here, Father." Clarissa spoke sharply from the doorway.

Lady Marlowe turned abruptly. Her niece was framed clearly by the hall tapers.

"You must sleep now, Father," Clarissa said, coming toward his bedside. "You have talked quite long enough for one day."

How much did the girl overhear? How long was

she standing in the door? Lady Marlowe looked at her niece closely and saw the answers in her face.

"You need not worry, Aunt Andrea." Clarissa answered her unspoken concern coldly. "Your sordid old secret is safe with me. You can go now. I will stay with my father while Mother rests. We won't need your attendance any longer." Her eyes were as hard and cruel as her words.

"I am sorry you had to hear this, Clarissa, so abruptly and unexpectedly, without any warning," Lady Marlowe said.

"Don't be sorry. At least now I know why father always had more affection for Francesca than for me. Not that I really cared. He gave me what I wanted."

Lady Marlowe hesitated for a moment, studying her niece, and then, squeezing Jeremy's hand one last time, she pressed it to her lips. "I will go and wake up Genevieve," she said.

"Wake Mother gently," Clarissa said with sarcasm. "Nothing sudden, or you might open her eyes to the truth after all these years. Knowing Mother, she probably still believes the old story you fed her about the French duke."

Lady Marlowe spoke kindly, ignoring her niece's tartness. "Perhaps you are too young yet to understand, Clarissa, that often fiction is kinder than truth. Would Genevieve be a happier woman today, if I had bared my soul to her twenty-five years ago? I think not."

"Forgive me if I fail to appreciate your duplicity, Aunt Andrea. I am sure you will find a much more receptive audience in your daughter. She seems to have inherited your talent for deception."

Clarissa's cold scorn masked a much more malignant sentiment. Eavesdropping on her father's deathbed confession, she could only think that she had been cruelly deceived again.

Francesca had claimed her husband—and now her father. Who was there left for her?

Chapter Thirty-One

Francesca did not want to return to the indolent life of London with its endless rounds of dinners and balls, country visits and tea parties. In Egypt she had important work to finish and infinite treasures still to uncover. She had grown to love the wild, barbaric place, which each day bore witness to forty centuries of history—the raucous, teeming bazaars of Cairo and the boundless desert at its door, the tempermental Nile that made the land habitable but refused to be harnessed, the mosques and the ancient monuments. Compared to England it was crude, undisciplined, unprincipled—but compelling and vibrant.

But Francesca had discovered more than ruined temples and pharaohs' tombs in Egypt. She had discovered the highest, richest human feelings and the lowest, most twisted emotions. She had learned the meaning of love and had been awakened to its limitless joy. And she had learned the meaning of terror. She knew what it was to be cornered like a beast, stalked and hunted and terrorized. She had suffered and she had lost. Yet from all she had experienced—the good and the bad, the tenderness and the torture—she had gained. For Francesca had learned to be a woman.

She was no longer the open, exuberant girl she had once been, no longer the shy, innocent girl who would blush at a word or glance. Her dark eyes still danced when she was excited, but her enthusiasms were channeled now. She was independent and self-contained. She had been tested painfully, and she had endured. There was an indefinable quality in her face, an inner strength that gave a stranger pause. She presented a cool, grave countenance to the world until she smiled. Then her wide, velvet eyes warmed and her face lit up like a million candles. The change was startling and not easily forgotten.

Mehamet Ali had not allowed such an unusual woman to slip through his clutches easily. He had grown so powerful, he did not fear British reprisals, but he did not want to be looked on as a barbarian by the Europeans whose friendship he courted. So he waited for Francesca to come around, much as Elfi Bey had, sure that her defenses would eventually weaken.

As long as she lived in his palace, Mehamet Ali was willing to bide his time. There was no rush in his loins for her. Just the timeless desire of a ruthless man to subjugate all he commands. But when Francesca announced her plans to return to England, he forbade her to leave.

Faced with his ultimatum, Francesca was forced to dare a perilous escape from Egypt. If she was apprehended, Mehamet Ali's vengeance would be too horrible to imagine. But she could not ignore her uncle's dying wish and she would not be the prisoner of any man—except Pierre.

With the faithful Osari to guide and protect her, Francesca slipped out of Cairo, disguised in the dress of an Arab woman. Leaving directly from her excavations in Memphis, without even returning to the palace to collect her belongings, they took the overland road to Alexandria. There were no sacred fakirs to impede her way this time and they arrived at their destination five days later without suffering any serious mishap.

Once in Alexandria. Francesca lost no time in looking up Sergeant Crawford. He was still manning his cherished post and still as pompous as she remembered him. Although he eyed her reckless escape as the utmost folly, he could not forsake a countrywoman in distress. and he secured passage for them on the S.S. *Gloria*, an English schooner that was sailing for Portsmouth at dawn.

When they reached the dock at daybreak, they found a dozen of Mehamet Ali's personal guards lying in wait for them. A fierce melee ensued between the pasha's men on one side and Osari on the other. The giant Nubian held them off single-handedly. Roaring like a mighty lion, he hurled men off the dock as if they were empty sacks and swung his long sword viciously, slicing off the arm of any man who dared to reach for Francesca. Although speared in the chest with a poisoned javelin, the brave Nubian battled on, never slowing until the dock was a crimson sea and all twelve men lay dead.

But the poison soon pierced Osari's heart, and he died in Francesca's arms on the voyage to England, a free man at last.

Francesca buried Osari at sea—the same day that Jeremy Dorset was laid to his eternal rest in London.

Chapter Thirty-Two

The Dorsets' brick mansion on St. James's Place stood as stolid and secure as the day Francesca had left it. But inside, the life of the old house had changed drastically, and it was not only Jeremy Dorset's death that made the difference.

Francesca mourned for her uncle whose last wish she had failed by seven days to fulfill. But it was the new lord and lady of his house whom she grieved for above all.

Not even her mother's letters had prepared Francesca for the change in Clarissa and Malcolm. Except for their shy, beautiful son Geoffrey, little had gone right since their marriage. Clarissa's angelic face had hardened like lacquer and her sweet, musical voice had grown brittle.

Although Clarissa's greeting was effusive, Francesca felt the change in her cousin as clearly as if she had been received with a slap rather than a welcoming kiss. Clarissa's embrace was too superficial, her enthusiasm too studied, her words too glib, for Francesca to be deceived. She felt the hostility behind her cousin's affected friendship and it cut her deeply.

But what disturbed Francesca even more than the hollow welcome was Clarissa's bold, boastful talk. From the moment Francesca entered the old Dorset home again, it seemed that her cousin began to brag about her infidelities. Clarissa seemed like a woman possessed. She could talk of nothing else. She asked only the most cursory questions about Francesca's Egyptian excursion and then launched into a full account of her own amorous adventures.

"You know, dear, I have become quite the darling of London in your absence. All the most desirable men—even the Prince of Wales himself—are simply dying to get their hands on me. But I have set my sights on a divine American," Clarissa confided gleefully. "The very first thing you must do now that you are home at last is meet him. You will be so envious. His name is Peter Barnes and he is the most gorgeous man in the world. He is madly in love with me, of course—has eyes for no other woman, although every girl in London swoons at the very thought of him—and he is the most marvelous lover!"

She paused, smiling invidiously. "Darling Francesca, I only wish that Peter could be copied so that you would know how wonderful he is. You look as if you could use a good lover yourself."

Francesca could not disguise her shock. Ignoring Clarissa's barbed words, she said, "But what about Malcolm? He is still your husband, is he not?" She had no way of knowing that more than half of her cousin's words were empty boasts.

Clarissa's forced laughter reverberated hollowly. "I am doing my utmost to repay my husband in full for everything he has done for me. But here he is now, darling; ask him yourself."

Francesca turned slowly to greet the man who had known her before any other.

"Malcolm!" she cried in stunned disbelief. She was not prepared for what he had become. Because of the unique bond they shared, she thought she would be moved in some special way when she saw him again. But all she felt was an immense pity.

Clarissa was hardened, but Malcolm was defeated. The long nights of drinking, glambling and womanizing had left their dissolute mark on his once handsome face. His blue eyes were vapid; his slender body had begun to bloat. The easy-going charm that had drawn her to him had disintegrated into mere weakness.

"Dearest Francesca," Malcolm said, taking both her hands in his and squeezing them warmly. "I have thought of you so often through these years."

His voice was thick with emotion and his eyes reflected the genuine warmth of his welcome. Overwhelmed with anger at Clarissa for what she had done to her husband and with loathing for the unknown Peter Barnes, whoever he might be, Francesca pressed Malcolm's hand in return.

"And I have thought of *you* often, Malcolm," she replied sympathetically.

Malcolm Lord Harrod knew that every detail of their reunion was being imprinted on his wife's spiteful mind. But at that moment, he did not care.

Malcolm loved Clarissa dearly. She could still enchant him when she wanted with her impish little ways and make him forget all the heartache she caused him. She'd cuddle up in his lap and make him laugh, and he'd agree to every wild plan she proposed or every mad whim she voiced. But her coldness in their bed, her revulsion at his tenderest caress, had sent Malcolm in search of a warmer, more willing woman.

Since the night of his terrible tirade, Malcolm had stopped drinking alone in the library and insisting on his rights as a husband. In the days, he concentrated on the business of Parliament and rapidly became one of the most promising young leaders in the Whig Party. In the evenings he became a regular at Waiter's, the Prince of Wales's favorite club, drinking and gambling until dawn, and in the intimate morning hours, he found solace in the arms of Harriette Wilson, the most desired courtesan in London.

When Harriette and her sisters drove in Hyde Park at five, their elaborate, baby-blue silk-lined carriage was always flanked by a cordon of gentlemen riders, hoping to set up a rendezvous. When they entertained in York Place, there was nary a duke or a prince who passed up the entertainment they proffered. When they hired a box at King's Theater, the performance on stage went unnoticed because all eyes were turned to see who was paying the Wilson ladies court and invariably the gentleman at Harriette's side was Malcolm Lord Harrod.

Harriette Wilson was the most sought after demimondaine in town, the fairest of the Fashionable Impures. Her artistry could satisfy the most demanding man, but she could never be the one thing Malcolm desired above all else. She could never be Clarissa.

Lord Harrod dreamed of possessing his wife's creamy flesh the way King Arthur's knights dreamed of the grail. He had not meant the angry words he had spoken. In spite of all the difficulties they had and all the heartache she made him suffer, Malcolm had never regretted marrying Clarissa—until Francesca came home.

Chapter Thirty-Three

Francesca no longer felt welcome in the old Dorset house where she had spent so many happy years, and so she moved into the house at Grosvenor Square that her mother had taken to be near at hand during Uncle Jeremy's prolonged illness. Although it was just across Hyde Park, she kept her visits to a minimum and, for the most part, left Lord and Lady Harrod to their own desperate devices.

The England Francesca returned to was far different from the one she had left just a few short years before. Leisure had become a way of life since she'd been away. After losing the American colonies, old King George had grown so feeble-minded that now the Prince of Wales was monarch in fact, if not yet in name.

Pleasure-loving Prinnie set the style for the country, and a lavish style it was. Rebelling against his father's stern, puritanical reign, he indulged himself extravagantly. No caprice went unsatisfied, whether it was for a pleasure dome in Brighton or for the pleasure of a plump new paramour between his royal sheets. He was the first gentleman of Europe, London was his playground, and Lord and Lady Harrod among his most exuberant playmates.

Lord Harrod was a favorite at the Prince of Wales's gaming table at Waiter's—and not only because Malcolm was usually so drunk that thousands of his pounds sterling invariably ended up in the royal purse. Lady Harrod's beauty and unbridled behavior added a sparkling, exciting note to his sumptuous soirees, and so their company was *de rigeur* at the extremely extravagant midsummer's night ball he was planning.

Dazzling though it was, Francesca had no interest in becoming a part of her cousin's social whirl. By the time she arrived in London, she'd lost the two men dearest to her, and her heart was locked away.

Uncle Jeremy was already dead and Pierre might just as well be. By fleeing from Mehamet Ali as she had, Francesca had relinquished any hope of ever being reunited with her love. Pierre might one day return to Egypt, but she never could.

In the weeks that passed, Francesca closeted herself in the house at Grosvenor Square and immersed herself in her Egyptian notebooks. From her meticulously kept diaries, she decided to fashion a book that would convey the wonder and mystery of the ancient, lost world to those who would never have the opportunity to see it with their own eyes. She would dedicate it to Uncle Jeremy, knowing that if he had lived, he would have enjoyed reviewing all she had discovered. He was the first to open her curious mind. The Egyptian book would be a personal memorial to him.

Engrossed in her project, Francesca remained aloof from the indulgent life of fashionable London. It seemed to her like a senseless carousel ride, twirling around and around in a dizzying succession of vacuous entertainments and going nowhere. She saw all too clearly what had become of Malcolm and Clarissa and she did not want to suffer a similar fate. But Francesca could not refuse the invitation to the Prince of Wales's midsummer's night ball.

It was not the elegant, engraved invitation with the royal crest embossed in gold that she found irresistible, but Malcolm's touching request, delivered as they passed each other on the front steps of the old Dorset house. Francesca was on her way in to lunch with her Aunt Genevieve. Malcolm was rushing off to the House of Lords.

He pressed her arm warmly as they passed. "I am so looking forward to the ball, Francesca. We'll have a grand time—just like the old days again!"

"But Malcolm," Francesca said in suprise, "I have no plans to attend the ball."

"Not attend the ball?" His astonishment was clearly sincere. "Why, you mustn't miss it on any account. I wager no one else in London has even considered declining. It is bound to be an unparalleled spectacle, and I have been looking forward so to the pleasure of your company," he smiled. "If you disappoint me, I shall be forced to ogle other men's wives. Surely, you would not want to put me in such a compromising position."

"Don't be silly, Malcolm," Francesca laughed. "Clarissa will save you from that, I've no doubt."

"Not at all. She is a restless butterfly at these events, flitting from guest to guest and lighting on whatever strong shoulder strikes her fancy. The lucky chap this time will probably be the American—I dare say Clarissa has told you all about him. He is quite a gambler, beats me with boring monotony at Waiter's, and is a favorite with the ladies. It's all quite harmless, really, but it does leave me quite alone."

Malcolm tried to speak lightly but a sad, wistful note filtered through his words.

Francesca's heart went out to him. He had become so pitiable, lost to both herself and Clarissa. She discovered long ago that their love was merely a childish fancy she'd outgrown, and Clarissa's only lasting interest seemed to be in taunting him.

Stirred by his pathetic request, Francesca ordered a new gown and steeled herself to brave the crush of guests. It was true: she did know all about Peter Barnes from Clarissa, and the more she heard, the less she liked the worthless rake.

"With my luck, Barnes will probably turn your head, as well," Malcolm had said jokingly. But Francesca was sure there was no chance of that. When she thought of how he was destroying Malcolm and Clarissa's marriage, her heart filled with anger.

Francesca hoped she would be introduced to the insolent American at the ball, because she looked forward with perverse pleasure to telling him exactly what she thought of his outrageous behavior.

"You have won our colonies, Mr. Barnes," she would say, "surely you should be content, without claiming any more of England's choicest property."

But, when Francesca met Peter Barnes at last, Malcolm and Clarissa's troubles vanished instantly from her mind.

Chapter Thirty-Four

Peter Barnes made the Prince of Wales seem as stodgy as old King George.

With his flashing eyes and curly black beard, the audacious American cut a wide swath through London society. He had the manners of a gentleman but the passions of a profligate.

Gambling and women were his favorite vices, and he excelled in both of them. In little more than a year, he'd become a familiar fixture among the gentlemen at Waiter's, where he delighted in stripping the English lords, who frequented Beau Brummel's elegant gaming club, of every pound they possessed.

Peter Barnes was equally fond of flirting with their lordships' ladies. After gambling into the early morning hours, he was still as fresh as a daisy and ready to take on the fairest of them.

Though restricted from Waiter's, the women reigned supreme over their own exclusive club, Almack's at St. James's Place. Entry was a privilege, guarded like the crown jewels by a covey of London's leading ladies. More intrigue went into getting one of the coveted invitations to the Wednesday evening supper balls at Almack's than went into Lord Nelson's plans to confront General Bonaparte. But Peter Barnes never had to inveigle for one. Every week without fail, his invitation was delivered by a liveried footman.

Talk was that Peter Barnes had been a riverboat gambler in America, which gave the older, more conservative Tory noblemen cause to wonder how he ever gained entry into their rarefied circles. No one could remember who introduced him into London society in the first place.

Was it young John Kent, physician to the royal family and half the English nobility, who brought him? Did Beau Brummel give him entrance because his elegant looks and fine wardrobe met the dandy's most demanding measure? Did he slip in on Lady Jersey's arm? Or was it Lady Harrod's?

Little was known about Peter Barnes. But he was so handsome and so attractive a companion—a challenge to both the sporting men at Waiter's and their sybaritic mates at Almack's—that nobody seemed to notice. All of the talk was usually on which of the fair ladies would garner his favor.

Almack's was a hotbed of scandal and gossip—and nothing was more scandalous and more gossiped about than the tug-of-war between the wicked Lady Jersey and the willful Lady Harrod to topple into Peter Barnes's bed.

Lady Jersey made no pretense about it: the handsome American was a prize she had set for herself. But then neither did the headstrong Lady Harrod. Even with her husband at her side, she proclaimed her attraction for the dashing young American.

At every dinner, every soiree, Clarissa clung to Peter Barnes's arm and monopolized his attention. Her gowns became more revealing each week, her behavior more like a courtesan's. She set the most timid tongues wagging, yet her husband remained unconcerned.

Malcolm watched Clarissa's shameless advances impassively, sure that she would never go beyond the public display. He knew all too well that she wanted all the play and none of the passion. Convinced without a shadow of a doubt that she would always be his wife and his alone, he allowed her to indulge in her harmless games.

Malcolm was supremely confident that no other man would ever know Clarissa. But he underestimated his wife's vindictiveness. Clarissa was determined to go to any lengths no matter how distasteful to her, to make her husband rue the night he threw Francesca's passion in her face.

Peter Barnes was the man she chose to revenge herself with. He was a double-edged sword: he was divinely attractive and, almost daily, he fleeced Lord Harrod at the gaming tables at Waiter's, often ending the night three or four thousand pounds richer.

Although Clarissa was determined to take Peter Barnes as her lover, she had formidable competition in the malicious Lady Jersey. Older than Clarissa and far more worldly-wise, Lady Jersey was stylish, witty and a shrewd judge of human nature. She instinctively knew what a man wanted and, in the rolling, pastoral setting of her famed country estate, she was more than willing to provide it. Her reputation was wide-spread, and her legion of lovers included many of the most powerful men in London.

Lady Jersey was ambitious. She could be cruel. But she was invariably discreet. Clarissa was beautiful, enticing and given to public outbursts of emotion. In his delicate position, Peter Barnes leaned toward Lady Jersey. With her there would be no tearful scene, no reproaches when the affair was over.

But he was a gambling man and the soft, voluptuous charms that Lady Harrod displayed so daringly tempted him to go for broke. Weighing the odds between the two ladies with relish, Peter Barnes decided to play his cards at long last at the Prince of Wales's midsummer's night ball.

Chapter Thirty-Five

The Prince of Wales's midsummer night ball was
the most sumptuous social event of the year. Two
thousand guests were invited and few if any failed to
attend. The came in barouches, landaus and victorias
through the welcoming gates of Carlton House,
passed the tall porphyry columns that lined its facade,
and entered the royal palace.

For sheer opulence Carlton House rivaled Versailles. A dining table some two hundred feet long
stretched the length of the fabulous Gothic conserva-
tory and in front of the table ran a gurgling
stream. Goldfish swam in its crystal-clear water and
thousands of flowers bloomed on its banks. Guests
stepped across gracefully curved bridges to reach the
table where a feast to satisfy the most discerning
palate was laid out. Hot soups, roasts of venison and
beef, whole salmons and turbots followed course after
course. Every platter and plate was of heavy sterling
silver and champagne flowed as freely as the stream.

The dancing took place in a gold-encrusted ballroom, hung with crystal chandeliers and enormous
mirrors that reflected the shimmering decor. The
splendor of the prince's palace was matched only by
the magnificence of the guests' attire. The men were
handsome in court dress or uniforms. The women out-
shone each other in the splendor of their dress and the

richness of their jewels. But none was more dazzling than the beautiful Lady Harrod.

Clarissa's white chiffon gown clung to her generous curves enticingly. Heavy gold braid embroidered the empire waist and plunging neckline. A wide gold choker gleaming with diamonds encircled her delicate neck, drawing the eye to the milky expanse she dared to reveal. Her full, creamy breasts rose tantalizingly, promising to escape any moment from the meager confines of her bodice.

Even in such a glittering assemblage, Clarissa stood out dramatically. Her violet eyes glistened as brightly as the diamonds. Her laugh tinkled as musically as the prince's priceless crystal. Her gaiety bubbled over like a fountain.

When she ordered her own new gown for the ball, Francesca thought she had never seen such a beautiful dress. Now, beside her dazzling cousin, she felt sedate and out of fashion. Her gown was designed like a Grecian toga instead of the empire style favored by the most glamorous women at the ball and, although it was chiffon like Clarissa's, instead of clinging, it seemed to float. Deep purple violets entwined on the pale lilac background and a panel of chiffon drifted from her shoulders. Her golden hair was piled softly on the top of her head and encircled with a single strand of amethysts. Otherwise she wore no jewels. Her fine, dramatic features were untouched by powders or rouge. Only her wide almond eyes were outlined in the Egyptian style.

"Francesca, darling," Clarissa's gay voice interrupted her cousin's thoughts. "At long last you will have the thrill of meeting my dashing new lover."

Even though Lady Marlowe had written about Clarissa's public displays, Francesca was not prepared for such a blatant performance. She was astonished

203

that her beautiful cousin would speak so boldly in front of so many, and she was embarrassed for Malcolm.

"Don't look so scandalized," Clarissa chirped. A snide, brittle note escaped through the gaiety. "Surely you will not have us believe that you are so pure you have never taken a lover." She could never forgive either Malcolm or Francesca for what they had done or for deceiving her with their silence and she hoped to make Francesca jealous by flaunting her handsome new conquest.

Peter Barnes excused himself from Lady Jersey when he saw Clarissa coming toward him, skirting the dance floor where elegant couples dared to embrace in the intimate new dance called the waltz, which was shocking London. *She looks ravishing—and ready to be ravished*, he thought with a stab of pleasure at the prospect that he was confident could be his whenever he wanted it. But it was the tall, honey-skinned girl at his side who held his eye. Simple and unadorned, she stood out in sharp contrast to the painted, powdered beauties that filled the room.

Clarissa looked like a ripe fruit ready to be plucked. In her revealing white gown all her ample charms were on display. But the other girl looked like a refreshing breath of spring, when the promise of magical summer days and fragrant nights is in the air, and everything lies ahead waiting to be discovered.

She seemed to be floating toward him through a field of violets. *Who can she be?* he wondered admiringly. Then she drew closer and for an instant he thought that he was caught in a terrible nightmare. He felt the blood drain out of his face. He could not move. He could not stop the tormenting trick his eyes were playing on him. He closed them tightly for a moment and whispered fiercely to himself, "She is dead, you fool, dead."

When Peter Barnes opened his eyes again, Clarissa was positioned provocatively before him so he could look down into her velvet breasts.

"Forgive the intrusion, Dr. Barnes, but I simply could not wait another moment to have my very favorite cousin meet you," she gushed. "Miss Fairchild just returned a fortnight ago from a lengthy sojourn in the Middle East."

Peter Barnes bowed to Lady Harrod then turned to the tall, slender girl at her side. Without a word, he took her in his arms.

For a moment his thick black beard had decieved Francesca. Then the room began to whirl like a tornado. She felt herself swooning just as his arms closed around her and he carried her into the swirl of waltzers.

Why had he left her? Why had he never returned? Never written? Never sent a word? Why was he here? Francesca did not ask. His gray eyes told her everything she wanted to know—everything she had longed to know and had despaired of ever hearing.

"Francesca, my love girl," Peter Barnes whispered.

"Pierre, *mon amour, mon cher amour,*" she answered. Tears of love and happiness shone in her deep brown eyes.

They waltzed around and around, lost in each other's arms. The noise and the guests melted away. They were alone. The long, lonely years of anguish and despair were forgotten and there existed only their love—then and now and forever.

Francesca's cheeks were flushed and her eyes glowed.

"You are even lovelier than my memories of you,"

he said brushing her cheek tenderly with his fingertips.

"No, it is you who is beautiful, even through that
great black forest that has grown on your face." She
smiled at him and drew his hand to her lips. "I have
kissed you so many times in my dreams, Pierre."

She felt his arm tighten around her waist and his
voice was low and urgent. "Not here, Francesca," he
said and he waltzed her out of the golden ballroom
into the quiet hallway beyond. He held her in the
shadow of a wide column, not daring to breathe, until
a liveried footman turned away for a moment. Then
he squeezed her hand and they darted across the hallway, up the winding marble stairway, taking refuge
in the first room they came to. It was an elegant sitting room with a wide bay of windows through which
the moonlight shone illuminating a handsome, inlaid
spinet piano and a damask-covered chaise lounge with
a low rolled back.

Francesca's heart was pounding wildly as Pierre
closed the door behind them and turned the key in
the lock. "I thought you had deserted me," she whispered.

"Never, my darling," he answered. His voice was
hurt and disbelieving as if to ask *how could you
doubt my love?* "Never for an instant have I stopped
loving you, wanting you, and despising myself for
leaving you. But there will be time to talk, to explain
everything. Now . . ."

He took her in his arms, crushing her against him
in the violence of his emotion, His hands caressed her
neck, her back, her buttocks, her breasts as if he had
to touch every inch of her again. His mouth rained a
torrent of kisses on her hair and eyes and cheeks, finally coming to rest on the lips that he had hungered
so long for.

All the women he had drowned his heartbreak in, all the women who had known his driving, torrential lust, ceased to exist. There was only Francesca. There had always been only Francesca, and she was his again, warm and alive and overflowing with love. Her lips parted and he tasted the moisture of her mouth and felt the sharp fine point of her tongue meet his.

His eyes blazed with a passion that nothing could restrain, no one could deny. "I want to kiss you, Francesca, and hold you close to me and make love to you until you cry that you can bear no more. And then I want to begin again. I want to bury myself between your lovely legs and sleep in the gently valley between your breasts. Do I shock you, my love? I don't want to—only to love you, to have you, to hold you."

All the passion, the love, the desire that Francesca had been holding back for so long was released in Pierre's arms. His touch, his lips filled her with an uncontrollable fire. She grasped his buttocks and pressed herself to him, undulating sensually against the hard, undeniable proof of his desire. The wild passion he had kindled in her seared his heart and made him her captive forever.

He raised her violet skirt and felt her silk stockings and above them the smooth, honey skin of her thighs, and his fingers came to rest between her legs.

A violent rush of desire filled Francesca. He felt her tremble in his arms and he gazed into her deep velvet eyes.

"Do you love me, Francesca?" he demanded passionately.

She answered him with her lips. Their tongues merged in a hungry, violent kiss and he tore away the fine, lace panties that kept her from him. He pressed his palm into her rich chestnut crown, until she cried out, "I have wanted you so long, Pierre. Don't make me wait for you another moment." Then he picked her up in his arms and carried her to the chaise lounge.

Francesca lay on her back, every fiber of her being burning with love, every inch of her flesh on fire with desire, had raised her lilac skirts for her love. She looked like some elegant courtesan, her beautiful gown pulled up to her waist, her silk stockings and satin garters still in place, her black satin dancing slippers still on her slender feet. The moonlight shone brightly on her smooth, flat belly and glorious chestnut crown.

Pierre gazed down on her loveliness, awestruck. Never had he known a woman so unashamed to give herself.

"You wild, wonderful love," he marveled, as she opened her legs to receive him.

Chapter Thirty-Six

Francesca paced the drawing room nervously, her arms folded at her waist, holding herself tightly as if she were trying by this simple posture to restrain the passions that had been loosed the night before. The house was silent except for the even tread of her footsteps.

Lady Marlowe had retreated to her country estate in Surrey to escape the London heat, and Francesca, in the flush of emotion from the evening before, had given all the servants a holiday. She had wanted to be alone when Pierre called at three, but now she was having second thoughts.

Francesca was beginning to regret her reckless behavior of the evening before and the foolish impulse that had made her dismiss the servants. She wanted to see Pierre again. She longed to see him, and yet she was afraid. There were so many unanswered questions.

She paused at the tea table and rearranged the silver plate of cakes, then she smoothed her dress. She had changed it twice already that afternoon before finally deciding on the simple yellow organdy.

Why was Pierre in London when he had promised to come back to her in Egypt? Why was he pretending to be Peter Barnes? Why had he never written? Never sent a word?

The grandfather clock in the front hall chimed three times. *He is late. Maybe he won't come*, she thought and began to pace the drawing room again.

Francesca was not sure whether she would be more relieved or more disappointed if Pierre did not appear. She kept thinking of Major Misset's sly words: "It is clear that Dr. du Bellenfant used you to gain entry to Elfi Bey."—and hearing Clarissa's proud boast. "Peter is simply dying to make love to me, but I am not going to be easy this time."

She marveled at the circumspection and control of women like her cousin who could say no when their hearts, their bodies, cried to surrender. But Francesca knew that if she had last night to live over again, she would do the same thing. Her heart would not allow her to do anything else.

The front door knocker clanked, interrupting her troubled reverie. She stood stark still in the center of the drawing room, listening to her heart beat and the blood rushing in her ears. The knocker banged again. The sound was louder, more insistent.

Francesca walked slowly to the front door and stood in front of it with her hand on the doorknob. She was trembling with fear and desire. If she opened it and Pierre came back into her life, she could never bear to let him go again. *Better*, she thought, *not to see him again, to pretend last night was a beautiful, impossible dream, than to give my love again and then lose him.*

But it was too late. The knocker clapped a third time and a fourth. Its insistent bang told her that he was not going to leave. Wiping her moist hands on her skirt, Francesca took a deep breath and opened the door halfway.

Pierre stood on her doorstep as roughish and devil-may-care as the young doctor who had been her guide and friend in Egypt. His devilish eyes and his brilliant smile gave no hint of the evening before.

"This is why I am late," he said gaily, producing a bouquet of creamy white gardenias from behind his back. "All for you—and one for me." He plucked a blossom from the bunch and put it in his lapel. "Aren't you going to invite me in, Francesca?"

Without waiting for her answer, Pierre brushed by her and, taking careful aim, he tossed his top hat at the stairpost. "Amazing shot! Perfect eye, don't you think? Almost as perfect as you in yellow," he said lightly.

From the instant Francesca opened the door, Dr. du Bellenfant had been examining his favorite patient and had diagnosed a case of embarrassment and regret for the night before and acute fear for what might happen this afternoon. Francesca seemed so shy and suddenly awkward, as if she did not know what to say or do or where to put her hands. Pierre had hoped that she would fly into his arms again, but he did not show his disappointment. Instead he played the rakish boulevardier as he had done when they first met in Egypt.

"Since the butler is not present to announce me to Lady Marlowe, may I have the honor of escorting you into the drawing room, Miss Fairchild?" He bowed with exaggerated formality and offered his arm.

Francesca blushed. "My mother is not at home this afternoon. She left for the country earlier today."

"I am disappointed to hear that. I was looking forward to tea with the lovely Lady Marlowe who, I am told, is almost as entrancing as her daughter."

"Oh, Mother is a million times more entrancing than I," Francesca said, trying to take refuge in light

211

chatter. "I always wished that I had inherited some of her beauty."

"I imagined that you looked like your mother," Pierre said as he followed her into the drawing room. "But, if what you say is not false modesty, then you must resemble your father more."

"I suppose I must," Francesca said, uncertainly. "Would you care for some tea?" She sat down on the sofa beside the tea table.

"Thank you."

Pierre stretched out casually in an armchair opposite her. "Why is it that you never talked about your father when we were in Egypt?"

"I never knew him." Francesca flushed again. "But I am sure you would much rather have a cup of tea than talk about my relatives. What do you like in it?"

Pierre ignored her question. "Lady Marlowe is in the country. The butler, I must assume, is indisposed. And the other servants?"

"I gave them . . ." she began and then she caught herself. "Also indisposed," she answered severely.

Pierre's gray eyes were laughing. "A marvelous coincidence, Francesca, wouldn't you agree?"

"If you are implying . . ." she began heatedly.

"Just a little sugar," he interrupted, "in the tea you offered me."

Francesca poured in silence and then filled a cup for herself. *How I must have hurt her to make her so afraid of me now*, Pierre brooded. But neither his face not his words revealed his dark, loving thoughts.

"Tea," he was saying casually, "is a British custom which I have not yet learned to appreciate. To me it is a tepid potion concocted to ruin a perfectly fine afternoon."

"Perhaps you would like a sweet cake, then, to make this dreadful potion more palatable," Francesca said, trying to maintain their light banter for as long as she could.

She passed the silver plate of cakes to him, but, instead of taking one, he caught her wrist. With his other hand he removed the plate from her grasp and placed it on the floor.

"Surely, Francesca, you did not dismiss the servants for the day to offer me nothing sweeter than a tea cake," he said. His gray eyes were as sharp as blades and they seemed to bore through her—to penetrate her heart. She felt as she had on the Nile that he could read the deepest desires in her heart.

Francesca tried to pull away but Pierre tightened his grasp. *What happened after I left her to make Murad swear she was dead?* he wondered. *What terrible things did she suffer?*

He pressed her hand against his mouth, sinking his teeth into her knuckles for an instant, and then he released her. When he spoke again, his voice was low and strained.

"Francesca," he said, "I do not know what you have done or how you have lived these last two years. But if you can say of me to any man, 'It doesn't matter who he was or is,' tell me this instant and I will leave without another word. We will call last evening a midsummer's night madness. We will blame it on the unexpected meeting, the sudden shock of finding each other again." He leaned forward, straining to be closer to her. "But never be afraid of my love, Francesca." He paused, his voice choked with emotion.

"My love is to cherish you, to caress you, to please you. It could never hurt you in any way. You must believe me," he pleaded.

The dashing young doctor was gone. Pierre was

once again the tender young man on the boat from Rosetta, the ardent lover in the Valley of the Kings.

"I was told you were dead and I believed it. I had reliable evidence—proof, I thought—that it was true. Nothing else could have kept me from you. Nothing but your death or my own."

Francesca looked away to avoid his pleading eyes. *How could he have thought I was dead when he left me filled with his love and his seed?* she asked herself. She wanted to believe Pierre and yet . . .

"Major Misset said you were a spy for Napoleon who would do anything you had to to gain entry into Elfi Bey's palace." She spoke flatly, trying not to let her words sound like an accusation. "And then," she hesitated, too proud to let him see how much his infidelities hurt her, "there are Clarissa and the others."

Pierre leaped to his feet, his gray eyes flashing with anger. "Major Misset," he shouted, "that cold, sly, bloodless fish. You accept his word but not my love. Was I a spy for Bonaparte? Is that what you want to know?" he demanded. "Very well, I will tell you.

"I was then—and I am now. What other reason would I have to take my mother's name and hide behind this forest of hair, pretending to be an American? I am Bonaparte's eyes and ears in England because we believe Nelson was not satisfied to destroy our fleet in Egypt. He is even now laying plans to destroy us completely."

He faced Francesca squarely, his eyes as cold and unyielding as steel. "Now you need fear me no longer. My life is in your hands. Denounce me to your good friend Lord Harrod, if it pleases you, and you can see me hang in Fleet Street tomorrow."

"I did not say that I believed Major Misset," Francesca said softly. His coiled violence frightened and thrilled her.

214

Pierre turned away angrily and paced the room like a caged panther. "Did I use you? That is what you are still asking me." He stopped in front of her again. His eyes had softened. His voice was low and taut. His soul was stripped naked, hiding nothing from her.

"Yes, Francesca, I used you in the beginning. I agreed readily to escort you to Cairo because it seemed like a golden opportunity to make an ally in the bey's palace. It did not hurt that I found you lovely to look at. But in my work that is just a lucky break. If you had been a witch, I would have escorted you anyway. That night on the Nile, though, when I told you I had never loved a woman, I was speaking the truth."

Pierre paused and a small, half-smile played on his lips. "Perhaps I told you that hoping that you would be moved to remedy my sorry situation. I know I wanted you that night and every night and every day thereafter. Or perhaps I already loved you then and did not know it. Who can say? Who can say at what moment one falls in love or if there is a single moment?

"Perhaps I loved you forever. I know I looked for you always and I know that I never made love until I made love with you." He looked into Francesca's eyes and saw the lingering trace of doubt. "What should I have done, Francesca, when I realized I loved you?" he asked her. "Should I have stayed away from the palace and never seen you again, because one day you might think I had used your love? If you believe that is what I should have done, then I can say nothing more. But then we would never have known our love. We would never have known that hour of joy under the shadow of the pharaohs."

Francesca held out her hands to Pierre and he drew her to him. She caressed his cheek lovingly and traced his classic features with her fingertips, lingering over each—the eyes, the curving brows, the noble forehead, the nose, the lips.

"And since that day, Pierre?" she asked hesitantly, not wanting to know, yet having to know the truth. "Clarissa has told me . . ."

"Yes, I have known other women," he said, silencing her with a finger to her lips, "too many others. But I have known no other love."

"I have acted so foolishly, Pierre," she said. "I have been so blind to what you are."

"No, no, Francesca, it is I who is to blame. I want too much from you." He held her tightly. "I do not want those years to stand like a barrier between us. I do not want to sit around a drawing room sipping tea and making polite chatter with you. I want to leap back across those terrible months to that day when our love was pure and strong and nothing stood between us.

"Last night was wild and abandoned and wonderful because we had no time to think or doubt, no time to feel guilt or hurt or betrayal. I want more than that from you, my heart," he declared passionately. "I want to see the sun angle against your naked breasts and shine from the deepest depths of your eyes, and I want to make love with you, slowly, totally, fully, so that we will both have time to think of every pain, to feel every cruel stab that the other has inflicted, every fear, every guilt, every ache of the heart, and I want our love to be so strong, so pure, so undeniable that none of it will matter. We will make love and hold nothing back. That is what I want for us, Francesca, nothing less."

Love and desire and excitement filled him. "Can we go back, Francesca?" he cried out. "Do you believe we can go back?"

216

Her answer came to him from the deepest recesses of her heart and each word rang with the trust and innocence he loved so in her. "Yes, Pierre, yes. Nothing exited before you or after you."

The house was silent except for the steady tick-tock of the grandfather clock in the front hall and the joyful cries of love in the bedroom upstairs.

Francesca and Pierre lay side by side, the sun warming their bare flesh, and with his hands and his mouth he made love to each part of her body. The frenzied hunger of the night before gave way to a prolonged feast of love.

He stroked her slender shoulders and kissed her long, swan-like neck. With gentle fingers he raised her eager breast to his lips. He kissed the small round globe, then took the rosy aureole in his mouth, sucking it tenderly until the satiny nipple grew hard and pointed like a tiny pyramid, and, as he did, his fingers moved smoothly down her belly until they found her sweet oasis.

Francesca moaned as she felt his searching fingers begin to explore her moist other lips. Her fingers entwined in his black curls and she pressed his head closer against her heaving bosom. Pierre continued to stroke her creamy mouth slowly, teasingly, driving her to dizzying heights of anticipation. She clutched him hungrily and arched her back higher to offer her delta of Venus to him, her desire too keen to control. He stroked her faster now and his teeth sank into her tender breast.

"Oh, Pierre," she moaned at the sweet, sharp pain in her breast and the fire greater than anything she had ever known that burned in her thighs, "I want you, I want you, my love."

He answered her desire with his own. Kneeling

over her, he entered her slowly, filling her with a passion so enormous, she cried out. Then drawing back, he thrust into her again and with each thrust he drove deeper until they were locked together in an exploding passion, every thrust harder, faster than the last, like great white-capped breakers crashing into the headland.

"I love you," Pierre cried aloud as the tidal wave of love broke over them and they exploded together, in a glorious, exultant song of love.

Francesca held Pierre's limp body in her arms long after, stroking his cheek with her tender fingers and murmuring sweet words of love in his ear until, weary and happy, he slept. The sun began to slip in the west and the crimson light of its setting glowed on Pierre's muscular body.

Francesca's eyes lingered lovingly, longingly over his nakedness, the broad chest and wide shoulders, the athlete's slim waist and powerful legs. She dwelled on each contour, each muscle, each dark hair, etching every detail in her mind for fear that she would never look on him like this again.

For Francesca could never allow herself to make love to Pierre again until she revealed the pharoahs' curse. She could not accept his gift of love again until she confessed her frightening, humiliating ordeal with Murad.

Francesca shuddered at the horrible memory, at the portentous ending to their first afternoon of love. *Would this afternoon end in horror too?* she wondered fearfully. Would Pierre turn away from her when she told him the terrible truth?

Chapter Thirty-Seven

Pierre opened his eyes and smiled at Francesca. Reaching over, he kissed her gently on the lips and eyes.

"I never want to wake up again unless my lips can reach yours," he said, and began to kiss her again, the fire in his lips kindling her heart once more.

"No, Pierre, please," Francesca whispered.

"What is the matter, my heart," he asked, drawing her close to him.

"I must tell you simething, Pierre."

"Mmm." He kissed her ear. "I am listening."

"No, Pierre," she said pulling away from him.

He laughed at her serious face. "Words can always wait for love, Francesca."

"Not these words, Pierre," Francesca said. She moved away from him and sat on the edge of the bed. "After you hear them you may never want to make love to me again." Although it was a warm evening, she shivered and pulled the blanket around her shoulders. "I have to tell you what happened after you left me that first afternoon."

Pierre got up silently and went to the window. The ominous note in Francesca's voice troubled him deeply. No matter what she had done while she waited for him, he could not bear to lose her again. This second life together was so unexpected. It seemed like a gift from heaven; a resurrection almost. But Pierre remembered the curse of the pharaohs and he felt it hanging over them like a shroud—like a destiny they could not escape.

"You don't have to tell me anything, Francesca," he said almost pleadingly. "We can begin again from to-day."

"I must tell you, Pierre, or it will always lie between us, an invisible, unspoken wedge in our love," she said.

Clutching the blanket tighter around her shoulders, Francesca began slowly, hesitatingly, to tell him of Murad. Her voice faltered as she related how he came into the temple where she lay still naked, his eyes wild, his swollen member exposed. She told him of how Murad boasted of following them and watching their lovemaking, and how she fled into the desert and he followed. She spared Pierre no detail, no matter how terrible it was to remember.

Francesca swayed on the edge of the bed, her shoulders hunched together, hugging herself as if to protect herself from the anguish of her narrative. "Finally, unable to bear any more of his blows," she said, "I stumbled and fell forward into the sand. I remember the curses he rained on his father's head ringing in my ears and his maniacal laughter. Then the world seemed to turn.

"The next thing I remember was the sun burning my bare back and legs. I opened my eyes and struggled to get up. But I could not move. My body ached. Sand filled my eyes and parched mouth and ground into the bruises on my back. All I could think of was water. Water," Francesca repeated. Her voice felt hoarse and parched, remembering.

"A khasmin blew suddenly out of the west. I lay on my face as it whipped at my back. I did not think I could survive it. When it passed, I tried to crawl again. I was desperate for water. I think I would have done anything at that moment for a single drop. And then, when I was sure I would die of the thirst, I saw a figure riding toward me in the distance. I strained to see him better. It was you, Pierre. You had come back and I knew I did not have to struggle any longer."

Francesca paused and moistened her lips. Pierre could hear her deep breathing, which sounded unnaturally loud in the still house.

"You were, of course, just a mirage," she went on. "I remember nothing else until I woke up in a tent with Osari at my side. He said he bought me for the price of a spear from a Bedouin chief who had found me in the desert." She smiled wanly. "It is a strange way to discover one's true worth in the world. When I was well enough to travel, Osari brought me back to Cairo. I lived as a guest of Mehamet Ali. I began to study and hunt for the ancient treasures you had told me about, and I waited."

Francesca huddled on the edge of the bed, her story finished, her head bowed low, waiting again. Pierre had not said a word since she began her story. She thought he was so disgusted by her humiliating story that he would never want to touch her, or even look at her, again. Their love had been profaned. She was so caught up in her terrible memories and dejected by her grim thoughts that she did not realize he was standing in front of her, until she heard his low, rich voice call her name.

"Francesca. Francesca, my love girl, can you ever forgive me for leaving you?" he begged.

She looked up at him. His gray eyes were cloudy and wet with tears and he pressed her head close to his belly and held her tightly against his nakedness.

221

"If one day you can, if one day you can forgive me, will you marry me, Francesca? I love you so much, my darling, you can never know. I would do any-thing—anything in the world—if I could make up to you for the terrible pain I have caused you. I will wait forever if need be, if one day you will be mine."

Francesca threw her arms around Pierre's legs and clung to him, weeping helplessly. Her heart opened up and all that was locked inside—all the anguish, loneliness and doubts, the torment of her humiliating ordeal and the pain of waiting—were washed away in her tears.

He held her tightly pressed against him until he felt her sobs begin to diminish, then he asked her again, "Could you ever marry me, Francesca?"

"Yes, Pierre," she answered, "today or tomorrow or yesterday, because I love you completely."

She smiled up at him through her tears and she kissed his belly and his legs. Then, impulsively, she reached and kissed what lay between his muscular thighs. It was small and powerless and wet with her tears. *How could anyone imagine the immeasurable bliss that this little thing can bring to me*, she thought, and she began to lick away her tears lovingly. He surged at the touch of her tongue and Francesca experienced the first exhilarating thrill of power. Then, with a combination of shyness and wanton passion, she took him in her mouth.

Overwhelmed by her abandon, Pierre murmured lustily, "I am so hungry for you, my love. Let me taste you too."

She moved back on the wide bed and he buried his face in her treasure, stroking her round, high buttocks and kissing the shadowed inside of her golden thighs. She wrapped her cool, tapered fingers around him, caressing him lightly, and he opened her with his tongue and began to drink from her sweet oasis.

Their bodies started to move together slowly, then faster, until they were making love with their mouths and their hands, arousing each other in ways Francesca had never even imagined, yet somehow knew instinctively without being taught.

Then he was mounting her, plunging headlong into her deep cave of love and riding her wildy until she surrendered with a sudden spasm of joy so intense it was almost too much to bear. Then he penetrated her again and again until lightning flashed and thunder pealed and the skies opened inside her and poured forth a torrent of love.

Francesca and Pierre lay together, spent and exhausted, their damp bodies still entwined, and listened to the hypnotic tick-tock of the grandfather clock. Finally, Pierre broke the silence.

"Do you think it was the curse of the pharaohs, Francesca?" he asked.

She smiled fondly at him. His superstitious Latin nature had begun to rub off on her cool, Anglo-Saxon soul. "At first I believed it might have been. But then I learned that soon after our meeting Murad was killed. Though the motive was never known and the murderer never apprehended, it seemed a sort of retribution that bespoke a more even-handed God."

Pierre listened silent and motionless. An eerie stillness seemed to envelop them.

"Are you asleep?" Francesca whispered.

"No," he replied. His voice was harsh. He pulled himself up and reached over to the chair for his waistcoat. Taking the scarab from his pocket, he placed it beween Francesca's breasts.

"I went back to find you, but I found Murad instead."

Her face turned ashen. "He is the one who told you I was dead?"

"Yes." Pierre lay back on the bed, looking up at the ceiling. His voice was flat and toneless. "I tore this from his bridle and killed him with his own sword," Pierre said as viciously as if he were murdering Murad again.

Francesca felt suddenly cold and empty inside. She knew so little about this man beside her who could hate as passionately as he loved. She had not yet even begun to plumb his darkest depths.

She fingered the little scarab. "Whose honor were you defending," she asked softly, "yours or mine?"

Pierre stared at her. His eyes were steel gray, merciless and unforgiving. "Both," he hissed, "and Lucy Barnes's."

He felt Francesca tremble and saw her fear. Putting his arms around her, he held her close to him. The mood was gone as quickly as it had appeared and his eyes were again as warm and frank as they had been the first time she met him.

"Murad is finished now, gone from our lives forever, Francesca." he said tenderly. "It will do us no good to keep remembering."

She leaned her head on his shoulder, and stroked the curly black hair of his chest. "Yes, Pierre," she said hopefully, "we will begin anew with today," and she wished with all her heart that nothing would ever again provoke his deadly wrath.

Pierre hugged Francesca tightly to reassure her, but even as he did, he was hearing her other words: "I staggered and fell forward in the sand." And he knew he could not yet forget the despicable Murad.

Chapter Thirty-Eight

Francesca and Pierre slept and woke and made love again and again. The moon came out; the stars twinkled and faded; the sun slid over the horizon, casting its mauve glow on the morning. They made love in every way. They luxuriated languidly in each other's bodies, frolicked playfully in love's nooks and crannies, consumed each other hungrily in abandoned desire. They would not get enough of each other, it seemed.

"Is this what you prescribe for all your women patients, Dr. du Bellenfant?" Francesca asked, half playfully, half seriously.

"Complete bed rest for a month," he teased her, "with the doctor of course in constant attendance."

"No. Tell me, truthfully, Pierre, are you this way with all the others'?"

Francesca tried to pretend she was joking. But she was jealous of every woman he had ever looked on with desire and she could not keep a trace of it from escaping in her voice.

Pierre took her in his arms. "Darling, there are no others. There is only you," he said gently. "Surely you must know that now."

"I hear tell that you are the most marvelous and sought-after lover in London."

225

He laughed and kissed her happily. "And do you agree—at least with the first part?"

But she would not be distracted. "That is not the issue."

"What is, darling? How much I love you?"

"Among others."

"You mean your cousin has entertained you with accounts of my amorous exploits." Pierre's roguish eyes twinkled. "Lady Harrod is very beautiful, and very imaginative. Despite what she may have told you, I have never kissed more than her pretty little hand."

Francesca looked up at him skeptically. "It is not only Clarissa."

"You imply that you have also heard tell of Lady Jersey. Ah," he threw up his hands in mock despair, "the wagging tongues of London! What can I say, Francesca—that I have never known any woman but you? Your cousin is beautiful and susceptible, and Lady Jersey is skilled. But they are not you, Francesca."

Pierre took her hand and kissed the open palm. He had dropped his gentle bantering and was speaking from the depths of his heart. "There is no one like you, Francesca, whose face haunts me waking and sleeping, whose kiss melts my heart, whose touch is magic on my body. No one whose laugh I treasure, whose smile lights my life, whose love is an honor that I accept with pride and that makes me strong and manly and free.

"Once I told you that I had never known love, never made love. Then I was only imagining. Today, I know how true those words were. You are my heart, my joy, and very soon I hope you will consent to be my wife."

Chapter Thirty-Nine

"Don't keep me in suspense another instant, Francesca. What did you think of the divine Dr. Barnes? I have been simply dying to hear your reaction all week and I know you have stayed away on purpose just to keep me on pins and needles."

Francesca took a long sip of tea. Whatever Pierre might think, she was grateful for the limpid concoction that afternoon as she debated how best to break the news to Clarissa that she had claimed "the divine" Dr. Barnes for herself.

"Come now, darling," Clarissa urged. "I can't wait to hear your verdict."

Francesca smiled. "I think Dr. Barnes *is* divine, Clarissa—and more than that."

Clarissa's gay laugh rang with a clear note of triumph. "Now it is unanimous. Every woman in London agrees Dr. Barnes is divine, but only one knows just how divine. He is simply insane about me. He has eyes for no one else. Did you leave the ball early? I lost sight of you in the dancing—so many guests such a marvelous fête."

Francesca sensed there was more than idle curiosity in her cousin's question. "Yes, I did."

Clarissa beamed happily. "Well, of course, after your dance, Dr. Barnes came right back to me. We waltzed until dawn. Oh, you cannot imagine how heavenly it was to be in his arms when the sun rose. Did he talk about me while you were dancing? Tell me every word he said."

"We talked mostly about Egypt, Clarissa," Francesca replied evenly.

"Of course, I should have guessed. How convenient to have a ready-made topic of conversation."

"Yes, and one that we both share."

"Share with Peter?" Clarissa asked in surprise.

"Dr. Barnes spent quite some time in Egypt before coming to England. That is what I came to talk to you about today."

"How marvelous! You must have had many notes to compare."

Francesca studied her cousin intently. The smile creases on either side of Clarissa's mouth had begun to harden and would in five years time be harsh furrows. Her full ripe breasts could no longer stand at attention without the assistance of corsets and stays. In the harsh light of day, her vivid violet eyes seemed to shine, not with gaiety, but with an almost hysterical glow. For the first time since she returned from Egypt, Francesca realized that her cousin was no longer the perfect, doll-like little girl it had always been impossible to refuse anything. Clarissa had always been headstrong and stubborn, but now she was a woman who knew no bounds.

What had Malcolm done to his golden girl? she wondered. Or had Clarissa destroyed herself? Francesca's heart went out to her cousin and she longed to help her. But Clarissa had erected an impenetrable wall between them. If there had been any chance of reaching beyond the brittle facade of friendliness, Francesca knew she would lose it when she told her cousin what she really thought of the divine Dr. Barnes. Another spark would be added to the hysterical glint in Clarissa's eye, but Francesca could not think of any way to avoid telling her the truth. She answered slowly, measuring the effect of each word.

"We do have many shared memories, Clarissa, because we were there together." Without giving her cousin an opportunity to say a word, Francesca plunged on. "When I was in Egypt, I fell in love with a wonderful young doctor. He was brilliant, handsome, dashing and kind. In short, you would have said he was divine. Two years ago he was called back to Paris on urgent business. I waited in Cairo for him to return, but he was never able to make the voyage. His name was Pierre du Bellenfant."

Francesca leaned forward and spoke softly, her eyes searching Clarissa's, praying she would understand. "Clarissa, your Peter Barnes is my Pierre du Bellenfant."

Clarissa looked at Francesca dumbfounded. Her face turned ashen. Her eyes grew as round as saucers.

"He changed his name," Francesca rushed on, not wanting to lie but unable to betray Pierre, "because he believed it would be easier to establish a practice in London if he had an Anglo-Saxon name. I guess the French are not too beloved in London these days, thanks to General Bonaparte.

"When you told me about Dr. Barnes, I never thought he might be Pierre. I had no idea he was even in London until you introduced us at the ball."

Clarissa regained her composure gradually as Francesca talked. The color returned to her cheeks and her scheming mind began to whirl again.

"Why, that is marvelous, Francesca," she gushed, "now that I am over the shock of your little surprise."

She laughed lightly. "It is really quite quaint. We

shared everything for so many years. Now we are sharing a new lover."

"Clarissa," Francesca hesitated, "Pierre—Dr. Barnes, that is—denied that you ever were . . . intimate."

Clarissa gave her cousin a quick, calculating glance. "But, of course, you always were so naively trusting, weren't you. All men say that, Francesca. Why even Malcolm says you and he were never lovers." She laughed again as if to prove how worldly-wise she was. "You can't believe a word any of them say. They are all alike."

Francesca flushed. She had never believed Clarissa knew about her night with Malcolm. It seemed so far in the past now, a foolish mistake she had long since regretted. To her the brief affair was dead and buried and now there was Pierre. Her heart beat faster just at the sound of his name.

"I don't want to hurt you Clarissa but I must make you understand. Dr. Barnes and I are going to be married. I love him so very much. Please try to understand," she pleaded. "We used to understand each other so well. We were like sisters. Remember how we learned to ride together and parse French nouns and curtsy to the king. Can't we try to rebuild that bond we once had?"

Clarissa eyed her distraught cousin sharply. "Of course we can, and we will, Francesca, but you should be thinking of your love now, not of me. My romance with Dr. Barnes was not an *affaire de coeur*. It was just a foolish dalliance with no heartstrings attached. But you—you remind me of my first days with Malcolm."

For an instant, Francesca wondered if Clarissa had said that intentionally to wound her—if her warmth was real or feigned. But then Clarissa gave her a loving sisterly hug.

"I am so happy for you, Francesca darling. You might begin right now and tell me everything about him," she insisted and soon they were chatting and reminiscing together like schoolgirls, Francesca's worry forgotten.

It seemed just like old times to her. Instead of losing her cousin completely, she had found her again. Francesca thought happily of her marriage to Pierre and decided she would do whatever she could to help breach the rift between Malcolm and Clarissa.

At the door when she was leaving, Clarissa hugged her again and kissed her cheek. "What did you say Dr. Barnes's names was, darling, when you knew him in Egypt?" she asked innocently.

"It was Pierre du Bellenfant," Francesca said.

"Of course. How stupid of me to forget," Clarissa smiled.

As the door closed behind Francesca, her false smile froze in a frightening grimace and her sweet voice turned savage. "Pierre du Bellenfant," she said aloud. "That name has a very familiar ring to it."

Before Francesca's carriage had reached the corner of St. James's Square, Clarissa had begun scheming how to destroy the lovers.

Chapter Forty

"I saw you before my eyes as clearly as if you were standing in front of me. The flames of the fire were flickering across your long silky thighs just as they did on that perfect evening, and you were calling to me. You wanted me more than anything in the world. You would have done anything to possess me again, and you did. You did. You made love to . . ."

"Stop it, Malcolm," Francesca cried angrily. "I will not hear another word of this talk."

But Malcolm was a desperate man. "Do I repel you, Francesca? You were not easily repelled then. Can't you remember when you wanted me so much you could not wait to have me?"

He was kneeling at her feet, clasping her knees. "It is true, every word. I lay on my wedding bed with Clarissa beside me and thought of you. My marriage was a mistake from the very first—from the wedding night. It is you I have always loved, Francesca, I swear it. I need you now more than ever."

"Let go of me, Malcolm. And stop groveling," Francesca demanded. She was disgusted with him and angry with herself for inviting him here to her mother's house.

She had hoped to persuade Malcolm to give up his paramour and try to breach the rift that had developed between him and Clarissa. But he had obviously misconstrued her intention, and now Malcolm would not be stopped. "Hear me out, Francesca, please, for old times' sake," he pleaded. "Is that too much to grant me?"

She remembered when Lord Harrod was effortlessly charming and self-assured, the envy and idol of all London. Now he was on his knees, pleading for a drop of kindness like a beggar for a scrap of bread. She could not bear to see him so reduced.

"Of course, I will listen to you," she said. "That is why I asked you here today—to hear your story and do what I can to help you and Clarissa. There is no need for you to prostrate yourself at my feet. Please, Malcolm, sit down and compose yourself, while I fetch you a brandy and soda."

In spite of everything, Malcolm still loved Clarissa as he had never loved any other woman. She could still disarm him with her impish ways when she had a mind to and drive away the bleak memories that kept them apart. But the moments when she cared to divert him grew less and less frequent, because what she wanted from her husband most, now, was revenge.

To Malcolm, Clarissa was still the most beautiful woman he had ever seen, but he was drawn back to Francesca like a moth to a flame. The girl who returned from Egypt was not the same one who ran away from him with a broken heart. He saw a haunting quality in her face which he had never been aware of before, a fluid grace in her every motion, and a magnetism in her glance that drew men of all ages to her. She radiated a strength and confidence that seemed to set her apart from other women of her class.

Seeing Francesca again, Malcolm rued his disastrous marriage, and in the weeks she had been back in London, his regret had grown until he could think of nothing else. He remembered her by day and dreamed at night of what might have been. Now he thought at last he had the chance to regain her.

Malcolm had stopped at Waiter's to fortify himself for this moment and in his dissolute state the brandy and soda Francesca gave him dissolved the last restraints of a gentleman.

"It is too late to help me and Clarissa, much too late," he confessed. "You came between us almost from the start. It was my fault—I should never have told Clarissa. I don't know what possessed me—months of accumulated frustrations, rejections, the terrible desire for her she would never let me satisfy, affections spurned once too often. I don't know . . ." His voice trailed off.

"You told Clarissa about us, Malcolm?" Francesca asked in disbelief.

"Yes, and worse." He bowed his head abjectly. "I always thought she knew or at least suspected. But it came as a terrible shock to her and she has never forgiven me for it."

"Nor me. That must be why she never wrote to me in Egypt, never once."

"I don't know about that, I only know I made a terrible mistake when I married Clarissa. Her beauty blinded me. I was like a man under a spell of enchantment. But my heart has always belonged to you. You must let me make it up to you, Francesca, we still have time.

"Dearest, Francesca," he said, taking her hand, "I wish I could make you my wife now, as I should have before but, I beg you, please try to understand my position. I cannot divorce Clarissa, even though all of London knows that she is flaunting herself before that notorious American gambler. I must think of my son. He is so young and so dear to my heart.

"But I will take care of you. You will have everything you desire—a flat of your own, a handsome carriage to ride in Hyde Park, the finest gowns and jewels. Of course," he went on, mistaking her silence for agreement, "it will all be handled with the utmost discretion. No one need know of our . . . our arrangement. There will be those who gossip, I suppose," he went on, trying to forsee her objections and answer them. "There always are. But this sort of thing is quite acceptable nowadays. Even the Prince of Wales openly maintains a paramour."

Francesca stared at the preposterous, dissolute man who sat holding her hand. She had been furious at first, but as he talked her anger changed to contempt and then pity, the worst of all. She looked at this man whom she once thought she would love forever, now grown so pathetic and concerned with propriety, and she felt like weeping.

Would we have ended this way if we had married? she wondered. *Would he be offering a proper, gentlemanly arrangement to some other young woman?*

Francesca could not bear to listen to his seamy little dream any longer and she answered sharply, hoping to put an end to his distasteful talk.

"I thought you were already quite comfortably established with a Miss Harriette Wilson."

"So you have already caught up on all the malicious gossip. I should have known that Clarissa would see to that immediately."

"It was not Clarissa, Malcolm."

"Well, it doesn't matter, in any case. It has nothing to do wih us, Francesca. Miss Wilson is artful and witty, but she is nothing to me except a sanctuary where I seek refuge from my wife's bitter tongue and

235

the satisfaction that she denies me in her bed. I am not a monk, Francesca, you of all people should know that . . . or have you forgotten? Have you forgotten the flickering fire in Jeremy's library, the passionate young girl and the loving young man we once were? Go back and look at the old Oriental rug; it remembers as well as I."

Drunken and aroused by the memory, Malcolm pulled Francesca into his arms. "I can make you remember," he insisted, searching for her lips.

"Let me go, Malcolm," she cried. "You are hurting me."

Francesca fought to escape from his embrace. But the drink and his long suppressed desire made him reckless, and he forced her to the sofa, falling on top of her. Her violent struggle and the feel of her lithe body beneath him again aroused him even more. He lurched hungrily for her mouth, her neck, her breasts.

Marriage to Clarissa had made Malcolm adept at taking women violently. But he was very drunk and Francesca was determined never to be abused again. When his mouth closed over hers, she summoned all her strength and shoved him away, sending him rolling onto the floor. Malcolm scrambled to his knees and lunged for her again. But she slapped him across the face with the back of her hand, first one cheek and then the other as hard as she could, until he staggered across the room.

The sharpness of the blows cleared the whiskey fumes from his brain and Malcolm slumped in a chair, burying his face in his hands, ashamed and utterly defeated.

Francesca looked at his sorry figure with a mixture of contempt and compassion. His touch had stirred not even a twinge of old desire in her and Malcolm knew it. He could see it in her eyes as she looked at him.

"Forgive me, Francesca," he pleaded. "I am no longer the man you once knew. What happened to us—you and me and Clarissa? We were so full of life and affection for each other once. Look at us now! Clarissa is filled with bitterness for both of us and I am a broken man. Only you—the one of us who was so ill-served—survived. You fled with a broken heart and now you have come home with new confidence and spirit. What did you discover in Egypt? Tell me your secret!"

Even as he spoke, Malcolm realized the answer. "Have you found someone else, Francesca?" he asked sharply.

"Yes, I have."

"And I mean nothing to you then? Nothing at all?" His voice begged her not to destroy even his memories.

"It was a long time ago, Malcolm," Francesca said gently, "and we were very young."

He studied her closely. "Just tell me one thing and I will not pry any further. Do you love him more than you once loved me?"

"Oh, Malcolm," she replied, trying not to add to his anguish, "it is never the same with anyone."

Malcolm saw the pity in her deep, wide eyes and he was filled with a terrible sadness. "You are a kind girl, Francesca, a wonderful, kind, generous girl—and whoever he is, he is very lucky indeed."

"His name is Peter Barnes," she said slowly. "I believe you have met."

Francesca did not want to be cruel to Malcolm. She could imagine how the name Peter Barnes must grate on his bruised heart. First Clarissa and now her . . . But Malcolm had his emotions tightly in check again.

If he was bitter and jealous, he was too much the stiff-upper-lipped Britisher now to let it show.

"Believe me, Francesca," he said, "I had no idea of your . . . your feelings. I have made a bloody arse of myself. Forgive me." Standing up, he took her hand. "Will you try to forget I was ever here today?" he asked. A wry, ironic smile played at the corners of his mouth. *Another gamble Barnes has won.*

Francesca gave his fingers an understanding squeeze. "I will, Malcolm. I promise."

"No, don't promise. Promises are made to be broken."

"Very well, Malcolm, I won't promise but you must believe that nothing that has happened tonight has changed my affection for you."

He looked down at the floor, suddenly shy and awkward, and Francesca saw a flash of the boyish charm that had once captivated her.

"I know I have no right to ask anything of you, especially after this evening. But there is one thing," he stammered. "You see Wednesday next I give my maiden speech in the House of Lords. Clarissa, well . . . Clarissa will not be attending and I was hoping you might, for old times' sake and all that . . ."

"Of course I will come, Malcolm," Her face lit up with a brilliant smile and she reached up and kissed him lightly on the cheek. "And I will sit in the balcony and clap and cheer louder than anyone else."

"You will?" he beamed delightedly and for a moment he was the engaging young lord again.

"I promise."

"No promises, remember?"

"Very well, no promises. But I will be there no matter what."

Francesca looked fondly after Malcolm as he skipped happily down her front steps. She did not notice the sleek black phaeton that pulled up behind his carriage as she closed the door, or the bouquet of white gardenias the reckless driver tossed angrily after her.

Chapter Forty-One

When it came to Francesca, Pierre du Bellenfant
was a fiercely jealous man. The memory of Murad's
perfidy rankled in his mind still and now the sight of
Malcolm Lord Harrod at her door enraged him.

Pierre could never forget the long, agonizing
months that he'd waited while Francesca pined for
her lost love. He could hear her yet on the boat from
Rosetta confessing in the darkness: "Once I loved and
I made love. It was not in the moonlight, but in the
light of the fire."

Pierre looked across the gaming room at Lord Harrod—wasted, dissolute and weak, drinking himself
steadily into a stupor. Was this the man she had
given her first love to? He could hear her as clearly as
if she was beside him, just before she surrendered to
his love in the Valley of the Kings: "His name was
Malcolm. . . ." Were they lovers again? Pierre could
not believe it and yet, only hours before, he had seen
Lord Harrod coming out of her house.

After leaving Francesca, Malcolm had come
directly to Waiter's and sat down alone with a full
bottle of whiskey. Now that too was gone but its spir-
ited afterglow emboldened him. Struggling to his feet,
he stumbled across the room to the table where Peter
Barnes and John Kent sat playing faro and planted
himself in a chair opposite the American.

Through his glassy-eyed stare, Malcolm saw not only a handsome man, but a cold, insolent one. He had never understood how the scoundrel had ever been allowed membership in Waiter's in the first place. Beau Brummel must have been drowsing in his milk bath when the doctor's name was proposed.

However he finagled it, the day Peter Barnes joined the club was a fateful one, Malcolm thought. He had lost thousands of pounds to the American—not to mention Clarissa's attentions and now Francesca's love. Fortified with the whiskey, he was prepared to settle the score.

"Barnes, you bugger, I have something to say to you." Malcolm leaned across the table, scattering the cards as he did so. His eyes were glazed, his speech slurred.

"I think I have had enough games of chance for tonight," John Kent said brightly, hoping to defuse the confrontation before it began. "What do you say, Peter, shall we leave his lordship to stew in his own alcoholic juices?"

But Malcolm was too drunk to be stopped. He pointed a threatening finger at Pierre. "You choose the weapons, Barnes. Whatever you want. You will have to fight me for her. I challenge you here and now to try to take her from me."

Pierre glared at Malcolm contemptuously. "I don't want your wife, Lord Harrod, no matter how much she may desire me," he sneered.

"Not my wife, Barnes," Malcolm mumbled, "not my wife. She will never have you. Her cousin Francesca, Francesca Fairchild. She is mine. I had her first. She belongs to me."

Pierre had been brooding darkly all evening and his ferocious anger was like a volcano ready to erupt. Blazing with rage, he turned over the table and

241

seized Malcolm by the cravat. "These are the weapons I choose," he swore, "these hands. I will kill you with them for even breathing her name." His grasp tightened with deadly force around Malcolm's neck.

Drawn out of his office by the sound of the shattering table, Beau Brummel saw the murderous glint in Pierre's cold, steely eyes and his blood turned to ice. The room was hushed, as if no one dared to move or speak.

It was said that Brummel spent five hours each morning on his toilet, longer than many women. He bathed in milk, then eau de cologne, and finally in water. He spent two hours having his hair coifed, and had his boots polished to a high gloss with the froth from champagne. But he was no sissy, for all that. Beau Brummel was as brave as the bravest man, and more shrewd than most. He walked calmly toward the two desperate men.

"What honor or satisfaction does it render you to throttle an inebriated man, my dear Barnes," he asked coolly as he came towards Pierre and Malcolm. "Lord Harrod's condition might best be described as advanced inebriation. Challenge him in the sober light of day, if you must, but do not take him on in his present state. A drunken brawl does credit to neither of you gentlemen."

Even through his furious wrath, Pierre recognized the truth of Brummel's words. He could not kill a helpless drunk—and kill him he would—no matter how great the murderous urge in his heart was. Letting go of his lethal stranglehold, he pushed Malcolm away.

"Get him out of here, Brummel," he warned, "or drunk or sober he'll forfeit his life."

"I will be delighted to see that Lord Harrod returns safely to the bosom of his family," Brummel replied evenly and, with the croupier assisting, he proceeded to escort his ranting, still struggling lordship to the safety of his carriage.

Pierre spent the rest of the night and early morning drinking and gambling with reckless abandon, but his thoughts never strayed from Francesca.

If she had nothing to hide, she would tell him without his asking what Malcolm was doing alone in her house in the evening. If she didn't say a word about his visit, Pierre would know they were lovers again. She would have ample opportunity to explain her meeting with Lord Harrod during the long carriage ride to Marlowe Castle that morning.

Chapter Forty-Two

"Is anything wrong, Pierre?" Francesca asked anxiously as they sat down to lunch. She had hoped the visit to Marlowe Castle would go well. But it was already off to a bad start and she had no idea why.

Pierre was unusually quiet and withdrawn on the long carriage ride from London, and she had no inkling of the cause of his dark mood. Hoping to dissipate his gloom, she chattered brightly, but he continued to brood. Then, when they finally arrived in the early afternoon, her mother was not there to welcome them. Lady Marlowe was lunching at the parish house and would not be back until after tea.

"The salmon could not be better," Pierre answered, purposely mistaking her meaning. "It is just that I have very little appetite today."

"We can return to London tonight, if you do not want to stay in the country."

"I would not even consider such a thing, Francesca. I am looking forward to meeting a woman more bewitching than you."

He gave her his most dazzling roué's smile, but Francesca had learned that this was a mask he pulled on to hide his deepest feelings and she would not let him brush aside her concern that easily.

"Have I done something to upset you, Pierre?" she asked softly, taking his hand and kissing it lovingly.

"Why do you ask?"

"Because you have been so distant today."

"I am sorry if my company does not please you. I shall try to do better after lunch."

Francesca was exasperated but nonetheless determined to salvage the day. She squeezed his hand affectionately. "It is such a beautiful day. Why don't we change and go for a ride before Mother returns. I will give you a guided tour of the grounds."

Lady Marlowe's estate was as vast and verdant as a park. Peacocks showed off their brilliant fans on the rolling lawns. Deer skirted through the tall shade trees to drink at the clear blue lake. Pastures of lolling cows and stud farms where once-swift racers took their lazy pleasure stretched farther than the eye could see. The land sloped into gentle hills and dales.

Francesca and Pierre reined their horses at the top of a crest and surveyed the countryside that spread around them. It was a clear, exhilarating fall day, a crisp nip in the air, the earth firm beneath the horses' hooves.

Francesca was wearing the kind of tunic and tight trousers that she had worn when they rode in Egypt. Her golden hair was tied back in a blue scarf.

"Do you like it, darling?" she asked.

Her face glowed and the day and the countryside were glorious. Overcome by the radiance of all three, Pierre smiled. "It is as beautiful as you described it."

"I have always loved it here. Ever since I can remember this has been my favorite spot in the world. I used to think you could see the whole world from this knoll."

Francesca laughed and the wind carried the notes across the broad green fields. "We never came here often enough, because Mother traveled so much of the year."

245

He looked at her lovingly. "We will make up for it this time. If Lady Marlowe will have us, we can stay through the week. I have no patients who cannot survive without my personal ministrations for a few extra days."

"Would you really like to Pierre?"

"I would."

"Then we shall. We are free as the wind," she cried, delighted that he liked this place as much as she did. Then she caught herself suddenly and her face dropped. "Oh, Pierre, I am so sorry. I forgot. I must be back in town by Tuesday evening."

"Surely any plans you have made are not so urgent that they cannot be changed."

"No, I really cannot stay. I am going to hear Lord Harrod address the House of Lords on Wednesday."

"Malcolm Lord Harrod?" Pierre asked icily.

"Yes, he is my brother-in-law—well, almost my brother-in-law. I thought I would take my little cousin Geoffery along to hear his father."

"Then we shall leave this evening. I would not want to detain you until Tuesday." He whipped his horse angrily.

"Wait, Pierre," Francesca begged. "Why are you angry?",

Her innocent eyes infuriated him. "Wouldn't you be?" he snapped.

"I can't imagine why I would be."

"You can't," he mocked and she saw in his steel gray eyes the same frightening look she had seen when he told her he had killed Murad. "Lord Harrod is your Malcolm, is he not?"

Francesca could not keep from smiling, although she knew it would only make Pierre angrier. "You remember?"

"Every word you have ever spoken."

"Then you should also remember that Malcolm is not mine. He never was."

"You loved him once. Perhaps you love him again."

"No," she answered easily. "I just thought I did—and anyway, he was different then."

"I cannot understand how you ever loved such a weak man."

"Since I met you, I cannot even imagine loving anyone else, let alone remember how or why."

He gazed at her. "I wish you had waited for me, Francesca."

"I did, love, in my heart."

He put his arm around her and kissed her hungrily. The horses whinnied and shook their manes.

"What is it about you that I love so much?" Pierre asked lustily.

"My irresistible attraction to other men," she teased.

"I can't joke about that, Francesca."

"I am sorry."

"Then you will stay the week?"

"No, I can't. I gave Malcolm my word. I must go."

"For old times' sake?",

"Something like that." she smiled. "Are you still jealous?"

Pierre spurred his horse. "Something like that." he shouted over his shoulder.

"Come on. I will race you back to the house." Francesca cried as she flew by him. She rode as if she was a part of the horse, one galloping machine, her thighs pressed tightly against the animal's sleek flanks.

He admired her natural, relaxed carriage and the way her body melded with the speeding steed, rising with it to clear a fallen tree that blocked the path.

But the horse stumbled coming down, throwing Francesca over its head.

Pierre dug his heels into his mount's flanks and, sailing cleanly over the felled tree, he leaped off his horse and took her in his arms.

"Are you all right, Francesca?" he asked anxiously; all the while his physician's hands were caressing her and at the same time feeling for any injuries.

"Just a tumble; nothing major, Doctor," she smiled, brushing herself off.

"Mmm, but you will ache in the morning, if you are not careful."

"What does the doctor order?"

"A very hot bath as soon as we get back, and you must soak in it for at least an hour."

"And what will you do while I am soaking?"

"I will find something to entertain myself."

"That is what I am afraid of," she quipped.

Pierre laughed. "I thought *I* was the jealous lover."

"Don't be so sure," she retorted as they remounted.

Happy and filled with love, they cantered back to Marlowe Castle.

While Francesca did what the doctor ordered, Pierre changed and strolled out to the verandah. The late afternoon was chilly but bracing, and he sat alone, wrapped in his thoughts; the lush lawns, green and hushed, spread in front of him.

His anger over Malcolm had washed away in the warm glow of Francesca's love and he chided himself for ever doubting her. *She is so compelling, yet so unaware of her singular charm, of the strange, hypnotic effect she has on men,* he thought. *If only she knew her powers, I would not worry so much. I would not be so afraid that she could be easily seduced again.*

Thinking he heard her approach, Pierre turned toward the house, his gray eyes brimming with happiness, a full, welcoming smile on his chiseled lips. Instead of Francesca, he saw a tall astonishingly beautiful woman standing in the doorway, studying him. She was wearing a forest-green dress with a high collar; long, tight sleeves; and slim lines that followed the exquisite curves of her body subtly yet unmistakably. A broad-brimmed hat of the same color with a fine mesh net, drawn down, shadowed her face.

He stood up and bowed deeply to her. "I have been told that Lady Marlowe was a rare beauty." His deep, rich voice was low with admiration. "But the reports I received were wrong. She is the most ravishing woman in all of Europe."

Lady Marlowe smiled and Pierre saw that its sudden radiance was indentical to Francesca's.

"Dr. Barnes," she answered and her voice was like a mountain spring. "You are a shameless flatterer, I am happy to see. May I join you?"

She glided toward him, taking the chair next to his and raising her veil. Francesca had inherited her mother's long body and golden hair, her graceful, fluid movements and full, sensual mouth. But Lady Marlowe was clearly more beautiful. Her skin was as fair and delicate as an infant's. Her eyes, as deep a green as her dress, were the kind that every man thought shone for him exclusively. Her nose was straight and partrician, her figure the envy of a twenty-year-old. She was slim, like Francesca, but her breasts were as full and ripe as a cornucopia.

"I hope you will forgive me, Dr. Barnes, for not being here to welcome you. But I am sure you will understand that luncheon with the vicar is a duty that I would gladly forfeit, if I could, on a much less intriguing excuse than meeting you."

"I envy the vicar his power to command your obedience," Pierre responded. His voice was like a caress.

Lady Marlowe laughed a low, earthy laugh. She was accustomed to being admired and desired, yet the thrill of first intimacies never waned. She appraised Pierre frankly. After a lifetime of study, there was little she had not learned or did not know about men, and she saw the deep passion and raw lust beneath his sophisticated grace. Fearful for an instant, she wondered if her daughter had discovered the full dimensions of this passionate man, and, even if she knew them, could she hold him?

He was handsome—perhaps more handsome than any man Andrea Marlowe had ever seen—and for a moment she allowed herself the luxury of imagining what it was like to be in his arms. It was the prerogative of a beautiful woman who knew she could command any man she wanted. But even as she felt a thrill of anticipation rush through her veins, Lady Marlowe banished the thought. Peter Barnes belonged to her daughter.

She looked away, studying the heavy rain clouds that began to gather out of nowhere in the east. The air turned chill, portending a storm, but Pierre was only aware of the tempest brewing inside him. Seduced by Lady Marlowe's tantalizing green eyes, he felt himself drawn to her against his will. Her beauty beckoned like a challenge that no man could accept without peril, or refuse without regret. He wondered how many others had fallen under her spell. How many had been drawn into her Garden of Eden, and been destroyed?

Lady Marlowe broke through his thoughts. "Years ago in Paris I knew a lovely American woman named Barnes—Lucy Barnes. You would not be any relation, would you, Doctor?" Her eyes seemed filled with promise and every word she uttered was rich with hidden meanings.

"Ah, mais oui. Francesca confided my identity to you," he replied with a slight raise of his black brows. "I did not know, madam."

Lady Marlowe's expression never changed in spite of his unexpected disclosure. Francesca had not told her anything about the young man, except that he was a physician named Peter Barnes whom she'd met in Egypt and fallen in love with. But now Lady Marlowe would not rest until she discovered what he was to Lucy.

Delving back in her memory, she resurrected faded pictures. Lucy's son was about four years old when Francesca was born—a devastating little boy with raven curls and startling gray eyes.

Andrea Marlowe smiled ingenuously. "So then it is Dr. du Bellenfant, is it not?"

"Francesca must confide everything in you, Lady Marlowe."

"She is my daughter, Doctor, or have you forgotten already?"

Pierre's gray eyes danced. *How well she must know men*, he thought admiringly. "I am sure, madam, that you have the ability to make a man forget everything. But no, I have not forgotten that Francesca is your daughter." He paused, meeting her inviting eyes boldly, "Unless you have."

Lady Marlowe smiled wryly. "Your father and I were once very good friends. In fact, I shall always be in his debt," she added cryptically.

"You disappoint me, madam. I would have thought that you were a woman who, once she accepted a debt, would pay it in full."

251

"He did me a favor once which nothing could ever repay."

"Ah, I fear you underestimate yourself, Lady Marlowe. Knowing my father as I do, there is nothing he could wish for or hope to exact in payment that you could not provide in abundance."

"It is you, Doctor, who are guilty of underestimation—both of your father and of the favor he granted. You judge him too harshly, I see. It is true that his eye strayed from time to time, as every man's does—even your own, I have little doubt. But his heart belonged entirely to your mother."

She paused, gauging his reaction carefully. "I pray that he is well and that you will give him my fondest regards."

"I have not seen my father, madam, since the revolution," Pierre said offhandedly. "But your sentiments are most kind."

"And your mother?"

Pierre did not permit even a flicker of emotion to escape through his cool mask. "She was killed, trying to escape."

"Lucy Barnes and I were very dear to each other once and your father was an esteemed friend of Francesca's late uncle, Jeremy. But that was all so very long ago, you cannot possible remember it."

"I cannot imagine ever being too young to notice you, but evidently, to my sorrow and eternal loss, there must have been such a time."

Lady Marlowe glanced away while Pierre was speaking and the smile froze on her lips.

"One day, Doctor, we must tell Francesca all this, but not today—not yet," she said urgently mysteriously, as she rose to greet her daughter.

The remainder of the day passed swiftly. They dined quietly, just the three of them, in the long, paneled dining hall. Afterwards the women entertained Pierre, Lady Andrea on the piano and Francesca at the cello. He sat sipping a brandy slowly. The stormy autumn night insulated them and his mind drifted aimlessly, wrapped in the sweet music of Mozart and in the beauty of the musicians. When he had drained the last drop of his cognac, he bade goodnight to Lady Marlowe and Francesca.

The two women sat alone in the cozy music room, listening to the autumn wind whistle through the dry leaves and the rain beat insistently at the windows.

"You love this young doctor very much, Francesca, don't you?" Andrea Marlowe asked her daughter gently.

"Very, very much, Mother," Francesca answered.

"You said the same about Malcolm, if you remember, not so long ago."

"But I was young then—and very foolish, and very wrong."

"What makes you think that in another four or five years you will not be saying the same thing about this young man?"

"How can you ask that, Mother, now that you have met Pierre?"

Lady Marlowe leaned back and let the evening shadows close around her face. Francesca was precious to her, more precious than life itself. She would not entrust her lightly to any man. She knew their perfidy and their weaknesses too well.

The years Francesca had been in Egypt were lonely ones but she knew they were no lonelier than the life to which she had relegated Francesca ever since she was four years old. She had made her fatherless—and motherless. At the time she had believed that living with the Dorsets would be the closest thing to a natural home she could ever provide for her daughter. But now she wondered if she had made the right decision. All those years she had stayed away, forcing herself to remain on the Continent for months at a time so that she would not disrupt her daughter's new life—could she have been wrong?

Perhaps, Lady Marlowe thought, *she should tell Francesca the truth at last.* She had promised Jeremy she would. But not now, not yet. There was still time and she was afraid to risk losing her daughter again.

"I can ask it, Francesca," she began slowly, "because I do not know if he loves you, and I do not want you to be hurt again. If he betrays you, what Egypt will you run to this time?"

"I will never need to run away, Mother. Peter loves me," she said firmly.

"And how many other women?" Lady Marlowe asked softly.

"No others."

"That is what he tells you?"

"Yes, and I know it is true."

Francesca had changed. She possessed a poise and confidence that came from being cherished—and knowing it.

Lady Marlowe envied her and prayed that nothing would happen to make her lose that confidence. But she knew that it was far better for Francesca to discover what Pierre du Bellenfant was now, than after they were married.

"We decided this evening," Francesca was saying, "that we would like our wedding to be here at Marlowe Castle—a very quiet, simple ceremony as soon as the arrangements can be made. Will you give us your blessing, Mother?"

Rain lashed against the windowpanes like the

knowledge of Pierre's lustful, compelling nature lashed at Lady Marlowe's heart.

"Your young doctor is beautiful, Francesca, but I wonder how well you know him," she replied mysteriously. "I wonder if you know how tempestuous and dangerous he can be."

Francesca looked at her mother curiously. Andrea Marlowe had never spoken so frankly to her daughter before, yet Francesca was not sure of what her mother intended by her words of warning. She wanted to talk further, as she had always imagined other mothers and daughters did, but Lady Marlowe cut her off brusquely.

"Come, Francesca," she said, picking up a taper. "It is late and we will talk more tomorrow. Everything looks different in the bright morning light—especially passionate men."

Chapter Forty-Three

While Pierre and Lady Marlowe parried on the verandah, at Lord Harrod's country estate to the east in Heretsford, Clarissa rode alone into the eye of the gathering storm.

Columns and pillars of murderous black clouds rose on the horizon. Bolts of jagged blue lightning sliced open the afternoon sky. Heavy winds whipped through the high grass.

Cropping her mount mercilessly, Clarissa galloped across fields and hills, driving headlong into the eye, reckless, callous, bent on revenge. She gathered the strands of a vengeful scheme in her mind as the black clouds gathered overhead.

The threatening storm mirrored the tempest in her heart. She would have Peter Barnes—Pierre du Bellenfant—in her bed, and pay back both Malcolm and her treacherous cousin Francesca at the same time.

Her horse's dark flanks were shiny with sweat as she whipped him again, urging him on. The fury of the storm was no match for her own. The delicate porcelain doll was as hard as granite. The angel face bore a malicious devil's grin.

Peter Barnes was Pierre du Bellenfant, son of Georges Duc du Bellenfant. Her evil laughter crackled in the chill air. She knew what she wanted and she would get it by hook or by crook. She wanted

Peter Barnes to lie in her husband's place as much as she had once wanted Malcolm Lord Harrod to lead her to the altar, and she would allow nothing—and no one—to stand in her way of having him, least of all Francesca.

The horse's galloping hooves pounded like her heart. Clarissa had recognized the name "Bellenfant." It was the name on her father's lips when he spoke to her Aunt Andrea before he died. At the time she'd wished that she had not overheard them. Now she was thrilled by her secret knowledge. She would twist it to her own advantage and use it to betray her cousin and revenge herself against her husband.

A lone rider exhilarated by the storm, Clarissa drove her mount recklessly on. Earsplitting claps of thunder burst in the heavens, crying out against her spiteful scheme. But she was deaf to everything except her own destructive desires. At last she would have the satisfaction she had craved for so long.

Andrea Marlowe had not revealed her secret in all these years. She would not give it up now—and no one else knew the sordid truth.

Clarissa's mount reared, whinnying wildly as thunder pealed again and lightning bolts rent the sky. But she would brook no opposition, Expertly she pulled the horse down, his bit white with froth and his flanks bathed in sweat, and dropped back into the valley. Exhilarated by her brilliant plot, she rode on, confident that Francesca would be stopped by the power of brotherly love.

Chapter Forty-Four

Francesca was lying in the darkness going over her mother's curious words, when she heard the bedroom door creak slowly open. She caught her breath, not daring to move.

"It is Dr. du Bellenfant come to examine Miss Fairchild." Pierre's low, teasing voice broke through the silent night.

Francesca's heart pounded wildly with excitement and trepidation. "Pierre," she whispered, "what if Mother . . ."

"I am just a dedicated physician paying a bedside visit to his patient," he interrupted. "How do you feel, Miss Fairchild, after your painful riding accident?"

She giggled guiltily at his boldness as he tiptoed across the room and sat down on the side of her bed.

"I had to kiss you goodnight, darling," Pierre murmured. "I could not sleep until I did."

"Is that what you prescribe for what ails me, Doctor?"

"Just the preliminary medication," he smiled as he bent over to envelop her mouth with his.

"I don't think I would ever have you for my doctor," she said, laughing happily. "I would not trust you to adhere to your examination."

"Would you trust yourself to let me?" he whispered.

"Never," she answered, touching his lips lovingly. "I

dreamed once that you did examine me. It was in Cairo—before we were lovers and the world began," she confided. "When you finished, I opened my eyes and you were standing beside my bed crying."

He caressed her hair and his gray eyes were smoky and filled with love. "It was not a dream, Francesca," he whispered, his voice low.

"Then why were you crying, Pierre?"

"Because I loved you and had been called back to France, and because your heart still belonged to someone else."

Francesca put her arms around his neck and drew him down to her, holding him close. "No, darling, my heart has never belonged to anyone but you."

Pierre kissed her hair as he had that first time. "I wish it were true."

"It is true, the truest words I have ever spoken."

"I love you, Francesca, more than you can ever know."

Francesca lay back against the pillows filled with happiness and a wild, daring desire to have him again, there in her own bed silently in the dead of night.

"Why don't you examine me again, Doctor, now while I am awake and can enjoy it," she whispered wickedly.

"You shameless wench," Pierre laughed sensually. "I intend to do just that. But first, Miss Fairchild, will you kindly remove your nightdress. I fear it may interfere with my examination."

Feeling naughty and abandoned, Francesca sat up and pulled the nightdress over her head. Her breasts shone invitingly in the moonlight. "I will catch my death of cold, Doctor," she shivered, with a thrill of dangerous expectation.

"Don't worry, Miss Fairchild, I shall see that you

are not chilled in the slightest. Now," he said critically, "does this hurt?"

Pierre bit her breast playfully and Francesca laughed softly, slipping her hand inside his silk dressing gown.

"Pierre!" she gasped in astonishment. "Did you come through the halls like this?"

He slipped off his robe and stood up, naked and alive with desire. "This is the suit I always wear when I call on a bewitchingly beautiful patient, Miss Fairchild. Do you like it?"

"You know I love it, you devil," she grinned, taking his hand and drawing him down on the bed. "It would not surprise me in the least if you did make your house calls like this."

Francesca kissed him reachingly, excited by his unexpected nakedness, but Pierre disengaged himself from her embrace. "Before you make me forget my duties, let me tend to your bruised muscles or you will be too sore to get out of bed in the morning."

"Then this really is a professional call," she laughed, "and all the while I have been thinking that you were a desperate lover posing as a dedicated doctor."

"If this is a professional visit, then it is not one the Royal Board of Physicians would look on too kindly," he quipped, taking a small jar of ointment from the pocket of his dressing gown. "Now, lie still and do as the doctor orders."

Francesca groaned appreciatively as Pierre began to work the cool ointment into her arms and shoulders. His hands felt firm and strong as he worked his way slowly down her body.

"Tell me truthfully, Francesca," he whispered, rubbing her breasts, "do you remember any other man's touch?"

She smiled up at him, radiant with her love. "You are so silly, Pierre. Who would I think of, who would I remember, but you? Don't you know there is no one but you? There never has been and there never can be."

"If I could believe that I would be the happiest man in the world."

"Believe it, Pierre, because it is true."

He had moved below her waist and was working his way across her hips and down her belly.

"Mmm," she smiled sensually, "lower, Doctor, that is where the trouble is."

"That's what worries me about you, you wench. You are hungrier for lovemaking than any woman I have ever known." He pinched her belly gently.

"Well, Doctor, what do you prescribe for it"? she murmured.

Ignoring her undisguised desire, Pierre continued applying the salve, working it vigorously into the muscles of her thighs and calves. Francesca's abandon thrilled him yet it disturbed him as well. He didn't want to share her with any man. Even her memories filled him with jealous rage.

"Were you ever like this with any other man?" he asked finally, his voice grave and dangerously soft, "so free and eager to be taken?"

"How could I be, love? There has never been any other man except you." All her trust and lustful love were mirrored in her gentle eyes. Pierre kissed her foot tenderly. "Turn over and let me do your back," he said. His words were simple but his voice throbbed with emotion. Francesca could feel the passion in his fingers as he knelt between her thighs and kneaded the cool ointment into her back.

"I can't bear to think of you with anyone else, I can't bear to think of anyone else touching you," he said fiercely. "I want to possess you completely and erase every trace of another man from your lovely body. Can you understand my terrible desire, love, or is that too much to ask of you?"

Pierre's hands were annointing her round, firm buttocks and the deep crevice between and moving down the back of her thighs. But his mind was with Murad. Francesca's words had rankled in his brain ever since she described her torturous ordeal: "I stumbled and fell forward in the sand and the world turned." He knew what Murad had done as vividly as if he had been a witness to the foul deed. Murad had known her in a way he never had.

Driven by something much more powerful than even a doctor's concern for his patient, Pierre began to work his way back up her legs, massaging the inside of her golden thighs and everything that lay between them, until Francesca's river of love began to flow in his hand and he felt the warm, sticky rush of her desire on his fingers.

"Don't stop now," she moaned, moved by his erotic massage into a dreamy, sensual state of arousal.

"I won't stop, darling, not now—not ever," he answered in an urgent whisper.

With trembling fingers, Pierre spread ointment over her smooth buttocks and into their deep divide, until they were as slick as ice. Then, gliding gently into her crevice with his love, he erased forever the last trace of Murad from her body.

Although she did not suspect the cause of his strange passion, Francesca gave herself freely to his urgent drive, sure of the rightness of their love and of everything they did in its name. Her innocent trust and surrender touched Pierre deeply and when he was satisfied that at last she was his alone, he held her cradled in his arms until she slept. Then covering her tenderly, he left her to her dreams.

A bright beam cut across the hall as Pierre stole out of Francesca's bedroom. He hesitated a moment then walked on slowly towards the light. At the open door of the master bedroom, Lady Marlowe waited for him, bathed in the tapers' glow.

Pierre caught his breath sharply. She looked as if she was clothed in a fine mist; nothing more. In the candlelight her sheer white silk nightgown seemed to melt away and he saw the shadow of her full white breasts, the high angle of her hips, and the soft curve of her belly. She was even more beautiful than he had imagined she would be.

Here is a woman who understands her power, and exactly how to use it, he thought.

Lady Marlowe smiled slowly like a cat. She knew that if Francesca discovered her, she would never be able to understand or forgive. Yet there was no other way that Andrea Marlowe could lay to rest her fears about this tempestous son of Georges Duc du Bellenfant. Better that Francesca find out now the true nature of the man she loved, than to marry, as Lucy Barnes had done, and have her heart broken bitterly each time the gossips tittered over another of his infidelities.

"What do you want with my daughter, Doctor?" her voice mocked Pierre gently. "You can have any woman you want, you know that."

Her voice was as inviting as a mountain stream and he could smell her special fragrance. The gray eyes that met hers were as cold as steel.

Instinctively Pierre knew that she was tempting him with her body to test his love for Francesca. But he was not a man to be toyed with by even the most beautiful woman in the world. *Very well,* he thought angrily, *if she wants to play games, I will set the rules.* His voice as cold as the steel in his eyes, he said, "You will get much more than you ever desired, if you trifle with me."

Lady Marlowe's green eyes glowed hotly. Now that she saw he would not be easily deflected, she was like an angry lion guarding her young. "What do you want with Francesca?" she hissed.

"I want nothing from her—and everything. I want to consume her, and be consumed." He pushed her aside violently.

"Don't try to stop me, Lady Marlowe," he threatened, "for I will not be deterred. I shall have your daughter."

Chapter Forty-Five

"Back at last!" Clarissa oozed with insincerity. "Darling Francesca, you were so kind to take little Geoffrey to hear his father."

Untying her bonnet, Francesca followed her cousin into Uncle Jeremy's old library. "You should have seen the boy. He was so proud I think he must have grown two inches. You would have been proud yourself, Clarissa," she said with a hint of remonstrance in her voice, "if you had been there. Malcolm was really quite splendid; very eloquent and impressive. Everyone was talking about his fine speech."

"I am sure I would have been simply bursting with pride, but I have been so distraught these past weeks, I just do not know what to do. I must talk to you, darling."

"What is troubling you, Clarissa?" she asked gently, taking a chair by the fireplace. "Let me help you if I can."

Clarissa clasped her hands to her mouth and her voice wavered as if she would break into tears at any moment. "It is not me, Francesca, it is you."

"Do not worry on my account. I have never been happier. We plan to be married as soon as possible— just a simple ceremony in the country. I spoke with Mother about it this weekend and she is already beginning the preparations."

"I know, dear cousin, that is what makes this all the more difficult."

"Is it something about Pierre . . . about Dr. Barnes I mean?"

"Yes, Francesca, something dreadful. I must tell you! It is my duty, yet I cannot. Your happiness, your life . . ." She broke off weeping.

Francesca went to her cousin and put her arm around her shoulder affectionately. "Come now, Clarissa, be strong. Whatever you have heard, it cannot be that terrible. Peter and I had a heavenly time at Marlowe Castle. Our love is so strong now, nothing can harm us."

"I don't know how to begin, Francesca," Clarissa said, daubing at her tears with a lace handkerchief. "The other day when you told me Dr. Barnes's true identity, I was so excited for you and overwhelmed by your romantic story that I did not think. I didn't make the connection at all, until you had left. Suddenly his name, his terrible name, rang in my head. I swooned from the shock and since that moment I have been tormented, knowing that I would have to tell you this—that only I could save you from a sin worse than death."

"I don't quite understand what you are trying to say, Clarissa," Francesca coaxed. "What dire thing can you have discovered about Dr. Barnes?" She was sure Clarissa had unmasked Pierre's true identity, but she did not care who he was a spy for, or why. She loved him anyway.

"I am trying to say that you can never marry Dr. Peter Barnes, née Pierre du Bellenfant," Clarissa declared portentously.

"Why that is ridiculous," Francesca said, trying to laugh off her cousin's dark words. "Nothing in the world could keep us apart now."

But Clarissa only shook her head like some ancient, all-knowing oracle. "One thing can keep you apart, Francesca," she insisted in a thin, shrill voice, "One thing that you do not know." Her big violet eyes glowed eerily in the fading afternoon light. "Pierre du Bellenfant is your brother."

"What are you saying?" Francesca cried, aghast.

"The father whom you always wanted to know was Pierre's father, Georges Duc du Bellenfant."

Francesca looked at Clarissa ashen-faced. Was there a note of malicious triumph in her cousin's words? She could never be sure. She felt the curse of the pharaohs hanging over her head again. If she and Pierre had obeyed the ancient law, they would never have come to this point. Now they were accursed—the most accursed sinners in the world.

"How do you know this, Clarissa?" she asked. Her horror-striken voice was scarcely more than whisper.

"I overheard Father on his deathbed, begging your mother to tell you the whole story. He would have told you himself, but Aunt Andrea would never allow him to and no one else ever knew the truth," she confessed. Her hateful plot was moving even more smoothly than she had expected. "When Father received word of your mother's predicament, he went to Paris to make any necessary arrangement he could. He and the Duc were best of friends and, although the Frenchman could not marry your mother, already having a wife of his own, he consented to give you his name. Aunt Andrea anglicized it when she brought you back to England. I was hoping she would tell you the full story herself this weekend. But since she didn't, I felt it my duty . . ."

Francesca listened to Clarissa's scandalous tale like an innocent victim hearing a life sentence. "Pierre—

my lover? My brother? My lover. . . . Oh God, forgive me," she cried, "what have I done?"

She felt as if she was screaming through a dense fog, which was closing in on her rapidly, but her voice was actually little more than a whisper.

Clarissa studied her cousin cautiously. "What will you do, Francesca?" she questioned.

But Francesca was too shocked to feel or think. She stared at Clarissa blankly as if she were a stranger. All she could do was repeat the words over and over in her mind. *Fairchild, Bellenfant.* How stupid she had been never to notice the coincidence.

"What will you do now?" Clarissa asked again.

"I don't know. I can't think. I must go away, someplace where Pierre will never find me again," she spoke distractedly. "He must never know this—never."

"Very well, if that is your wish, but now let me help you, darling," Clarissa smiled warmly. "Let me think for you. What else are cousins for? Malcolm will know where you can go—he should be good for something at least. Just leave it to me. I will arrange everything."

In her shocked, distraught state, Francesca never imagined the poison that coated Clarissa's sweetness. "What would I do without you?" she cried gratefully, opening her arms to embrace her cousin.

Clarissa caught Francesca as she fainted. A triumphant, evil smile wreathed her beautiful face and lit up her cruel violet eyes. *There is only one thing left to do*, she gloated. Tonight at Almack's she would sow the seed of doubt in Peter Barnes's possessive heart.

Chapter Forty-Six

"Let me be the first to welcome you into the family, Dr. Barnes," Clarissa said gaily, taking Pierre by the arm proprietarily and drawing him away from the chatter of admirers.

"You are most gracious, Lady Harrod," he responded.

The Wednesday supper dance was as desultory as always and Lady Harrod was as desirable. If a beautiful woman wanted to monopolize his attention, Pierre was not the man to refuse her. But this did not prevent him from observing Clarissa closely, noting the calculation behind her welcoming words, the suggestion of cunning he always sensed beneath her most spontaneous outburst.

He took her soft, milk-white hand and tucked it in his arm, determined to find out what game she was playing.

"I confess that I am quite dazzled by the prospect of becoming a member, if only by marriage, of a family that claims so many beautiful women. Each is an exquisite family jewel and none is more breathtaking than you are this evening."

Behind his glib words and suave manner, Pierre was thinking that Clarissa was fast becoming like her Aunt Andrea—a woman capable of anything. But despite her beauty and bloom of youth, she lacked

Lady Marlowe's aura of mystery. There would be no challenge in the conquest of Clarissa because she contrived to spread her charms indiscriminately. There was little left for a man to discover from a woman who displayed her assets so blatantly, for all to see.

"I wonder," Clarissa chimed, a bright gleam in her violet eyes, "if my cousin told you how very intimate—and understanding—our family is?"

"Francesca did say that you have always been like a sister to her, Lady Harrod."

Clarissa laughed gaily. "She always is *so* discreet, isn't she, Doctor? But now that you are practically one of us, we should not keep family secrets from you any longer. I look forward to having you join our little family affairs," she looked up at him slyly, "you and Francesca, Malcolm and myself. A quartet is so much more interesting than a triangle, don't you agree?"

Pierre glared fiercely. "Lady Harrod, what are you trying to insinuate?"

Clarissa could see from the smoldering anger in his gray eyes and the barely repressed rage in his tense body that she was playing with a deadly fire. But she had gone too far to stop now. Her malicious scheme was moving so successfully she would not give it up.

"Nothing to take offense at, Dr. Barnes. As your prospective sister-in-law, I was only extending welcoming arms," she demurred, fluttering her eyelashes innocently. "Now, if you will excuse me, I must attend to my duties as a hostess. There are so many guests here this evening—so many beautiful women, I must not monopolize the most charming man in the club."

"Just a moment, Lady Harrod," Pierre held her arm. "Where is Francesca? She said she would be here this evening."

"Why, didn't you know?" Clarissa said, moving away from him. "Francesca is indisposed this evening. Curiously enough," she added "so is Lord Harrod. But then Francesca and I always shared everything, as she probably told you. We still do." She smiled wickedly and melted into the crowd.

Pierre did not believe Clarissa's invidious innuendoes. He could see that behind her angelic face she was a cunning, calculating woman. But he was angry that anyone could even intimate a liaison between Francesca and Malcolm. The memory of her first love—the knowledge that, even in a moment of youthful folly, she had once pledged her love to another man, and one as weak and unworthy as Lord Harrod—was a scar that would never disappear from his heart. With Murad she had been an innocent, helpless victim. With Malcolm she had been a willing, generous loving accomplice—a partner, a mate. Could she be again? His Francesca, his heart who was soon to be his wife? Was some long-buried emotion aroused when she saw her first love again?

Pierre did not believe it was possible, but he was so wildly, so completely, in love with Francesca that even the thought of it drove him insane with jealousy. He tried to banish the dark thoughts by immersing himself in the dancing and chatter of the evening. But finally he could not stand the uncertainty any longer. He had to know without a doubt.

Clarissa had planted a poisonous seed in Pierre's mind—the poisonous seed of doubt and mistrust—and it grew with each moment until it threatened to strangle his love. Determined to uproot it, he rushed out and, leaping into his black phaeton, he whipped his horse through Hyde Park, heading for Grosvenor Square. There was only one way to resolve the dreadful uncertainty—to find Francesca.

Chapter Forty-Seven

When Francesca revived she was lying in her old room, where each nook and cranny was as familiar as her own face and where she had dreamed so many innocent, girlish adventures.

Nothing mattered now, not whether she lived or died. Only that she get away. She had committed the most unforgivable of sins. She had made love to her brother. Even now, as she was filled with revulsion at the sin she had committed, she was also filled with a terrible lust for his forbidden flesh.

Francesca rose like someone sleepwalking and descended the broad stairs. She looked like a ghostly apparition. Her eyes were dark burning hollows sunk in a gaunt, deathly pale face.

"Where are you going, Francesca?" Malcolm's firm but gentle voice stopped her and she turned to him still dazed and distant.

"I am going away, far away," she whispered ethereally. Her voice was like a dry breeze.

He walked slowly toward her, afraid that any quick movement might frighten her and took her in his arms. "I will take you, Francesca," he said.

She sank gratefully into his secure embrace and did not protest when he lifted her in his arms and carried her out to his carriage. Malcolm held her cradled tenderly in his arms as they rode through the quiet London streets.

"What has happened to you, Francesca?" he asked gently.

"Where is Clarissa?"

"She has gone to the supper dance at Almack's. It is Wednesday night, don't you remember?"

"Yes, Wednesday night," she repeated abstractedly.

He smiled at her sadly and held her closer. The color was beginning to return to her cheeks and the fog that shrouded her mind seemed to be lifting.

"Where are you taking me, Malcolm?"

"I am taking you home." He stroked her cheek. "Tell me what happened, Francesca. Clarissa said you received some very bad news this afternoon."

"She is very kind."

Malcolm studied her drawn face closely. "Why are you running away again, Francesca?"

Suddenly her eyes blazed wildly and she clutched him desperately. "I must, Malcolm, I must and you must help me. Please help me get away."

"Ssh," he soothed. "Of course I will help you. I will always help you." He smiled at her sadly. He had never seen her like this before—so distraught and helpless. "Is it another wounded heart?"

"Not wounded," she cried fiercely, "dead. Stone dead," and she began to weep inconsolably. She clung to him, sobbing, her pain and grief pouring out in her tears.

"Who was it this time, Francesca?" Malcolm asked angrily. "Who did this to you? That scoundrel Barnes?"

"I still love him," she sobbed. "There can never be anyone else. I cannot live without him—and I can never live with him."

Malcolm clutched her possessively. *Peter Barnes,*

the bloody bastard! First Clarissa and now Francesca.
I should never have allowed Brummel to come be-
tween us that night, he thought indignantly. But he
spoke gently.

"You cannot keep running away, you know."

"I must. I can never see him again—ever," she cried,
frantically.

"Where do you want to go?" he tried to soothe her.
"Back to Egypt?"

"No, not Egypt, Malcolm. Anywhere but Egypt."

He stroked her hair pensively. "If you really must
leave England, you could always go to my mother's
home in Ireland. It is high on a cliff overlooking the
sea. The land is rough and windswept, but it is secluded and I think you would like it there."

His sheltering arms and reassuring words seemed to
calm her.

"I know this is terribly selfish, Francesca," he murmured, "but I am glad he is gone. I cannot bear to
see you hurt like this. You will forget him—as you forgot me."

Francesca knew Malcolm was wrong. She would
never forget Pierre du Bellenfant. Even as she
thought of their sin—the worst of all sins—her body
ached for his. She could never see him again or feel
his special touch on her yearning flesh. But could she
live without him?

They were riding through Hyde Park, crossing from
St. James's Place to Grovesnor Square. The night was
bright and clear with a full moon. The park, which in
the afternoons was filled with the most fashionable
ladies and gentlemen of London, was deserted except
for a sleek black phaeton that was gaining on their
carriage rapidly.

Wrapped in their melancholy memories and impossible dreams, Malcolm and Francesca were oblivious

274

to the approaching vehicle. Their coachman pulled the carriage to the left to let the phaeton pass. But as it drew alongside, the driver reined his horse sharply. The full moon shone in the carriage window.

Malcolm pressed Francesca closer in his arms. "It could have been different," he whispered, looking into her tearful eyes.

"Yes," she said dreamily, "it could have been. Everything could have been."

Chapter Forty-Eight

Francesca spent the next day alone with the terrible truth, trying to understand her own tattered and tangled feelings. With a wrenching vision, she realized that she was hopelessly trapped. The day before she had been dazed and uncomprehending. She felt as if she was caught in a nightmare from which she would surely awaken. But in the harsh light of day her love glared like the most repelling sin. The perverse logic seemed even worse than before—Bellenfant anglicized to Fairchild.

The pharaohs' curse had not been Murad's defilement, but this sentence worse than death under which she must live the rest of her life, this unbearable destiny to which she was doomed, this living hell from which she could never escape. The love which even now consumed her was forbidden, yet she could never banish the illicit passion from her heart.

Disgusted by the unforgivable sin she had committed, ashamed by the dreaded desire that still raged within her, Francesca decided to leave for Ireland as soon as possible.

Yesterday Pierre was her love. Today his flesh was forbidden fruit—and every day for all eternity. Over and over all through the day, the sad, lonely words he had whispered on the Nile echoed in her heart: "Somewhere I have a sister named Francesca . . ."

276

Touched by his tenderness, she had replied: "Let me be your sister, Pierre."

Now her words had come back to haunt her in a way she had never imagined. Her innocent sentiment seemed pregnant with dire portent. Did she know, from the very beginning, that in some deep, mysterious sense they belonged together? Did she sense, somewhere deep within her unconscious self, that they shared the strongest, most undeniable tie of all—the bond of blood, of brotherly love?

No! No! No! she cried to herself again and again. But even as she did, her own words came back to haunt her: "Let me be your sister, Pierre . . ."

Tormented and grief-stricken, Francesca sat down at the library desk and wrote to her mother. After Lady Marlowe had guarded her secret for so many years, Francesca could not confess that she knew at last who her father was and wished desperately that he had been any other man in the world. Surely she would be forgiven one small deception in the face of her awful truth.

Mother dear,

I am leaving as soon as the arrangements can be completed for Malcolm's home in Ireland. I hope to complete my Egyptain notebook there in the peaceful countryside where the excitement of London cannot tempt me from my work. Since returning from the country, I have been thinking of your wise words. Dr. Barnes and I have decided not to rush into a hasty marriage at this time. Sometimes are hearts are too eager. I look forward to the tranquility of Ireland.

Your loving daughter,
Francesca

Francesca read the note over slowly. Why did her mother have to be so beautiful no man could resist her—and her unknown father so weak? What lust had driven him from his wife's bed into her mother's open arms? What perverse blood coursed in her veins?

Francesca folded and sealed the letter. Then she took a fresh sheet of paper, dipped her quill in the alabaster inkwell, and began to write, "Dear Pierre ..."

If she left him without a word, he would search for her. But the letters she penned blurred in a sea of tears and ran like the Nile, making a river on the paper. She had confessed Malcolm's seduction and Murad's savagery, but she could never tell Pierre of their shared sin.

What cruel twist of fate had brought them together? What evil burned in her thighs that made her lust for her own brother? She was trapped by her blood and her birthright, by her heart and heritage. Drowning in grief, she prayed for the only possible release—death.

The light dimmed. Day turned into night. Still Francesca sat like a prisoner chained to her desk. A mound of crumpled papers, each with the same salutation, lay scattered around her. She struggled and wept, then struggled again, but she could not find the right words to write to Pierre—words that would force him to forget her, but would not hurt him too deeply; firm words that would make him realize her decision was irrevocable, yet gentle words that would not turn his heart bitter.

The servants had retired. The house had grown silent. Francesca had not eaten all day and she was weak from hunger and from the emotional toll of the past thirty-six hours. Her eyes were red-rimmed, her face pale, but she could not rest until the painful task she'd set herself was done. She shivered, although the evening was warm, and, rubbing her arms together, she pulled her shawl closer. She had not bothered to dress all day and still wore the same blue cotton duster she'd pulled on without a thought that morning.

Francesca sighed deeply. Dipping her pen in the black India ink, she began once again, "Dear Pierre . . ." Suddenly a loud rapping interrupted the evening. She leaped at the startling intrusion and huddled in her chair, not wanting to see any living soul that night.

Francesca sat and listened tensely, refusing to open the door to anyone. Her heart pounded. Her pulse raced. The angry knocking resounded eerily in the quiet house. There were no other sounds except the monotonous tick-tock of the grandfather clock and the furious beat of her heart.

Edward came to the door of the library to ask if he could be of assistance. But Francesca said no, she did not want to be disturbed that night and, whoever the caller was, he would soon give up. But she knew by the impetuosity of the knocking that it had to be Pierre.

She listened motionless, not even breathing, unable to respond to the urgent demand of her heart. This was her last chance, her only chance, to ever see him again. She fought the lustful voice of passion within her that begged her to say yes to her heart. Just a glimpse, a last word, one final embrace—the innocent farewell of a brother and sister, nothing more.

But Francesca knew that, if he knocked all night, she could not admit him. She could never again open her door to Pierre du Bellenfant. She could not trust herself with him again.

Francesca covered her ears in a vain attempt to block out the sound of her love calling to her with the wild, abandoned passion he swore no woman had ever made him feel before. More than life itself, more than heaven or hell, she wanted to answer his call—to fly into his arms and forget everything she had discovered in his embrace. If only they could be innocent lovers again and erase the knowledge of who and what they were.

But their terrible sin held her back. She sat poised, like a bird ready for flight, until the fierce knocking ceased. Then she uncovered her ears and listened to his receding footsteps, until his last step faded and silence once again enveloped the lonesome old house.

Francesca turned back once more to the letter she could not write. It was over. Her life, her love. "Dear Pierre . . ." she began for the umpteenth time. Sighing deeply, she leaned back and stared out into the dark garden not seeing, but searching for the right words, which would say what was in her heart.

Suddenly she turned a ghostly white. She tried to scream but her voice caught in her throat and no sound came out. Staring at her through the French doors, a black cloak thrown across his shoulders, shrouding him against the night, stood Pierre du Bellenfant. With a violent thrust he broke open the doors. His dark, furious presence filled the room. His eyes burned with the murderous glint she had seen when he confessed to Murad's killing. The hint of danger, the strain of controlled violence she had always sensed in him, was now as real as his cloak.

Francesca shuddered uncontrollably in apprehension and excitement. For in that instant, she knew that she possessed this beautiful, dangerous man as no other woman ever had, and very few ever could, and she was overwhelmed by a thrilling, frightening sense of power that she had never known before.

Suddenly she knew that he belonged to her body

and soul. He was hers to command. With her embrace she could turn his anger to joy. From his fury she could bring forth the passion that so many other women craved. *He would kill for me. He had. He would die for me. There is nothing he will not do for me,* she thought. And then in the next breath, she realized there was one other thing: He would never let her go.

Would he stop at anything to keep her? Would he allow the terrible truth about them to prevent him from having her? Suddenly frightened by the unknown power and passion of this man she loved, Francesca pushed away from the desk and darted for the door.

But Pierre was too fast. He moved with the speed of a jaguar. He struck with the suddenness of a cougar. He was as graceful and lithe as a panther. Crossing the room in a single stride, he caught her by her long golden hair.

"Where are you going, Francesca?" he asked. His voice was hard and low. "Why are you running away from me?"

He turned her around, pulling her hair painfully and yanking her head back.

She looked up at him, her eyes brimming with tears and with the love she could never disguise—not even then.

"Please, Pierre, go away! Go now! I cannot bear to hurt you or see you hurt," she pleaded.

He slapped her hard across the face. She looked so innocent, so vulnerable, so much in love. *Even now,* he thought bitterly, *she is using all the ruses she knows have worked so well. How well her mother taught her! How many men she must have deceived with her lustrous eyes and innocent, blushing cheeks! What a damn fool I have been.*

281

"Don't look at me like that," he spat. "It won't work anymore, Francesca."

"Let me go, Pierre," she cried desperately. Her eyes were enormous dark pools like lakes on a moonless night. "You don't know what you are doing. You don't know the truth about us."

He gave a short, curt laugh. "Ha! Do you think I am both blind and a fool? How long did you think you could deceive me with your innocent looks and false promises?"

"No, no! Clarissa would never tell you," she gasped.

"Ah," he cried enraged, "so you do not even attempt to deny it, you audacious whore."

She flinched at his cruel words as if he had struck her again. "How can I deny it Pierre? I can't. Oh, God, I wish it were not true," she cried. "I would do anything in the world if I could make it not be true. I did not know. I never suspected. You must believe this, Pierre."

"You never knew until last night," Pierre said in a cold, mocking voice. He was seeing her again as he had the night before, cradled in the arms of Lord Harrod in Hyde Park.

"Yes," Francesca nodded in answer. She was hearing Clarissa's fateful verdict again: "You can never marry Peter Barnes. He is your brother."

"And now," Pierre said sarcastically, picking up her letter from the desk, "you are composing a last farewell."

"I was writing to beg you to forget me—forever," Francesca whispered.

"Forget you, Francesca? But of course," he laughed cruelly, his lips curled in a disdainful smile. "Throw your letter away, darling. It comes too late. I already forgot you—last night."

282

She stared at him, hurt and helpless, stunned by his cruelty. But he went on unmoved.

"But you, Lady Andrea Marlowe's well-trained daughter, you will not forget me so easily," he promised and the threat of violence was no longer veiled.

His hands closed around her long, swan-like neck and she felt them tighten. Closing her eyes gratefully, no longer caring to live, she waited for him to release her from the living death to which she was doomed by their forbidden love.

But he released her suddenly and, seizing each side of her cotton duster, he tore it off her, exposing her smooth shoulders and firm breasts. Francesca screamed and tried to cover her nakedness. But he grabbed her arms, twisting them behind her back. She tried to escape from his grasp but he held her fast.

"You won't run off until I am finished with you," he warned angrily.

She fought wildly to be free of his embrace. But her struggle only aroused him further.

"I am going to make you want me, Francesca," he swore, "as no woman has ever wanted a man before. After this night you will remember me, whenever a man looks into your eyes or touches your flesh with desire."

He pulled her to him, crushing her body against his. Francesca felt his hot, quick breath on her face and the rough wool of his cloak scratching against her bare breasts as he bent and kissed her savagely, bruising her lips with his own.

"Let me go, Pierre," she cried, twisting away from his mouth.

Pierre du Bellenfant smiled cruelly. "I will when I am finished with you. Then you can go as far as you like—to the ends of the earth if you want—but I will always be with you." He turned her face towards him so she could see the threat and the challenge in his smoky eyes. "Always," he repeated softly, his mouth just inches from hers. "You will never be able to forget me."

He kissed her again, forcing her lips apart with the hard thrust of his tongue. She bit down sharply, tasting his warm blood on her lips. But he did not seem to notice the pain. Reaching for her breasts, he cupped them in his hands, raising them up and pinching her nipples between his fingers while his tongue drove deeper into her mouth.

Francesca fought desperately but Pierre would not be stopped. He was a man possessed by a consuming passion. Ignoring buttons and hooks, he ripped at her clothes, tearing them off with his rapacious hands, claiming her naked flesh with his burning fingers. His searing lips were everywhere, enflaming her breasts, her belly, her neck, her hair.

Francesca struggled fiercely to contain the passion surging within her. But she was like a drowning swimmer miles from shore. Her body craved for his. The violence of his desire, the threat of his stormy passion, the searing flame that was now forbidden her aroused her in a way she had never known before. Her tender nipples stood out audaciously, proclaiming her body's willingness. The hot springs of love were surging between her thighs.

Francesca pressed against Pierre, meeting his embrace with her own desperate one. His cloak was rough against her bare skin but she didn't care. Her mouth answered his lustfully and, in the wildness of their kiss, their mouths mimicked the forbidden act their loins craved. She could not resist him now, and she would not let him resist her.

"What do you want, Francesca?" His voice, his body demanded her surrender.

"I want you," she whispered, her voice as urgent as his own.

Pressing his fingers deeply into her soft cheeks he thrust her against his enormous desire. "You want a man—any man," he said savagely.

Pierre's scowling face was darkly beautiful, more beautiful in its fury than she had ever seen it. His angry mouth curled sensually at the corners. His eyes pierced her heart. Francesca looked into their smoky depths and was filled with an exhilarating sense of the power she wielded over this man. He was hers to command, to enslave, to conquer, even to destroy. She thrilled with her strength and with an overwhelming lust not to surrender, but to seduce. She wanted to draw the anger from his sensual lips, the fury from his savage manhood. This man who could have any woman he wanted was hers to possess completely. She had driven this beautiful, untamed man whom women on three continents desired into a wild, ungovernable tempest. A burning lust for his forbidden flesh, and for the power it gave her, overcame Francesca.

"No," she answered hungrily. "I want only you. I want to take you, to have you, to possess you." She felt his enormous desire harden against her.

"Can you wait, Francesca?" he asked as he had asked once, so many lives before, his voice deep and intense.

"No, not a second," she answered.

Her anxious fingers were quick at his trousers, sure and deft. He felt her long, cool fingers coil around his throbbing desire, drawing it out and traversing the length of his swelling shaft. He throbbed uncontrollably as her fingers locked around him and she began to move up and down, along his shaft, in a slow rhythmic motion.

"Can you wait, Pierre?" she whispered triumphantly. She looked up at him, and he saw in her velvet eyes a smoldering passion—and a naked challenge.

He stared at her a long instant, then he laughed, deeply, dangerously, her challenge answered in its ring.

"You bitch, you virgin bitch, you daughter of Eve," he whispered lustily, savagely, "We'll see who surrenders."

He hoisted her over his shoulder. His fingers tangled in her auburn forest, then moved slowly, teasingly away from the silky hair and circled the entry to her mossy cavern, as he carried her into the hall. Mounting the stairs, his hand demanded entry into her secret passage, delving deep inside her, searching for the answer to the mysterious power that held him in her thrall. Trembling from his ecstatic touch, she clutched his back in her hungry passion and sank her teeth into his shoulder, stifling her cry of delight.

"Don't stop," she whispered, as he carried her into her room. He tossed her down on the bed, where she lay motionless in the darkness, her arms thrown over her head, her body arched hungrily waiting to meet his, and watched him strip off his clothes.

What is love? she thought passionately. *The need to possess? To own? To take? Is this love? To punish? To master* But all questions and answers, all good and bad, all right and wrong were forgotten as Pierre loomed over her, his naked, muscular body poised and ready. In the dim light his sex towered dark and dangerous—a raw challenge, both a threat and a promise.

Francesca's hands trembled with anticipation and wild desire as she caressed the length of his body and drew him down to her. For a moment they lay still, their bodies pressed together, locked in a loving embrace or in mortal combat—they did not know which. Then they began to kiss and nothing else mattered.

There were no restraints now. They were like Adam and Eve returned to Paradise. Their tongues and fingers were everywhere. It seemed as if they each had a hundred hands and mouths.

Love and hate, anger and lust, were all one. There were no barriers, no distinctions, nothing they would not or could not do. They made love in ways Francesca never dreamed of yet knew as naturally as a flower knows to open in spring. Their bodies were continents and they were explorers, eager, passionate discoverers claiming new gardens and valleys.

Francesca and Pierre abandoned themselves to a torrent of desire that no man nor woman, blood nor blandishment, would contain or come between. They were furious and gentle, cruel and loving, violent and tender. She was victor and he vanquished, she was lover and he beloved. And then it was the other way.

When giving and taking, possessed and possessing, they had satisfied every desire; when they had driven out the demons of jealousy and guilt and answered the deep, secret hungers they had never even admitted to themselves before, then they began slowly, gently to make love.

They were alone in the universe, kissing and caressing; tongues on eyes, nipples, thighs; fingers gently probing, coaxing ever new secrets from each other's bodies; revisiting the special places where a touch or a kiss turned flesh to fire.

Francesca raised her body to meet Pierre's thrust as

he entered her yet again. He was a shooting star in her milky way, a lightning bolt in her dark heaven and they were at the beginning of creation. Nothing existed except the two of them and their love. He thrust slowly, deeply into her mysterious abyss, then faster, harder, the two of them moving together—one, inseparable, driving wildly, exultantly: surrendering totally, holding nothing back, exploding in torrential ecstasy.

Love triumphant, Francesca and Pierre slept—their bodies still entangled, exhausted, moist with passion. Pierre dreamed that the night never ended. Daylight never intruded and he and Francesca lived forever, loving and making love and never tiring. He woke up with a smile on his lips and reached out lovingly for her.

Through the open window he saw the sun beginning to rise. It was the dawn of a new day and the beginning of a new life. For Francesca was gone.

Chapter Forty-Nine

Castle Glenreagh—where Malcolm's mother was born and his cousin, Robert Adair, still lived—stood high in the mountains, surrounded by thousands of acres of lakes, woodlands and fields. It was situated in one of the most desolately beautiful corners of Donegal, wrapped in mist, buffeted by ocean winds, and colored by the memories of its native son, the courageous St. Colmcille, who more than twelve hundred years before slew the terrible monster of Lough Swilly.

Lough Swilly, or the Lake of the Eye, is a long sea inlet that cuts into the heart of Donegal. The monster that once lived in its depths had one hundred eyes glowing from its head in every direction. The people lived in terror for miles around, not daring to fish or swim in its waters, or even stray far from their homes, for fear of being visited by the dreaded creature. But Colmcille knew no fear. He killed the monster of Lough Swilly in a bloody duel, then he left Ireland to carry the word of Christ to distant lands.

Although Colmcille died in the seventh century, his legend was still very much alive in Donegal when Francesca sailed into Lough Swilly, a week to the day after leaving Pierre. She had awoken just before daybreak in Pierre's arms, his lithe, handsome body still thrown across hers.

What she had blotted from her mind and heart in the frenzied passion of that night seemed in the bleak light of day to be unforgivable, perverted and damned. Before, their love had been pure. They were innocent of their sin, unaware of the bond of blood they shared. But now, knowing who they were, they had committed the unpardonable sin. They had made love, abandoned, passionate love again and again as if in jubilant celebration of their crime. Ashamed of her lust yet still very much in love, she'd slipped out of his embrace. With tears brimming from her eyes, she'd kissed his raven curls and ran her hand lovingly down his broad, muscular back. Then, not daring to stay another moment, she'd fled. She had to put as much distance between them as she could, for she could never risk seeing him again.

Francesca roamed alone, lovely and haunted, through the grounds of Castle Glenreagh, frightened by the strange passions Pierre had aroused within her and tormented by guilt for their incestuous night. Yet even now she knew that she would do it again. If he touched her again, no will, no restraints, would be powerful enough to control her response. She could not forget that night of forbidden, illicit love, that shameless night of utter abandon.

What has he made me? Francesca wondered. But she could not blame Pierre. Her desire was as strong as his, her demand to know the secrets brothers and sisters can never share was urgent. That night revealed a side of herself she never knew she had, and a power she never expected to possess. It had made her, in a way she had never been before, her mother's daughter.

Lady Marlowe's eyes, her poise, her presence, conveyed a daring challenge to every man that drew them against their will to test themselves and prove they were invulnerable. It was the sure knowledge that she could command their hearts. Now Francesca possessed it too.

She wondered if this quality was what brought the Duc du Bellenfant from his wife's loving arms to her mother's fertile bed? And yet Lady Marlowe had loved Francesca's father alone among all the men she'd known. She would never speak of him. But once she said, "Francesca, you will hear many stories about me, some of them true, some not. But there is only one thing you need to know and to remember always. I have loved only one man in my lifetime and that man was your father."

How did she live without him? Did they see each other again through the years, did they make love again? Now that she had renounced Pierre, Francesca wondered increasingly how her mother had survived. She did not even want to try and yet she knew she had to live without Pierre. She tried to establish a routine for herself there in the lonely northwest corner of Ireland to keep herself from brooding.

In the mornings she worked on her Egyptian notebooks, trying to convey a sense of the enormity of Egypt's past and the raw, sensual power of its present, saved from the devouring jaws of the desert only by the munificence of the great river Nile. In the afternoons she rode fast and furiously, her golden hair flying behind her, the wind in her face, the horses' flanks sleek beneath her.

But memories of Pierre and the frightening passions he had unleashed within her intruded on her, waking and sleeping, working and riding.

Sometimes at night, alone in the secluded castle, a prisoner of destiny, Francesca would feel Pierre beside her as clearly as if he were there. She would moan to him softly, pleadingly in the night and open

291

her legs to receive him. In that unreal state between sleeping and waking, she would touch herself as he had, but it would do no good. She could give herself no relief from the aching desire.

Their last night of love had aroused such passionate demands within her that she thought she would never be able to contain them. The longest walks, the fastest, freest gallops did not quiet her urgent needs. She felt as though her body had become something apart from herself with a will of its own. It was a machine separate from her heart that drove her where it wished.

For the first time Francesca began to understand her mother and the life of loneliness, the depths of isolation, she had endured, trapped in the cold, barren world of lust without love.

Gradually though, after she had been in Donegal for a couple of months, the urgency in her loins began to subside and her body took on a new focus. Unbelieving at first, Francesca watched her belly start to swell with a mixture of awe at the life taking place within her and of horror at the enormity of the sin she had committed. For Francesca was pregnant.

After discovering that she was carrying the child, Francesca lay awake night after night trying to decide whether she should abort it. She feared that an incestuous child might be born feeble-minded or monstrously deformed, yet the seed growing in her belly was all that she would ever again posses of Pierre. She could not kill it, but neither could she dispel the nightmare.

In the days she tormented herself with her fears and at night she dreamed that she gave birth to a child as fearsome as the monster of Lough Swilly, a punishment for the sins of its parents, acursed by the incestuous union in which it was conceived. She'd wake up screaming, alone and frightened. Then, in the fourth month of her pregnancy, Robert Adair returned to Castle Glenreagh.

Chapter Fifty

Pierre waited for Francesca to return as she had once waited for him—in vain, without a word of explanation, without a letter or a message.

To him that night had been like no other. He had already discovered her sensuality, her quick desire, her uninhibited gift of love. But that night he discovered even deeper, unsuspected levels of passion in her—a fierce demand, an insatiable hunger, that he knew he alone could slake.

He had broken in on her in a furious anger, believing she had deceived him with Lord Harrod. But she had consumed his jealousy in the fury of her passion. After that night, he did not believe she could return to Malcolm—or to any other man. She loved him. It was as clear and incontestable as his own desire.

When Pierre awoke that bleak morning to an empty bed, he had begged, bullied and ordered Edward to tell him where his mistress had gone. But the butler remained stalwart and silent. He had ridden to Marlowe Castle to look for her. But the big estate was empty. Lady Marlowe had left for London only hours before his arrival, and there was no trace of Francesca.

Returning to London, Pierre confessed his anguish to his friend, John Kent. "Don't worry, Pierre, no woman can resist you. She probably escaped for a few days so she wouldn't be burned alive by your legendary blazing passion." Dr. Kent smiled at his friend's distress. So *the notorious lady-killer is smitten at last!* he thought.

"You may be right at that," Pierre grinned, accepting his friend's joshing without rancor. "I suppose I must have been an alarming sight, appearing out of the darkness at her window like a burglar and then . . . well, I needn't tell you anymore than that," he concluded discreetly and he smiled to himself at the memory—the private, treasured memory of their wild desire and even wilder capitulation.

And so Pierre plunged into his work and waited for Francesca to come back. He stayed away from all the social events, refusing every invitation proferred. Every afternoon he drove his phaeton to Grosvenor Square and rang the doorbell to inquire if she had returned, and each day Edward opened the door and greeted him with the same message.

"No, Dr. Barnes, I regret to say Miss Fairchild has not returned or sent any word to pass on to you." As the days followed one after the other and Pierre continued his lonely vigil, Edward began to have pity on the young doctor and one afternoon invited him into the empty house for tea. Gradually tea at the kitchen table and a simple game of chance became a daily routine with the two men. When Pierre discovered that Edward had a secret passion for gambling, they began to liven their teatime with a simple game of chance.

One day, after Francesca had been gone a month or more, Pierre challenged Edward to a game of One-and-Twenty, wagering him a twenty pound note against information about Francesca's whereabouts.

Edward had served Lady Marlowe since she was first widowed, but he was a gambling man at heart.

More than that he had grown genuinely fond of the doctor, who had so clearly fallen in love with his young mistress. He could still picture Francesca's red-rimmed eyes as he helped her into Lord Harrod's carriage that fateful morning. "Dr. Barnes is asleep upstairs," she'd blushed and touched his arm. "Take care of him for me, Edward," she'd said, then she was gone.

Miss Fairchild could do a sight worse than Dr. Barnes, Edward thought as he turned up the corner of the card which Pierre had dealt to him. It was the ten of clubs.

Pierre dealt again, this time laying the cards face up. Edward looked at the knave of diamonds in front of him and the seven of spades in front of Pierre.

"Very well, Dr. Barnes," he said conspiratorially. "But I warn you, you will have to have some bit of luck to win your wager."

Pierre looked at the butler ruefully. "May I assume then, Edward, that you do not wish another card?"

"An excellent assumption, Doctor," he replied mischievously. "I shall stay with the cards you have dealt me, as befits a good servant."

"I could never hope to be as circumspect as you, Edward," Pierre laughed "so I will take another."

Without so much as glancing at the card that lay face down beneath his seven of spades, Pierre dealt himself a third one. It was the three of spades.

He leaned back in his chair. "Well, Edward, let's see what you have."

"Twenty it is," the butler said heartily, turning over his ten, "and I'll be twenty pounds richer for it, thank's to you—a kingly sum for a butler if I say so myself."

Pierre drained his tea. Then slowly, without a word, he turned over his bottom card.

"One-and-Twenty," he said.

Edward's face paled as he looked at the doctor's card. It was the ace of hearts.

"You lose, Edward," Pierre said evenly.

Edward cleared his throat awkwardly. "Well, Doctor," he said finally, trying to muster a hearty tone, "a wager is a wager, but are you quite sure you want to hold me to this one?"

Pierre leaned across the table. "Where is she, Edward?" he demanded, his voice low and urgent.

Edward hesitated. "Ireland, sir," he finally said reluctantly. "Donegal, in the northwest corner."

Pierre stood up and shook the butler's hand. "Thank you, Edward. You are a man of your word."

Edward followed him to the door. "Will you go after her, sir?" he asked apprehensively.

"This very night."

"Please, sir, not a word about me."

"Not a word, Edward," Pierre promised solemnly. "I will carry our secret to the grave."

Riding for three nights and three days, pausing only for fresh mounts, Pierre galloped north through England to Scotland. At Ayr, he slept fitfully for a few hours; then, hiring a boat, he set sail for Donegal.

He could not imagine what worry or fear had taken Francesca from him and kept her from writing during the long months he had endured without her. But now her haunting face, the touch of her hands, the taste of her lips, the smile in her eyes were within reach again, and his heart quickened with remembering.

The sea was stormy and the crossing from Scotland to Ireland was rough. Heavy rains swept down on the small boat, drenching him through to the skin and the north wind howled.

Pierre believed in omens. Deep down, beneath his

sophisticated grace, ran the blood of a true Latin. He believed there were powers beyond those any man could know, superhuman forces that he could neither control nor understand. As a physician he had explored the human body, studied its construction, and marveled at the complex way it worked and the divine genius that invented it. The infinite variety, yet basic sameness, of the human form and the astonishing attention to each minute detail that went into its creation filled him with awe. With each patient he treated, his respect for what he could not understand deepened. He knew that in centuries to come, many of the mysteries which had perplexed men from the earliest times would be unraveled. But he also knew there was much that would never be fully comprehended or explained away by the limited, earthbound mind of man.

Love itself was a mystery as profound as creation. Where does it begin? How does it happen that one particular man and woman come together, innocent magnets drawn by the force of destiny into each other's arms? What happens with them when they couple and mate that happens with no others?

He had done nothing in that last night of love with Francesca that he had not done before with dozens of others—the same caresses, the same fevered kisses, the same inescapable lust. Yet it seemed as if they were adventurers discovering a new world that no one had ever known existed before. They had entered a realm that transcended any other, and been consumed together in love's eternal flame.

Pierre gripped the rudder tighter and stared out over the horizon trying to catch the first glimpse of Donegal. He had not known another woman since that night. He did not want to touch or taste anyone but Francesca. Her smile, her surrender were all he desired. He had dreamed that she was a beautiful, unexplored island known to no man and he was the sea, strong and fragrant, lapping at her shores, pounding in again and again on her smooth beaches, surrounding her, oozing into her every nook and cranny, crashing boldly—an enormous, crested, white wave rising higher and higher, rolling, driving slowly toward her, moving faster and faster and breaking with a great roar, spilling white, salty foam in her dark sea cavern.

Now, as she filled his mind again, the desire so long denied him was almost more than he could control. He could taste her and smell her and feel her beneath him as surely as if she were there, and he concentrated on the stormy sea, trying to hold back his need.

Was love created in a man and woman in seven days as in Genesis?—not seven calendar days but seven days of the heart. For the first six time stood still and waited, and on the seventh day they lay down together and their world was born.

The dark, empty sea stormed, as full of turmoil as his soul. He was alone, as far as he could see. The day was black, or had the evening set in and daylight faded? The angry clouds would not permit him even this scrap of surety. The furious sea hurled itself against the hull, tossing the little vessel helplessly like a discarded love note blown in the wind.

As he tried to hold the boat on the course his heart would never veer from, Pierre wondered ominously if all the powers beyond man's control were conspiring to keep him from Francesca—the dark skies, the angry sea, the blinding fog. Could a force greater than either of them—greater even than their love—have drawn her away from him after that night of love? A bolt of thunder split the heavens and Pierre felt the curse of the pharoahs through the fog that enveloped him like a shroud.

Francesca, with her linear, Anglo-Saxon mind, was intrigued by the ancient curse as she was intrigued by all the myths and customs of that people who filled their elaborate pyramid tombs with priceless jewels and fine food to ease the transition to the other world, and buried favorite wives and servants with kings to make them comfortable in their journey. But she did not believe it and she had teased him for being superstitious. He was the man of the world and she the simple, innocent girl. But in this they were opposite.

"Why, Pierre," she'd laughed merrily, "you almost sound as if you believe those ancient mummies could hurt us."

"Are you so sure there are no powers we do not know—that the dead sleep forever undisturbed and undisturbing?"

She'd laughed again. Francesca was too rooted in the solid brick and mortar of London where the only mystery was how they lost their American colonies to the upstart Yankees, to be afraid of ancient curses.

As he guided his boat through the treacherous storm, Pierre was filled with dread that he had brought the ancient curse down on their love with his challenging words. Now the pharaohs were punishing them for celebrating life in their death chamber, for mocking their darkness with light, their loss with eternal love.

Pierre possessed the soul of a romantic and the imagination of a poet. He was under the spell of everything mysterious, fantastic and enchanting. It was not so much that he believed with his mind. But whatever was inexplicable and otherworldly was food for his soul, enriching him like the silt from the Nile

300

enriched the delta crescent. In a subtle way it was what gave him that extra measure of charm—that unfathomable quality—which, as much as his handsome face and masculine beauty, drew women to him.

Pierre had thought they'd paid in full with Murad and the desolate years of separation. Finding each other again seemed like a gift of the gods and their last night of love, a final absolution—all misunderstandings, guilts and betrayals whether real or suspected, erased with their love.

Now, as he sat alone on the storm-tossed sea, he wondered if the pharaohs were still exacting their awesome price—if he and Francesca would ever be free of their curse or if they were doomed.

But the storm abated at last and a new day began to dawn, pushing the fog and dark clouds out of its path. Once again Pierre was filled with new hope. He found himself only miles from shore and sailed on calm waters into Lough Swilly. Without taking time to rest or eat, he set out to find his love.

An old fisherman, mending his nets on the quay, pointed Pierre on his way to Castle Glenreagh where an English girl with golden hair was visiting. The road was steep and tortuous, over a rough mountainous terrain, relieved occasionally by patches of woodland. But Pierre rushed on, in his exhaustion and excitement imagining that he was climbing higher and higher to a secret kingdom of the heart.

Finally, flushed and breathless, he reached a clearing where he could see spread below him pastures of lolling cows, a blue jewel lake like a sapphire, and above, the ghostly castle spires lost in the low clouds.

"Good morning to you, sir," a voice said.

Pierre traced the sound to a tree trunk against which an old man in a patched jacket and knickers rested. Behind him a mule of equal age munched flowers and grass indiscriminately.

"Good morning to you," Pierre said. "I did not see you resting there."

"I am an old man and the road to Castle Glenreagh is long and steep. If you are going there too, sir, I would be grateful for your company."

"You are most kind. I am new to these parts and could use a guide."

The old man struggled to his feet, eyeing Pierre sharply. "Meself, I be carrying a letter to the castle. What be your business there, if it is not impertinent of me too ask?"

Pierre hesitated. He did not want to discuss his business with this old man. Any word he said would surely be repeated to everyone in the country.

"I am on a holiday," he smiled disarmingly, "and I was told that Castle Glenreagh is one of the most beautiful spots in all of Ireland."

"It be that all right," the old man agreed, unhitching his mule.

"Do you know the place well?"

"I have been coming here ever since I could walk, and me father before me."

"Then perhaps you can tell me something of the history of the place as we walk."

They stood together, surveying the countryside, which stretched out before them.

"Every blade of grass, every rock and tree as far as the eye can see," the old man said, waving his arms expansively as if to embrace the entire world, "belongs to the lord of the castle, Master Robert Adair."

"A fortunate man, indeed. I would like to make his aquaintance," Pierre answered, amused by the man's apparent pride.

"Robert Adair is a hard man to pin down. He is

away for long months at a time," the old man said guardedly. "Are you English, sir?" he asked suspiciously.

"No," Pierre smiled, "I am a mongrel like your mule there—I am French and American on my mother's side."

"St. Colmcille be praised," The old man said. Then lowering his voice as if there was some possibility that they might be overheard even here, he said, "Between you and me, governor, I hope that your little General Bonaparte gives them English a sound thrashing."

"Is that a commonly held sentiment in these parts?" Pierre asked curiously.

"To Robert Adair and his men it is," the old man said proudly. "A brave man, Robert Adair, and a fine son of the sod he is."

"I am doubly sorry not to meet him, then." Pierre knew he should quiz the old man further to find out how far Bonaparte could count on these insular people, but he was too anxious to find Francesca. She was so close at hand, yet still so far. An inch beyond his reach was a world apart. "Is no one living in the castle then?"

"It is empty now, sir, except for a young English woman."

"A friend of Robert Adair, is she?" Pierre asked trying to make it sound like a casual question.

"There she is, sir," the old man pointed, "over there by the lake."

Pierre followed the old man's finger with his anxious eyes. Yes, she was there, silhouetted against the lake, her fine golden hair as bright as the sun, her figure a pencil of blue—too far away to see more clearly, yet unmistakably his love.

Pierre gazed at Francesca hypnotized. "What is she

303

doing here?" he asked as much to himself as to the old man.

"She be waiting," the old man said, with an undisguised hint of suggestion in his voice, "but not for Robert Adair, if that be what you're thinking." The old man spoke confidentially, eager to show the aristocratic gentleman that he knew everything that went on in the country, even among the privileged few. "She be waiting for his cousin, not a bad young lordship, even though he's English on his father's side."

The blood ran cold in Pierre's veins. "What is his lordship's name?" he demanded coldly.

"Why, Lord Harrod, sir," the old man said, taken aback by the sudden change in the fine gentleman's manner. "I . . ."

Pierre whirled and, grabbing the man by the jacket, raised him off the ground. "How do you know that?" he demanded angrily.

The old man cringed with fright. "Please, sir," he stammered, "cook at the castle told me so herself."

"Liar," Pierre spat fiercely, shaking the old man until the few remaining teeth in his head were almost lost.

"It is the truth by Holy Mother Herself," the old man pleaded. "Lord Harrod is a cousin to Robert Adair. His mother was Robert Adair's only sister and a beauty she was in her day, I remember her well." The old man spoke faster, hoping somewhere in his outpouring would be the right words that would save him from this wild stranger.

Abruptly Pierre let him go. What had the old man done after all, except boast too much? Pushing the frightened creature aside, he looked for the last time at the solitary figure he would love to the death.

What a romantic fool he had been to think that it was an ancient, ridiculous curse that drew her from him, when it was the oldest curse of all—the treachery of the female heart. How could he have been so blind that he did not see that beneath the veil of innocence, the generous, giving nature, Francesca was nothing more than her mother's daughter?

Now, her every word sounded false; every caress seemed to have been a mockery of his love; every act of love a lie. "I want to take you, to have you," he heard her say and saw the challenge gleam again in her haunting brown eyes.

She had risen from their bed of love, leaving him still warm with the sweet scent of her body, and slipped away to Malcolm. Why else was she here? No love, however deep, however consuming, could remain blind to this incontestable proof that her truest affections belonged to Malcolm Lord Harrod.

Now that he had come so close, Pierre turned back. Francesca was too far away for him to see more than her distant outline. He could not see that she filled the lake with her tears, nor the new roundness of her belly where now she nourished the fruit of their union. All he could see, in his mind's eye, was Francesca in Malcolm's embrace. Rushing back down the mountain path, Pierre ran away from his love, away from himself.

He spent that day and night at a small inn by the quay. At dawn the next morning he returned to England, determined in his bitter anger to pay back Lord Harrod in the only way he could—by granting Lady Harrod the pleasure she had so long desired.

Chapter Fifty-One

The return of Dr. Peter Barnes added an unaccustomed zest to the usual Wednesday night supper dance at Almack's.

"Where have you been, Doctor?"

"London was simply dead without you."

"How could you desert us without a word?"

The phrases were slightly varied, but the sentiments were the same as the handsome young physician passed among the jeweled, powdered cream of London society, looking for Lady Clarissa Harrod. The women's eyes, bright with thinly concealed desire, were as hard and polished as their nails—*so unlike Francesca's*, he thought. *Beside them she would be aloof and regal, and eminently more desirable.* But he banished the thought as quickly as it came and resumed his stalk of his prey.

"Lady Harrod," he said, coming up behind her, "I have been searching for you all evening." His low voice was like a caress.

She turned, her violet eyes shining with triumph. "Welcome back, Dr. Barnes," she purred in her little-girl voice. "To the fray, that is."

It had been weeks since Pierre had looked at any woman except Francesca with desire and he appraised Lady Harrod admiringly. Her delicate beauty so much more obvious than Francesca's, the daring

306

degree of her décolletage, her flirtatious manner which suggested her readiness to be plucked, promised a sweet revenge. He recognized the canny, dangerous woman behind the elfin charm—the woman who knew exactly what she wanted and invariably got it. This time he would not disappoint her.

He took her in his arms, holding her lightly as they danced. "I trust I am not too late, Lady Harrod."

His steel gray eyes bored through her, sending a tiny shiver of anticipation up Clarissa's spine. Her scheme had worked like a dream, more perfectly than she had imagined possible.

"Patience has always been one of my many virtues, Doctor," she laughed, and the tinkling music sounded pleasantly to hin.

She felt his hand tighten at her waist and his voice low in her ear. "I am more interested in your vices than your virtues, Lady Harrod."

His dark beard tickled her forehead. "I am afraid I must disappoint you then," she replied coyly, "for I only have one."

The music stopped but he held her a moment longer. "I hope it is the one weakness that interests me most," he quipped.

Clarissa laughed again more wickedly. "That is for you to discover, Doctor."

He took her hand and raised it to his lips. "When may I begin my explorations?" he asked, feigning her own bantering gaiety.

She felt a rush of excitement and daring. At last she would pay her husband back with the most devastatingly handsome man in London. "Tomorrow at three?"

Pierre held her hand just long enough for Clarissa to know that he understood perfectly what she was offering. She sensed the promise and the threat in his strong grasp, and a sudden pang of fear and regret struck her heart. Francesca was devastated. Malcolm's turn was now only a day away. Then her revenge would be total. But instead of being elated that her scheme was proceeding so flawlessly, Clarissa felt a sudden wave of apprehension and tried to retreat.

"Actually, Dr. Barnes," she said quickly, "I have been in some pain in recent weeks and have wanted to consult with you . . ."

"I shall not be disappointed, Lady Harrod," Pierre interrupted. He was smiling, his white teeth gleaming, but his eyes glinted coldly. "Until tomorrow at three."

Lady Harrod lay on a chaise lounge in her setting room. The curtains were drawn against the afternoon sun, casting the room in shadows. She wore a shell-pink robe edged in delicate lace and tied demurely at the neck with a satin bow. A deeper pink lap rug was drawn up to her waist.

"Oh, Dr. Barnes, at last," she cried weakly. "I have been in such distress."

"You seemed quite well last night, Lady Harrod," Pierre said lightly, closing the door firmly behind him.

"It comes and it goes, Doctor," she sighed dramatically.

"Ah, I see," he said, advancing slowly toward her.

"Is there anything you could prescribe. I have tried tonics and . . ." Clarissa looked up at Pierre as he stood at the foot of the chaise and read the frank, bold message in his steely eyes.

"Surely a doctor and a gentleman like yourself would not take advantage of a woman's helplessness," she whispered with false coyness.

"Last night, Lady Harrod, you wanted a man, not a doctor." A cruel contemptuous smile played on his lips. "As for my gentleness, I shall allow you to be the

308

judge of that," he said, pulling the lap rug off her legs and throwing it carelessly on the floor.

"My husband," Clarissa cried shrilly. "Think of my husband, Dr. Barnes. He will be returning for tea at any moment."

Her words were a blatant falsehood. The afternoon session of the House of Lords was just convening. But looking into the cold, arrogant eyes of Peter Barnes, she wished with all her heart that it was true.

"I am thinking of your husband, madam," he replied drily. "It it because of him that I am here."

Clarissa did not understand his cryptic remark, but she did not have time or an opportunity to puzzle over it, because Pierre had had enough of her devious, tantalizing family. He believed that Francesca, Lady Marlowe and Clarissa had each, in her seperate way, used their very considerable sexual charms to try to force him to do their perverse will. He had had his fill of all of them. The fury and passion boiling inside of him erupted. The mask of debonair man-about-town was dropped and he was revealed as a man of raw, naked passions. To toy with him was to play with fire.

"You wanted a man, Lady Harrod, and I fully intend to honor your desire," his low, controlled voice seethed.

Clarissa cringed as if his words were a blow. He seemed to breathe fire from every pore and, at the same time, to be wrapped in an icy resolve. Clarissa knew that at last she had gone too far. She had gambled, and she had lost. She had conspired ruthlessly to bring Peter Barnes into her bed without really considering the consequences, and now that he was a step away, she realized too late that she had chosen the wrong man to play with. She had thought he was

a dashing rogue. She did not know he was a dangerous man.

Clarissa was caught in her own trap, and she was
frightened. Her game was over. Peter Barnes was
calling her bluff. She could see in his coiled, primitive
passion that Malcolm's most urgent demands as a husband and lover—even his drunken thrusts—were
child's play compared to what this man would expect—would insist on.

At last Lady Harrod was going to get the full, unrestrained heat of a man's fire—and her blood ran cold
at the thought. Beneath the selfishness that led her to
such cruel excesses, Clarissa was just a spoiled, petulant little girl, play-acting at being a woman. But
now, instinctively and in a flood of terror, she knew
that the pretending was over. Peter Barnes had come
for a woman, and he would have one.

In this way, Lady Harrod, six years a wife and
once a mother, was rudely awakened to womanhood,
against her every desire.

Peter Barnes loomed over her. "Get up, Clarissa,"
he commanded.

She cried out in fright and sank deeper into the pillows of the chaise, her arms crossed protectively over
her breasts, her eyes huge terrified pools.

But Pierre had been taken in by too many of the
Dorset women's ruses to be moved again. He believed
Clarissa was just pretending fear. He thought her
alarm was a pose and he was in no mood to coddle a
capricious woman. He would not play her coquettish
games or coax her fickle heart.

"Get up!" he repeated, and this time his command
was so furious she dared not refuse him.

Standing before him, her hands shot up instinctively to her bosom but he was too fast. He yanked
the ends of the pink satin bow. Her robe opened and

310

his hands were inside it, pressing against her bare flesh, drawing her up to his demanding mouth.

"Please no, please stop!" Clarissa pleaded. But she was too late and he too unforgiving. He thought she was still teasing him.

Pierre smiled cruelly at her, wanting to punish her, to hurt her, to savor the sweet taste of revenge. "It is time I gave you what you have so long desired, Lady Harrod," he mocked.

His hands were sure and insistent as he stripped her bare and held her naked flesh at last. Her skin was as fine and pink as a rose petal. Her figure, though too full for her tiny size, was the kind of body that invited a man's most erotic fantasies—lush and voluptuous. Clarissa was a sweet, ripe peach waiting to be plucked and Pierre was hungry. He had not touched or looked on a woman since Francesca had left him.

He did not undress. He wanted to give nothing to this woman, only to take—to take everything she had so long flaunted at him, everything her husband had once claimed as his own. He threw her down on her bed and rose over her like a vengeful, unforgiving god.

Clarissa cried for mercy, but he had none. Pierre drove his enormous lust inside her. Every thrust of his violent passion was a blow against Francesca and Malcolm. But there was no sweetness in his revenge, only bitterness and regret, for he realized, as he lashed her with his ungovernable desire that she was beautiful but passionless. She had been teasing. She had wanted nothing more. But by then he could not stop himself.

He struck her harder, faster, deeper, with each relentless blow insisting on her complete, abject surrender, until with the final drive of his terrible lust Clarissa's body convulsed.

Pierre disentangled himself from her desperate clutch, angry and disgusted with himself. Why had he punished this pathetic woman for the pain in his heart? She had done nothing except play her little charades—harmless games, he thought, still not suspecting her true treachery.

He stood over her for a moment. She lay as he had taken her, legs open, round thighs shining with the glaze of his lust. "I am sorry," he said gruffly and, covering her nakedness with her robe, he left her as she lay, motionless except for the great swell of her breasts, heaving uncontrollably, wracked by terrible sobs.

"House calls seem to be the major part of your practice, Dr. Barnes." Lady Andrea Marlowe's sarcasm greeted Pierre as he came down the stairs. She was standing in the drawing room, framed in the sunlight as she had once been framed in the taper light of her own bedroom. But now Lady Marlowe was quite properly attired, not in a transparent nightdress, but in a chic cranberry crepe gown with long tight sleeves buttoned at the wrists and a low, square neckline that revealed the gentle rise of her bosom to advantage.

Pierre looked at her, his face white with contained anger, much greater than any that Clarissa had aroused in him.

"And your family, madam," he responded icily, "are my most obliging patients."

Lady Marlowe glided as gracefully as a swan to the foot of the stairs.

"Why is it that all your patients are so young?" she mocked.

"Do I detect a note of envy in your voice, madam?" he asked contemptuously.

She stood in front of him, facing him squarely. Each was fully aware of the power of the other, of the fire behind their barbed words.

"You have missed your true calling, Lady Marlowe, that of a teacher. I congratulate you on the skill with which you have schooled your daughter. Judging from her performance, it would be a loss to mankind if you allowed your specialized knowledge to go to waste."

The thin veil of sarcasm was lifted with his bitter words. Their swords were drawn—poised to cross and not to parry any longer. Lady Marlowe's green cat's eyes flashed dangerously and she raised her hand to strike him, but he caught it, twisting her arm behind her back.

"Let me go," she hissed.

Pierre's suppressed desire for Francesca was like a raging fever that drove him deliriously to have, to hurt, to take, to destroy every woman who crossed his path.

Andrea had not wanted him to have Francesca. She thought he was too violent, too passionate, too demanding for her warm, loving daughter. She would only be hurt, and her premonition proved correct; Francesca had fled to Ireland.

Pierre du Bellenfant belonged to no woman now, and Francesca to no man.

All this flashed through her mind as he held her powerless, her arm still painfully twisted behind her back.

As if to put him to the final test, she reached up and kissed his mouth, not with the glancing caress of a mother-in-law but with the urgent, hungry lips that no man had ever refused.

Pierre tasted her burning kiss and answered it with

his own. Then he pushed her away savagely. Unprepared for the force of his thrust, she lost her footing.

"Like mother, like daughter," he grated and left her where she fell.

In that fatal kiss, Francesca died for Pierre du Bellenfant.

Chapter Fifty-Two

Robert Adair was not at all like his cousin Malcolm.
Older by almost twenty years, he was square and
stocky, a powerfully built man with the fair skin and
ruddy complexion of the Celts, clear blue eyes, and
blond hair just beginning to gray at the temples. He
was a shrewd judge of men, a leader of the Irish
rebels since Wolf Tone's death and as full of blarney
as any true son of the sod. Although he tried to pass
himself off as a simple country squire, no one who
knew him was fooled. Beneath his country tweeds,
Robert Adair was an intelligent, complex man—a man
of strong convictions and few fancies. He was a
widower, his only daughter married and a mother
now herself; as attached to the land of Donegal as a
root to a tree, and fiercely loyal. A skeptic, who nonetheless believed in the old myths on which Ireland
was built, he never went to church, but he never
mocked St. Colmcille either, or ventured far from
Donegal without touching the Sorrowing Stone on his
way.

Robert Adair never questioned Francèsca about the
child in her womb or about its father, and she never
volunteered any information. But his genial companionship made the long days of her confinement bear-
able. If she woke up screaming in the night, he would
sit by her bedside and soothe her. If the day seemed

to stretch on interminably, he would think of some entertainment to divert her.

Although Francesca refused his urgings to enlighten her family about her delicate condition, under Robert Adair's understanding care her torment eased and she became engrossed in the life that was developing inside her. The last four months were passing more easily than the first when she received a letter from Lady Marlowe.

My Darling Francesca,

I have hesitated to write this letter to you for many months now, but I can no longer postpone the unpleasant task. Upon receiving your brief note eight months ago announcing your trip to Ireland, I rushed back to London in the hope of seeing you before your departure and ascertaining the true reasons for this sudden flight.

I must say your note took me completely by surprise, following as closely as it did your visit to Marlowe Castle with Dr. Barnes. From our talk and from the few words I exchanged with him, I believed it was your mutual intention to wed. The time is passed, when I might have, under different circumstances, presumed to tell you how to conduct your life or dispense your favors. I have not set an example for you to emulate. However, it is far, far too late for me to do anything about that now. I should have thought of all this many years ago. Alas, I did not see life so clearly then as I do now.

As you know, I found Dr. Barnes an attractive even exciting young man, yet I had certain reservations about the constancy of his affections and I feared the grief a man such as he could bring to you. I can only assume from your hasty flight and brief, noncommittal letters that my worst intuitions were proven true much sooner than I had ever anticipated.

I hope, Francesca, your heart is not too sorely bruised and I write the following, not to increase that pain but rather to eradicate any hope you might still harbor to be reunited with that man. He has, since your departure, become a cause célébré in London, the scourge of every pretty girl and handsome woman. Lady Jersey is his constant hostess, but when in London he is surrounded by the most daring and desirable young women, and I have every reason to believe he does not disappoint them. He sports his conquests with an ease that would do credit to Lord Nelson and compounds his winnings by taking their husbands' fortunes at the gambling tables.

Dr. Barnes has proved himself to be a man with passion but little heart. If you still cherish any love for him, I urge you to abandon it now while there is still time. If your intention is to return and try to claim him for a husband, pray reconsider. . . .

The letter went on about family and friends, but Francesca did not read on. Pierre had wiped her out of his life.

That night, before the doctor could be fetched from Donegal, Francesca went into premature labor, and Robert Adair, assisted only by his faithful though sharp-tongued cook, delivered a beautiful, perfectly formed child with honey-colored skin like her mother's and her father's gray eyes and black curls. She named the baby Lucy Barnes Fairchild.

Three months after giving birth, her breasts still enlarged with milk, giving a new ripeness to her slender figure, Francesca entered Robert Adair's bed. But, even though he was a thoughtful and exuberant lover, he could not make her forget Pierre.

Lucy was a daily reminder of their incestuous love and her hunger to possess him again grew with his child.

During Robert Adair's frequent absences, when the memory of Pierre became so acute that she could feel his forbidden flesh as surely as the child at her breast, Francesca tried to drown it by taking yet another man.

Exploring a new body with a different scent and a different touch, taking him repeatedly until she fell into exhausted sleep, relieved the fire in her loins. But it did not touch the ache in her heart.

Francesca was repeating all her mother's mistakes, yet she could not stop herself. She had to force herself to forget Pierre for Lucy's sake. Time and new faces, other kisses, healed everything, she told herself. But she knew it was not true. Some pain only deepens. Some sins damn us forever.

Even when Robert Adair was away from Castle Glenreagh, his friends and fellow rebels retreated there to rest and reconnoiter, to scheme and dream. During her confinement, Francesca had seen little of these men but now she would sit with them at dinner, listening to their talk of their courageous fallen leader, Wolf Tone, who had been defeated off Lough Swilly and was hanged for his troubles.

They were the ideal men for her. Lusty rebels, almost strangers, wanting nothing more than a fond memory perhaps. Francesca had discovered the power to command men's hearts and she used it selfishly. She took possession of their souls as well as their manhoods, and many were drawn back to Castle

318

Glenreagh and the seductive enchantress who held them in thrall.

Robert Adair was the acknowledged leader of these Irish rebels, now that Wolf Tone was dead. He knew that Francesca's favors were dispensed to his men as well as to himself, but he held his tongue. She was exorcising a devil, using him and his men to free herself, punishing herself for some sin real or imagined, and Robert Adair knew that he could never have her himself until she was free. But there came a time when he could no longer watch in silence.

Returning home unexpectedly, he found Francesca lying alone in her darkened room, her wide eyes vacant and staring. He skin still glowed from another lover and the unmistakable scent of their spent desire still hung sickeningly in the heavy air.

Robert Adair looked down at the girl for a long, angry moment—at the smooth, honey skin he had rushed home to kiss, at the long, slender body he had yearned to embrace.

"Ah, girl," he said brusquely, have you not had enough? What ever have you done, what ever has been done to you, you cannot make it disappear by punishing yourself this way—or by giving men cause to do it for you."

His curt tone masked his fury. His harsh words concealed his bleeding heart.

Later that night he came to Francesca again. She was lying in her darkened room just as he had left her. Robert Adair took her hand tenderly and his voice was like a loving caress. "I blame myself for leaving you alone so much, Francesca. But I must if we ever hope to see Ireland free."

He looked at her pale, drawn face silently for a moment. "Why would you be taking strange men into your bed—brawny, lusty men who give not a fig for

319

you—like some village tramp? Have you been so hungry to punish yourself for some unexpiated sin? God forgive you, and them for having you."

Robert Adair's accusations were hurled softly but they struck Francesca with the force of thunder bolts.

"I can see in your eyes you have known a living hell. But it is over and finished now," he said firmly. "I'll not be standing by silently any longer and watching you give yourself up to men's basest desires. And that is final, me girl, for as long as you stay in Castle Glenreagh."

Silent springs of tears overflowed from Francesca's eyes and ran down her cheeks.

"Ay, I did not mean to be too harsh on you, Francesca. But can't you see what you are doing to yourself and how it breaks my heart to watch you?"

Robert Adair knelt beside her bed and embraced her, burying his face in the blankets that covered her nakedness.

Chapter Fifty-Three

Looking up at the demanding man who towered over her, blazing with rage and desire, Clarissa had wished for Malcolm. When she saw the violent passion, the naked, consuming desire smoking in Pierre's eyes, she realized what a gentle man she had married.

There was no more sweet taste of revenge in her surrender to Pierre than there was in his conquest. There was only regret. Her infidelity did not settle her account with Malcolm, it proved the truth of his bitter words. She was just a plaything, no better than a porcelain doll. In the demand of his loins, Pierre had forced Clarissa to look at the spoiled, selfish girl who had lured him to that point of no return.

When Malcolm came home for tea, he found his wife still weeping hysterically. He hated to see his golden girl sad and he sat with her, holding her on his lap like a baby and drying her tears. He could feel her nakedness beneath the dressing robe and was stirred by it. It had been so long since she had allowed him to touch her, or even hold her innocently like this.

"Hold me, Malcolm," she begged through her tears, and he pressed her closer.

"No, hold *me*," she whispered.

Surprised and excited, Malcolm slipped his hands

inside her dressing gown and felt the luscious contours of her breasts which he loved so much.

"I cannot hold you like this, Clarissa—not after I have dreamed about it for so long. I cannot trust myself not to do more."

"I want you to do more, Malcolm," she whispered, looking up at him, her big violet eyes brimming over with tears.

"Oh, Clarissa, don't do this to me," Malcolm begged. "You are killing me. I don't want to force you ever again. I would rather not have you," he said, drying her tears with his gentle fingers.

She caught his hand and kissed it. "I want you, Malcolm," she said, looking down to avoid his eyes, and she slipped the shell-pink dressing gown off her shoulders.

"Clarissa, what are you doing to me?" he cried, overcome by an almost unbearable blend of ecstasy and anguish. She was so beautiful. He wanted to get lost in her wonderful hills and valleys.

"Please, Malcolm," she whispered, kissing his lips timidly.

He carried her to her bed where Pierre had just lain and, for the first time since they had been man and wife, Clarissa opened her thighs willingly to receive him. He entered her in awe, as if her body was a sacred temple, and made love to her tenderly, touchingly, afraid that with any violent motion or thrust he would lose her again.

When he was finished, she held him against her bosom and stroked his hair. "Can you ever forgive me for being such a terrible wife?" she asked.

"Only if you can forgive me for being such an impatient husband," he smiled, sure that in a moment he would wake up from this heavenly dream.

"I have been so selfish—and so scared."

"And I so stupid."

"Do you think it is too late for us to try to start again?"

"Not if you want to, dearest. You know you are my only girl, as enchanting to me today, that is if you want to be," he smiled again, "as the day I married you."

"I do want to," Clarissa whispered.

She nestled his head in the soft valley between her breasts and Malcolm kissed their snowy peaks hungrily.

"I cannot share you with any man, Clarissa," he warned fiercely.

"I never want you to," she answered, and he fell asleep, hoping that he would never discover what had happened to her that afternoon to change her—what or who.

Clarissa did not change overnight, but she did see that she must try to—for herself, for Malcolm and for their son. By forcing her to stop playing the make-believe games that had sustained her since childhood, Pierre made her look at herself clearly, and she did not like what she saw. Her spiteful, willful behavior was destroying everyone she cared about. She wanted to salvage her family before it was too late, and the best way to do it, she thought, was to get away from the dizzy, superficial world of London high society.

Clarissa had always wanted to see Italy and so, impulsively, they closed up the Dorsets' stolid old house and sailed for Genoa. Although they took Genevieve Dorset and little Geoffrey along, Malcolm and Clarissa were as filled with excitement and anticipation as young lovers. It was a second honeymoon, which had to turn out better than their first.

In the warm, Mediterranean sun, Clarissa and Malcolm began slowly, often painfully, to rediscover each other. Perhaps because he was older now, Malcolm had more patience and made fewer demands, and, if Clarissa did not grow into a passionate woman, at least she learned to be a more willing wife.

Released from the pleasure-hungry world of London society, they began to cement their family ties. Her golden curls were bleached in the warm sun and her fair skin tanned to a rich copper brown. He seemed to shed a dozen years. He regained some of the boyish charm and carefree, easygoing manner that had once made him the most sought-after young lord in England.

She no longer needed to flaunt her ample charms in revealing clothes to prove that she was a desirable woman and taunt her husband. He no longer needed to seek solace in the arms of anyone but his wife. Her special little ways, known only to him, thrilled Malcolm more than the caresses of the most skilled courtesan.

Clarissa was happier in Italy than she ever remembered being. She felt almost as if they had been given a reprieve—a second chance—and in a certain way she thanked Pierre for it. Although she was, if anything, more pampered and spoiled than ever, her experience with him had jolted her out of her blind selfishness. She was still determined and willful and canny, but now she considered first the full consequences of her selfish desires.

She was sometimes as capricious and difficult as she had ever been, but it was just these unpredictable ways that had enchanted Malcolm from the first, and he would not change her for anything. They slept together now each night and, if they made love less frequently than most husbands and wives, he did not care. He tried not to press Clarissa and she tried not

324

to refuse him, and slowly, at his gentle coaxing, her body began to respond to his desire.

When their three month honeymoon was nearly over, they decided to extend it for three more. Leaving Genevieve and little Geoffrey at their villa in Leghorn, they visited Venice and Florence. One afternoon, strolling through the gardens of the Pitti Palace, she let him have his way in the tall, flower-strewn grass overlooking the banks of the Arno. The sun was warm on her face and Malcolm's love was warm between her legs and, for the first time with her husband, Clarissa knew the convulsive burst of ecstasy. This time there were no sobs. In the lovely Renaissance city she discovered what poets and lovers had sung of since creation.

The only thing that marred Clarissa's new happiness was the knowledge of what she had done to Francesca. Rediscovering Malcolm, she realized at last the depth of her cousin's—her sister's—love. She had relinquished this kindest and gentlest of men to Clarissa without a word of bitterness. In return, Clarissa had committed an unforgivable treachery. Her deed was too terrible to ever admit. Even Malcolm would turn against her if he knew what she had done. At first he would be incredulous, then gradually he would begin to see the truth clearly, and he would spurn her in disgust, shocked by the malicious lie she had invented.

One thing eased Clarissa's guilt. After tasting Peter Barnes's violent lust, she was sure gentle, generous Francesca could never truly love such a man. No matter how dastardly the deed she'd committed, Clarissa consoled herself with the knowledge that she had saved Francesca from an even crueler fate. She wrote warm, happy letters to Francesca in Ireland, but she gave no hint of her deceit.

Malcolm, too, was filled with guilt when he remembered Francesca. He had had his own very selfish reasons for dispatching her so readily to his remote family castle in Ireland, where, he was sure, she would be safe from Peter Barnes. He had fully intended to visit her there as often as he could, and his pulse had raced when he imagined how she would repay him for his kindness. But instead, overcome by the abrupt change in Clarissa, he had abandoned Francesca again—just as he had the first time.

Although she was never far from their thoughts, Malcolm and Clarissa rarely mentioned Francesca to each other. But once, as they sat in the garden of their white stucco villa overlooking the blue-green Mediterranean, another glorious Italian summer day coming to a close, Malcolm asked his wife what Peter Barnes had done to Francesca to cause her such bitter grief. As he spoke, he saw her fleetingly again in his arms in the carriage and heard the words on her lips: 'It could be.' The picture faded with Clarissa's evasive answer and Francesca was forsaken again, left alone in Ireland, and the only two people who could save her—Lady Clarissa Harrod and Lady Andrea Marlowe—were determined to keep her from Pierre du Bellenfant.

Chapter Fifty-Four

Francesca passed her hand lingeringly over the ancient Sorrowing Stone where, local legend said, St. Colmcille sat and grieved before exiling himself from Ireland. Since then emigrants bound for the ships at Derry have always stopped at the worn rock slab to pray.

"So you are still homesick, still longing to return to whomever it was you left your heart with, are you, Francesca?" Robert Adair said in his soft lilting voice.

"Did the good saint ever come home?" she asked, though they both knew the answer was no.

"And would you be planning to live like a saint for the rest of your life?" he chided her gently. "A lass as young and lovely as you does not have a chance, not when she looks at a man as you do with eyes that tempt him to do what he should not and dare him to dream that all things are possible."

"I don't know what I would have done without you to tease and comfort me," she answered evasively. It was true she had not known a man's caress since he had shamed her with the truth of his accusations and, though she knew his desire very well, she was grateful he never pressed her to answer it.

"And I do not know what I would do if you ever take it in your head to go home again."

Francesca smiled sadly. "You have little to worry

about on that score, Robert," she said, as she started to walk back to the castle, picking blossoms from the hedges as she went. "I like it here in Ireland. It is wild and free . . ."

"Free of memories?" he interrupted drily.

"Yes," she said slowly, toying with a flower she'd plucked. "My book is finished now. It was, I suppose, a final testament, a memorial to all that I left behind. Now that it is done, there is nothing behind me. Everything lies ahead. I must begin to build a new life for Lucy's sake."

Lucy! Francesca knew all too well what the child's life would be like. She knew the mystery, the uncertainty, the loneliness her child would live with, never knowing her father—or even who he was. And she feared that Lucy would inherit the same fateful destiny as her mother and herself—doomed to love a man she could not have. Francesca almost wished she had given birth to a son.

As the path grew steeper, Robert Adair reached out to help Francesca up the difficult mountain terrain. "Francesca, my girl," he said, only half-joking, "give me your hand, for heaven's sake. Must you always go it alone?"

Catching the other, more serious note behind his light words, she turned to him and their eyes met. For a moment they stopped still. The lightness was gone.

"I don't know, Robert," she answered honestly. "Perhaps I must."

He studied her closely for a moment, trying to fathom the sorrow that shadowed her dark eyes, then he drew her slowly to him.

"Can't we go on together, Francesca, as man and wife?" His brogue was as soft as a morning mist.

Francesca looked away. From where they stood,

she could see for miles—the lake in the distance shining like a sapphire in the afternoon sun, the spires of the castle reaching up to heaven, and beyond it all the cruel Atlantic stretching on and on, in an infinity of blue.

Of all the men who had fallen under her thrall since Lucy's birth, Robert Adair alone remained his own man, although he was in love with her. Perhaps it was his age, or the fact that his first and final love would always be the green, verdant land of Ireland.

"Francesca," he said, "You have given me your body and held back your heart. But I am a patient man. I can wait and, in time, after we are man and wife, you will finally forget and come to me."

"I can never tell you . . ." Francesca hesitated.

"I will never ask," Robert Adair said, reading the warning in her eyes, "who he is or why you fled from him, carrying Lucy in your womb. I want no explanations of the past." He paused, giving her time to absorb his words. "Think of Lucy, Francesca. Doesn't she deserve a mother *and* a father, and even perhaps her own brothers and sisters?" He took both her hands in his. "I don't want to force you, Francesca, or rush you. I only ask you to think about it. Do not refuse me outright. I do not require an answer today or tomorrow. I told you I am a patient man, but I am also a man who knows what he wants."

Francesca looked at him with sad, troubled eyes. She did not want to go on living like her mother, a restless roamer taking men as other women took tea. Yet Pierre had made her too passionate to ever live a barren life. Her body would rebel, and of the lovers she had known, only Robert Adair was the one she was truly fond of.

Was it fair to him, though, to accept his offer and give so little in return? She could tell him nothing of

329

her past and offer him nothing of her future except her body. But was it fair to Lucy to refuse him?

Francesca sighed deeply, unsure and unresolved. "If you would allow me a month, Robert," she said, "by then my book will be published in London. It is in a way a testament to what I have been and to those whom I have loved. With its publication, that chapter will finally be closed, the last link severed forever."

"You may take as long as you need, Francesca," he answered, "as long as you promise me that you will think about it, as I do each day."

"I promise you my answer in a month," she hesitated. "But I don't think I would be a very good wife to you. I have so little to offer."

Robert Adair pressed her hand tightly in his. "Let me be the judge of that, Francesca," he said.

She smiled, warmed by his tenderness. "A month then from today."

But before the month ended, Francesca received an urgent message that Lady Marlowe was seriously ill, and she and Lucy were on their way to England. Robert Adair watched them go, knowing in his heart that he would never see mother or daughter again.

Chapter Fifty-Five

Lady Andrea Marlowe lay on her back in her high oak four-poster, her exquisite face like an alabaster mask against the white linen pillow slips. Her breathing was labored and heavy. Her once coveted body had thinned and the luster had faded from her green eyes.

"Mother," Francesca whispered, bending over her bedside, her anxious eyes straining for some flicker of recognition, some sign that her mother was aware of her presence, "I have come home."

"It is Francesca, Mother," she said again, taking her mother's long tapered fingers in hers. "I have come home at last."

Lady Marlowe opened her eyes slowly. She was tired; very tired. She had grown weary of the social intercourse, the ceaseless games of hide-and-seek and blindman's bluff and catch-me-if-you-can that she had played with so many men over so many years since loving Francesca's father. She had grown increasingly lonely since his death. She had no desire to live on through years that would do little except claim what remained of her legendary beauty, and nothing to live for now, except to tell her daughter the truth as she had promised Jeremy on his deathbed.

Lady Marlowe had been caught in a sudden burst of spring rain, the first of the season—a heavy, unexpected shower that had drenched her to the skin—and she had returned to Marlowe Castle shivering and rain-soaked, her wet clothing plastered against her glorious frame, her flaxen hair dark with the wetness. The next day she had complained of pains in her legs and arms, and of a terrible soreness in her throat.

The doctor in the village had been called but, in spite of his most earnest ministrations, Lady Andrea's condition worsened. When she continued to slip rapidly, Edward summoned Dr. Kent from London. By then, however, there was little the young doctor could do except relieve her discomfort and maintain a patient vigil at her bedside.

Lady Marlowe's moments of alertness grew rarer each day but, when she was conscious, her mind was remarkably clear. At one point she had opened her eyes and looked squarely at Dr. Kent.

"Exactly what am I suffering from, Doctor?" she'd questioned.

"My diagnosis is a severe case of influenza," he replied quickly, surprised by her sudden sharpness. "There is an epidemic of it sweeping out from London. I believe you are one of the first to be stricken in this county."

"Am I going to die, Doctor Kent?" she demanded, her candid eyes insisting on an equally candid reply.

"I hope not, Lady Marlowe," the young man hesitated, "but I simply do not know."

"In that case, Doctor, call my daughter home immediately," she ordered imperiously. "I refuse to go peacefully to my grave until I have seen Francesca."

Now Francesca was back home at last, but Lady Marlowe wondered, how long would she stay this time? She could not insist, or even ask her to remain. If a mother ever possessed that right, she had relinquished it many years ago when she left the little girl

332

in her sister Genevieve's drawing room. It mattered little now that her intentions had been the best or that her overriding concern at the time had been her daughter's happiness. All that mattered now was that, at that moment, she had given up her precious daughter.

Lady Marlowe squeezed Francesca's hand weakly. "I am glad that you have come," she whispered.

The soreness in her throat made speech painful, yet she had so much to tell her daughter now, before it was too late. She hoped Francesca would not judge her too harshly for what had been done in love—and in lovely innocence.

If only she had not played such silly games then—absurd pretendings not very different from Clarissa's, pretending she was someone other than she was, the whims of a foolish girl who had been forced to be a woman too soon. If only she had not played those games with him, they would never have allowed themselves to fall in love. *So many ifs in a lifetime,* she thought. *So many traps that can break a heart.*

"You will love Ireland, Mother. It is very beautiful this time of year, and Castle Glenreagh is like something in a storybook. It is set high in the mountains with a lake and great woodlands, and pastures and flowers everywhere. Beyond it all the Atlantic, fierce and cold and somehow thrilling, stretches infinitely, uninterrupted all the way to America. You must come and stay as soon as you are well again, and I will hear no more of your excuses.

"Of course, nowhere is as dear to my heart as this old place. But the change—the sea air and the rugged power of Ireland—would be a marvelous new experience for you."

Francesca spoke a little too fast, a little too eagerly,

333

as if, with her words, she could drive death away from her mother's bedside and give her new strength to fight on. She seemed to be telling herself that, if she kept talking lightly and happily about anything but the palpable aura of finality that hung in the room, she could prevent death from claiming her mother.

Although Dr. Kent told her she would be shocked by her mother's appearance, nothing could prepare Francesca for what she found. It was not that her mother looked so terribly weak or feeble. She was still beautiful. Her fine features were unaltered. The first hint of gray colored her temples, otherwise her hair was still like flaxen silk. But her spirit was gone. It was as if a beautiful room was decorated with the utmost care and lavished with the finest furnishings; each feature of the room was in perfect harmony with every other and the whole was brilliantly lit. Then suddenly the lights went out and all that was visible was a dim shadow—a vague reflection of the splendor that had once shone so clearly.

"Francesca," Lady Marlowe said. Her voice was pained but the timbre was still strong. "I am going to die. The only thing that has kept me alive these past few days is waiting for you to come home. I promised your Uncle Jeremy on his deathbed that one day I woud tell you the truth about your father, and I cannot die until I have fulfilled my pledge. I have been lying here gathering the courage to tell you at last. I cannot wait until tomorrow, darling, it may be too late, and I may become a coward again as I have been all these twenty-six years."

"Do not be silly, Mother, neither of the two will happen," Francesca said gently. "Anyway Dr. Kent made me promise I would not let you tire yourself with too much talking. I plan to remain with you for as long as you need me, so we will have plenty of time to tell each other everything that is in our hearts."

"Please, Francesca, hear me out," she entreated. "Now that I have steeled myself at last, I suddenly cannot bear my awful secret any longer."

Lady Marlowe looked at her daughter lovingly, and longingly. She wished they had been closer through the years and she wondered if Francesca loved her Aunt Genevieve more than she loved her own mother.

"I have waited a lifetime to hear you say those words," Francesca said softly, and she spoke the truth. But now she was filled with anguish not anticipation. She was not sure she could bear to hear the full story of her father, for it would tear open again the wounds of her incestuous love.

"Sit beside me, Francesca," Lady Marlowe said, "and have patience. For I must begin at the beginning, some thirty years ago, with a seventeen-year-old girl as innocent and carefree as a summer morning.

"I am sure Genevieve has told you parts of my story, but still they will bear repetition. We lived in a comfortable, though far from elegant, manse a few miles beyond the village of Heretsford, which, as you know, bounds the farthest western edge of the Marlowe estate. We were of what was called the gentry class, respectable but poor," she added, whether with bitterness or mockingly Francesca was not sure.

"Genevieve and I had none of the lovely frocks or horses or governesses with which you and Clarissa grew up. We each had one Sunday dress, which mother cut and stitched for us herself. I can still see her squinting by the candlelight to put the final ruffle on my first grown-up dress. Alas, I have since regretted that she ever finished it, although at the time I was overjoyed. I thought it was the most handsome

335

dress any girl had ever had." She smiled, still fond of the memory yet amused at her own sentimentality.

"Father died when we were very small, fighting the French in the Colonies. He was a major in his Majesty's fifth platoon, a gorgeous man, tall, handsome and broadly built, but something of a scoundrel. He was a gambler, a drinker and a less than faithful husband. He gave Mother many a tearful night alone, I am afraid, but I adored him and she did as well.

"When Mother was carrying Genevieve, and I was three, Father went off to war. He was as full of dreams and schemes as ever, but he never came back. The little allowance that was due Mother was hardly enough to feed and clothe two little girls, but somehow she always managed, although to this day I have never understood how she did it.

"She gave piano lessons to the girls in the village to augment our meager income, but there was never enough. The butcher was always demanding his due, and if it was not the butcher, then it was the eggman or the peddler. Still we were happy. There were pastures to roam through and books to read.

"We grew up freely. We were a little wild perhaps, with no father to rein our natural high spirits, but our mischief was always good-natured. Mother was very much like your Aunt Genevieve. She was a pretty, kind woman, who grew plump as she grew older. It was her sweetness, though, which I remember most about her. That is what won over our father and kept him returning to her after he tired of the others. Miraculously her sweetness never left her, although it must have been a difficult life, alone and almost penniless with two small children to sustain. It never occurred to me how heartbreaking Mother's life was, until after she died. I had left Heretsford and her far behind me by then. But she looked the same in death

336

as in life. Not even that final arbiter could change her from the dear, kind woman she was. She exasperated me often, much the way Genevieve does now, but I must have not been easy for her. I was headstrong then and filled with dreams.

"I was my father's daughter in every way. I inherited his looks and his instincts as well. I think Mother suspected this and was frightened by it. What may be accepted in a man is frowned on in a woman. Maybe that is why she agreed to marry me off when I was just eighteen. Perhaps she wanted to tuck me safely away before I discovered my true self, or perhaps she was only concerned with securing a safe, comfortable life for me.

"Mother was a dreamer in her own way. I know that she envisioned me as mistress of Marlowe Castle—with heaps of fine dresses and jewels at my throat, the belle of His Majesty's balls, with footmen and servants to command, and travels on the Continent—because that is the picture she painted for me from the very first."

Lady Marlowe sighed deeply. "I have never understood how Mother could think I would be happy married to Lord Marlowe. For many years I could never forgive her."

Lady Marlowe looked at her daughter keenly and Francesca saw a silent entreaty in her mother's eyes, which she did not understand.

"It is only in these past months that I have begun to understand for the first time. I did not know then that what a mother wants for herself is often what she wants, above all, to protect her daughter from. She can see the suffering that lies ahead for the girl, because she has known it, and she wants to spare her daughter. She *must* spare her daughter," Lady Marlowe repeated firmly.

The strain of speaking and of the emotions she had aroused were more than she could bear in her weakened condition. She began to cough, wracking, strangulating sounds that brought Dr. Kent rushing in.

"Lady Marlowe," he said sternly, "I must insist that you end your daughter's visit and get some rest. Now that she is home, you will be able to see her each day. But you must keep the visits short until your strength begins to come back. If you don't, you will only tire yourself and slow your recovery."

He smiled at her. "I can see that you are not used to obeying, but this time I must demand that you do."

Francesca laughed. "You are most perceptive, Dr. Kent, and a very strong man, indeed, if you can make my mother do your will." Bending down, she kissed her mother's forehead. "Don't be afraid," she whispered, "we have time now—so much time."

Lady Marlowe watched Francesca and the young doctor go out. Then, spent and exhausted from the strain of her story, she lay back in the pillows and slept.

The worry that Francesca had tried to hide in front of her mother overcame her as soon as she shut the door behind her.

"Dr. Kent, is my mother going die?" she blurted.

He took her arm reassuringly. "Your mother is still young and strong. She has a severe case of influenza, but, if she fights to live, then there is a good chance that she will come through this illness."

They walked out to the verandah and sat where, just a year before, Lady Marlowe had sat with Pierre.

"What are you trying to tell me, Doctor?" Francesca asked.

"In order to recover, your mother must *want* to live, she must fight hard."

"You are trying to tell me that my mother has no desire to overcome her illness?"

"Yes, I suppose I am. She was determined to stay alive until you returned . . . but after that . . ."

Francesca closed her eyes. The setting sun was a vivid ball dropping from the sky, turning everything it touched brilliant orange and crimson. "I know how Mother feels," she said.

John Kent sat silently watching the girl for a moment. The reflections from the crimson skies caught her cheek and shimmered like a mirage. Suddenly she opened her eyes and, catching him staring, she smiled. Her strong, dramatic face glowed brighter than the sunset and he saw, in that radiant instant, why his friend Peter Barnes had fallen in love with her.

"I am being morbid, Dr. Kent. Will you forgive me?"

"I think a man could forgive you almost anything, Miss Fairchild," he replied earnestly.

He was not sure if she flushed slightly, or if it was the setting sun.

"You are a flatterer, Doctor. That may be true of Mother, but not of me."

"I am not a flatterer," he demurred. "I am a loyal friend."

"I know you are, Dr. Kent, and I can never tell you how grateful I am for the care you have given my mother."

"You misinterpret my meaning, Miss Fairchild. I meant that I am a loyal friend to you and Peter Barnes."

"Peter?" Francesca said. "I did not know how close . . ."

"I have no friend I value more."

Francesca turned away, more upset than she could ever let him see. "And did he tell you? . . ."

"Only that you had gone—not why or even where."

If she could never see him or touch him or hear his voice again, at least, Francesca thought, *at least she could know him from afar without guilt or fear.*

"How is he, Doctor? Tell me everything about him," she urged, trying to make her words sound lighthearted. "I have heard that he has become the scourge of London. No woman's heart is safe from him and none can resist him—nor he them."

Dr. Kent smiled sadly. In spite of her brave front, it was clear to him that love had not died in Francesca's heart any more than it had in Peter's.

"It used to be said that a man grew tamer as he grew older. Wildness was thought to be a symptom of youth, but Peter seems hellbent on disproving the theory. For more than a year now, he has been drunk all the time on wine, gambling and women—trying to forget that he is a man with an incurable illness."

Francesca blanched. "What is wrong with him?"

"He is suffering from a broken heart," Dr. Kent said softly. "Nothing he prescribes seems to alleviate the pain."

Francesca turned away, her own heart torn in two, and sank back in the broad porch chair. The last traces of pink had faded in the west. The evening shadows obscured her face and hid the helpless tears that shone in her eyes. Somewhere from a far field came the deep, contented sound of a Jersey returning to pasture after the evening milking. Otherwise the night was quiet. They sat in silence, Francesca lost in her thoughts and love of Pierre, John Kent waiting, letting his words register fully in her heart.

"Do you know of any cure for Peter?" he asked finally, nudging Francesca gently with his question. "I have used up my doctor's bag of remedies."

Francesca did not reply for a long time and, when she did, John Kent was taken back by the vehemence of her answer.

"There is nothing—nothing," she repeated, "that I can ever do for your friend." And in her words and in her voice was the cold finality of a death knell.

Although there was no chill on the evening air, a quick shiver ran through the young doctor.

"In that case," he said slowly, measuring each word, "it will not disturb you to know that Peter has announced his engagement to Lady Warwick. The wedding date is set for two weeks from today."

Francesca could not disguise her shock. Although she could never have Pierre again, she had never thought of him marrying. She fought back the jealous wave that was rising in her heart, but it was too strong. "Why is Lady Warwick in such a rush?" she asked acridly.

"It is not Lady Warwick who insists on the early date. It is Peter," Dr. Kent paused, studying Francesca again, "but I would hazard a guess that if he knew he had fathered a pretty little girl, he might well change his plans."

Francesca leaned forward in the chair and stared at Dr. Kent, her dark eyes glowing angrily like hot coals.

"If you are referring to my daughter, Dr. Kent, her paternity is of no interest or concern to your friend Peter Barnes. There is no reason he need ever know she even exists."

"That can hardly be avoided now, Miss Fairchild," he said quietly. "I am considering asking him for an opinion on your mother's condition. I value his consultation highly."

"No," Francesca cried sharply, "he cannot come

here." Then she caught herself, forcing down her longing and her fear. "It is more than selfishness that makes me insist upon this, Dr. Kent. I have full confidence in your ability as a physician. But, if you believe another opinion is required, I am sure you can call on a doctor of skill and dedication other than Dr. Barnes. I would hate to interrupt his wedding plans," she added coldly and with her tart, jealous words, she closed the subject of Dr. Peter Barnes forever. Lady Warwick would have him for better for worse, from that day forward.

Chapter Fifty-Six

"The dress that Mother made for me was white muslin, very simple and modest with a ruffle at the throat and hem, but when I put it on I felt as if I was a cloud floating across a clear summer sky. I knew I was prettier than either Mother or Genevieve, but I did not know then that I possessed the physical gifts that would make men's blood rush. And I don't think I was vain, although the swell of my breasts and the smallness of my waist pleased me.

"My white dress was the first that had ever shown them to advantage and I saved it to wear to Easter Sunday service. It was one of the most festive days in our little village and I so wanted to look grown-up and perfect. There was a young lad—the dairy farmer's son, as fair as I, and blue-eyed—who sometimes came to our door with a fresh pitcher of cream for Mother. When I thought of him, my cheeks would flush."

Lady Marlowe smiled at the memory. She felt strong and rested—better than she had since the onset of her illness. Beginning her story at last had lifted a terrible weight from her soul and she'd slept soundly. The crushing burden of guilt she had lived with for so long would not follow her into the grave. She had looked into Francesca's eyes and seen the change in her, and she knew that her daughter had suffered enough to understand and forgive.

"With a wide-brimmed bonnet that matched my dress and little Genevieve by the hand, I set out for the village church. We were late, because I had lingered over my toilet, and so we took a shortcut that we had used many times before. Instead of following the road to the village, we cut through the lower pasture of old Lord Marlowe's estate. Mother had told us repeatedly to stay off of his land, because he had no mercy on trespassers—even young, perfectly harmless ones.

"Alas, I was reckless and disobedient. We cut through the copse where you have ridden so many times and came out into the farthest pasture, face to face with the old lord himself. I can still see him now. I thought he was at least one hundred-years-old. He was short and wiry, with a wretched face as pinched and wrinkled as a monkey's. He was grinning meanly, his lips pulled back and his teeth bared horribly. They were as yellowed as his skin, and on his chin a great black mole grew with white hairs protuding from it like pins from a cushion.

"We stood stock still like statues, our hearts in our mouths. Then we turned and ran. His high, dry voice followed us: 'Run away if you like, I'll catch up with you, girly, soon enough.' And then we heard him laugh, a brittle cackle that was more frightening than the direst threat.

"We ran and ran as fast as we could. Even when we thought we could not go any further, we forced ourselves on, propelled by the picture of that wizened, nasty old man at our heels. We arrived at Easter service just before the church doors closed, dusty and exhausted. But I did not care that my beautiful new dress was soiled and my face was red and streaked with dirt. We had escaped. That was enough. Or so I thought. But I was wrong, so terribly wrong, for the next week Lord Marlowe came to call on Mother.

"Genevieve and I were walking up the road from the village one afternoon when we saw at our modest gate a shining carriage drawn by a pair of matching roans, the most beautiful horses I had ever seen. A coachman sat in the box as motionless and unseeing as a statue. Instinctively we knew it was Lord Marlowe's carriage and we hid behind the house.

"We dared not even think what horrible punishment he was demanding for our crime. To us, crouched in our hiding place, it seemed that he remained in the house for hours. Finally we saw him shuffle down the path. We waited until the horses' hooves were a distant echo then, frightened and contrite, we crept home to Mother.

"She was sitting alone in the parlor. The tapers were not lit, yet in the dim light, we could still see clearly that she was crying. We went to her shyly, ashamed for causing her grief but scared of the punishment we would surely receive. For mother was a kind woman but not a lenient one. In this she was the opposite of your aunt. She was quite stern with us girls, not at all the spoiling, doting mother that Genevieve has always been to Clarissa—and to you, Francesca, I have no doubt."

Lady Marlowe paused and patted her daughter's hand, the old regret again strong within her. But she went on with her tale.

"To our surprise, Mother did not have a word of scolding. Instead she took us both in her arms and hugged us tightly to her bosom. We felt the sobs rise in her chest but she held them back. Her silent grief was much worse than any punishment could have been.

"'What did the ugly old lord want, Mother?' I asked apprehensively. 'Nothing but good for you Andrea,' she said slowly, but there were no glad tidings in her voice. 'I will tell you about it in the morning, when the surprise of His Lordship's words has worn away and I have thought clearly about his request.' She released us and stood up to light the candles.

"As you can imagine, I was curious and excited, but something in Mother's face kept me from pressing any more questions on her. That night Genevieve and I lay in bed, inventing all kinds of wonderful fairy tales about Lord Marlowe's beneficence. We imagined lovely new dresses for Mother and sleek horses for ourselves. We were so simple," Lady Marlowe sighed.

"Needless to say, the morning shattered our childish dreams. Mother sent Genevieve out to play and sat me beside her on the parlor sofa. I could see from her tired face and the dark shadows beneath her eyes that she had gotten little sleep that night.

"'Andrea,' she began, and I can hear her words today as clearly as I did that day, 'you have grown into a very beautiful girl with a special loveliness that would soon be extinguished if you were constrained by our modest means to live the life of a yeoman's wife. I have always pictured you as a fine lady, with elegant gowns and a devoted husband to frame your radiance.' She took both my hands and squeezed them so tightly that she hurt me, but I said not a word. 'Yesterday a way was opened for you to escape from this impoverished life.'

"I held my breath, thinking that the dreams that Genevieve and I had harbored the night before were about to come true. 'Lord Marlowe came here to ask for your hand in marriage,' Mother said. 'When he saw you in his pasture on Easter Sunday, he was so taken with your beauty that he wants to make you his bride.'

"I must have turned ashen because Mother hurried on, trying valiantly to make me see the advantages of the privileged position I had been offered. 'Think of it, Andrea,' she said, 'you would be Lady Marlowe, mistress of the vast estate. You would have all the finery a girl could hope for, everything and anything your heart desires. You would go to sumptuous balls and dance with the king's young sons, and you would be the envy of every fine lady in London because you will be the most beautiful girl of all.'

"Mother envisioned a marvelous future for me, but all I could see was Lord Marlowe's dreadful face, leering like an evil gargoyle, his yellow teeth barred in a gruesome grin. I felt the horror surging inside of me. 'No, no! Never Mother! I will die first,' I screamed and ran blindly from the house.

"Mother let two days pass before sending a note to Lord Marlowe, saying that, after weighing his offer carefully, she had decided that her daughter was too young to wed. Lord Marlowe replied immediately, but he did not press his suit to Mother. If he could not get what he wanted as a gentleman, then he had no compunction about getting it in another way. That same afternoon I received a missive embossed with the Marlowe crest. It was not a letter but an ultimatum. If I persisted in refusing the honor Lord Marlowe was prepared to confer upon me, our house would be demolished within the fortnight to provide additional pasture for his Jerseys, and my mother, sister and I would be put out on the street. If I accepted, Mother would be presented with the deed to our home and she and Genevieve would be provided for in every way. A sworn statement from our landlord was enclosed, saying that he had, on that same day, sold our home to Lord Marlowe.

"Three weeks later, a pale, trembling bride stood at the altar, her heart filled with hatred for the man who was claiming her hand. I had little knowledge of the duties of a wife except what Mother had told me the night before—that marriage gave a husband the right to intimate knowledge of his wife. She said that the act of love out of which Genevieve and I were conceived was a sacred and wondrous thing. But she could not say more, knowing that I would never bear any affection for the menacing old man, fifty years my senior, whom I was destined to wed."

Lady Marlowe closed her eyes and Francesca sat silently, listening to her labored breathing. She had never imagined that her glamorous mother was once a helpless, frightened girl, and her heart bled for the young Andrea.

"Perhaps you should rest for a while, Mother," she said tenderly. "We can continue your story this afternoon."

"No, darling. It is not the weakness of the influenza that gives me pause, but the bitter memories I am resurrecting from their dusty tomb."

She reached for the glass of water on her bedside table and Francesca held it to her lips, raising her shoulders and steadying the glass in her shaking fingers. Then she went on.

"I prayed that my husband's age would prevent him from claiming any more than my hand and, for a while, I believed that my wish had been granted. Lord Marlowe did not insist on his rights at first. He showered me with costly gifts and responded eagerly to my every whim. Instead of seeing that he would expect to be repaid in full, I began to think that I had misjudged him terribly. Behind his ugly visage, he was probably a kind and decent man.

"Lord Marlowe and I were married exactly one month when he decided the time had come to collect his dues. As I bade him goodnight that evening, I detected a chilling, lecherous note in his tone. 'Thank you, my dear,' he said, offering his withered cheek to be kissed, 'and a very goodnight it shall be.'

"I sat for a long time on my bed, not daring to undress for fear he would visit me at last. But, alas, I did not wait long enough. I had just slipped into my nightdress, satisfied that my fears had been misplaced, when I heard the key turn outside my door, locking me in. I listened intently, too scared to move, as the minutes ticked by. Then, just as I feared, the adjoining door creaked slowly open.

"Lord Marlowe was dressed in a wine-red dressing gown, a white scarf at his throat, his sparse hair freshly brushed over his forehead. A strong scent of cologne wafted from him and his small, beady eyes shone like glowworms. 'It is time that I became better acquainted with my sweet young wife,' he said, coming slowly towards him. His teeth were bared in the same gruesome grin that I had seen that first Easter Sunday in the pasture and all I could think of were the words he spoke that day: 'Run as far as you like. I'll catch up with you soon enough.'

"Terrified and repelled by the odious old man, I backed away from his advances. 'Come, Andrea,' he urged. 'I have been a generous husband. Did you think you could go forever without returning my favors? I do not believe in works of mercy, you know.'

" 'Your Lordship,' I pleaded, 'I will repay you in a million other ways. Ask any favor of me—anything, I beg of you.'

" 'What else do you think you have to offer,' he

asked cruelly, 'except your soft, virgin flesh? You cannot deny your lawful husband, girly.'

"He had, by then, backed me against the wall and was trying to embrace me. For a man of his years, he was surprisingly spry, but I twisted free of his grasp and ran as fast as I could. I heard him panting behind me but he was too old to keep up. I flew through his bedroom that I had never entered before, through hallways and wings that I had not yet explored, never stopping until I felt the carpets give way beneath my bare feet to the cold, wood floors of the servants' quarters and I landed, breathless and exhausted, in Edward's surprised arms.

"He was a young man then, newly come to His Lordship's service, but he took pity on me. Without embarassing me with too many questions, he hid me in his room that night. I shudder to think what would have happened if we had been discovered. Dismissal would have been the least of the punishments that Edward would have paid. But my husband had given up the chase—at least for that night.

"I slept in Edward's bed and he in his reading chair. In the morning I returned to my mother. But Lord Marlowe was a stubborn and miserly man. He had bought and paid for me. I belonged to him and he was determined to have me anyway he could.

"My husband had in his employ, then, an immense, dumb-witted servant by the name of Gordon—a Goliath of a man whom he had trained to obey his every command without question—and he was sent to bring me back. There was nothing poor Mother could do to spare me. She was as helpless against Gordon as I was, and she could not very well appeal to Lord Marlowe to refrain from his husbandly rights. Faced with no other alternative, she begged me to endure his desire, consoling me with the knowledge that a man of

350

his years could not be too demanding. But my husband's touch was repulsive to me. I could not bear to even think of his caress.

"Back at Marlowe Castle, I was locked in my room and allowed to see no one. That night I did not undress. I sat wide awake and ready to fight to the death if I had to. I will not go into the details of that evening, except to say that it was much the same as the previous one—except this time the wily old man was better prepared. When I tried to escape through his bedroom, I found Gordon's massive frame blocking the doorway. I pounded on his chest, begging him to let me pass. But it was to no avail. He stood like a block of granite as if he had no eyes, no ears, no heart.

"The old lord cackled triumphantly. I was trapped at last. 'Bring her here, laddie,' he ordered Gordon, thumping his bed with a bamboo cane, 'I have a mind to teach the vixen a lesson she'll not soon forget.' I screamed and struggled but I was helpless. Gordon brushed aside my pounding fists as one might brush aside a mosquito and threw me across the bed face down. He pinned me in an iron vise while Lord Marlowe brought his cane down across my back. I screamed at his blow, but this only seemed to excite him. The louder I cried out, the harder he thrashed me.

"I am sorry, darling, to have to tell you the brutal details of my story. I never wanted you to know, or even imagine, the degradation to which I was subjected and to which many men subject their women simply because they are able to dominate us with the raw strength of their bodies. But you must always remember what I learned that night. Though the body may be forced to comply, the heart and mind can never be conquered against one's will. They are

351

indomitable. But I shall not preach to you, Francesca. I am only telling you these details so that you will understand everything that led up to your birth.

"When my noble husband was done with his whipping," Lady Marlowe continued drily, "he ordered Gordon to strip me naked. To allow Lord Marlowe to have his will was mortification enough. But to be exposed to that human monster was a humiliation that will never be washed from my mind. He was not, I discovered, totally devoid of human—or at any rate bestial—feelings. He chuckled lewdly as he tore open my corsets and only His Lordship's sharp command stayed his hand at my bosom.

"Struggling fiercely beneath Gordon's great, rough paws, I managed to break free and reach my own room where I slammed the door shut and planted myself against it in the vain hope of barricading it. Gordon pushed it open easily. Following the orders of my husband, he dragged me to my bed and bound my arms and legs to the four posts with His Lordship's silk scarfs. When I was secured firmly, my naked body and all its secrets opened to the ogling eyes of master and servant, Lord Marlowe dismissed Gordon, and had his way at last. That, Francesca, is how I became Lady Andrea Marlowe in deed as well as in name."

Lady Marlowe related her story as matter-of-factly as if she were telling her story about someone else. It was difficult for Francesca to see the innocent, young girl of the story in the sophisticated, alluring woman she had always called "Mother." *How little we know of those nearest and dearest to us*, she thought, and at that moment, she felt closer to her mother than she had ever before.

Lady Marlowe smiled ruefully at her daughter. "It is heartening to remember there is some justice in this world, Francesca. The exertion of that night proved so great for my husband, he never lived to pleasure himself on my body again. As his widow, I, of course, inherited everything he owned, which amounted to a considerable fortune.

"In the past years I have grown to love Marlowe Castle as you have, but my first and only desire then was to escape from here. I put Edward in charge of overseeing the estate and I moved to Paris. I was a very bitter young woman. I held my mother at least partially to blame for what had befallen me and I broke my ties with her and poor little Genevieve.

"All their letters went unanswered. I wanted to remember nothing that had gone before—nothing of that dreadful experience. I even assumed a false name. I did all the things a woman does to forget a profoundly horrifying experience."

Lady Marlowe paused and eyed her daughter shrewdly. "All the things you have done, my dear, and then some," she said, making the color rush to Francesca's cheeks. But she went on as if she had noticed nothing.

"I had been living on the Continent for about three years, quite content with my decadent, new life, when I met your father. I have known men more striking in their appearance, more elegant in their dress, more experienced in their approach to a beautiful woman, but never one more charming.

"He was tall and slender, and a little bashful, with a grave face and blue eyes that stated clearly here was a man who could never willfully bring grief to another. After my diet of Parisian boulevadiers, he was refreshingly sincere, like a bowl of fresh fruit after too many rich desserts. But I do not begin to do him justice," she sighed. "How can one explain what draws us to one man above all others? How can one ever understand the mystery of love, or why it always is the one forbidden man who attracts us above all others?"

Francesca looked at her mother sharply. *Which one of us is she talking about? Could she have known Peter Barnes's true identity all along and remained silent*, Francesca wondered? But she held her tongue and waited in torturous anticipation for the revelation that she was sure would come.

"Your father was like a dream come true," Lady Marlowe went on in the same deliberate tempo. "He was disarming. He was passionate. He was the most marvelous friend and companion I had ever known and, by the end of three glorious weeks, we shared a love that transcended everyone and everything—or so we thought.

"He told me quite frankly that he was recently married to a dear, loyal girl but now there was no vow more important than our love." Lady Marlowe spoke slowly now, like someone picking her way through a bramble patch. "What I did not know, nor ever suspect until it was too late, was that the dear, loyal girl was my own sister, Genevieve."

Francesca turned so pale that Lady Marlowe thought she would faint. Her voice sank to a whisper and she reached for her daughter's hand. "Yes, Francesca, it is true. Jeremy was your father as well as Clarissa's."

"Why didn't you tell me, Mother? How could you keep this from me all these years? Uncle Jeremy, dear Uncle Jeremy!" Francesca cried in anguish. He was all she had ever wanted in a father. If only she had known . . . Wild unquenchable grief for the father she had loved so dearly yet had never known overwhelmed her.

"How could we ever tell you this and hope you would understand?" Lady Marlowe implored. "How

354

could we tell you without making Clarissa loathe her father and Genevieve despise us both? If there was a way, it eluded us, and so we did the only thing we could. We kept silent. Even now, after all these years, I did not know a gentler way of breaking it to you, Francesca. But I promised Jeremy just before he died that, one day, I would confess everything to you. He thought you should know who you are . . . but I, I was never sure. I should never have told you. The terrible shock, darling . . . I won't go on . . ."

Agitated and distraught, Lady Marlowe turned away. She could not bear the terrible expression on her daughter's face. It was just this that she had never wanted to see—that had kept her from revealing her secret for so many years.

"No, Mother," Francesca squeezed Lady Marlowe's hand imploringly. "I want you to go on. I want to know everything. Please hold nothing back from me now. I must know the truth, the whole truth."

For an instant the intensity of her shook and grief had blotted out everything else. She felt like a fighter stunned by a blow. Her head was reeling and she could not sort out the implications of her mother's confession. *If Uncle Jeremy was her father, how could Pierre de Bellenfant be her brother?*

Francesca's desperate, pleading voice was more than her mother could refuse and, gathering her waning strength, Lady Marlowe continued.

"When Jeremy returned to London, he found that Genevieve was carrying Clarissa. He had promised to come back to me, but he had not anticipated his wife's condition.

"You must remember, Francesca, that Jeremy still did not know my true name, nor I the identity of his wife. When he visited Paris again, it was only to tell me that we must relinquish our love forever. But by

355

then you were growing in my womb and I felt compelled to tell Jeremy my full story.

"I can still see him, as the terrible truth of who I was and what we had done dawned on him. He buried his face in his hands and a cry more anguished than any sound I have ever heard before or since escaped from his clenched jaws. Then he looked up at me and, his tortured face shining in the moonlight, he told me that his dear, loyal wife was my sister, Genevieve.

"I was sure of only one thing," Lady Marlowe whispered. "Genevieve could never know what we had done."

Weary from the long narrative and from the deep emotions she had rekindled, Lady Marlowe sank back into the pillows. A silence deeper than any sleep enveloped mother and daughter—the one exhausted from her memories, the other suspended in a state of incredulity. Francesca dared not think or hope, until she knew everything no matter how shocking or painful.

"Go on, Mother," she begged. "You cannot stop your story now."

Lady Marlowe summoned her strength and began again. Now that the worst of her revelations were told, she sounded more like the cool, controlled woman Francesca had always known.

"Jeremy had an old friend in Paris, a very dashing nobleman who gallantly agreed to accept paternity for you. Unfortunately, his wife, a sweet, fun-loving American girl, believed the story he invented to save my honor and he was too much of a gentleman to deny it, even to her."

Lady Marlowe paused pensively. "I think that to this day Genevieve has never suspected the truth. But in sparing her, I am afraid we sacrificed that other innocent."

She coughed painfully and waited until the attack had subsided. "When you were four, I anglicized your name and brought you to England. I left you with Jeremy and Genevieve so that you would have the family life that I, alone, could not provide. The rest of the story you know."

Francesca stared at her mother, still stunned and confused. Her dark eyes held a hundred questions and harbored twice as many doubts.

"Does anyone else know your secret, Mother?" Her strained voice was scarcely more than a whisper.

Lady Marlowe hesitated, not certain of how Francesca would react to this additional shock. "Only two people know: your adopted father whom, I understand, may not have survived the bloody revolution, and . . . Clarissa."

"Clarissa knows that Uncle Jeremy is my father?" Francesca gasped. "She couldn't! She couldn't possibly."

"Do not think that I confided in Clarissa before telling you," Lady Marlowe hastened to reassure her daughter, misconstruing her impassioned reaction. "You cousin overheard her father's deathbed confession."

She hesitated and for the first time that Francesca could remember her mother's eyes were filled with tears. "Try not to judge Jeremy too harshly, Francesca," she begged. "At the end when he knew he could not hold out until you returned, he asked you to forgive him for never publicly acknowledging you as his daughter, although in his heart you were always his dearly beloved."

"Are you *sure* he was my father?" Francesca demanded fiercely.

"Who would know better than I?" Lady Marlowe smiled through her tears and her eyes filled with love at the treasured memory. "Clarissa knows it as well. You can ask her, darling, although I begged her to let me tell you myself."

She daubed at her tears with the back of a slender hand, her long, tapered fingers brushing gracefully across her lovely face. "I hope Clarissa kept that promise."

"She did, mother," Francesca blurted in a tear-choked, broken voice. "Oh, she did."

Lady Marlowe scrutinized her daughter intently, trying to read in her dark eyes the emotions that were churning in her heart. But Francesca could not look at her mother. Her confession and Clarissa's horrifying revelation crashed together in her brain like jarring cymbals. She was too numb to think clearly. She could not comprehend the full meaning of her mother's words or her cousin's malice. She had to be alone to sort out the stunning truths and terrible lies. Rising unsteadily, Francesca turned away, but her mother reached for her hand and held her back

"You know, darling," she said, "in one of those odd coincidences of which this life is full, you were once engaged to your adopted father's son, although he used his mother's maiden name.

Lady Marlowe felt her daughter's fingers tighten, urgently.

"Tell me his name, Mother," she whispered.

"The father's name was Georges Duc du Bellenfant and the son was . . ."

Francesca did not hear her mother's last words. She felt the room begin to whirl and lost consciousness with the name Bellenfant on her lips.

Chapter Fifty-Seven

"Francesca, Francesca, can you ever find it in your heart to forgive me?"

Clarissa knelt at the side of the bed, holding her sister's limp hand in her own. Her big, violet eyes were red-rimmed, her pretty, heart-shaped face was swollen and blotched from her bitter tears. Although she feared Francesca was already too far away to hear her, still she sobbed out her painful confession.

When Francesca fainted at her mother's door, Dr. Kent had thought at first that she was overcome by exhaustion, but by nightfall it was clear that this was just a contributing factor to a much more serious illness. Francesca had caught her mother's influenza.

For six days she had lain in her bed, her face deathly pale. Each day Dr. Kent watched helplessly as her strength ebbed further, but he could not reach her. It was almost as if an invisible curtain had been drawn over her, sealing her from the world. Francesca's influenza was a mild case, nothing as severe as her mother's, and yet she sank fast until now she hovered on the brink of death.

After the weight of her guilty secret had been lifted from her bosom, Lady Marlowe gained strength rapidly, but Francesca grew weaker and weaker. It seemed to Dr. Kent that the mother was draining life from her daughter, but, of course, he knew that could not be. He was letting his emotions color his professional duties to a dangerous degree.

The truth was much simpler. Francesca had even less will to live than her mother had had. The man she loved, the father of her child, was at that very moment preparing to make another woman his wife. With the best of intentions, Dr. Kent had divulged this information to Francesca. Now he felt responsible for her precarious condition as surely as if he had infected her himself. He had to save the girl—but how? What could he do to make her want to live again?

With each passing hour Lady Marlowe continued to grow stronger and Francesca faded deeper into a seemingly endless sleep. Lord and Lady Harrod, recently returned from Italy, had been notified of her grave condition. Rushing from London as soon as they received the urgent news, they arrived at Marlowe Castle at dawn.

Now Clarissa knelt in Francesca's darkened room, her bitter tears staining the linen bedclothes as she begged forgiveness for her terrible lie.

"Please, Francesca, don't die with my awful treachery unabsolved. Don't leave me like this without a word," she cried.

Francesca opened her eyes for a moment and held Clarissa in a distant gaze. It was too late for reproaches, too late to hold fast to any bitterness. Then too, she had always forgiven Clarissa everything, and it was too late to change that now. She pressed Clarissa's hand weakly.

"Take care of my baby for me," she whispered. Then her soft, luminous eyes closed and she drifted away again.

"I will, I will," Clarissa sobbed, "as if she were my own." Burying her face in Francesca's limp hand, she

360

wept helplessly, her whole body wracked with anguished sobs.

Clarissa stayed at her sister's bedside until Malcolm tiptoed into the darkened room and gently raised her up. Putting a strong arm around her trembling shoulders, he led her outside and then returned to take her place beside Francesca. As he studied the motionless figure he had seduced and abandoned twice, he felt as if he were keeping a death watch. With a freshness and vividness that surprised him after so many years, he remembered again the cool touch of her flesh, and the shy generous gift of the love that she had given him once so many years before.

How different all our lives would have been, he thought, *if I had kept that first vow I made to her. For better for worse, until death doth part us. . . .* But these were the words he had finally sworn to Clarissa instead, and he wondered if that was, in part, why there was no man at Francesca's bedside now except himself.

While Malcolm was keeping his solitary vigil, Lady Marlowe was confronting Dr. Kent with her deepest fears.

"I trust you are a sensible enough young man not to feel that what I am about to say implies any lack of confidence in you, Dr. Kent," she began slowly.

The young doctor made no reply. He had already decided what he must do for Francesca but he had been worried that Lady Marlowe would oppose his plan. Now he waited expectantly for her to continue.

Lady Marlowe was sitting at her bedroom window, watching her granddaughter being wheeled through the manicured gardens below in Francesca's old pram. The child had come as a great shock to her. She was hurt that Francesca had not confided in her. But even more, she was deeply afraid that she had

361

somehow bequeathed this pattern of unhappiness to her daughter—that Francesca was doomed to relive her own bitter past.

When Edward told her the child's name, her fear deepened. Lady Marlowe knew that there was only one reason why Francesca would christen her baby Lucy. And she knew instinctively what she had to do, no matter how humiliating it might be for her, to save her daughter. "I never thought I would come to this day," she said grimly, turning back to Dr. Kent, "but I have. I believe my daughter requires a second doctor's opinion—and not just any doctor." She paused, remembering his brutal mockery, and she steeled herself visibly. "I believe Francesca needs the opinion of your colleague, Dr. Peter Barnes."

John Kent smiled slowly at his imperious, beautiful patient. "I agree with your diagnosis precisely, Lady Marlowe. Perhaps you missed your true calling."

"Then you will call Dr. Barnes?"

"I took the liberty to dispatch Edward to London this morning," he answered blandly.

Lady Marlowe considered the doctor more closely than she ever had before. He had the kind of face that would always look boyish, even when it had grown deeply furrowed, and the kind of body that would never turn to fat. He was scarcely older than Francesca, yet she trusted him with her dying daughter's life.

"So, Dr. Barnes should be here by midnight," she said, letting him see clearly her relief and gratitude.

John Kent turned away so that Lady Marlowe could not read the worry in his face. "It is possible, of course. But I don't think we should expect Dr. Barnes at Marlowe Castle for a day or two at least. He has a very busy practice in London, you know."

Dr. Kent did not want to deceive Lady Marlowe

with false hopes, yet he could not tell her his worst fear. He could not tell her that he suspected his friend was secluded yet again at Lady Jersey's pastoral estate—or how skillful the future Mrs. Barnes was at making Peter forget everything but the pleasures of the flesh.

Chapter Fifty-Eight

Clarissa was sitting on the verandah, cradling little Lucy in her arms. Ever since Francesca's whispered words, she had hardly let the child out of her sight. Now, as she watched a sleek black phaeton come up the long gravel drive, she hugged the baby tighter.

"Look, Lucy," she cried to the child, "here comes the doctor who will save your mother."

Although Malcolm had assured her that Dr. Kent had done everything possible for Francesca, still Clarissa believed that there must be something more the new doctor could—and would—do, and her heart skipped hopefully as his carriage drew nearer.

Dr. Kent had told her that he was summoning a distinguished colleague from London but it was not until the phaeton drew up in front of Marlowe Castle and Edward helped the new doctor out that Clarissa realized the man upon whom she had pinned all her hopes for Francesca was Peter Barnes.

"Lady Harrod, what a charming picture the two of you make," he said, bowing with a flourish. "My congratulations. I was not aware of the happy event."

Clarissa had not set eyes on Peter Barnes since the afternoon he ravished her, and now, believing she saw mockery in his eyes, she was filled with shame once more.

"What are *you* doing here?" she blurted out.

Pierre still deeply regretted what he had done to Clarissa and now, seeing her embarrassment, he tried to ease it by adopting a clearly professional air.

"I am looking for Dr. Kent, Lady Harrod; perhaps you would be kind enough to direct me to him."

Clarissa looked at him aghast.

"You mean *you* are the distinguished colleague he sent for?"

Pierre could not help smiling at her bald words.

"I am not sure I am deserving of such a flattering sobriquet, but yes, Dr. Kent did ask me to look in on Lady Marlowe."

"Oh, no, it's not Aunt Andrea," Clarissa said, quickly forgetting her own chagrin in her anxiety to see her sister well again. "*She* has made a quite remarkable recovery. It is Francesca, Dr. Barnes. You must save her, you simply must!" Her eyes filled with tears and her voice broke.

"Francesca!" Pierre echoed hollowly. He felt every muscle in his body tense with fury and he turned to Edward sharply. "Why didn't you tell me it was Francesca?" he demanded sharply.

Edward remained unruffled. "Begging your pardon, Dr. Barnes," he replied diplomatically, "I believed it was best this way, what with your, er, your plans for the future such as they are."

Pierre stared at Edward with eyes of steel. He had tarried at Lady Jersey's and had only agreed to come to Marlowe Castle with the greatest reluctance. In fact, only Edward's insistence and the memory of their lonely afternoons of tea and cards at the kitchen table in the house on Grosvenor Square had finally swayed Pierre.

Discovering so abruptly that the patient was

Francesca and that she was holding onto life by the slimmest thread, those terrible months of loneliness and bitterness, the desperate nights of women and gambling, his wedding the next week—all were forgotten in his overwhelming love. He had tried his best to kill his love for Francesca, but he had succeeded only in burying it for a while. Now only one thing mattered: saving her.

"If you will excuse me again, sir," Edward went on, ignoring Pierre's fierce look, "there will be ample time to upbraid me later, but Miss Fairchild has no such luxury. She is very poorly, Doctor," he said gravely. "Let me show you up to her room. The sooner you look in on her the better."

Edward turned to lead the way, but Pierre rushed past him. He remembered well where Francesca's room was and he bounded up the broad stairway, deaf and blind to everything but the fearful love pounding in his heart.

"I have no desire to be trampled upon, Dr. Barnes," a cool, arrogant voice said.

Pierre stopped cold. Lady Marlowe stood just four steps above him, blocking his path.

"I seem to recall that you always did look on my housecalls with disapproval, Lady Marlowe," he said.

"Perhaps I once did, Dr. Barnes," she replied, but no longer. You are most welcome at Marlowe Castle."

"It was Lady Marlowe who asked me to send for you, Peter," Dr. Kent said, coming up the stairs behind his friend. He had just caught Lady Marlowe's last words, but he sensed that he was interrupting something much more than a chance encounter.

Lady Marlowe laughed softly. "Now that I am a grandmother, I intend to behave like one. Surely, Dr. Barnes, you would agree that it is about time I did."

A grandmother—not likely, Pierre thought. It was

clear from the special way Clarissa held the baby that it was hers.

"Perhaps you saw the child on the verandah with my niece," Lady Marlowe went on cooly. "Lady Harrod has been taking care of little Lucy ever since Francesca's illness."

Pierre moved up the stairs until he was so close to Lady Marlowe that she could feel his fiery breath on her cheek. His eyes blazed dangerously and his voice was low and taut with emotion.

"Why wasn't I told?" he demanded.

Lady Marlowe drew in her breath sharply and fought to overcome the sudden weakness in her legs. She clutched the bannister tightly, her knuckles turning white from the force of her grip.

"None of us knew, Dr. Barnes." Her clear green eyes filled with tears. "I believed, until this moment, that only Francesca and the child's father were aware of its existence. I see now I was wrong in assuming even that much."

"If the two of you insist on resolving the child's future here and now," John Kent interrupted again sharply, "little Lucy will soon find herself an orphan."

At his harsh but honest words, Lady Marlowe stepped aside to let Pierre pass. "Dr. Kent believes my daughter has no will to live," she said gently. "I hope you can give her back that desire."

Pierre could not trust himself to speak. On impulse he pressed Lady Marlowe's shoulder as he passed, then hurried down the hallway to Francesca's door. Slowly he turned the knob. *Dear God, what a fool I have been*, he thought as he entered the silent room and looked with fear and longing at the slim, motionless form on the bed.

But as his eyes gradually adjusted to the dim light, Pierre became aware of a still figure sitting alone in the shadows, and he was seized by a rage as great as his love. Marcolm Lord Harrod was maintaining his anguished death watch.

Together from the first to the last, Pierre thought bitterly. Could he heal Francesca for this man? Could he let her die because of any man? As much as he wanted to save Francesca, Pierre wanted to destroy Lord Harrod.

"I imagine you would like to examine the patient, Doctor," Malcolm said. At Pierre's curt nod, he stood up and with a last worried look at Francesca, he started toward the door. But before he reached it, he stopped and faced Pierre squarely.

"I owe you an aplolgy, Dr. Barnes, which I fear is long overdue." Malcolm cleared his throat awkwardly. "When I challenged you at Waiter's in an inexcusably inebriated state, I wished at the time Francesca was mine. She never truly was, you know. In fact, that very night she had told me of her deep feelings for you. I was angry and jealous, though I had no right to be.

"Neither Lady Harrod nor I have seen Francesca since she left London so hastily, and now . . . now I only hope nothing either of us has done anything to bring her to this fearful point."

Pierre studied Malcolm coldly. "You have not been in Ireland, Lord Harrod?"

"No, Lady Harrod and I have been in Italy for most of the year and I am ashamed to say we never did make the visit to Francesca. Now, of course, we both wish we had not neglected her so. Why is it, Dr. Barnes," he said dejectedly, "that our regrets always seem to come too late?"

"It can never be too late for Francesca, Lord Harrod, never," Pierre replied fiercely, and it seemed to

Malcolm as if he was hurling his defiant words at death itself.

"I share your hope and I pray that your faith will be justified," Malcolm said.

Pierre extended his hand and Malcolm accepted it with a firm, forceful grip, then he left the doctor to his patient.

Closing the door tightly behind Malcolm, Pierre leaned against the frame for a moment and tried to compose himself. *If she did not run away to be with Lord Harrod, then why did she go,* he wondered. His heart had not been touched since their last night of love. The only emotions he had known were angry ones or shallow ones. He had known no warmth, tenderness, or love. Now everything he had held back for so long threatened to engulf him.

He walked slowly across to the bed. Francesca was whiter than her pillow. Her cheeks were hollow, her lips pale, yet she was as beautiful to Pierre as she had always been.

"Francesca," he called, willing her to hear him, willing her to wake up as he had once done so long ago in Elfi Bey's palace in Cairo. But she did not stir.

With trembling fingers, he drew back the sheet and began his examination. He gazed at the slim, spare body he had longed to taste again, and he was filled with an unbearable sadness. What madness had possessed him to let her escape from his love? What madness had made him think he could ever belong to any other woman?

Pierre lay his head on Francesca's bosom and felt her small, round breast against his face as he strained to hear the beat of her heart. Her skin was warm as if the sun were burning down on it, and as white as alabaster.

The oath Pierre had sworn as a physician was forgotten. He was both doctor and lover. Each touch of his skilled hands was a caress filled with a tumultuous desire and a terrible despair. He was everything and he was nothing, for she seemed so far away—so utterly beyond his reach.

Overcome with grief, Pierre took Francesca in his arms and clung to her desperately. He kissed her closed eyes, her pale lips and cold forehead. Burying his face in her golden hair, he whispered hoarsely, "*Adieu, adieu, mon amour.*"

At Pierre's special touch, the touch of her love, Francesca dreamed that the sun reached down from the sky and caressed her naked breasts and belly. Wherever it touched, the rays seeped into her body and warmed her, and she basked in their healing power. Then she dreamed that the sun leaned down from the sky and kissed her hair. Warm drops rained on it like a summer shower through the woods, and she opened her eyes slowly.

Pierre's gray eyes were soft and he was crying. Then Francesca knew it was not a dream, and nothing would forbid her total surrender.

PREVIEW

STORM OF DESIRE

Paula Fairman

Storm of Desire *is the story of beautiful, high-spirited Reesa Flowers, innocent of the ways of the world, but beginning to feel the stirrings of her budding sexuality when the story opens. Both tempted and repelled by the woman-hungry men in the railroad camp where she lives with her telegrapher-father, Reesa is no match for the sophisticated city ways of Ted Foster, builder of railroads, a young man with a dream.*

Ted and Reesa will clash swords, wits, and passions, will love one another and hate one another, and Reesa will make a disastrous marriage before she and Ted reach the maturity that transcends their physical and emotional involvements with others.

Storm of Desire *is by far Paula Fairman's best work to date. Set in a tumultuous era, when a young country was feeling the growing pains of its adolescence, and a woman's life was directed by her father or her husband with no consideration for her own feelings,* Storm of Desire *tells the story of one young woman who refused to become a pawn in men's games and a victim of her times.*

Following are the opening pages of this latest novel by Paula Fairman (author of Forbidden Destiny *and* In Savage Splendor), *to be published in February, 1979.* *

Had Miller Flowers but known the indignities to which his daughter was nightly subjected, he wouldn't have continued to send her with the crew orders for the midnight train. Reesa was a voluptuous young woman of eighteen, and she couldn't help the fact that men found her beautiful. She had black hair, the color of burnished ebony, coupled with green eyes to make a rather unusual but striking combination. Her face was dusted with a light spray of freckles, an effect which enhanced, rather than detracted from, her beauty. And as she pushed through the crowd to stand near the twin steel ribbons that connected Albuquerque to civilization, her full breasts and well-rounded *derrière* would attract awkward and seemingly accidental touches.

Miller Flowers, who had returned from the battle of Shiloh minus one leg, found that he was also a widower with an infant daughter to raise. He had been Reesa's sole parent since she was three months old, and he still looked upon her as a young, innocent child. Young she was, and thus far innocent as well. But Reesa was no child.

Despite the pinches and grabs she had to endure, there was an excitement to meeting the midnight train that Reesa relished. There was always a carnival atmosphere about the crowd: laughter, good-natured joking, the constant cry of drummers who hawked their wares to midnight customers, and, usually, music from guitars or an occasional band.

What Reesa liked best, however, was the approach of the engine. The whistle could be heard first, far off and mournful, a lonesome wail that never failed to send chills through her body. Reesa would stare down the track, waiting for the train. The first thing to come into view would be the light—a huge, wavering, yellow disc, the gas flame and mirror reflector shining brightly in the distance. That sighting would be closely followed by the hollow sounds of puffing steam, like the gasps of some fire-breathing, serpentine monster. As if to add to the illusion, glowing sparks were whipped away in the black smoke clouds which billowed up into the night sky.

As the train pounded by, something inside Reesa's body throbbed in rhythm with the engine's powerful beat, and she felt herself drawn to it as a woman is drawn to her lover. When the train was compeltely still, Reesa would stand there for a moment, feeling her body bewilderingly alive, yet hauntingly hollow, as if craving something more. It was a bittersweet sensation, and she allowed herself to drift with its pleasurable waves, though a small, unheeded voice often cautioned against it.

After the train was completely stopped, Reesa came out of her reverie and walked along the side, headed for the engine. Sam Norton was the engineer, and as Reesa approached his cab, she could see through the window the maze of pipes and valves that were Sam's controls.

"Hello, Miss Flowers," Sam called down.

"Hello, Sam," Reesa replied. "Did you have a nice trip?"

"Sometimes better'n fifty-five miles per hour," Sam said proudly. Then, "Do you have our orders, girl?"

"Yes, here in this envelope," Reesa said. She strained and stretched, reaching up to hand the envelope to Sam. The action brought her dress tight against her body, and those who were standing nearby took visible notice of the curves thus accented.

The envelope slipped from Reesa's fingers and bounced under the engine.

"Allow me, miss," a man's deep, resonant voice said.

The man who spoke was a stranger to Reesa. He was tall, dark, and well dressed in a russet-brown jacket and brown riding breeches tucked into highly polished boots. A ruffled shirt did nothing to hide his powerful chest, nor did the jacket detract from his broad shoulders. His eyes were a warm brown, and Reesa noticed with some surprise that they nearly matched the shade of his jacket. He had an easy smile and a handsome face, and Reesa couldn't help but feel a quickening of her pulse as she looked at him. Her reaction surprised and frightened her somewhat, and she found that for a brief moment she couldn't speak. Finally she found her voice.

"I fear I'll cause you to soil your clothes, sir," Reesa said.

374

"Then I shall wear the grime as a medal of honor for having served you," the man replied. He handed the envelope to Reesa, then smiled as she stretched to hand it up to the engineer.

"You are staring, sir," Reesa said, flustered.

"Yes," the man answered easily. "And I'm enjoying every minute of it. Fully as much as you are, I suspect."

"Sir, you are impertinent!" Reesa exclaimed indignantly, but her cheeks flamed in embarrassment, giving credence to the man's comment.

"I apologize. I meant no disrespect," the man said. "I was so taken by your charming ways, and meant only to speak honestly. Please forgive me if I offended you."

"Miss Flowers, this here is Ted Foster," Sam said from the cab of his engine. "He's goin' to build this here railroad clear on to the Pacific Ocean."

"You're Ted Foster?" Reesa asked. For she had heard of him, as had everyone in Albuquerque. The news that a new railroad, the Southern Continental, was going to connect Albuquerque with Phoenix and San Diego was on everyone's lips. But that a man so young could do all this? Ted Foster couldn't have been over twenty-eight.

"I see you've heard of me," Ted said. "I also see that I don't come up to your expectations. You, on the other hand, are everything I was told you are."

"You've heard of me?"

"Of course," Ted said easily. "You are Reesa Flowers, the beautiful daughter of the man who is going to be my superintendent of station masters and telegraphers."

A yard worker approached them and stood back

quietly, awaiting recognition. Ted saw him, smiled broadly, and stuck out his hand. "My name's Ted Foster," he said. "Who are you?"

"Arnold Blair, sir," the man replied, surprised that he had been asked. "I've come to tell you that your private car has been detached from the end of the train and pushed onto a sidetrack."

"Good. Thank you, Arnold. I appreciate that."

Reesa was impressed with the way Ted spoke to the man. Many, she knew, would have barely acknowledged him. Ted had taken the time to introduce himself, learn the man's name, and use it.

"That was nice," she said after Arnold had left.

"It was nice of them to take care of it for me," Ted agreed.

"No, I meant for you to take the time to speak with him."

"Friendliness is an investment, Miss Flowers," Ted said. "One which costs little, and often gives great returns. Like now, for example. I'd like to make a friendly gesture and invite you to join me in my car for a small drink before I turn in. Would you be interested?" Ted saw the shock in Reesa's eyes, and he laughed. "No? Very well, then perhaps some other time. In the meantime, Miss Flowers, I bid you good night."

Ted gave a small bow, almost mocking in its lack of movement, though made gracious by his style.

"Good night, Mr. Foster," Reesa said.

As Reesa left the train, the image of Ted Foster stayed with her. She could still see his broad chest and wide shoulders, and the even, white teeth that smiled at her from the tanned, handsome face.

Reesa's innocence went as far as her virginity.

376

No man had known her, though there were many in Albuquerque who had privately vowed they would pay any price for the privilege. Reesa, though still a virgin, already knew herself to be a woman with a passionate nature. Sometimes, unbidden, erotic thoughts played their temptations in her mind. As she was completely without experience, there was no form or substance to these fantasies, but there was an insistent longing for something more.

There were even times when she secretly enjoyed the attentions of the men in the crowd, and their gropings, and took a measure of pride in the fact that she could stir men so. But such feelings were rare, and were always followed by a sense of guilt. Reesa was determined to dominate the sexual side of her nature. She realized that decent women were not ruled by their passions, but controlled by their minds, and she vowed to keep her lustful feelings in check.

But even as she thought of her determination to be pure of thought, she found herself thinking of Ted Foster. The throbbing feelings in her body that were stirred by the arrival of the engine seemed, somehow, to intermix with thoughts of the handsome young man. She felt a spreading warmth in her body, and a weakness in her knees. No man had ever made her feel this way. What was it about this one that affected her so?

* * *

Reesa and Ted will soon come to know one another better, as lovers and as friends. But there will be others who come between them: Joaquín de Mendoza, fiery young Mexican rebel, who will fight to the death to keep the gringos off his family's land, and who wants Reesa in the way she wants Ted; Warren Leland, dissolute son of the banker who controls Ted's destiny by virtue of his financing, who sees in Reesa the perfect weapon to use against Ted; and beautiful Lyrica Montoya, who, loving Joaquín, betrays Reesa.

In Storm of Desire *Paula Fairman has created powerful, flesh-and-blood characters whose strengths and weaknesses, good and evil, passions and lust, are skillfully blended in an absorbing story that, once started, will be difficult to put down.*

From the publisher of *Love's Daring Dream*
In Savage Splendor
and *Legacy of Windhaven*,
3 new historical romances . . .

Samantha, by Angelica Aimes

☐ 40-351-8 $2.25

"A fine magic carpet ride, with a courageous heroine, and a fascinating hero whom I believe few women will be able to resist. I enjoyed it enormously."

—Patricia Matthews, author of *Love's Avenging Heart*, *Love's Wildest Promise*, *Love, Forever More*, and *Love's Daring Dream*

ssion's Proud Captive, by Melissa Hepburne

☐ 40-329-1 $2.25

From the moment she saw the bold, dashing Lancelot Savage, Jennifer was in love with him. And when he was arrested for piracy and sentenced to hang, she knew she would do anything to save him—for he was the man she loved, the only man she would ever love.

Tropic of Desire, by Antoinette Beaudry

☐ 40-344-5 $2.25

Exquisite passions explode in savage ecstasy when young, lovely Mercy Carrol and brave, proud Clifford Hawkes are shipwrecked on the exotic island of Cuba.. But this tropic of desire is seething with rebellion, and Mercy and Clifford must risk their lives for their freedom . . . and a love that even fate dare not deny!

PINNACLE—BOOK MAILING SERVICE
Box 690, Rockville Centre, N.Y. 11571

Please send me the books I have checked above. I am enclosing $ _____
(please add 50¢ to cover postage and handling). Send check or money order—no cash or C.O.D.'s please.

Name _____

Address _____

City _____ State/Zip _____

Please allow approximately four weeks for delivery.